The Forgotten Sister

Krystal
You are loved
you are beautiful
and you are eternal
Dalila
Caryn

Dalila Caryn

ISBN: 1533464251
ISBN 13: 9781533464255
Library of Congress Control Number: 2016910591
CreateSpace Independent Publishing Platform
North Charleston, South Carolina

For my family, without whom I might never have followed my dreams. I love you all.

With much gratitude for the encouragement, anticipation, and coffee of the Daily Brew Crew:
Scott, Kali, Lauren, Lindsay, Ashley, Alex, Matt, Joe, Amanda, and Geneva.
Thanks a latte.

A Curse Is Born

*T*here once were two princesses, sisters, as different as a mountain and the wind. Rowan, the elder, was as firm and strong as any mountain and equally determined not to bow down to the forces surrounding her. Roisin was born under different stars, wilder and more changeable ones; she was more than willing to bend to the wills of those around her because she knew they could not alter her deepest self. The differences did not end there; where Roisin was a petite, delicate creature, Rowan was tall, with broad shoulders and a strong back.

Different. The princesses were so different in everything from looks to personality to circumstance that no one would ever think them sisters. But they had between them a deep and abiding love. Where fate would keep them apart, they found each other, and where fate saw fit to curse them, they fought it.

It began as most curses do, with a broken heart.

"You should not sit here so long. Your time is near, and it looks like rain." Maureen, midwife to the queen, spoke from just over her shoulder. "It would not do for you to be stranded here."

Maureen was a medium woman in all ways but temperament, of medium height and weight, with warm brown hair that fell in gentle waving curls and eyes of a similar shade. It was in those eyes that her true nature could be seen. They swam and flashed with knowledge as old as the earth, and very little patience.

"I could never be stranded here," Queen Sinead said softly. She looked out on the garden she had planted with meandering rows of roses. She had begun the project, along the eastern side of the palace, in the first month of her marriage, lonely for the companionship she had known in the Fairy court. Two years later, the saplings were growing in great spears toward the heavens.

"Even you aren't immune to a rainstorm." Maureen watched the young queen with worried eyes. Her water had broken hours ago. Maureen had suggested a walk to speed things along, but now Sinead refused to leave the garden.

Sinead was a delicate thing, slight in build, with long, flowing blond hair and eyes of a nearly clear green that shifted fluidly with her moods and the moods of the earth. Maureen was not sure she had ever heard the girl raise her voice in anything but laughter. She was so very gentle. What would happen in the birth? The queen did not seem quite up to the challenge of bringing a child into the world. Not today, at any rate. Curse the king!

"My mother was born in a thunderstorm," Sinead said in a faraway voice, almost oblivious to the growing darkness.

Maureen half nodded, half rolled her eyes at the comment. The Fairy queen was a storm herself. A wild, beautiful, painful one. "I can well believe it." Maureen's hand found Sinead's shoulder and tightened reflexively as her own heart contracted with grief. "But you and Desmond were born on a fine spring day on a soft feather bed. And I think your child deserves a bed, as well."

"Ohhh." The queen sighed, rubbing a circle over her belly with a wistful smile and teary eyes. "My daughter is a sturdy one. She won't be cowed by a bit of stormy weather."

The women drifted into silence and their own thoughts. Sinead would be such a better mother than the Fairy queen had been to either of her children. But for all that, Sinead could stand to have just a bit of her mother in her. The Fairy queen never gave in.

Sinead's hand continued its circular trek around her belly. "Do you think he loves her?"

"What nonsense," Maureen snapped.

Sinead laughed over her shoulder, eyeing her dear friend. Their friendship was so different here than it had been in the Fairy court. "Not the Lady Gwyneth. Though we both know it isn't nonsense. Ugh!" The queen bowed forward suddenly, both her hands clenching around the bench.

"There, there." Maureen crouched in front of the queen, mopping her brow. "You must come in now."

"*No!*" Sinead sat up, showing uncharacteristic defiance and looking every inch the queen. "My daughter is not some insipid princess to be petted and groomed and made a tool for a man's ends. She is a child of the earth and the air. She is a fey creature; she will be born in the light and the air—and the storm, if need be." Her voice was fierce and sharp, but the tears slipping down her cheeks were not for her physical pain alone. She must see that her daughter never felt this way.

"All right." Maureen stood, rubbing the queen's shoulders. Perhaps she was up to the task. At least she was finally fighting back.

"I mean my baby," Sinead said more firmly. "Do you think he loves her?"

"Of course." Maureen's stomach clenched, catching hold of her breath. She looked over her shoulder toward the palace. The king was there, flirting with the daughter of a visiting noble, instead of looking to his pregnant wife.

Sinead heard the doubt in Maureen's tone. They were not meant for places like this. They were born to the earth, as her daughter would be. Fairy people called them *fey folk*—delicate, odd, changeable creatures. But the truth was, they were old. Centuries old, even if they had only lived a few short years, because they were eternal. The eternal servants of the earth. Never meant to be shut away from nature to play games of power and intrigue. Not Maureen, not Sinead, and not her daughter, who would be born within the hour.

"Bring him to me."

"What?"

"He will give me a quarter hour of his time. Here on my territory. Tell him he owes me nothing less." Sinead's voice was firm, harsh even. She had never seemed so like her mother.

"Of course. But let me send a servant, or speak to him once she is born."

Sinead looked over her shoulder, taking Maureen's hand in her own. "It must be now." Maureen's hand tightened so suddenly and so tightly that Sinead nearly cried out. The fear in Maureen's eyes all but defeated Sinead's tiny strength. "Please, Mo. I trust no one but you."

Maureen nodded with damp eyes and hurried off, on foot, as the king preferred. Sinead turned back to face the garden, cradling her belly in both hands.

This place, this life was nothing like the Fairy court. Not so simple or carefree. She and Maureen had been more like daughter and slightly deferential mother when they first arrived in Stonedragon. Two lone fairies in a realm of humans. They grew every day lonelier and turned to each other for comfort, becoming friends. Better friends even than Maureen had been with Mama.

Sinead leaned back, and a smile painted her face. There were so few ways she would ever surpass her mother—not in looks or power or ability to hold a man's devotion—but she certainly loved Maureen better than Mama ever had, and Maureen loved her better as well. Maureen would look after Sinead's baby. Her beautiful girl.

Sinead closed her eyes, laying both her hands against her baby, and saw in her mind the pulsing light of her daughter's heartbeat. Already she was so strong, so good. She would be better than all of them. Her heart was such an open thing.

"I planted this for you, little one. I did not know it at the time, but it was all for you. You will be a child of great strength. The daughter of a king and a Fairy princess. In all of time, there has never been another like you. I have felt my love for you since long before I met you. It was so large, I did not understand."

She leaned her head down, intending to kiss her large belly, but could not reach, so she carried one hand to her lips for the kiss and laid it against her daughter's thumping heart. It was hard to believe now that Mama had not seen this enormous love in Sinead's future.

"You must always remember, more than anything else, that you are a child born of love. Love will always be your greatest ally."

She bent forward again, gripping the bench through another pain.

"Patience. I will let you out soon."

"Sinead?" Maureen came rushing forward to lean in front of her.

"Please, Maureen, a little decorum," the king snapped, following along at a properly sedate pace. "That is not the queen's proper address."

4

Sinead's head shot up, and her eyes pierced her husband. "It is the address I prefer," she snapped, gripping her friend's hand. "I would speak with you, Your Majesty."

"Of course." He bowed his head to her, shooting Maureen a look until she stood.

"I will be just over there." Maureen nodded her head toward the roses a few feet away.

"Could you not have waited until a more appropriate time? I was in the midst of a very delicate negotiation," the king said, once Maureen was out of hearing.

"Our daughter comes now. I would have an understanding with you before she is born."

"An understanding? You cannot hold my son hostage in there forever."

"This child is a girl. I have seen her in my dreams."

"You know I do not believe that. Out with it. Why did you call me here?" Balder's mild brown eyes snapped, and his jaw clenched. His eyes darted anywhere but Sinead, anywhere but her belly.

Sinead closed her eyes, gripping the bench. She thought maybe the pains were closer together, but she couldn't be sure; time always passed differently when Balder was near. She looked up in time to see Maureen start forward and shook her head, halting her where she stood.

"You are not happy in this marriage." Sinead spoke slowly, looking up at her husband. They were so very different. He was a tall man and so...unyielding. He wore his height like a weapon with her, and a shield with others.

"I have had most of what I wanted from our marriage. I will have the rest with my heir." He spoke coldly, but Sinead knew he was not so at his core. He knew he was in the wrong but would never say as much, so he lashed out.

"Well, you will be free of me soon enough," she whispered, her entire being tight and yearning for him to only meet her eyes, for him to fight to keep her. "But I need certain assurances from you first."

Balder drew up to his full height. He did not like being asked for favors. King Balder nodded.

Sinead's heart dropped as her last hope died. Had he no love for her then, none at all? When she had freely and happily given him her own. Was he so enraptured with his new love that he did not even care?

Beyond him Maureen stood like a tightly coiled muscle, pulsing against the wind, her fists locked, her eyes piercing the king while tears streamed down her face. She seemed even to be growing blue from holding her lungs so tight.

"To terms, then." Sinead swallowed her tears. "This child, male or female, is to be crowned your successor."

Balder drew back, rolling his eyes with a disbelieving smile. "That is silly. Women do not rule alone in human realms. That would mean abandoning my line to the control of an outsider."

"She will rule on her own. Any husband she might take would be purely ornamental. You can relate to this idea, I think."

"No *man* would accept it."

"Then no man will have her!" Sinead set her teeth and clutched the bench to ride through another bout of pains. "Why do you argue?" She panted as it passed. "If my dreams are nonsense, it costs you nothing to give in."

"Fine," he tossed off, annoyed to have been outwitted by a silly fey princess, as he was fond of referring to her to amuse his palace friends. "My word: the child will be crowned my successor, male or female. Is that all?" He threw up his hands, angling himself toward the palace.

"Not quite. My child will not be a tool to be bargained away. Any marriage contract will be of her making."

"As she is apparently the future queen, that seems a small thing," he said snidely. "Perhaps you would like me to say she can take power before my dotage, perhaps when she is twelve. No? Younger?"

"Your word that you will make no arrangements without her consent will do." Sinead watched her husband; when he hesitated, she spoke again. "Would you have your child as unhappy as we? Only think, had your father but allowed you a say, you might be married to your Gwyneth."

He looked made up of steam and embers standing there huffing as the wind grew wet. Sinead could barely feel the wind brush her face, carrying away the damp strands of hair that wanted to cling to her. The pain was back, but she did not possess the strength to cringe or scream.

"Come inside, Sinead," Balder said with concern in his voice. "You have my word; I will let her choose. You need a bed. I will take you."

"Thank you."

Balder bent forward to lift her, but Sinead stopped him with a hand against his chest. "No. For the promise. Thank you for the promise. Agh!" She fell forward over her belly, protecting it as the rain beat down.

She felt Balder's arms go around her to lift her, and fought back.

"No. No, I need one more promise. The most important."

"What? What? Anything." Gone was his stiff demeanor; he looked like a desperate child now.

Sinead took her husband's hands and placed them over her daughter's rapid, determined heartbeat. "This is your daughter. You must love her. Promise me you will love her!" She screamed it, nearly crushing the king's hand beneath hers as the pain claimed her.

The king did not move. He stared down at his wife as though he had never met her before. Perhaps he had not. The sky was growing dark, and the rain was falling in earnest, but she seemed untouched by it, shimmering with an amber light, like the tips of a blazing fire.

"Promise me," she pleaded.

"I promise," he whispered.

Sinead smiled, her breath sobbing raggedly out of her as tears streamed down her face. "I knew it." She breathed the words quietly and melted from exhaustion. Everything would be all right now. Her daughter would be loved, she would have Maureen, and she would be master of her own fate. Her life would be wonderful.

"I will take you in."

"There isn't time." Maureen's choked voice rose from the ground at the queen's feet. "You've a suddenly impatient child." Maureen wanted to lie down and sob, or shake Sinead and demand she *fight*, but as it had been the day she delivered Sinead and Desmond for the Fairy queen, Maureen felt Sinead's little girl crying out to join the world.

"But…we must get someone." Balder jerked around like a skittish rabbit.

"No, stay." Sinead sighed. "She will be fine. She will be marvelous." Sinead gripped her husband's hand tight and leaned her back against the tree, sheltering the bench.

"Now, my darling, you must push," Maureen ordered.

There were tears and yelling, and through it all, the queen grasped her husband's hand in one of her own and the tree at her back with the other. Thunder raced into the night, and rain pelted the garden. Every other minute the sky lit with lightning.

The princess arrived amid an explosion of thunder and lightning at once. Fiery blue light of Fairy magic filled the garden, waking the roses so they stretched out their vines, peeking over Maureen's shoulder at the child. Sinead lay slumped against the tree with a weary smile on her face and tears running relentlessly from her eyes.

"It is not true, you know," Sinead whispered, drifting in and out on the pain, her arms aching impatiently for Maureen to clean the baby and place her in her arms. "Mama wasn't born in a thunderstorm. She was born in her mother's bed, as is proper for a princess. But not my girl." She chuckled softly.

In the magic blue light weaving its way through the garden, Sinead saw her little girl. With a wild mop of hair and a smile like the moon, warm and wide—and safe. The light shifted, and she saw her again, a young woman, with a shy smile on her lips and her legs curled beneath her on this very bench, reading a letter. The light shifted between two rosebushes, and Sinead saw her daughter as a woman, so tall and regal and sure. She wore a suit of armor like a dress, with a sword at her waist and a crown on her head, speaking to a gathering. A leader. Sinead's blood tingled with the wonder of it.

"She is huge." The king regarded the puffy alien thing that was his daughter as Maureen lifted her into the queen's arms.

Maureen eyed him firmly. "Hold them, both," she ordered, crouching back down. "Sinead isn't strong enough."

Balder's arms came around Sinead hesitantly, his right hand supporting the baby from beneath Sinead's. He shook, breathing heavily.

"Oh." Sinead sighed, running a finger down her daughter's cheek, oblivious to all but her girl, her heart. She *was* huge. Sinead couldn't quite believe something so big had come from her; she had puffy little cheeks and five little reddish curls on the top of her head. Her baby's eyes shifted between golden brown and clear green, reflecting the earth. "She is perfect. I shall call you Rowan. For the tree that sheltered us as you were born. What do you say, my love?" she whispered into her daughter's ear.

Rowan cooed up at her mother, and they regarded each other with the warmth of old friends.

"Rowan it is, then. You," she sighed, breathing deeply between each word, "are loved, you are beautiful, and you are eternal. Now Mama must rest for a moment, my beautiful love."

"Sinead! Sinead?" The king shook his wife as best he could, clutching his suddenly screaming daughter to his shoulder. He yanked at Sinead with one hand, but she only slumped further against the tree. "Sinead."

"Don't shake her," Maureen snapped with all the force of a general.

"Sinead. Sinead!"

The last words Queen Sinead spoke were to her daughter amid the storm and the chaos of life and death combined, but between them there was only love and peace.

Though the king had not loved his wife in their short marriage, he truly mourned her loss. He shut himself away in his castle, refusing visitors for the first two years of his daughter's life. He invited only one guest, and she came only once, though she was invited much more often. It was the girl's grandmother Sorcha, the Fairy queen.

"That baby is no family of mine," Sorcha declared, staring into the cradle with wide, horrified, angry eyes. That couldn't be her grandchild. She had foreseen no children of this marriage. "That is a changeling, a monster sent to destroy you and your family."

"Sorcha." Balder lay his hands gently on the Fairy queen's shoulders and urged her closer to the baby. "This is Rowan, Sinead's daughter."

No. Sinead was meant to long outlive her husband. Meant to return home to the Fairy and rule them when her mother tired. How had this happened?

"That *thing* is no granddaughter of mine." She threw off Balder's hands, glaring at the baby. "She is a poison. She poisoned my daughter's blood, as she will poison all you love."

Balder drew away in shock, his hands retreating to his sides. He wanted to yank his daughter into his arms and hide her from the woman's gaze. But he couldn't move.

"Sinead loved her more than anything," Balder insisted.

"You do not understand love! You never will. I want nothing to do with that creature." Sorcha swept away from the cradle and her granddaughter, throwing words over her shoulder. "Keep her away from me." Balder's skin crawled with fear, but he still could not move.

It should have sounded like a threat, but Sorcha's parting words rang in his ears like a plea. Was she afraid? Of Rowan?

Moments after leaving King Balder, the Fairy queen appeared in the soft morning light of the rose garden. Maureen had been waiting, had felt her coming; at her arrival Maureen sank into a curtsy and waited. The Fairy queen did not look Maureen's way, just wandered among the roses, touching them, and perhaps seeing Sinead's death from their perspective.

"This is where it happened," the Fairy queen whispered.

Maureen, still crouched in a curtsy, watched her move. There were tears running down Maureen's cheeks, but she didn't make a sound, her eyes fixed on the scepter in Sorcha's hand. Sorcha held the scepter so that the crystal atop it nearly trailed the ground, so the boy trapped inside nearly touched the ground. Desmond. Maureen's heart clenched, and her fingers followed suit, closing around the fabric of her skirt.

This was what he feared when he challenged his mother—Sinead dead.

Sorcha must have sensed Maureen's feelings, because all at once she stood over Maureen. The Fairy queen laid a hand on Maureen's shoulder and squeezed, and tears rushed out of her eyes.

"She is gone, Maureen," the Fairy queen sobbed, turning her face away.

Maureen stood and wrapped her friend in a tight hug. "I know. I know."

They cried together for a moment, the Fairy queen burying her face in Maureen's shoulder. But she was never one to accept comforting for long. She pulled free of Maureen's arms and moved around her toward the tree and the bench before it.

"This is where that *thing* killed my girl," she snarled.

"King Balder?" Maureen asked at a loss. She was well used to the rage, even the venom in her friend's voice, but there was a tremor there as well. Grief, Maureen thought, and perhaps a bit of fear. But the Fairy queen had nothing to fear from the king of Stonedragon.

"Ha!" Sorcha's eyes sliced the air, seeking Maureen, and a chaotic, purple irradiance surrounded the Fairy queen. "As if something so paltry as a mere human could kill her. No, not he. But his blood, his offspring destroyed my daughter from within."

"Rowan is nought but a babe." Maureen's voice was so tight with restrained anger the whisper barely made it out. Her eyes sought the crystal again, to remind herself: Sorcha was no longer her sweet girlhood friend. "Rowan killed nothing; she simply survived."

"She killed my child!" The garden flashed purple, and the air filled with steam.

Maureen stepped back.

"You would defend that monster? It is your magic protecting her father; do not deny it." Sorcha's magic moved out before her, slowly evaporating the air in the garden.

"I have guarded him from death at your hand," Maureen choked out. "Sorcha..." Tentacles of steam closed around Maureen's throat. Maureen raised a shocked eyebrow at the Fairy queen. Against one person Sorcha had never turned—the one person who would never turn on her, Maureen.

"Why are you protecting him? He betrayed my child. Tell me you do not want him dead. Tell me he does not deserve it." Sorcha's voice was no more than a whisper.

The steam holding Maureen's throat released, so she could speak once more. "He deserves to die for his crimes, but Sinead's girl deserves a father more."

"That *thing* is not my daughter's baby!"

"Yes, she is." Maureen's voice quivered, and her tears returned. "I will not let you take Rowan's father away while there is power within me to stop you, but...Your Majesty," Maureen pleaded, "I know you are grieved; do not let that steal the last of your family from you."

"She is not my family. Nor your charge," Sorcha snapped, flicking out a hand to close the subject. "Come; we are leaving. At home, among your kind, you will see. Come."

Maureen took a step away, her entire body shaking, mostly of sorrow, but there was fear as well. In a rage, there was no saying what Sorcha might do. Maureen had known this woman since they were girls, when the world was carefree and certain. She had known Sorcha when she was soft and sweet, loved by the world—and when she was betrayed, frightened, and enraged. The one thing that held true of every version of this beloved friend was that Sorcha never went back. There would be no forgiveness if she saw Maureen's choice as betrayal. And that meant not only failing Sorcha, but Desmond as well.

Maureen took another step away, shaking her head slowly. "I am staying. Sinead wanted me to care for her girl, and I will do so."

"You dare refuse me? I who elevated you, elevated all the water sprites, made you the most honored of our people? Be careful you do not make me change my mind."

"Sorcha." Maureen covered her mouth with a hand, forcing herself to take one step after another away. Sorcha wouldn't do it, would not be so cruel. "Please, it is not too late. Hold Rowan; look at those eyes. Sinead's eyes."

"I am through discussing that creature!" Sorcha shouted, her voice quivering. "That she will live should be enough for you. Now, come home, and all is forgiven."

"I am staying with Rowan," Maureen said as firmly as she was able, but she could not help pleading with Sorcha one last time. "She will need Fairy with her; she will need her grandmother."

The purple light of Sorcha's magic surged, scorching bright, and for half a second she bared her teeth in a snarl; then all was calm again. The Fairy queen stood, small in height but giant in presence, wholly serene.

"Stay then," she said so sweetly they might be discussing a change in the weather. "I see you've made your choice in the end. But I am through with traitors. I wonder if it isn't a trait of your kind."

Maureen bit her lip and stared at the ground, shaking; she forced her fisted hands to her sides. It was her people's comfort, or a baby abandoned to a world that would not understand her—Sorcha would make her choose. For she could not protect both. Maureen held silent; her people at least would have one another.

"I find I cannot trust the water sprite; they have no home any longer in my domain—lesser beings all."

"They are your kind as well, Sorcha."

"I am no water sprite."

"You are Fairy; we are Fairy. It is the same."

"No, my dearest friend, that is what I have always allowed you to believe. Because I loved you. But I cannot love a traitor." Sorcha's eyes darted away from Maureen for the barest of instants, eyeing the crystal atop her scepter. When she looked on Maureen again, all trace of Maureen's old friend was gone. "I am Fairy. Her guardian, her maker, her queen. And your kind are no longer welcome among us."

The Fairy queen vanished. Maureen dropped to her knees, sobbing.

Though it seemed the Fairy queen would never return, King Balder tried for many years to heal the breach for his daughter's sake. Sorcha never responded, and the king ceased his attempts just months after the celebration of his second marriage, to the lady Gwyneth, when Rowan was four.

Lady Gwyneth had not visited the castle much in the years after the queen's death, but she and the king had been nearly constant correspondents. And Gwyneth was the first guest when the castle reopened.

Balder was careful to be sure that Rowan was comfortable with Lady Gwyneth before he proposed. And she was a kind stepmother. Still, none were more aware than Rowan and Gwyneth that they were not mother and daughter. They liked each other, they were friendly, and they both loved the king, but there was no motherly and daughterly affection between them. It seemed that Rowan would not suffer from the lack of it. But things changed.

The Last Rose

On the night of Rowan's sixth birthday, she wandered into the garden where she was born. She waited for Maureen to visit her as she did every year at this time to tell her the story of her birth.

Maureen remained in the kingdom, but not the palace. She visited often, but was too heartbroken to live in the place she lost her girl.

As Rowan wandered through the rosebushes, running her fingertips along the petals and feeling the wind against her face, she played over and over in her mind the words of the story. Tonight, more than any time before, they shimmered inside her.

You are loved, you are beautiful, you are eternal.

No one thought a six-year-old could understand such things, but tonight Rowan did. Because she was eternal. Some secret of the universe had unwound within her.

"Rowan?" Maureen's voice startled her out of her thoughts. She spun around so quickly, she scraped her arm along the thorns. Three little drops of her blood fell to the ground beneath the roses and winked up at her like rubies met by moonlight.

"Rowan?"

"I'm here," she said wonderingly. She watched as the blood was absorbed into the ground.

"What have you done to yourself?" Maureen chuckled, lifting Rowan's scraped arm and smoothing away the last of the blood, healing the scratch. Rowan was prone to little accidents, clumsiness. Maureen wondered if there was not more of the king in this little creature than her mother. Sinead had been an ethereal creature—soft, graceful, slight, almost as ephemeral as a ray of light or a warm breath in the snow.

Rowan was none of those things. Her feet were too big for her body, she broke something every time she turned around, she had a mop of lightly curled auburn hair that no one could do a thing with, and she was far too solid to ever be viewed as ephemeral. But Maureen couldn't help loving her, clumsiness and all.

"It's nothing," Rowan said dismissively, well used to her reputation. "I'm to have a sister," she said with a sly smile.

"Are you, indeed?" Maureen asked once she had caught her breath. There it was. Every so often Rowan would look up at a person, and her mother's eyes would be looking back. Nearly clear, they held little flecks of color, lights flashing across the surface of still water. "And how do you know it will be a sister?"

"I dreamed it. She will be beautiful, Maureen. With lovely blue eyes and three little freckles just here." Rowan ran her finger just under her right eye. "And she will have a sweet voice, and everyone will love her."

"That is a beautiful dream, dear. I had no idea you wanted a sister," Maureen said neutrally. It was possible Rowan was finally showing signs of her heritage, but it could just be the dream of a lonely girl.

Rowan shrugged, walking away from the roses to sit on her bench. Maureen did not believe her. Father had not believed her, either. They would see soon enough.

"Would you like to hear the story of your birth?" Maureen asked.

"No." Rowan ran her hands up and down the trunk of her tree. "I know it."

Maureen sighed; she was such a serious child, so old for her age.

"Will you be married *soon*?" Rowan complained impatiently. It must have been months since Maureen told her. What was taking so long?

"Yes," Maureen chuckled. "Will you come? I will miss you if you are not there."

"Of course. Then you will have children of your own, two boys and one girl. The boys will stay, and she will go away. She will go to the Fairy court."

"I…" Maureen caught her breath, and her mind went blank. Rowan had never seemed so completely Fairy; it made Maureen's heart race, panicked. "How do you know?"

"Because I will ask her to," Rowan said simply.

Maureen stared at her openmouthed. She felt the power of Rowan's happiness flutter through her, and resisted it. This made no sense. Maureen, more than anyone, longed for Rowan to show signs of her Fairy heritage, but so suddenly, so impossibly, Maureen could not let herself believe. She had long since given up hope of having her own children. She spent her time loving and mourning the children of others.

Now, her heart trembled with hope and fear combined. And hope could shatter a heart.

Rowan turned up her nose at Maureen's skepticism. "I love my sister. I will take good care of her."

"I am sure you will, dearest." Maureen stared at this little creature, a bit lost. "Are you sure you do not want to hear the story? Sometimes it is nice to hear a story even if you have heard it a million times and know exactly how it ends."

"All right." Rowan shrugged, scooting over on the bench for Maureen to take a seat next to her.

Maureen wrapped one arm gently around Rowan's shoulders, pulling her close, and began her tale with a troubled mind. "You were born into a raging storm. Your mother had gone out into the rose garden, as she did every day, to be among her friends."

Maureen made a point to never say the roses were Sinead's only friends or to mention the extent of her sadness that day. Rowan was already so serious, she should hear joyful things. "They smiled, always welcoming, a sea of roses of every different hue. She sat among them as the sky grew dark and the wind grew wet. And I at her back begged her to 'come inside' and have her child in a bed 'as is proper.'"

Maureen watched Rowan's little head rise in pride, knowing what was to come. She was such a sweet, innocent child. Maureen ran a hand along her cheek—her beloved little girl, could she be right? After everything, could Maureen become mother of her own children?

"Your mother would not back down," Maureen went on, smiling though her eyes stung. "She said…"

"My daughter is not just some insipid princess." Rowan knew the words by heart and spoke with regal confidence. "To be petted and groomed and made a tool for a man's ends; she is a child of the earth and the air. She is a fey creature, and she will be born in the light and the air and the storm if need be."

Rowan's tone of voice was so fierce Maureen had to chuckle. Her smile lingered as she continued her story. "Sinead was always a gentle creature, delicate as a wisp of spider thread and charming as a baby's laugh." Maureen pulled a few of Rowan's curls forward, tickling her neck in the process, so she giggled and gazed up at Maureen with sparkling eyes. "But on that night, with her back to the blazing fire of the rowan tree's leaves, she was as firm as any mountain. She called for your father, the king, and told him what would be." Maureen slipped a finger under Rowan's chin and gazed proudly down into her eyes. "That you would be queen of his people and would choose a king to sit beside you.

"The wind grew fierce and cold, and the rain came down in waves, shedding tears for what nature knew was to come. But still your mother would not move. Her girl was something special. Her girl would not be frightened by a little storm."

Rowan stiffened her spine as though she would stand against the storm in the story.

"And so it was, in the hour of your birth, the winds raged to welcome you, and the rain fell to bathe you, and thunder and lightning shook the very air of the world, for here was a *special* child. And your mother laughed for the joy of it, saying that even her own powerful mother was born in a bed as is proper for a princess, 'but not my girl.'" Here Maureen always had to stop; the tears were too great to go on without kissing Rowan on the forehead. But her sweet Rowan, she really did see only the good. Even though Maureen was recounting her mother's death, Rowan's eyes shone with joy for the few moments shared by mother and daughter.

"When your mother held you in her arms, her fire blazed more brightly than the strongest flame. She looked into your eyes, your eternity, and came to know you in an instant. She told you that you were perfect and named you for the tree that sheltered you as you were born. And you gazed into each other's eyes, of one mind in that moment, and she whispered her last words, 'You are loved, you are beautiful, and you are eternal. You are my beautiful love.' Then she shut her eyes to this world, leaving it to you, and became one with eternity."

Rowan snuggled into Maureen's arms as the story came to an end and laid her head against Maureen's chest. "Maureen, I think she is happy I'm to be a sister."

Maureen bit her lip and allowed a few tears loose. "Yes, dearest, I am sure she is."

Six weeks later, a cautious king sat his daughter down to inform her that the queen was pregnant. Rowan smiled and pretended to listen, imagining what a good sister she would be.

Balder watched his daughter as he would a prowling dragon. Sinead had known Rowan would be a girl, and he hadn't believed her, either. But this was different. Sinead plucked knowledge from the air, in bits and pieces, as though she had seen them drifting past. But Rowan…she sat him down over breakfast and told him the day his next daughter would be born, how tall she would be, and the color of her eyes and hair. She told him not to worry, that Gwyneth would not die in childbirth. She knew so much, and none of it seemed to disturb her. She just smiled serenely, like a mystic of fifty instead of a child of six. What did one do with this?

What was he to do with her?

The roses lining the eastern wall grew three feet that week and filled out like climbing vines rather than bushes. They linked branches, forming an impenetrable wall around the eastern side of the castle. The gardeners could do nothing about it; the branches refused to be cut, growing hard as metal when threatened.

Balder's fears about Rowan's powers only increased in the months leading up to the birth of his second daughter. Time after time, odd calamities befell the castle. It began small enough: Gwyneth was cold, and Rowan brought her a blanket, only to have it catch fire as she laid it over her stepmother's legs, though there were no flames near. Gwyneth jumped away, kicking the blanket to the floor. She fled into her husband's arms, staring at Rowan as though she were a monster as the round-eyed child stomped the flames out. Or when Rowan said she wished she could see the bird perched in the rafters more closely, and an entire flock came swarming into the great hall through an upper window and dove just in front of a giggling Rowan. Then the calamities grew bigger.

When the king refused her permission to go to Maureen's wedding, Rowan threw a fit and was sent to her room. Minutes later, her nurse rushed down the stairs, screaming about demon children. Fearing the worst, Balder raced to his daughter and found Rowan sitting with her legs dangling in the air. She stared into the village, defiantly unconcerned that her entire wall had crumbled into the garden.

He couldn't bring himself to move from her doorway. With every new incident, Sorcha's words haunted him. Even with the roses, whenever he spoke with the gardeners about them, Rowan would smile secretively. He had no idea what to do with this.

The king closed that wing of the palace, moving the family to the south side, facing the sea. Every day he watched and hoped for a way to understand and help this new Rowan.

By the time Gwyneth was four months pregnant, the roses reached as high as the castle roof. Gwyneth was so distraught over the incidents, she stayed locked in her room, refusing to see her stepdaughter.

King Balder understood that there were things he could control and things he could not. So he took charge of the things he could, ordering the rose garden burned to the ground.

He stood watching the progress, so he was there to see Rowan come running from the castle, screaming at the top of her lungs.

"No! No, you can't kill them," she sobbed, running forward. Balder caught her when she would have run past him to the gardeners and their torches. "No. Please. Mama planted them for me."

"Rowan, you must stop this. I cannot let it go on anymore."

"Don't burn them." Rowan did not even hear her father, her eyes on the burning roses. Every time she smelled them, she heard her mother's spirit whispering, *I planted this for you, little one.*

"Rowan!" The king shook his daughter until she focused on him. "You *must* stop. You are frightening people. Enough! Tell me what is upsetting you."

"You're burning Mama's roses," Rowan wailed.

"They will overtake the entire castle. You must stop."

"It isn't me," Rowan pleaded with her father. "I'm not making them grow."

"No? And the blanket, your wall, were those not you, either?"

"I...I didn't mean to. I don't know how they happened. But I am not making them grow."

"Who is, Rowan? Perhaps these are accidents, too." He waved to the smoldering roses. Rowan shook free of her father, running straight into the clouds of falling ash.

"Rowan. Stop!"

She dropped to the ground, clutching one stem and the barely singed pink rose attached to it.

"Mama," she sobbed; the rose lay in her open palm. "Aaaaaaa!" A burning limb collapsed on her shoulder, and the flames caught on her gown. Rowan clenched her hand shut in shock, screaming in pain and sending the jagged thorns deep into her palm.

"Rowan." The king stooped into the pile of cinders, jerking his daughter into his arms and patting out the flames. "Come here, okay, okay. You'll be fine. I have you now."

"I'm not poison," she mumbled through her tears. Her breath was ragged, and there were angry red burns across her back.

"No, you're not poison. You're marvelous," Balder whispered, cradling his daughter gingerly.

How did she know about that? He never told her. No one else could have, because he told no one. But he had been thinking about it. About all of it, wondering if there wasn't some truth to it.

He had no right to wonder.

Rowan slept for five days, recovering from the burns on her shoulders and back. The king did not leave her side; his hand rested over hers, where she clutched the rose. He had tried to pry it from her fingers, but she only clutched it tighter, thrashing about and moaning in her sleep.

The roses, which had burned all the way to the ground, grew back the first night. And were climbing the walls halfway up the castle by the second.

Balder ordered a wall built around the garden, with only one entrance. When it was finished, he ordered the roses burned daily. Between burnings they grew back up the palace walls, every day faster. He kept the key to the garden on his person, allowing it off only so the gardeners could get in to burn the roses.

When Rowan woke, Maureen was at her father's side, whispering quietly.

"Good morning, little love. I've a surprise for you," Maureen said as Rowan's eyes fluttered open. Maureen leaned in to kiss her on the head. "Your father is building a home for me and Colum where the old stables were. So I can always be near you."

Rowan looked between them, saying nothing. Her father was smiling expectantly, as though he thought she would jump from the bed and hug him. Maureen too wore a cautious smile.

You're scaring people, Father had said. Scaring him. And Gwyneth, and it seemed Maureen, as well.

Rowan looked down at her hand and the last rose trapped in it; several petals had fallen off, and what remained were dry and shriveling. She pried her fingers apart, wincing. Her skin had started to close around the thorns, as though they would become a part of her body. She yanked the rose out with two fingers, making sure to avoid the thorns. Rowan stared down at the little puckered holes of skin.

"My sister won't have scars. She'll be perfect like Mama, like a princess."

"Rowan." Her father leaned forward, brushing back a stray hair that fell over her eyes. "You are a princess, and you will be a queen. Just like your mother."

Rowan looked up and caught Balder's eyes. He startled. Rowan's eyes were so clear, sometimes he could see himself in them; it was unnerving.

"I will like having Maureen nearby." Rowan rolled over, holding the rose between two fingers.

The gardeners couldn't explain how she did it, but every morning when they arrived in the walled-up rose garden, Rowan was sitting on the bench where she was born. She did not move, did not speak; she simply sat and watched as her mother's roses burned, clenching her fingers so tight they dug into the thorn scars in her palm.

Maureen moved into the castle until her home was built, spending hours each day trying to teach Rowan to use the magic she suddenly found herself wielding. It was slow going.

"All right, dearest." Maureen massaged Rowan's shoulders gently from behind. She tried to focus this little bundle of nerves; Rowan was always so afraid of being imperfect. "See the candle before you?"

Rowan slouched her shoulders noncommittally. Maureen kissed the crown of Rowan's head with a patient smile Rowan could not see.

"Imagine your mind is an extinguisher; then lay it over the flame and put it out."

Rowan held her breath, clenched up her shoulders, and scrunched her eyes, focusing on the flame. She felt full of little magical charges rushing to get out, and all they had to do was snuff the flame.

Nothing happened. Why couldn't she make it work when she tried?

A maid walked through Rowan's new room, gathering up her dirty laundry. Rowan watched her work, waiting, the magic pounding to get out, but if there was someone watching...nobody liked Rowan's magic.

You're scaring people.

"Aaaaaaa!" The maid cast aside her basket as flames jumped from the laundry. "She's trying to kill me."

Rowan cowered back into Maureen's arms.

"Get out." The entire room vibrated with Maureen's rage at the young maid, but her arms wrapped Rowan gently closer. The maid fled, and as Maureen kissed Rowan's head again, the flames went out.

"Well," Maureen chuckled, "at least you moved the fire."

There were more little incidents as Rowan was learning control than there had been when magic simply flowed out of her. Maureen was sure if she could only figure out Rowan's magical talent, things would improve. All she really needed was confidence. Her talent did not seem to be with fire, and when she'd taught Rowan to call the rain as water sprites could, there was a monthlong drought. Most animals attacked when Rowan tried to soothe them, and not for the life of her could Rowan make herself invisible—though it was clear she wanted to be so, every day more. Perhaps magic worked differently when one was only half Fairy.

When Gwyneth came out of her room at last, the king made sure Rowan was there. Gwyneth approached Rowan cautiously, watching her feet more than her stepdaughter.

"Rowan," Gwyneth said, with a voice as thin as a summer breeze. She was a delicate-looking woman; everything about her seemed to drift gently. "I am sorry I overreacted. I know you would never mean to hurt me."

Rowan looked between her father and stepmother, chewing the inside of her cheek. She wasn't fooled; Gwyneth was still afraid. And Father had allowed her to hide for nearly two months because he thought she was right to fear.

Rowan sighed through her nose, releasing her cheek from the cage of her teeth only long enough to say, "I am sorry, Gwyneth; I only wanted to help you."

Father smiled. "Good. That's behind us now."

Rowan knew he was wrong, so she kept her distance from Gwyneth.

Rowan saw caution in many eyes. Only one pair seemed never to look on her with fear—Maureen's husband, Colum. As days passed with more and more people looking at her guardedly, Rowan spent more time following Colum around as he trained the young knights.

"So, these sons I'm to have, will they be big men like their father, knights?" Colum was just a bit taller than Rowan's father, with shoulders that looked quite used to lifting heavy burdens. He had welcoming brown eyes, but more than anything, it was his deep, rumbling voice, like thunder or magic, and the smile that came along with it that Rowan loved best about him.

Rowan smiled. She was hiding behind a bale of hay in the stables, but Colum always knew when she was there.

"No," she teased; only he understood her humor. "One will be a gardener, the other a tailor, and both very sickly and poor."

"Ah. Good, good. A man wants his sons to forge their own paths." He chuckled. "And my daughter, she will be ugly, I trust, to scare away all of the men."

"No. She will be the most beautiful woman, save my sister. But a terrible shrew."

"Ah. Good. A man wants his daughter to take after her mother."

Rowan fell over laughing. He was always pretending to insult Maureen.

"Well, Princess, are you going to lie there uselessly laughing? Or will you help me train my men?"

Colum kept Rowan active, putting her to work feeding horses and carrying around sparring weapons. When the king would have objected, his daughter's smile halted him. There were only two times she smiled: when she spoke of her sister, and when she was "training" young knights. So he let her be. Colum would never let any harm come to her. What was the danger in a six-year-old dragging a bag of weapons after his knights?

Desired above All

On the night of her sister's birth, Rowan stole into her stepmother's birthing room to watch. She wanted to be a part of welcoming to the world this child, who was desired above all.

Rowan wasn't nervous. She knew what would happen; but even knowing how it would end, the wait was unsettling. She crouched secretly in a corner between the wall and a cabinet. Gwyneth had three nurses around her, and Father stood by, awaiting his new daughter. It was a clear, warm night, and Rowan could see stars out the window behind Gwyneth's bed. She looked at them in the frightening moments, when Gwyneth would scream or cry. The eternal stars, she looked on them and wished.

"Let her be eternal, too. Let her be eternal, too," she begged in nearly silent breaths, and her magic raced out into the night with the words.

When at last she heard her sister cry for the first time, Rowan started forward, too overcome to remain hidden. She ran up to the midwife and pulled her arm aside.

"Princess!" the woman screeched. "Where did you come from?"

"Over there," Rowan said, gazing rapturously at her sister. "I knew you would be perfect."

Rowan's eyes were only for her sister. She did not notice the reaction of the adults around the room—the fear on the midwife's face, the panic on Gwyneth's, or the resignation on her father's.

"Rowan." The king bent down beside his daughters.

"She is perfect, Father. Isn't she perfect?" Rowan asked, dotting a finger to each of the three jewel-like freckles under her sister's right eye.

"That she is. Just like you said she'd be. Shall we let her mother see her?"

"Oh, yes." Rowan stepped back so her father could lift his new daughter away from the midwife and carry her to Gwyneth.

"She is perfect, Gwyneth!" Rowan effervesced. "Everyone will love her."

The moment her child was in her arms, all the panic that had gripped Gwyneth melted away. She held her as though she was made up of no more than bits of stardust and would crumple away if held too tightly. Gwyneth's lips lay on her daughter's forehead, and her eyes drifted shut as she offered a prayer of thanks.

Rowan watched the perfect mother-daughter moment and felt tears overwhelm her. She tried to look away but could not seem to move. Rowan rubbed the scars from where she had gripped the last rose. She wished she could remember her mother, even for one moment.

Balder's hand came down on her shoulder and gave her a comforting squeeze.

"What is she to be called?" he asked Rowan.

"Me?"

"Did you not dream her name?"

Rowan shook her head. Her sister had walked into her dreams a fully formed being. She had never even wondered what her name would be.

"Then you must name her," Balder insisted. "You have known her longest."

Rowan felt a great swelling of pride, but in the same instant, a wave of caution. She looked at Gwyneth. Her stepmother seemed wary of her even now.

"Yes, Rowan," Gwyneth nodded. "You must name her. Come here; hold her."

Rowan climbed onto the bed with Gwyneth and held out her arms. She looked down at her sleeping sister and saw her as a girl dancing barefoot in a field, and a woman holding her hand out to fate with a smile.

"Roisin," she said at last. "For the rose garden."

Gwyneth's eyes shot to Balder, unnerved and resistant, but the king did not notice. All he saw were his girls, so perfect together.

"What do you think of that, Little Rose?" Balder asked with a soft smile. His new daughter blinked twice and drifted to sleep.

Rowan leaned down, placing a kiss on her sister's forehead, and whispered, "I have ever loved you. I will never let anything harm you. You are loved. You are beautiful. And you will be eternal."

For some time, it seemed everything would be better. Rowan had never been as angelic as she was standing over her sister's crib. Gwyneth's fears slowly retreated. She looked upon Rowan kindly again, and there were no more incidents.

But on the anniversary of Roisin's sixth month, the palace opened in a great celebration of her birth. Kings, queens, and leaders from the thirteen nations of the known world filled the palace, bringing gifts and offering blessings. Only one nation had no representative, the Fairy. But she was not missed.

It was a joyous gathering. From her place beside her sister's crib, Rowan watched as person after person came forward and fell under Roisin's spell. She watched the dignitaries, noting with wonder all the beautiful and exciting differences, the ways their voices flirted with the air, the various clothes they wore, and all the special things each considered gifts.

A man in a bright green robe stepped forward, and Rowan could barely resist running her hand along the shimmering fabric and the little golden threads within it, catching the light. He was more beautifully garbed than half the women. He lifted Roisin high so her feet kicked the air and her laughter filled the room. When he laid her back in her cradle, he intoned in a rolling voice, "She will be blessed with a joyful spirit."

A quiet man caught Rowan's attention next. He was simply garbed, with a shaved bald head and a voice so low and steady it barely disturbed the air when he ran a finger over Roisin's forehead and pronounced her blessed with compassion.

A tired-looking old woman, with quiet green eyes and her hair wrapped beneath a dark scarf, pleasantly startled Rowan by laughing aloud while doing playful battle with Roisin over her finger. "This child is blessed already with strength of conviction."

There was a little round woman dressed in clothes so heavy with fur Rowan wondered if she could be quite comfortable. But she regarded Roisin with a wide smile before turning away and saying, in a fluttering sigh, that she would be a woman of deep goodness.

When a willowy woman of dark looks and a soft voice leaned near to the crib, Roisin cooed and rolled so that her little noises sounded like a song. "You must have a lovely voice to sing that heart song, child," she told Roisin and winked at Rowan. "Don't you think?" Rowan nodded, excited to be included in the blessing process. The woman walked to rejoin her husband and small son, with ringing steps that made Rowan want to dance and sway as well.

One after another, the guests came to her sister and offered her their blessings. Beauty, wealth, grace, honesty, wisdom, an affinity with nature. Every imaginable offering was laid before her sister. Rowan had never seen or heard so much to spark her interest. And she was nearly overcome with pride; it was her sister who had brought about all this togetherness and celebration.

"You are eternal," she whispered into Roisin's crib during a lull in guests. How could she be anything else, with all she inspired?

Rowan had been standing in one place for hours; her feet hurt, and every so often her eyes drifted shut. But when her father leaned down to ask her if she would like to sit, she shook her head. She felt cold suddenly. Not on her skin, but in her blood—a prickling cold, like icicles floating through her veins.

Rowan stretched out a hand and gripped the side of the crib; her other hand balled into a fist around her scars.

As the hall fell slowly silent, Rowan peeked around her father's legs to see what was causing the quiet.

A woman's soft voice sliced through the hush. "Have I arrived too late?"

And the World Will Never Be the Same

*I*n the middle of the parting crowd of palace guests stood a woman so short, she'd have been obscured had the crowd reformed. Yet Rowan sensed the need of the crowd to give her even more space. She had bright green eyes, and her hair was even paler blond than the soft curls on Roisin's head.

"You must forgive me," she said bitterly. "It seems I was overlooked on the guest list. Though it is my right to be here."

"Queen Sorcha." Balder stepped in front of his daughters. He bowed. "It is our great honor to have you, of course. My apologies for overlooking you."

The woman drifted closer, bringing the cold with her. Rowan found it hard to breathe. She couldn't make out the woman's steps; she simply floated. She was horribly beautiful—so much so that it was hard to look away from her. She was like a bird, fluttery and small, surrounded by light, as though passing the sun at its apex. She had wings! One moment Rowan could see them, and the next, because they were so thin, they vanished into her light. And her waving white gown might have been made of a thousand white feathers stitched together.

Rowan reached her free hand out to her father's back. Her eyes burned from the magnitude of the woman's beauty.

"Make her leave," she whispered. She did not know why. She did not want to know. But Rowan was certain if the woman was allowed to remain, something terrible would happen, and the world would never be the same.

"It will be all right." Gwyneth pulled Rowan's hand off her father. "I am sure your grandmother only wants to meet you."

Rowan's eyes shot to where the woman had been only moments before. Empty. She was nearly upon them.

Her grandmother?

"No." This horrible woman couldn't be her grandmother. "No. Take Roisin away and hide her."

"Rowan." The stinging lash of her grandmother's voice struck Rowan.

Too late.

Rowan turned to face the woman who was her grandmother.

"A boy's name." She looked Rowan up and down critically. Seven now, Rowan was more than half her grandmother's height. "I had rather hoped it would stop suiting you. But you do take after your father, don't you?"

Rowan was sure she should be hurt by the words. Perhaps she would be, later when she was gone and Rowan could banish this feeling of impending doom.

"Are you dumb as well, child? Answer me."

"Do not speak to her that way," Balder ordered in full kingly force. But Rowan's grandmother only smiled.

"You shouldn't be here," Rowan said at length, her eyes locked with her grandmother's.

"No. You shouldn't," she spat out; her face felt mere inches from Rowan's, though she had not moved. "You should have died at birth. But you poisoned your mother—like you poison everything you touch."

The prickles of cold in her veins raced all together to stab at Rowan's heart. She winced away from the pain, straightening her back and forcing the feeling into the darkest recesses of her mind, so she could guard Roisin.

"Just as your father does." Sorcha twisted toward the king. He was frozen, whether by magic or from fear, Rowan could not tell. Her grandmother was so beautiful. In every move, she was graceful, soft, and womanly. Yet beneath it all, Rowan felt a deep ugliness. She was here to inflict suffering.

"You and your whore broke my child's heart." Sorcha paused, and her eyes pierced Rowan into place, though no one else seemed to notice. "Then *you* killed her. Now I will do the same to you."

"No." Rowan started forward, the lone person in the hall not trapped by the woman's terrible spell.

"You may have sixteen years from the night of her birth. Sixteen years for the *little rose* to grow in beauty and goodness. And for you to love her more with each passing day." Sorcha spoke in a silky voice, drawing every ear to her.

"No." Rowan blocked her sister's crib bodily, as though it would make a difference. "Leave. Make her leave! She shouldn't be here."

"And on the first night of her sixteenth year, you will break her heart." Her eyes were all for Rowan. They bore into her, so she could do nothing but stand futilely blocking her sister, with tears running down both cheeks.

"Then you will poison the one you love most, pricking her finger on a spindle, so she falls dead at your feet. That is my gift to you." She jerked her gaze away from Rowan. "To you all. I will take from you what you love most. As you took it from me."

As suddenly as she had come upon them, she was gone, leaving not so much as a ripple in the air. Nothing but the crushed spirits of every member of the gathering betrayed her.

Rowan remained as she had been, panting for breath, her body before Roisin's crib like a shield. She sobbed even as sound exploded back into the hall, even after Gwyneth yanked Roisin into her arms as though the simple act of holding her child could undo the curse.

No, that terrible woman could not be her grandmother.

"We must do something."

"Send a battalion; kill the witch. Surely that will undo the magic."

"Hide her."

"Destroy all the spindles."

Ideas were flung from all sides of the room. Only Rowan and her father remained silent. Both knew there was no undoing this type of magic.

"Give her Rowan."

It was spoken in a wretched whisper, torn from her very soul. But as Rowan looked over her shoulder and into the eyes of her stepmother, she knew Gwyneth meant the words.

"I am sorry," she said to Rowan. "I am so sorry. But it was you. It was Rowan she spoke to; we all saw it." Gwyneth looked into the crowd for support. "It is you Sorcha wants to punish. If you aren't here, there is no reason for her to curse your sister." She looked back to Rowan.

"You mean kill her, I think." Maureen's voice rang strong and clear over the din of the guests. She had not been at the celebration, Rowan was certain. She had just appeared. "Nothing short of Rowan's death—if that—would satisfy the queen's thirst for vengeance. So, Lady Gwyneth"—she used her old title, infusing her voice with anger and insult—"would you have us kill one child to save another?"

"Rowan will not be killed. Nor sent away." The king spoke for the first time from out of his stupor. "We will not, now or ever, descend to the evil that has been cast at us."

"You would doom our child to save yours?" Gwyneth demanded, half-mad with fear.

"She is not yet doomed." Maureen stepped up to the crib and knelt in front of Rowan, brushing a stray curl from her cheek. "You blessed your sister in the hour of her birth. What did you say?"

"That I would keep her safe."

"No, that is a sister's promise." Such a promise could not have so altered this human child that Maureen could feel its distress from her cottage. She knew Rowan, her open heart, so like Sinead's. "The other. Say it again."

"I said, you are loved, you are beautiful, and you will be eternal," Rowan whispered. Her hands slipped from the crib to drift to her sides.

"You will be eternal," Maureen repeated, blinking back tears. "She will not die; she will sleep." She walked to Gwyneth and held out her hands for the baby. "Now all that remains is for me to offer my blessing."

"Will it help?" Balder asked.

"It will help. How much, I cannot say." She took Roisin in her arms for the first time, running a finger over the freckles Rowan had foreseen. "You are loved. Everyone says it, and now it is for you to earn it. You will be saved by love. Only the purest and strongest of loves can set you free and wake you from your sleep. Find love, little rose, and you shall wake eternally."

Rowan watched Maureen's eyes as she blessed the baby. They were sad, and somehow—cold. This was all they could do? Truly?

"Those are nothing more than words!" Gwyneth shouted. She marched to the king and shook him.

"Then so were the queen's." Maureen's voice was so angry, it reminded Rowan of her grandmother's. She wanted to reach out and hold Maureen, to be sure she was still herself. But Rowan couldn't touch anything; she balled her hands and dropped them to her sides.

You poisoned your mother, like you poison everything you touch.

Her grandmother. Had that really been the mother of her mother? Was it possible someone so horrid could be mother to someone so wonderful? Or had it all been lies?

"The queen? The queen! I am your queen! Or do you still serve the hag that would kill my child?"

"I do not serve the Fairy queen. But *you* will never be my queen." Maureen's eyes raked across Gwyneth viciously, but her arms rocked the child with innate tenderness.

"Balder! Why do you just stand there?" Gwyneth shouted, advancing on her husband like a wild animal, waving her arms and shaking. "Do something. She will kill our child! Does that mean nothing to you?"

Still the king held silent. He stared at his daughter, his first. Rowan returned his stare, tears wetting her cheeks.

I am poison, Rowan thought, looking into her father's eyes. *He will die of his love for me, and so will Roisin.*

"I will go to her, Father," Rowan said in a small voice.

Her tears dried on her face as she spoke. She looked around her: Maureen and Gwyneth would kill each other with their fears; Father was frozen; Roisin lay crying in Maureen's arms, trapped between the battling women. Rowan wanted to go to her, to carry her away from all the anger and fear, but she couldn't.

You poisoned your mother, like you poison everything you touch.

"No, Rowan, you will not." Balder walked calmly to Maureen and lifted his new daughter from her arms, carrying her to crouch in front of Rowan. "Hold her."

In the same instant, Rowan jumped backward, shaking her head, and Gwyneth rushed forward, intent on grabbing her daughter.

"Stop," the king ordered his wife, pinning her in place with a stare. "I made allowances for you during your pregnancy. No more. Rowan is my daughter, your future queen. If you cannot show her affection, you will at least show her the proper respect."

Gwyneth jerked back as if slapped, with wide, injured, frightened eyes, and her shoulders slunk in toward her chest. Rowan glanced between her father and stepmother, her stomach twisting with a sharp shock. Didn't Father fear her as much as Gwyneth?

Balder faced his daughter, softening his features into a gentle smile. "Rowan, step forward and hold your sister."

Rowan took two hesitant steps forward, but made no move to take Roisin. "I can't."

"You will," he said firmly, stretching a still crying Roisin toward her sister. "You are not poison; lift your arms. Now."

Rowan did as her father instructed, flinching when at last Roisin settled in her arms. Terrified her sister would die right then, Rowan squeezed her eyes shut and held her breath until she couldn't any longer, and it escaped as she gasped for new air. Nothing happened. Slowly she peeled her eyes open and looked down at her sister. Roisin returned the gaze; suddenly calm, she let out a little coo, snuggling into her sister's arms and into sleep.

Gwyneth cringed, her hands fisting around her skirt to hold herself still.

"You see? With you, she knows she is safe; you are her protector. If you went to the Fairy queen, who would keep her safe?" Balder's voice shook.

Rowan looked slowly up at her father. "I am her protector?"

Gwyneth flinched, taking an involuntary step forward and releasing her skirt; her arms reached out for her child. Balder barely glanced her way, but the rage in his eyes held her in place. He blinked, and when his eyes found Rowan again, they were warm, comforting pools of certainty.

"Yes. The Fairy queen is trying to trick you." Balder laid a hand on Rowan's shoulder and squeezed firmly. He barely managed to clear the tears from his throat before he spoke again. "She knows only you can keep Roisin safe. Do not be fooled."

Rowan nodded slowly, firmly, regarding her sleeping sister. "I won't let anyone hurt you."

Balder rose from his crouched position and looked at his girls. He could not lose them, either one. Rowan, sweet, quiet Rowan; she needed her sister almost more than he did, more than Gwyneth.

"Hold her close," the king said, taking Rowan by the shoulders. "Do you have her?" She nodded. "All right; kneel, Princess. I will help you."

Rowan knelt, holding her sister tight to her chest. The king stepped back and lifted the ornamental sword he wore from its sheath. Rowan startled, suddenly afraid.

"You have not been to a knighting ceremony, have you?" Balder chuckled. "You are safe." He laid the tip of his sword on Rowan's right shoulder, noting with pride the way she bent her entire body around her sister, protecting her from the sword. He lifted it from one shoulder to the other.

"Rowan, future queen of Stonedragon, arise Rowan the Eternal, Knight of the Rose." He smiled down at his daughter and dropped the sword to assist her rising with a hand beneath each elbow.

He expected Rowan to smile excitedly, but while there was a gentle curve to her lips, Rowan was ever serious.

She looked firmly into her father's eyes. "I won't fail you."

With Spindles All in Ash

There were few celebrations in the palace after that night. Although Balder had grown greatly in his belief in magic since Sinead's death, he could not simply trust that Maureen's blessing had done the trick. So he took nearly every piece of advice he was given. He sent soldiers to kill the Fairy queen, but uninvited, they could not reach her kingdom. He consulted every mystic or fey creature he could find, doing them great favors so they would be in his debt and bless his child. He outlawed spindles, dispatching soldiers to gather them from every home in the kingdom, casting them all in a pit together, and setting it ablaze, not content until they all lay in ash. The kingdom's entire woolworks were sent by sea to the kingdom of Ulm. Ulm returned the trade with a supply of prepared cloth, all of which was painstakingly inspected for spindles before it was allowed off the ships and into the kingdom. But still Balder was afraid.

Every day that passed, he grew to love his new daughter more. And the more he loved her, the more his every thought revolved around keeping her safe.

What began as a way to convince Rowan she would not poison her sister took on a life of its own. Rowan the Eternal was not content to sit and wait. Every day for three hours before dawn, she went to Colum for training to be a real knight.

She wanted to fight with a sword right away, but he would have none of it. "It won't do for a sometimes clumsy girl to run around with a blade twice her size," Colum teased, resisting the urge to comfort her when the crinkle at her brow revealed the tears she was fighting. "You must learn a bit of balance."

First, he insisted, they needed to train her body. She ran laps around the palace and strengthened her arms by climbing ropes and pulling herself up over

37

increasingly higher bars. She practiced riding astride a horse, as knights did, on a daily basis; it was by far her favorite kind of training, galloping off with the wind tugging at her hair. The worst training was for balance. It began with the pit, a log stretched out over a pit of hay that she must walk across, slowly, balancing a quarterstaff. Which wasn't so bad until Colum added the tiny buckets of water to each end of the staff and insisted she not spill a drop.

She had not even come close. So Colum put her on firm ground; she walked every day three laps around the palace, balancing the buckets on the staff. Still she could not manage to make it around without spilling some, and Colum always knew, even if it was only a drop and he was nowhere near to see it.

"Psst."

Rowan jerked around, and the buckets hit the ground with a plunk.

"Fill them up and start again." She heard Colum's shout, but could not see him.

Bran walked over, grinning. He was among the newest batch of knights; none of the others took him very seriously. His father was a sheep farmer, and his mother had spun wool until the spindles were burned. The other knights thought the son of peasants would never match them in skill, but he showed them. Rowan glared at her friend, though she rather liked the interruption, just not the way he spoiled her second circuit without spilling a drop—she was nearly there.

He laughed and bent to retrieve the fallen buckets. He carried them a few feet away and dipped them into the horse trough to fill.

Rowan screwed her face up in disgust.

"What?" He laughed. "You're not going to drink it. Now"—he took the staff from Rowan and slipped the bucket easily over it, holding it out casually—"stop trying to balance the staff."

Rowan planted one hand on her hip and glared up at her gangly friend. "I am going to be a knight."

"Of course you are." His easy agreement startled Rowan. Was he trying to trick her? "I'm helping you do it faster. Hold your arms out straight." He placed the staff in Rowan's grasp, holding it lightly until she had it balanced. "Now when you walk, don't look at the staff. Trust me."

Rowan held her breath and took one step, and Bran kept giving instruction. "Close your eyes and feel your arms staying straight, feel your feet moving smoothly, and your head reaching for the sky. It's you that needs to be balanced."

It only took her a day and a half to master it after that. When she stood before Colum, dancing and clapping with excitement, he patted her on the head and smiled proudly. But the minute her back was turned, he pinned Bran in place with a glare.

The next day Colum informed her she couldn't hold a sword until she did five circuits around the palace, spinning the staff without hitting anyone or anything, including herself and the ground. But Rowan was not discouraged; she knew the trick now and would be holding a sword soon enough.

Maureen continued trying to help Rowan develop her magic. Trying to help her see it in the world around her, so she might take control. Rowan spent time each day with her sister, and even found time for lessons from her tutors; on every subject from reading and writing, to geography and memorizing the last three generations of royalty from all the kingdoms on the island. At the end of each long day, she returned to Colum for more training.

Rowan was determined not to let anything harm Roisin. So much so that her entire life was consumed with the quest to be the very best sister and the very best knight in the land. None but Maureen knew that with every passing day, Rowan's magic slipped further away. She could do no spells—right, accidental, or purposeful.

When Maureen tried to show Rowan to use her magic like a giant breath to fill the garden with wind, she managed to rustle a few leaves, but only with her real breath. Or when using it like a hand to draw a book from across the room, all she managed to draw was a headache from concentrating so hard.

Nothing caught fire or crumbled off the palace anymore, but no spell seemed to work, either.

Maureen decided to try a different tactic. Rowan had seen the future before; perhaps that was the only gift her Fairy magic chose to extend her. "Rowan, when are my children to arrive?"

Rowan jerked away from the snail she was studying, startled. Her eyes met Maureen's momentarily and skidded away. "I don't know."

"No? What of your sister? Will she have children?" Maureen encouraged.

Rowan bit her lip, and her focus fled back to the snail. "Probably." Her voice was distant, flat, and heavy. "If she doesn't die."

Maureen walked to Rowan and gathered her into her arms. Not the future then.

It worried Maureen. This girl who had been so very powerful and open was wearing out. Or perhaps, closing off.

When Roisin was three, the Fairy queen grew impatient. Magically glowing spindles appeared before the tiny princess. She was drawn to them all. She had been stopped from touching each one, but that only magnified her desire. It would only be a matter of time before Roisin touched one.

All it took was one.

"It will not work!" Gwyneth pleaded with the king one evening after Roisin had been saved from touching a spindle. "She is only three. She hasn't found love yet. The Fairy queen is changing the rules. We must do something. We were nearly too late today."

"I know. We must do something," Balder mumbled.

"Balder." Gwyneth knelt beside the king, taking both of his hands in her own. "I know it is wrong and you will never forgive me, but I cannot continue watching my daughter grow closer to death because we do not give the queen what she wants. I will do it."

"No." He flung her hands off. Coming to his feet, he paced away from her. "Who stopped Roisin today? Rowan! The *child* you would kill. She is all that stands between our daughter and death. Sorcha will not stop with taking her revenge on Rowan. She wants to destroy us all. She uses Rowan so we will do her work for her."

"Kill me, if that will stop her. Kill me," Gwyneth begged; she looked desperate, pathetic, with wide, swollen eyes. "Don't let my daughter die. She has done nothing wrong."

"What has Rowan done wrong?"

Gwyneth shook her head. "If it is her life or my daughter's..." She shrugged, looking wraith-like with her pale, thin skin and sunken eyes.

"I cannot see you." Balder walked to the door and leaned into the hall. "Guard, escort the queen to her chambers and remain there. She is not to be left alone at any time. For her own safety."

The king left his wife in the hands of his guards and walked away, absent-minded with rage. He did not notice Rowan slip out from the curtained alcove behind his desk. Balder did not stop walking until he was through the door of Maureen's home. She had taken to her room, due to deliver her triplets any day.

"Your Majesty." Maureen attempted to rise when the king walked, unannounced, into her bedroom.

"No; rest. I must ask for your help." Balder took a seat next to the bed, facing Maureen intensely.

Maureen leaned back against the bed, shifting the blankets around her, embarrassed.

"Will she stop? If I killed Gwyneth and myself?" Balder begged. "Would that appease her?" He was panting with just the effort to get the words out, his stomach knotted and roiling. He couldn't even consider how he might do the thing, focusing only on how to save his girls. He couldn't fail them.

Maureen smiled sadly, resigned now to the insanity and desperation that gripped this kingdom. He would never go through with it; men who asked were not men who acted. "It doesn't work that way. The curse has been laid. And, no. It would make no difference to her type of anger. She wants you to suffer as she does. Every day—for eternity."

Balder shrank before her as his last hope died. He bent forward, burying his head between his hands. Maureen watched, startled; this was not the king she had known. Even in his darkest moments, he never failed to appear every inch the sovereign before inferiors. Once it would have pleased her to see him brought low. But she no longer saw him as Sinead's husband. He was Rowan's father. Though he had failed his first wife in every other way, he had been true to his promises.

"Do you find it so very hard to believe in good magic?" Maureen asked quietly. "It doesn't always seem so, but blessings are stronger than curses."

Balder's muffled voice slipped out between his hands. "It is not that I don't trust your magic, or Rowan's. But I feel that if I do not move, do not work to protect her, something will take one or both of my girls from me. The curse, it was put on Roisin, but it is Rowan it will kill in the end."

"That was its intent." Maureen's voice fell like lead through the air. "Not for her to die and be buried in the ground. But for her to die as the queen has— inside. Where there can be no peace."

Balder looked up and met Maureen's gaze with wet, shattered eyes.

"She's farther away every day," Balder's voice shuddered. "Do you remember when Rowan would just gaze into your eyes silently? Reading the very nature of your soul? It unnerved me; not her, but that she could see into me. There is a distance in her stares now."

"As though she doesn't want to see your soul." Maureen's gaze drifted away from the king. She felt the distance as well.

"I cannot let her destroy my girls. Rowan is consumed already in a need to protect Roisin, and every day a new spindle appears. Roisin may never reach sixteen this way, and if she does, Rowan will be so worn down…" His words failed, with his waning hope.

"These spindles," Maureen sighed, shaking her head. "Having laid the curse, Sorcha cannot alter it but to take it back entirely. I will not say the spindles cannot hurt your girl, but they cannot kill her. I believe they are serving their purpose perfectly, driving you mad with worry and wearing Rowan down until she is too tired and broken to resist the curse," Maureen's words fell flat and she shut her eyes a moment, fighting back tears. Her poor Rowan, Sorcha had such suffering in store for her.

Balder took Maureen's hands between his own, drawing her eyes, and did what no royal had ever done with this simple servant: begged. "Please; I will take any punishment, give up anything. I know you have hated me, blamed me for Sinead. And you were right to. I was selfish, smothered her fire. I knew what I was doing, but I didn't care. I will never stop feeling the weight of my crime. But please, you must help my daughters. They are the only innocents in this."

Tears ran down Maureen's cheeks as she returned Balder's grip.

"She was my girl, Sinead. I never expected to have children." Maureen's voice was flat as she looked into the past to her own little girl. "So she was my girl, and I did hate you. But...it passed. When you knighted her Rowan, saved her from her fears, it passed. I will help any way I can."

"Tell me, what can I do that I have not already done?" He leaned forward, his entire being hungry and clawing for help.

"I don't know. The queen is a powerful foe. If anyone threatens her power, she crushes them. She had a sister, four actually, but I mean her twin, Nessa. Fairy tend to come in groups." Maureen rubbed her belly. "Nessa was born first, by all of three minutes. But those three were enough, and she was to be queen. Was for a short while. They always fought, quietly, underhandedly, playing tricks and blaming each other." Maureen stopped. It had been a long time since she'd thought this far into the past. She never spoke of it to anyone but Colum. Didn't want to think of it.

"It wasn't a problem until Nessa married the man Sorcha loved," Maureen went on. "They barely spoke afterward. When Nessa died of fever, there were those who said Sorcha had a hand in it. Fairy rarely die of fevers. And Sorcha had always been the most skilled of the Fairy. She came to power, but Tyrone, Nessa's husband, accused Sorcha of her sister's death. That is how the Fairy war that led to your marriage with Sinead began. And Sorcha crushed all who opposed her."

"Why are you telling me this?" He shook his head, dismissing the information.

"This is who you mean to challenge. She banished her younger sisters for sedition. They were triplets, inseparable. Different as could be. They fought quite openly all the time, but if one was challenged, all three took up the fight. Together they were as powerful as Sorcha, maybe more powerful."

"And they challenged her?"

"Never." Maureen laughed. "But it didn't matter. Sorcha knew if they decided to, she would have the fight of her life. And Cianna's husband had died in Sorcha's fight. So, to eliminate the threat before they became one, she found a way to be rid of them. They can never return to the Fairy kingdom; if one tries, all three will die." Maureen looked out her window; she should have stood up to Sorcha then. Fought her banishing her sisters and the fairies who took Tyrone's side. How many times had she remained silent, rather than speaking for what was right? Who would help Rowan and her sister? Everyone was the same.

"They were not the only ones. She cast out the water sprites after Rowan was born and I refused to return to her. She called us lesser creatures, undeserving of a place in the Fairy kingdom, a place in the waters we *belong* to." Maureen shook with the words, and her hands would not release her blanket. Her eyes were red and stinging, but dry from too many tears spilled already over too many years. "Sorcha cursed the entire Creelan nation after they took Tyrone's side in the war, said they must walk the earth as wolves, and they were never seen again. She has enslaved the fowl as her spies. No one will challenge her," Maureen bit off, as angry with the world as she was with herself. "She keeps too many in fear."

"I do not care to defeat Sorcha." Balder leaned forward with feral intensity. "Only to see my girls survive. Is there no way to gain help without it being a threat to Sorcha?"

"No." Maureen pushed herself up, so angry she was unconcerned with appearances. Was he even listening? "For one of Sorcha's curses to go uncompleted would start an uprising. Fairies she banished after the war would seek to return home. The kingdoms of Creelan and Turrlough as well would seek an end to their share of the punishment. Perhaps even the water sprites would challenge her. Seeing it made possible, everyone would seek to be free. She knows this. She cursed her own son!" Maureen released the words in a sob. "Sinead's twin. She has regretted it every day, but cannot undo it."

"Would he help?"

"He cannot." She collapsed against her pillows, looking away. Her boy—he had been so sweet and deep, such a good soul she helped to raise. He was the only one who ever stood up to Sorcha, and what did it get him? "She trapped him in a crystal, carried on her scepter. He will likely never be freed."

"What did he do?"

"He spoke our names," three voices said in unison.

The Aunts

*B*alder jerked around so quickly, he nearly fell out of his chair. Three women stood behind him, all of different looks. There was a glow of soft light surrounding them, like the setting sun releasing the last vibrant colors of the parting day.

"I told you we should knock. It will take forever to calm him," the shortest of the three said. She was so small, she looked childish, with bright green eyes and a playful golden muddle of curls. She stood to Balder's far left, looking at him like he was a fool.

"Nonsense. A silent man is a good man," the woman in the center said harshly. Nearly as tall as Balder, she had something of Rowan's looks in her pale, almost translucent eyes, and had straight brown hair that fell nearly to her knees.

"Only if he is also listening," the first countered.

As the first two women spoke, the third moved to the side of the bed where Maureen was struggling to kneel and simply lifted her back onto the bed. She was of medium height with short, choppy, black hair and eyes of a darker blue than any Balder had ever seen; they seemed to smile. Silly, how could eyes smile, but hers did. Seeming to promise all would be well.

"No. Silent is still better than speaking." The tall one looked Balder over sharply.

"Or fighting," the short woman added.

"Or thinking. Remember, it is men we're talking about." The tall woman used a dead serious tone, but beside her, the first, childlike woman cackled.

"Come back to bed, good sister," the third said to Maureen. "Nephew." She looked at Balder. "You've tired her with your begging. Fetch water."

Unable to explain why, Balder got up to do as she instructed. The other two women stepped out of his way, walking to the bed.

"Triplets," the childlike one exclaimed. "You are blessed for your years of service."

"She isn't blessed until they are out," the tall one argued.

"How would you know?"

"Why have you not called us?" the middle woman asked. "Did you think we would not help?"

"I had no right to ask. I did not help you," Maureen said as Balder returned to the room.

"She is ours to protect also," said the tallest. She turned to face only Balder; removing the glass from his hand, she passed it behind her without looking. "I am Bride, and these are my sisters, Alma"—she indicated the shortest—"and Cianna," indicating the medium woman. "We are the aunts of your deceased wife."

"We can introduce ourselves, Bride," Alma said. "You may be the tallest, but that does not make you our leader."

"No? Only when we're walking, perhaps, and you can't see over the tall grass." She tilted her head to the side with a jaunty smile on her lips.

"Why you…" With an expression halfway to a smile, Alma jumped at her sister, yanking on her hair.

Cianna walked forward to where Balder stood and smiled at him sweetly. "Where is our great-niece?"

Balder looked out the window; the sun had already set. To his left, the women continued fighting, pulling on hair and clothing, laughing every once in a while. "Rowan would be with her sister now."

"Good," she replied, ignoring her sisters. She nodded, and a warm pink light filled the room.

As soon as the light faded, all five members of the party were in the nursery, bed and all. Rowan had been on the ground rolling a ball back and forth with her sister. She jumped to her feet and drew the broadsword that leaned against the wall. It was more than half the length of her body, but she waved it slowly between the strange women, shielding her sister.

"Who are you?" she shouted.

Alma laughed. "I like her. She has spirit."

"So young, and already a warrior." Bride drew to her full height and stared Rowan down. "We are your aunts."

If anything, announcing that they were relatives made Rowan's stance only more vigilant. She cast a glance behind her.

"Roisin, behind the chair, quickly."

Happy to play the game, Roisin ran behind the chair. She peeked out every few seconds to giggle.

"We didn't come to hurt you. Bride enjoys intimidating people with her height, but I think you will be taller one day." Alma chuckled. "I will enjoy that."

"If she is taller than me, she will thoroughly dwarf you." Bride smirked, one eyebrow reaching for the ceiling.

"Enough teasing. Really, you two." Cianna rolled her eyes.

"Rowan," Balder said, recovering from his shock, "these women are no friends to your grandmother."

"She has no friends," Rowan said fiercely. "But that does not mean they don't serve her."

"Fat chance." Alma snorted. "I'd sooner serve Bride."

"We are not here to harm your sister. We are sisters," Bride said impatiently.

"Who insult one another?" Rowan threw off.

Cianna stepped out in front of her sisters, right up to the tip of Rowan's sword; smiling serenely, she met Rowan's eyes. "All sisters fight, eventually. But we would gladly die for one another. Something you understand, little mother."

Rowan looked between them, not ready to lower her sword yet. In the years since Sorcha's visit, Rowan had come to understand something that she would not share. There was something bad inside Fairy.

It was immediately apparent in Sorcha. At times she could see it in Maureen; when she defended Rowan, the room grew cold, and the air shook violently. And when she blessed Roisin, there had been a sad sort of anger about her. Rowan even saw the badness in herself; when her magic ran away from her, it always found a way to frighten the people who were hurting her feelings. Fairies were bad. These women might not work for Sorcha, but if they had her blood, they were a threat.

"Why are you here?"

"Because your father begged," Bride replied, "that you both be safe."

Rowan glanced at her father, disbelieving. *Begged?* That did not sound like him. Rowan felt a chill run through her veins. Knowing the feeling, she spun toward her sister, nearly cutting Cianna in the process. But Alma was already there, lifting Roisin playfully into the air away from the glowing spindle.

"Mustn't touch that, darling," she cooed, tossing Roisin into the air only to catch her again.

"Put her down," Rowan ordered.

"Rowan, trust them," Maureen called out.

"If you want her, take her," Alma teased. "I don't think your arms can do all the work, though. Why not use your magic?"

Rowan flinched, and her hands tightened on the hilt of the sword. She fought to hold the magic back; it always came out wrong. She might hurt Roisin by mistake.

"Are you certain she can?" Bride asked. "Bring the child to me. I want to see something."

"Will you never learn any manners?" Alma demanded, tickling Roisin far away from her sister.

"No." Bride appeared before Alma and took Roisin into her arms.

Rowan swung the sword back and forth. She did not want to strike them, but they had Roisin. Her heart beat fast in fear, but the cold wasn't returning.

"You are an interesting creature, aren't you?" Bride said to Roisin. "Cianna, come and see her. It is all very strange."

Rowan was near tears with fear; she dropped her sword, pulling her shoulders back. The third woman was there now, touching her sister, poisoning her.

"I am Rowan the Eternal, Knight of the Rose. If you do not release my sister, I will kill you." Rowan's every muscle was stiff, her head held high, even her heart frozen anxiously in her chest, and her eyes bore into the women so powerfully they hurt.

Behind her, Maureen and Balder drew back in shock. Rowan was a vigilant protector of her sister, but until this moment, she had not seemed up to murder.

"Rowan the Eternal." Alma chuckled. "Spirit. And without her shield, no less."

"I don't carry a shield," Rowan hissed between her teeth.

Bride bent to put Roisin on the floor. "Run; go to your sister. Your shield is that blade," she said, holding Rowan's gaze.

Roisin ran to her sister and tugged on her legs, "I want up."

Rowan bent and pulled Roisin to her. She was shivering inside and out, but with Roisin in her arms, her heart beat again, banishing the cold of badness.

"You are very generous, little mother." Cianna watched Rowan and her sister warmly. "Have you any idea what you've given away?"

"Anything that's mine is hers," Rowan said simply. Of course she had given Roisin a share of her eternity. They were sisters. Eternity would be empty without her.

"Well." Bride smiled warmly for the first time. Her sisters drew close around her. The individual glows of their Fairy light melded, forming a sunset halo around them, so it was impossible to tell where one began and the other ended. "Sorcha was never particularly generous."

"Wouldn't share a thing," Alma agreed.

"Do you share your toys?" Bride asked.

"What toys?" Cianna pointed out sadly. "Look at her, still a child and more comfortable with a weapon than a ball."

"How old are you now?" Alma looked Rowan up and down like one would a strange animal.

"Ten. Just yesterday." Rowan remained angled toward the aunts, but her eyes darted left, for her father and Maureen.

"Yesterday." Balder sighed. "Rowan...I am so sorry."

Rowan bit her lip; fighting the sudden urge to cry, she looked down at the floor.

"I forgot to tell you the story," Maureen said, almost in the same instant.

"I know the story." Rowan shrugged. "There were three attacks on Roisin yesterday; we all forgot."

"Rowan." Her father stepped forward and took Rowan's face in his hands. "You are just as important to me as your sister. I should never have forgotten. Can you forgive me?"

Rowan gave a stiff nod, pulling her head from her father's grasp. She knew he loved her, would die to keep her safe. Still, there were moments when she wondered if she really was quite as important to him as her sister.

"Rone." Roisin petted her sister's face; she hadn't mastered the pronunciation of Rowan's name yet. "Don' be sad. I give you a present."

Rowan laughed and kissed her sister on the cheek. "You are my present."

"Oh, Sorcha has no idea what a mistake she's made with you," Alma said with a wide, marveling smile.

"But she will." Cianna spoke quietly, her eyes searching the room, as if fearing an imminent attack.

"Soon. We must move quickly. She isn't ready yet," Bride said in her usual take-charge voice.

"Sorcha is not a patient woman," Alma said, thinking aloud.

"Odd then that she gave them sixteen years," Bride remarked. "What is the significance, do you think?"

"My mother was married at sixteen," Rowan answered. This was an answer she figured out long ago, with Colum's help.

He said nothing was random with vengeance. The best way to defeat an enemy was to understand them. So they sat together and figured out everything they could.

"So she was." Bride nodded. "Much too young."

"As if you could say. When were you married, again? Oh, I remember, never." Alma stuck out her tongue.

"And what of it? Neither were you." Bride yanked her head up, offended.

"I don't act as if I know everything." Alma shrugged, her eyes darting away.

"Sixteen is too young. I remember that year distinctly, and I was an idiot," Bride snapped superiorly.

"Well, you have my agreement there." Alma smirked; she nudged her sister in the shoulder until Bride rolled her eyes and returned the smile.

"What's the matter, little mother?" Cianna silenced her sisters with a look.

"Will you keep her safe?" Rowan asked almost sadly.

Roisin smiled in the direction of the aunts every moment more and stretched her arms toward them.

Rowan had felt it coming for some time now, the day when they would be separated. She did not want it. But Roisin would be safer for it.

"You have made her safe," Bride replied. "We came for you."

"What?" Balder started forward. Beyond him Maureen shoved higher in her bed, leaning forward anxiously.

Rowan looked from the aunts back to her giggling sister, reaching toward them. The day Roisin was born, Rowan had envisioned her as a small girl, dancing in a field. There were no fields like that here.

"No, you didn't," Rowan said flatly. "If I did not know she was safe, I would never stay in any protection."

Maureen sighed with relief, but her hand covered her lips as her heart reached out for Rowan.

"You worry too much about toys, Cianna. The sword suits her quite well," Bride said with a wry look, accepting without question the truth of Rowan's words.

"We could separate," Cianna suggested.

Balder's hands dropped down, one to Rowan's shoulder, the other to Roisin's head. His gaze flew among the women anxiously, but he could not make his mouth work.

"We cannot. Sorcha would have no trouble finding or defeating us," Bride pointed out.

"But she isn't ready. She will not use her magic," Alma put in.

"Cannot, I think."

Rowan stiffened, shrugging off her father's hand and the curiosity she felt from him. She pointedly avoided Maureen's gaze. Everyone was looking at her; she wanted to curl into a ball and hide.

"As usual, you think wrong. Doesn't she, Rowan?" Alma held up her hand to stop her sister's inevitable protest. "You do not let the magic out. Why?"

Maureen gasped, and a few tears went rolling down her cheeks. If Rowan was resisting magic, she knew why.

Rowan closed her eyes, wishing that meant no one could see her.

Cianna walked forward, laying a hand on Rowan's cheek. Rowan's eyes popped open, and Cianna leaned in, letting her magic slip out and come to know Rowan. "You were so open before. You couldn't hold the magic back; you believed so much. What has changed, little mother?"

Bride came closer, looking deep into Rowan's eyes. She smiled sadly, sinking to her knees so Rowan had to look down to meet her gaze. "So much anger. It won't do. Sorcha has made anger her weapon; you'll never match her at it."

"No?" Rowan shoved her chin into the air.

"No." Alma gently took Rowan's chin in her hand, searching her gaze. "We must find you a new weapon. Something Sorcha will never understand."

"Love is not a weapon!" Cianna shouted, guessing the direction of her sister's thoughts.

"She never said that it was," Bride defended. "But it may be the best she can come up with."

"That isn't what I meant." Alma held Rowan's eyes sadly. "Sorcha knows love. She's only forgotten it."

"You don't want her defeated." Rowan tightened her hold on Roisin.

"I...do not want her to die," Alma countered.

"None of us do," Bride added. "She is our sister."

"But we will not let her harm you," Cianna added. Stepping back, she smiled. "We will do as you ask."

Bride moved to stand beside her sister. "She will want for nothing."

"What do you mean?" Balder demanded behind Rowan, only to be ignored.

"You must accept that the magic is not poison. You are not poison. Only the whole of you, Fairy," Alma said with gentle encouragement.

"Warrior," Bride said with a stiff, soldierly nod.

"Queen," Cianna added.

"Sister," all three said in unison.

"Can break the spell," Alma finished.

Cianna reached out to take Roisin in her arms. Rowan reluctantly released her sister, but would not let go of her hand. Roisin seemed to trust the aunts. That more than anything convinced Rowan, but she did not want to let her go.

"You will answer me." Balder tried to sound forceful, but his eyes were wide and frightened, and his voice quivered uselessly.

"Auntie C," Roisin said, drawing everyone's shocked attention.

"Yes, little love? We shall go for a trip now."

"Who is we?" Balder sounded truly panicked now. "You cannot take her."

Rowan held on to her sister's hand. She was sure Roisin would be safe with them, and yet…she would not be there. She would not be there to protect her sister; it felt like abandoning her post. Worse, Roisin would forget her. They would not be sisters as the aunts were. They would not know each other's stories and thoughts. They would be strangers and sisters. A sick, swirling mass was growing within; she wanted Roisin safe, and she knew this was the way, but already Rowan felt empty for the loss of her sister.

Rowan laid her forehead against Roisin's and whispered, "I love you eternally. Be happy, little sister. You are loved, you are beautiful, you are eternal."

Roisin kissed her sister's cheek. "Love you, Rone."

Rowan released her sister's hand and stepped back. She could not watch, so she looked at the ground and bit the inside of her cheek to keep the tears from coming.

Cianna carried Roisin to her father and handed her over.

"What is going on?" He pulled Roisin tight against his chest. Cianna's smiling eyes were no longer such a comfort.

"You asked for our help," she said soothingly, laying a hand over Balder's. "We will hide your daughter where our sister's curse cannot find her."

"But you cannot take her without her family," Balder said, holding his daughter closer.

"Bride," Alma muttered. "The mother."

"Ohhh, yes," she replied ominously. "I will get her."

Balder's gaze jerked Alma's direction, and his arms tightened on Roisin; he'd forgotten about Gwyneth. He couldn't let them take his baby without her sister, without her mother, without him. What would become of her?

"We cannot hide so many," Cianna explained. "Sorcha has many spies. If so many were to disappear, there would be many people, even those who Sorcha has no hold on, who would tell her to win her favor."

As her sister spoke with the king, Alma took Rowan's face in her hands once more. "Nothing is impossible. You must learn to think of magic not as something separate from you, but as a limb."

"Like the sword?" Rowan asked. "Colum says if I think of it like a part of my body, I can control it, even though it is far too heavy for a girl my size."

"Exactly." She examined Rowan hesitantly. "You must come to it on your own, I imagine, but magic is no more evil than people are. We all have bad—and good."

Rowan nodded without agreeing.

"My baby." Gwyneth appeared with Bride. She ran to Balder's side and tried to yank Roisin from his arms. "Don't let them do this. You cannot trust them. They are Fairy; they work for the Fairy queen."

"They don't work for her." Balder kept a firm hold on his daughter. "She killed their sister and banished them."

"Killed our sister?" Bride said, incredulous.

"Telling tales, Maureen?" Alma said with a resigned chuckle.

"She did not kill Nessa," Cianna said. "They were two pieces of a whole."

"It was as much the accusations that she had killed Nessa as the loss of her other half that has made Sorcha so cold," Alma said with a sigh. Her sister's faults were many, but it hurt to hear people speak of her in this way.

"Nessa took a fever. It is heartbreaking, but that is all there is to it."

"Well, she took a fever by being a fool. It was her own fool fault. Dancing naked in the snow all night." Bride scoffed.

"Don't speak of her that way," Cianna ordered. "You know it was her habit to welcome spring so."

"That's neither here nor there," Alma interrupted. "The point is, Sorcha did not kill her."

"They are defending her. They will give her Roisin," Gwyneth shouted, waving her arms around with wild eyes.

"You really must calm down, dear," Cianna said kindly, laying her hand on Gwyneth's shoulders, holding her so she could not look away. "You are not being your best self."

"It must be terrifying," Alma remarked, "being powerless to help her."

"But you aren't the only one who worries. Do you understand what this little girl did? This little girl, whom you would sacrifice?" Bride demanded, standing beside Rowan.

Rowan allowed herself to be drawn to Bride's side as Gwyneth calmed slowly and her eyes found Rowan. Gwyneth looked at her for only the briefest of moments, flatly, as if she couldn't really see Rowan. The same way she had looked at Rowan every day since Sorcha's curse. But just now, Rowan felt too heavy with sorrow to worry about Gwyneth.

"It is not what I want," Gwyneth said with a broken sob. "But if it will appease the Fairy queen, I must do it."

"Nonsense." Alma sounded as though she would chuckle at the stupidity. "They draw together." She indicated Rowan, Balder, and Maureen. "They plan and worry and fill your daughter's life with light—together."

"While you suffer alone, going insane. As Sorcha wants." Cianna's voice was so soothing, it held Gwyneth in its thrall. "You cannot combat a curse with fear. You could have had two daughters to love and cherish."

"It is too late for that," Bride interrupted. "Now you must sleep in the bed you made out of your fears and lack of character."

Gwyneth jerked away from Bride's sharp tone; crossing her arms over each other protectively, she looked away.

"Bride," Alma sighed. She turned to Gwyneth. "You will say good-bye to your daughter. Between us and the gift Rowan gave her, your girl will be quite safe."

"We will return her to you on the day after her sixteenth birthday," Cianna said. "But you will never survive that long if you do not learn to trust."

The aunts led Rowan over to Maureen's bedside and allowed Balder and Gwyneth to say their private good-byes to their child.

Gwyneth reached out once more, latching onto Roisin's arm when Balder refused to relinquish her. "I can't do it," she whispered. "I can't let her go."

If anything, Gwyneth's hysteria settled Balder; this must be done. For both his daughters' sakes. "She will be safe." Balder kissed the crown of Roisin's head. "You will be happy. And when you return, we will pull you close and never let you go."

Roisin giggled at this and wiggled as if trying to get free already.

"But..." Gwyneth laid her head against her daughter's back and listened to her tiny breaths. She whispered, "How can you trust them? How can you just give our child away?"

"How could you suggest I offer Rowan as appeasement to her grandmother?" he hissed.

Gwyneth closed both arms around Roisin, still trapped tight in Balder's arms. She closed her eyes, speaking to the ground. "Balder, I do not know what I am saying half the time. My daughter, this beautiful life we created, is threatened with death." Tears ran down her cheeks, striking Balder on the arm, and slowly his features and his hold on his daughter relaxed.

"I do not...I never want to hurt Rowan. I only—"

Balder cut her off. "This is how we see that they are both safe." He kissed his daughter on the head once more and held her out to her mother. "Go to Mama now, my rose. Give her a giant hug; we will not see you for a very long time." He choked the words out over a tear-clogged throat.

Gwyneth pulled her daughter greedily to her and buried her face in Roisin's hair. "Oh, my darling girl." She kissed her again and again. "My perfect, beautiful baby. I love you so much."

"Thirteen years," Rowan whispered with her back to the good-byes. Maureen reached out and took Rowan's right hand, squeezing it tight. "She will not remember us. Will she even want to come home? She will be so happy with you!"

"Why do you say that?" Bride demanded.

"I saw it when she was born. She was seven or eight and dancing in a field. She was in a Fairy circle—two, really. There was a perfect circle of trees surrounding her, and right in the center where she danced, there was a circle of mushrooms. There were sounds of a brook in the distance. She was so happy, carefree as she danced. I think she was waiting for someone."

Maureen caught her breath; her eyes rose excitedly from Rowan's face to the aunts. Rowan had never shared so much of the vision before.

"A circular field, with a Fairy circle at its center." Cianna sounded awed. "This is powerful magic."

"An excellent hiding place," Alma agreed.

"Is that not where you live?" Rowan asked, confused.

"No," Bride said excitedly. "But it will be. Tell me, the trees—what kind were they?"

"They were my trees," Rowan replied.

"A field in the rowan-wood forest. Oh yes, very powerful magic." Alma's voice was practically giddy. "Didn't I say I liked our great-niece? Very wise."

"But..." Rowan stared between them, baffled.

"When you first come into your powers," Cianna said, "you understand the meaning of eternity without your mind. It simply is."

Slowly Maureen released Rowan's hand, and her gaze sought Rowan's with growing concern.

"Because of this, you can see and do and understand things without even knowing," Alma interrupted excitedly. "That is what you did."

"You made her a safe place. Without even knowing it," Bride said with pride. "That is why we will be successful."

Maureen was not so excited. Did none of them see the danger? Did they believe so completely?

When all that must be defeated was Sorcha's desire for vengeance, there was room for hope. Given time, Sorcha might change her mind, come to love Rowan even. But this was great power. Power enough to threaten Sorcha's throne. If Rowan still wielded it, there was greater cause for concern, not less. Sorcha would never let such a threat stand.

"Before Sorcha cursed her, you protected your sister," Cianna finished, glowing all the more.

Rowan nodded; she wasn't certain she understood, but it didn't matter. Roisin would be safe. What did it matter if she didn't remember them as long as she was safe?

"She will remember you," Bride said firmly. "Perhaps not your face, but she will remember the warmth and safety of your love. And she will love you."

Rowan dashed away her tears; burying her face in her hands, she began to sob. Maureen reached out, intending to comfort Rowan, but was beat to it.

"Rone! Rone!" Roisin struggled in her mother's arms, reaching out to her sister. Gwyneth let her down, watching in surprise as her daughter ran across the room to hold her sister. She had made a point not to see them together. She didn't want to see their love, because all she saw when she looked at Rowan was the necessary sacrifice to save her child.

Rowan sank to the floor, knowing Roisin was coming. Roisin wrapped her tiny arms around her sister's neck, petting her head.

"Don't cry, Rone. Don't cry. 'Member, you are love, you are beautiful, you are 'ternal. Like me."

"I remember," Rowan said, wrapping her arms around her little sister and clinging tightly.

"Do you see?" Cianna asked Gwyneth. "Who you will hurt most if you harm Rowan?"

"Keep that firmly in your mind, Queen." Bride threatened with her stance, her tone, her very essence.

"We will know if something happens to her," Alma added.

"Gwyneth." Cianna pulled her focus once more. "Be your better self, for your own sake. When we return, we will each have one question for you."

"Endeavor to answer them all with yes," Bride warned cryptically. "Balder, enough with the fire. Sinead's roses are no threat to you."

"And they are Rowan's connection to her mother," Cianna added. "Leave them be."

Rowan was tiny and empty inside. Heartsore. She never wanted to let Roisin go. No mother, and now no sister. Eternity was such a wide, bare existence.

Balder nodded, but his eyes were not on the aunts. He watched his daughters. Without thinking, he walked the short distance to his girls and knelt down with them, wrapping his arms around them both.

"My girls. We will all be together again. I know it."

More Loved with Each Passing Day

2,791 days until Roisin returns

For most people, the days passed more slowly with Roisin gone. It was always understood that Roisin was loved by all, but it was never as apparent as it became in her absence. Most of Stonedragon's inhabitants forgot the days of the week and the months of the year, days were counted by when she would return; today was not October seventeenth, it was 2,791 days until Roisin returns.

Artists and craftsmen from around the kingdom spent their hours making gifts for the absent princess, painting her face on the sides of buildings or carving it into chairs. There never lived a person as loved as this absent child.

It was a great comfort to Gwyneth that she could not walk down a hall or around a corner without seeing her child's likeness. She had been a good, if somewhat distant, queen, but now she would spend great portions of her day with the lowliest of her citizens, regaling them with stories of her child.

The king as well seemed pleased with the outpouring of love for his lost daughter, not just from his subjects, but from other royalty. Every kingdom with a son to its name made an offer for his daughter's hand upon her return. Gifts were sent of money, jewels, poetry in her name, and offers of soldiers to march against the Fairy queen. All were put off, but none were rejected. The king said only that they would see once Roisin returned. After having missed her so long, he would not be immediately ready to part with his girl. Every kingdom accepted this, but it did not curtail the offers.

All anyone in the known world could think about was the return of the "Rose Princess," as Roisin had become known. It was suddenly predestined that she would return safely. With her gone, no one was concerned about paltry little things like curses or the queen of the Fairy. No one, save Rowan, Maureen, and her family.

Rowan hated the paintings, sculptures, and banner in the courtyard, every day counting one day closer to the return of the Rose Princess. She hated that all anyone ever wanted to talk with her about was Roisin. She hated that when she closed her eyes at night, she saw horrible visions of Roisin, a beautiful young woman, with her hand stretched out toward the spindle Rowan offered. But what she hated most of all was that with each passing day, as her father's love grew for her sister, she could feel it fading for her. By the time Rowan was fifteen, it seemed the only time her father remembered who she was and that he loved her was when she stood right in front of him.

It hurt too much, wondering when the day would arrive that he would forget his love entirely. So Rowan spent less and less time near him and more time with Maureen and her family.

"They have carved her face into the banisters now," Rowan grunted, swinging her broadsword down to connect with the practice dummy to her left. Colum's five-year-old son Ferdy was clinging to her back. "It's disgusting. Treating her as if she is dead."

Colum said nothing. She was getting stronger every day. It was she who had first suggested practicing with extra weight to hold her back. At this rate, she would be as good as half his men by the end of the year. But that wouldn't be enough for her.

"They are planning a party. Now! She isn't due home for over seven years, and they are planning a party for her triumphant return." With each word, she swung the sword harder, faster. As if destroying a straw and leather training post would solve her problems.

"Do they have any idea what kind of trouble they are courting? Ferdy!" Rowan screamed, halting midswing when Ferdy, chuckling evilly, reached up and covered her eyes.

"Enough." Colum walked forward, easily lifting his son off Rowan's back.

"Tell me again why we can't use your good son." Rowan made a face at the wildly chuckling boy.

Colum ignored the comment and sent his son running home to torture his mother. And torture her he would; Ferdy had gotten all of the Fairy trickster energy. All three of his children were so different: Keagan with his quiet strength and wisdom; Ferdy with his brilliant mind and trickster's spirit; and Petal, his sweet, peacemaking, fun-loving, eternally optimistic Petal, who never met a problem she couldn't solve. Colum had never expected to be a father, and now he had three children.

What would he do if he lost one of them? What would they do if they lost one another? He looked at Rowan, in the middle of the practice ring with her eyes shut now; she hit the targets with such accuracy, he knew the ring was far too easy for her. She was like one of his children, and every day he watched her growing more alone.

"Come sit, Rowan."

Rowan looked to where Colum was sitting on a hay bale outside the practice ring. She knew that tone; he was worried about something, and she was about to hear what. Sheathing the sword, Rowan walked to the edge of the ring and shoved aside the front flap of her skirt to climb out.

It was a dress of her own specifications, more of a long tunic than anything else. From the top it was all things proper and ladylike, but the hem stopped in the middle of her calves, with long slits running up each side to just below her thighs, to make it easier to fight. Beneath it she wore thick stockings, like boys. Wearing a squire's uniform would make fighting much easier, but Father already resisted her training; he would never approve of her giving up dresses entirely, so this was their compromise.

Rowan sat with her friend. Through everything that had happened, Colum had remained her truest and most trusted friend. Many people thought it odd that she would follow around this man who was at least twenty years older than her own father, but she didn't care. Colum didn't seem to care, either. They met and knew at once they would be forever friends; nothing could change that.

"Rowan, you are an incredibly accomplished swordswoman, the best I have ever seen. I think it is time you started focusing on something else," Colum said slowly.

"I am already fairly handy with a bow. And you refuse to teach me to fight hand-to-hand."

"I don't mean another kind of soldiering," Colum said. "Do you honestly think you will one day face the Fairy queen on a field of battle?"

"No." Rowan shrugged. "But isn't it foolish to assume if it comes to that, the Fairy queen would be the only thing I must face? She is powerful partly because she holds so many under her influence. I will have to fight them to reach her."

"Yes, that is likely true." Colum nodded. "But even the most accomplished of knights does not expect to go into battle alone. You consider nothing else."

"Well…I have given some thought to forming a company of knights," Rowan said, looking across the courtyard to where the real knights trained. Real knights—she would never be one, and everyone knew it. "The trouble is I don't trust any of those sycophants."

Colum laughed. "Is that what they are?"

Rowan had a way of expressing herself that most found off-putting. But Colum had always seen the humor in it. She could easily be called severe. Her hair, which once had had a softening effect, she now wore in a constant braid, pulled away from her face. It hung nearly to her waist. She was so tall now, she reached just above Colum's shoulders, and he was a tall man. Rowan was no longer clumsy; that insult had been replaced with aggressive. Her steps were always long and purposeful, and her expression tended to dare the world to challenge her. But Colum saw the lonely girl beneath, and he loved her, all of her.

Rowan sighed. "They're victims of the curse. But…I don't trust anyone who not only falls under my grandmother's curse, but also cannot see it. It was there, in her words, that we would grow to love Roisin more with each day."

"Do you?" Colum asked, as if merely curious, but Rowan felt the slap of the question.

Every day, some person questioned her love for her sister. Because she did not sigh Roisin's name as she walked around every corner, because she did not sob every time she came across a new portrait of her three-year-old sister. Rowan heard them whisper that she was jealous. Saw them watching for signs that she would indeed, as the Fairy queen had said, break her sister's heart and kill her. The more she heard it, the more Rowan began to wonder if she wasn't under the spell too, just in a different way.

They sat in silence; Rowan hadn't answered, and Colum was a patient man.

"Perhaps you could suggest some knights," Rowan said after a moment. To her shame, she did not know how to answer. One thing she knew: whether she loved her sister more every day or not, she was as determined as ever to see her safe. Her love had never diminished. She looked up at Colum; he was one of only a handful of men in the kingdom who were taller than she. "I should prepare to fight wisely, and that means I cannot do so alone. And it would be good to have a sparring partner who is not afraid to harm me."

"You think any of your subjects more willing to risk hurting you than I?" Colum asked.

"I know it," she said, recalling the looks people threw her way.

"Then I cannot suggest any of them to you," Colum said. "Do you think I would allow you to spar with someone who means to harm you?"

"Will you let Ferdy when he comes of age, or Keagan?"

"That is different."

"Because they are boys and must become men? I can handle myself. If anyone must learn how to, it is me."

"What makes you so certain there will be a confrontation?"

"Every night I dream of her dying at my feet. I feel my grandmother's malevolence in every new painting they make of Roisin, every present that arrives in her name. When they asked me if I would help them plan a party for her return, I felt a chill throughout my body that I have not been able to banish. Sorcha, queen of the Fairy, has not been defeated because we found a way to conceal Roisin. Let us say we have defeated this one curse. What is to stop her coming and making another?" Rowan said fiercely; tears were gathering behind her eyes, but she had not shed a tear in public since the day her sister was taken, and she was not going to start today. "There will be a confrontation, because I will never trust Roisin is safe until I have one."

Colum nodded, looking at his feet. "I will find you knights. I will teach you to fight with your hands and any weapon in our arsenal," Colum said slowly. "But you must find something else to put in your life, Rowan. Something that makes you smile—as this used to."

Colum stood and walked away without looking back. He had not wanted to agree to that. He wanted the teasing Rowan back, the still hopeful child. Rowan watched him walk home; she would follow in a moment, but not just yet. She knew what would happen when he opened the door.

Ferdy would be the first on him, screaming excitedly and throwing himself at his father's legs. He always did this—wrapped his entire body around his father's legs so that he was clinging onto his own feet and Colum couldn't move. Then Petal would jump at her father and float right into his arms. Keagan would come and hug him gently around the waist before simply taking his father's free hand. They would all laugh and hug, and Maureen would come over and playfully complain that no one loved her, until they all attacked her with tickles.

The first few times Rowan had seen this little tradition, she had been too overwhelmed by the beauty of it even to move. But eventually she couldn't bear to look anymore; it hurt too much.

"Princess?"

Rowan glanced around, startled. A little man in a vaguely familiar livery of a knotted barley stalk stood to her right.

Rowan stood; perhaps the man was not so very short. After all, she was now taller than most men in the kingdom. Few men were not at least a bit shorter than she. Although he did appear a bit lower than the average man.

"Yes?"

"I was sent from Turrlough to extend this offer to you." He held out both hands with a rolled-up bit of parchment between them and bowed low, so that his face was no longer visible.

Rowan looked down at the parchment and the royal seal on it. Another marriage offer. She had received three since turning fourteen. Rowan's reply was always the same. She could not entertain any offer until her sister was home. Most offers came in conjunction with offers for Roisin. In fact, all had until this one.

The very first offer she received had been from Turrlough; they were the most determined. It had arrived after their fourth offer for Roisin had been put off. They had offered, if the king would but consider a marriage between Roisin and their crown prince on Roisin's return, "the second son of King Thaddeus and Queen Aya would be honored to be consort to the future queen of Stonedragon."

Rowan lifted the scroll, wondering what tactic Turrlough was using now. They were a poor country and could certainly use the money that would come with such a marriage. She understood their desperation better than the others and had always looked on their offers more patiently as a result.

The man remained bowed low as Rowan opened the letter. She could not explain why, but she didn't like the little man. She wanted him out of her presence, so she read the letter quickly.

> *Dear Princess Rowan,*
>
> *I am told you are more commonly known as Rowan the Eternal, Knight of the Rose. It presents an interesting challenge, I imagine, when one addresses you in person. Tell me, do they call you my lady, sir, princess? For I cannot imagine people actually address you with your entire title.*
>
> *I apologize if this letter seems a bit forward, as we have not met, but I was told you have control over who you marry, so it seemed foolish to address your father. You must know of my kingdom's many deficiencies. I am well aware that a union between our two kingdoms will appear to be an act of charity on your part. However, being as I was raised to understand the burden of a king, my pride is not as important as what might help my people.*
>
> *I understand you will not entertain offers until you are certain of your sister's safe return. A wise and sisterly notion. Therefore I suggest, rather than entertaining my proposal at this time, you merely accept my open invitation to visit Turrlough castle and become acquainted with one of what I'm sure must be your many suitors.*
> *Your Servant, Gavin, High Prince of Turrlough*

Rowan was confused. She had been made an offer by the high prince, and in his own hand? How flattering. She nearly laughed. It was certainly a new tactic, playing on her vanity. She looked at the servant in front of her; as she read, her distaste for the little man had faded, only to return stronger.

"You may wait in the great hall." Rowan dismissed the man coldly. "I will pen a response immediately and send it to you there."

He looked up then, catching Rowan's eye; there was knowledge there, deep knowledge. He winked and walked away.

Rowan watched him go stiffly. Only realizing once he was gone that her hand rested on the hilt of her sword. Something was very wrong about that servant.

She threw a quick glance over her shoulder toward Colum's home. She would not be missed. Rather than going straight to write a response, Rowan steeled herself to speak with her father.

The king was in his strategy room, surrounded by advisors and Gwyneth, when Rowan found him. "Do you have a moment, Father?"

"Of course, Rowan," Gwyneth answered instead of her father. "We are planning for Roisin's celebration. Would you like to help?"

Rowan looked at Gwyneth skeptically.

Since the aunts took Roisin, Gwyneth had been nothing but kind and courteous to her. Never a foul word spoken. Rowan preferred Gwyneth when she was offering her up as a human sacrifice. This new Gwyneth was so false, it was hard to know precisely where one stood. Rowan imagined it was somewhere near where she stood in the past. No sacrifice was too great to save the Rose Princess.

"No. Thank you. I need to speak to the king about another matter."

"Of course, dear." He sounded very loving.

Rowan let out a breath she had not realized she held.

"Does it need to be private?" he asked, coming around his table toward her.

"No." She shrugged. "I have just received another offer from Turrlough."

"Ah," he nodded. "They are very determined. Surely they realize we have no motivation to move quickly."

"As to that, the offer came from the high prince."

"Really!" Balder was impressed. "They would force him to give up his throne for a favorable bargain. It is clever. Are you…considering this offer?"

"My answer will be the same as ever. Still…I know Turrlough is a poor country, but I wonder just how poor. This seems like an act of desperation."

"Rowan"—the king shook his head, coming to give his daughter a brief hug—"you underestimate what a desirable catch you are. Any man would consider himself lucky to have you."

Rowan barely caught it, but Gwyneth rolled her eyes at the comment, looking down at the table. Rowan straightened; she was used to slouching because she was so very tall. All the women commented on it when they thought Rowan could not hear. That she was tall, with mannish features, too large to be appealing. It should not bother her; she had no time to worry if she was appealing to men, but…Every so often, she would walk into the portrait gallery and look on her mother. How soft and elegant she was. In those moments, she remembered her grandmother saying she took after her father. She thought about how the knights looked on her as something not quite man and not quite woman, and she would wish she could be just a bit more womanly. More like her mother.

"That is not the point. I've no intention of accepting the offer," Rowan said stiffly. "They are desperate enough to offer me the heir to their throne and to accept that I will not marry for at least another eight years. He admits they have nothing to tempt me. Throwing his kingdom at my mercy. I had not thought their situation so dire. Am I wrong?"

"Well, we've known for some time that they struggle."

One of the king's advisors, Vance, spoke. "And the rain last year, so beneficial for the rest of us, caused the river to flood several times on their farmland. They lost a good deal of crop."

"I see."

"And…" Balder said thoughtfully, "if we know of their troubles, we must assume they are quite bad." When Rowan looked at him questioningly, he only shrugged. "Were I king there, I would not want my enemies or allies knowing the full extent of my weakness."

"So they are likely in dire need." Rowan began to pace. "And we are allies."

"A relationship only they benefit from," Vance commented.

"How so?" Rowan asked. "The wars among kingdoms have been over since you were a boy, Father. We were meant to be helping one another since then. Yet we offer them no aid in their time of need."

"They should ask if they have need," Vance said.

"As allies, we should know and offer. Would we make them beg if their need was military?"

"We…"

"Rowan is right." Balder interrupted another of his advisors; he looked concerned. "We should have offered assistance as soon as we knew the river flooded."

Rowan saw bits of light dawning on various faces. She wondered if all the dignitaries who had attended Roisin's celebration had been as badly affected, or if it was only here. Sorcha might not be able to reach Roisin, but that did not mean she would not gain her revenge another way.

"How many more allies are struggling as a result of the rainy season?" Rowan asked.

"None…" Vance said slowly. "But there are a few other problems."

"And we are flourishing," Rowan commented.

"It is good that we flourish."

"Not when we fail to help our struggling allies. All the Fairy queen need do is point out our selfishness, and we will quickly find ourselves the enemy of every kingdom on this island."

"You are right," Balder said. "How have I not seen this?"

"We are under a spell, Father," Rowan said in exasperation. "Did you think that because Roisin was safe, the Fairy queen would simply give up her revenge? We love Roisin more with each day. And the more we love her, the less we care for anything else."

"Why are you not swayed?" Gwyneth asked. It was the first time she had as much as questioned Rowan.

"It affects me differently," Rowan replied, not meeting Gwyneth's eyes. "What are we to do about Turrlough and the others?"

"Well, we must offer them aid. But we should be careful how we go about it. It will seem like condescension now that we have waited so long."

"What of Liadan? The river passes through their kingdom to reach Ulm." Rowan walked to the map wall. She always felt a breathless sense of insignificance when she looked at it; it was oddly comforting. In the vast expanse of the world, Stonedragon was such a small thing, and she was only one of its two hundred thousand people. Surely that meant Sorcha was not so large and unconquerable as they made her out to be.

Great Island, as it had been dubbed by early sailors from the south, sat at about the center of the world, not its largest landmass, but its most important. The island was split into six equal portions some three hundred years earlier after several years of warring over control. Already split into north and south by the Gray Lady, the river Liadan, each half was then divided among three of the ruling factions at the time. To the north, from east to west, between Anwyn, Fairy, and Ulm. And in the south, between Stonedragon, Creelan, and Turrlough.

The kingdoms had kept their general positions, but over the years, little aspects of the boundaries had changed. Beginning with Anwyn.

Rowan smiled, stretching out a finger to run along the edge of the enchanted forest that was meant to be part of Anwyn's kingdom. They never managed to settle it. No one could. The rowan trees refused to be cut, and whenever people tried to settle within the forest's boundaries, the trees picked up and moved, losing people within their wood. Rowan often came here and examined the map, wondering where in that dense forest there might be a circular field with a Fairy ring at its heart and a brook at its edge and a little girl spinning around. Perhaps it got up and moved every day to keep itself well hidden.

Anwyn had demanded compensation, accusing the Fairy of trickery, and was given the island's smaller of two mountains, renamed Mount Anwyn, as compensation. Making them just slightly larger than Stonedragon and the Fairy land as a result.

Rowan let her finger drift down a bit and run along the river. Moving against the rivers current Rowan's finger traveled west, away from Stonedragon and past what was once the nation of Creelan, now a nearly empty hilly mass of contested land. After the Fairy War, the nation inexplicably disappeared; there were rumors that they were made into wolves by the Fairy queen in vengeance for taking sides against her. Or that she simply killed them all. No one knew for certain; they were just gone. Every year a few more of Stonedragon's citizens worked their way into Creelan, and likely so did the citizens of Turrlough, on its western border. To the north the river passed the Fairy land, where it sat at the feet of Mount Kieran, the highest point in the world. Of course, even the Fairy had only managed to settle about halfway up the mountain before the air was too thin.

Beyond those lands the Liadan cut through Turrlough, now the largest kingdom on the island, but not for warring—they barely had a standing army. For some reason, not a year before the Fairy War, the king of Ulm ordered the construction of a wall around his kingdom, blocking it from all landlocked sides and cutting off a quarter of his own land to do it. He gave the land to Turrlough in exchange for supplies to build his wall. Now the only way into that kingdom was by boat, at one of their ports, or through Gray Lady Gate, the river's feeding point from Lake Noomah, which rested within Ulm's wall.

After the wall was built, the king constructed a single tower in the center of the lake and locked himself within. Most thought he was mad, but oddly no one had ever tried to overthrow his rule. He must be dead now; though none had been invited to mourn him, his son ruled from the port city.

It was all so neat and civilized; every kingdom touched the sea in some way, and every kingdom had access to Liadan's waters. But still every fifty years or so, another battle broke out, and the borders changed by mere inches. How silly it all was when each kingdom had something the other needed.

"We trade by sea with Ulm." Rowan explained her thinking. "But the Liadan would be much faster. What if we offered to pay for passage?"

"We've traded comfortably by sea for years," Vance commented.

"If we worded it right, it might work." The king looked excited, ignoring his advisor. "And we might convince Anwyn to do the same."

"Exactly," Rowan said, pleased to see her father out of the haze of Roisin fever.

"Excellent, excellent. Clear this table," the king said.

"But the celebration!" Gwyneth screeched as her preparations were shoved aside.

"Is many years coming. We have time yet. Bring me everything we know about our neighboring kingdoms. Rowan"—Balder turned to his daughter—"it was your suggestion; would you like to arrange your first treaty?"

"I would love to. But I must write a response first. I will return shortly."

"Will you mention the treaty in your response?" the king asked.

"I do not think so. They will know when it comes why it has happened. I think…" Rowan gazed out the window beyond her father. "I will simply respond to the letter; there's no need for anything else."

The king nodded with a gentle smile and began issuing orders to his advisors.

Rowan went straight to her room to rush a response. She was half-worried she would return to find her father planning Roisin's party once more.

> *Dear High Prince Gavin,*
>
> *As I understand it, you are a knight as well, or is that merely a courtesy title they extend to royalty in your kingdom?*

Rowan paused, nearly crumpling the letter. No one understood her humor. It was probably best not to insult the future ruler of an allied kingdom. On the other hand, the prince's opening remarks could be viewed as equally sarcastic.

Rowan decided to leave it. Let him take it as he chose; he would anyway.

> *I must thank you for the courtesy of your somewhat vague offer; I am aware of the very great honor it is.*
>
> *I would love to see your kingdom firsthand. I am told there is a particular passage of the Liadan from which you can see both the ocean and Mount Kieran. I have often wondered what it would be like to travel along it. However, things are not as well here as they might seem. I see it as my duty as high princess of Stonedragon to remain and assist in any way I am able.*
>
> *Since you were kind enough to express an understanding of my hesitation to accept any offer, I will thank you and say I have great respect for your willingness to help your kingdom whatever the personal cost. When the time comes, I would be honored to consider your offer first.*

*I am "Princess" to my servants, "Your Majesty" to my subjects, and
"Rowan" to my family and friends. My knightly title was given courtesy
of my father when I was too small even to wield a blade.
With thanks and much respect,
Rowan, High Princess of Stonedragon*

Rowan reread the letter twice. She couldn't believe that she had offered to give
his proposal first consideration; it was as close to accepting as she had ever come.
But she couldn't bring herself to take it back. He was willing to shame himself
to help his people; no prince she had met so far was equally devoted to his duty.

Far more troubling was the end—her claim that her knightly title was a
courtesy. Implying she was not really a knight, did not really train, was not a
towering mannish figure. It was true the title had been a courtesy when she was
a child. But Rowan worked day and night attempting to earn that honor.

Did it really matter so much that a prince she had never met, far away in a
crumbling kingdom, not think of her as ugly? Or was it just that she wanted one
person who didn't think so? Even if they would never meet. Or did it matter not
at all and she was simply wasting time?

Rowan folded the letter, refusing to read it a third time. She sealed it with
the ring her father had commissioned for her the year before on her birthday.
Today was her birthday. No matter.

She ran her hand across the ring again. It was beautiful; the image was the
dragon of their family crest clutching a sword with a rose hilt. He had given it
to her with a note that called her the knight of the family, its eternal protector.

Shaking off her thoughts, Rowan stood and rushed down the stairs, careful
to avoid touching the unnerving banisters with Roisin's head. Rowan turned the
corner into the great hall. Immediately she noticed the messenger, who had so
disturbed her earlier, with his head bent close to Gwyneth's.

Seeing Rowan across the room, the servant winked once more, and Rowan
knew suddenly what it was that unnerved her about him. It wasn't knowledge
she saw in his eyes. It was eternity. He was Fairy.

She had tried, very hard, to stop thinking of Fairy as inherently bad. But seeing his head bent next to Gwyneth's, Rowan could not help but feel threatened.

She drew her shoulders back so stiffly it hurt and walked forward, her steps ringing across the stone floor. Gwyneth glanced over at the sound and smiled sweetly at Rowan, a swindler's smile.

"I was inquiring about your suitor," Gwyneth said. "I have never met the high prince. A flattering offer, don't you think?"

"To a lady." Rowan struck Gwyneth with her words. "But as high princess myself, it is only fitting."

"Of course." Gwyneth executed a brief curtsy before storming out of the room.

"Put her in her place, didn't you, little queen?" The fairy laughed, throwing off all deferential behavior and giving Rowan a wide grin. He leaned back against the wall casually. He had dark, tight curls despite his age, which must be over fifty—how much was hard to say with Fairy. His eyes were of a deep earthy brown, and his grin was so wide, it took over his face. How had she not realized before?

"I am Rowan, of the house of Maeve, and as such I have power over you. Speak the truth or suffer, Fairy," Rowan ordered, holding his eyes and exerting all her will over him as Maureen had taught her. "Do you truly serve the house of Turrlough?"

The little fairy laughed. "Not got the hang of that, have you?" he teased. "Be this the response you promised me? Kept me waiting some time."

"You owe me your deference." Rowan tried again, getting annoyed rather quickly. "Answer my questions."

"I owe you nothing, little queen."

Annoyed with her ever greater lack of magic, Rowan drew a dagger and shoved the little man against the palace wall.

"I am not the little one here," she snarled. "You will answer my questions."

"You are little in power, little in age, and little in understanding. I only hope you improve before the Fairy queen comes for you. Or we are all doomed. I'll take this." He grabbed the note and disappeared, leaving Rowan threatening a stone wall.

Little in power, little in age, and little in understanding.
Was she?

An Evening for Surprises

By the time Rowan found her way back to her father, nearly two hours had passed. She paused outside the door, taking a deep breath, preparing to pull him out of the haze of the curse.

When she opened the door, her father was waiting for her.

"Is it so time-consuming sparing a man's dignity?" he asked with a smile.

"You've no idea," she replied, pleased he had remembered what she was doing. "How are the plans?"

"I am having the information compiled. You and I shall work on the particulars tomorrow."

"But don't you think…"

"No. I made myself a promise when I forgot your tenth birthday never to do so again, and I meant it."

"I didn't…"

"Think I knew. Yes, I realized that. Come with me; we have somewhere to go." He turned his daughter with an arm around her shoulders and led her from the room. "Your birthdays have rarely been moments of joy for you. It is something I have always regretted. It is a difficult thing to combat, the sadness we all feel remembering your mother today."

"I know," Rowan said flatly. She felt like a terrible person for thinking it, but just once, she would like it if people didn't make her birthday about her mother or her sister or the battle between good and evil. She didn't remember her mother more today than any other. She missed her every day.

"However, I thought today we might try."

"Oh?" Rowan chewed her lip, doubtful he'd have any luck.

"Yes." There was a smile in Balder's voice at Rowan's skeptical tone. "I thought we might go for a ride together over to the west hills."

"That would be lovely. I love to ride."

"I know. I do know a few things about you, Rowan. Today I learned one more."

"What?" Rowan raised a cautious brow. *That I think I know everything? That I'm pushy? That the curse affects me differently because I'm a bad sister?*

"I have always known you would be queen one day. Today I discovered you will be a very good one."

"Thank you." Rowan was shocked. He had always loved her and spoken well of her, but it had seemed most times that he did it only to make her feel better.

They rode out alone together, very slowly until they were outside the walls of the palace. Once they had passed them, Rowan looked to her father; at his nod, she set her horse, Yseult, off at a wild gallop. She couldn't think of a thing she loved more than her daily ride. Galloping away from the palace, as fast as she could, as though she never had to go back.

When she eventually slowed Yseult to a walk, she was smiling broadly, not really thinking of anything but the hills in front of her and what must be beyond them. Her father trotted his horse up next to hers and reined it in to a walk.

"You always were terrifyingly mad on the back of a horse." Balder had trouble catching his breath. Rowan just laughed. "Why do you ride so fast?"

"When I go fast enough, I can only see or hear or feel or think that one moment. Nothing before it; nothing beyond it."

"And other times you feel the rest?" the king asked, confused. "I was not aware you did any longer."

Rowan was surprised again; it seemed to be an evening for it. Her father was bringing up magic, something he never did.

"It isn't the same as before." Rowan considered as she spoke. "Before, I knew everything. Even things I couldn't understand. Now, it's just out of my grasp; and it haunts me, this knowledge I know I could have if I reached out and took it."

"I see." He said it so slowly, Rowan wondered if she had frightened him, as she used to. "Have you considered simply letting it go?"

"No," Rowan snapped. She would never stop trying.

"I don't mean you should stop being part Fairy. You could never do that. I wouldn't ask you to. But perhaps if you do not try so hard, it will come naturally."

"Maybe," Rowan sighed, reaching out to pet Yseult. *Just let go*—she wasn't sure it was in her to do that. "I know everyone thinks hiding Roisin has defeated the curse. That Roisin is safe and we will get her back in eight more years, but I don't believe that. If I do not figure it out, the Fairy queen will win."

Balder chuckled. "Well, I shouldn't be surprised. You were born fighting. When I remember your mother and her magic, it doesn't seem like something she did; it seems like something she was."

It was more than her father would generally say about her mother, and Rowan waited with bated breath for him to expand. She half hoped, half dreaded hearing more about this nearly perfect woman. Did he wish Rowan were more like her?

"Did you love her?" Rowan whispered into the silence, leaning toward her father, searching him.

"Your mother?" He knew exactly whom she meant. "Not as I should have."

Not a real answer; never a real answer.

"People don't speak of her often." Rowan shifted on Yseult, looking away. "When they do, it's all about how graceful and beautiful and gentle she was. I am not much like her."

"You are like her in some ways," Balder said. "Your mother was only one year older than you when we married, and only two more older than she died. And she was so much more childlike than you have ever been."

Rowan nodded. She had heard this from Maureen.

"You have your mother's eyes. They were changeable like yours, nearly clear one moment; then they would turn green or blue, gold even. They looked straight into a person, reading their soul, as you have done since you were born. And she loved to ride."

"She did?" A joyful tingle ran beneath her skin, tickling out a smile. "Truly?"

"I wouldn't lie to you," he said softly. "She loved to ride, faster than the wind, just like you. She would laugh her head off. She wasn't as poetic about it; she just said it was fun."

Rowan smiled. It *was* fun. Perhaps she should learn to put things more simply.

"She was also much stronger than she seemed. For someone she loved, she would do anything. Like you, she did not fight quite as firmly for herself."

Rowan shrugged dismissively. "I fight for myself if I need to."

"No, you don't. You never have." Balder shook his head, smiling sadly.

Rowan let her gaze wander into the distance as the hollow within grew a tiny bit. She worked hard never to feel it, the hole that had been growing since Roisin left. But perhaps it had been in her longer, waiting to be filled. Was she supposed to fight to fill it? Weren't other people just born without holes?

"Here, now look what I've done." Her father spoke almost playfully, chastising himself. "This was meant to be fun."

"It is," Rowan insisted. When he shook his head again, she shut away the void and smiled for the parts she had enjoyed. "It is fun. I never knew her like you did, like anyone did. Hearing about her, what she was like before the night she died, I like that. It makes her more than just a dream."

"Good." Balder nodded. "Now come along. I have one more surprise for you." He led his horse at a slight trot just ahead of Rowan to veer off the path they followed and down a little hill.

At the bottom of the hill, Maureen, Colum, and their family sat under a canopy, with a small feast spread out in front of them. Rowan was thrilled, and shocked. It was a rare thing for her father to go anywhere near Maureen's family. He had certainly never sat on the ground with them and behaved as though it was enjoyable.

It might have been the best birthday Rowan ever had. She learned about her mother, went riding with her father. She ate with the only people in the kingdom she loved. Played with the children late into the evening and was given an array of wonderful gifts.

From her father, she received a full suit of armor in the lightest metal she'd ever felt. It was made to look like a lady's dress and had her personal crest, matching her ring, beat into the breastplate.

Colum gave her a new sword, made of a similar metal. Topping its hilt, just above the grip was a magnificently carved wooden rose with open petals that he made himself. When Rowan held it, with the brown rose sticking out at the bottom of her clenched hand, it looked like she was gripping onto a long, bladed rose stem.

Maureen said Rowan was old enough to dress like royalty, instead of only wearing the old gowns she practiced in. So she gave her a long, shimmering, hooded dress woven out of blue Fairy silk, and a woven leather belt with a rose clasp. Between her mother's garden and naming her sister *Little Rose*, roses had come to represent Rowan.

Her favorite gifts came from the children. They were such different little creatures in nearly every way. But all of them were incredibly loving and generous and beautiful. Every one of them was so beautiful.

Ferdy was first, because he refused to be anything else. He walked right up to her looking smug; he rarely wore anything but a smile, this little devil. He had light sandy hair like his father's was between the spreading gray, and his mother's brown eyes, but the evil smile was all him. He handed Rowan a wriggling bag.

"Oh dear, do I dare open it? It won't attack me, will it?" Rowan's playful smile fed Ferdy's already broad grin.

Ferdy shook his head. "I caught it for you, and now it is your servant."

Slightly horrified already, Rowan opened the bag cautiously and peeked in. Her breath hitched in sudden pained sympathy. An apparently wounded and tied-up barn owl lay inside. As gently as she was able, Rowan slipped the bird out of the bag and untied the cord around its wings, laying it on the grass beside her to examine its injured foot.

"You poor thing," she whispered, rubbing its wing, trying to sooth it. "What did he do to you?"

"I didn't do anything." Ferdy stomped his foot, well used to getting into trouble. "I found it that way; that's how I caught it."

Rowan smiled at Ferdy, her secret favorite, simply because she could sympathize with having perfect siblings. She pulled him into a tight hug with one arm and kissed him loudly on the head.

"I love my gift. Thank you, Ferdy. Now you must help me nurse it back to health."

"All right," he said, sounding slightly crestfallen, and moved out of the way so his brother could have a turn.

"Happy birthday," Keagan said very properly, holding out a rolled-up scroll. This one had his father's green eyes and hair of a similar shade to his brother's, but a bit darker. He rarely gave a real smile, but when he did, it stole the room to silence.

"Thank you, Keagan." Rowan gave the boy a kiss as well before unrolling her present.

It was a painting of Rowan holding her sword, with Ferdy on her back. Keagan had captured his brother's spirit perfectly—Rowan's too. It was a bit unnerving seeing her own focus and intensity beside Ferdy's open enthusiasm. Keagan was quite the artist.

"Why, Keagan, this is lovely; did you do it?"

"All by myself." His pride overtook his shyness.

"Thank you; I'll treasure it forever."

Smirking, he went to stand beside his brother. Rowan fought to restrain a chuckle.

Petal walked forward, the very image of a fairy, slight with wild red curls and bright intelligent green eyes. She had an innate confidence that only a well-loved child could, and an apparent understanding of everything. She looked straight at Rowan, her eyes twinkling, not unlike Ferdy's would when he played a trick, and held out a tiny box.

"It took me days and days to find it. Then I had to trap it in the magic bubble, but it will bring you luck."

"Ooo. Luck, huh?" Rowan reverently opened the box to find a perfect little shamrock floating in what looked like a water-filled bubble. "How lovely, Petal. Thank you very much." Leaning forward, Rowan pulled Petal to her for a quick hug and a kiss.

"It's much better than their gifts," Petal confided with a whisper in Rowan's ear. "More useful. Keep it close."

"I will," Rowan said over a smile. "Always."

There didn't seem to be anything more Rowan could have wished for from the day, except to see her sister. It was near midnight when Rowan found herself alone in her rose garden; she wore all of her gifts but Keagan's scroll, which she left in her room, and Ferdy's owl, which she was carrying in her hand, trying to sooth.

"Oh, Ferdy. What will I do with that boy?" She laughed, petting the bird's head. She walked to her bench and sat smiling at the clink of the armor against the stone bench. She shivered a little. "Who knew armor was so cold?"

From the day the aunts had taken Roisin away, the roses had grown normally. Rowan rather liked the wall around the garden now; it made it her private retreat. Father had given her the key, and no one was allowed in without her invitation.

Rowan held the bird close to her and sat breathing in her roses. She couldn't understand why the bird was suddenly calm. They gazed into each other's eyes; the bird had shining golden eyes, similar to Rowan's in candlelight.

"I was thinking of what I should call you. It's silly, I suppose, but what do you think of Mother?" The bird made no response.

"Well, you could at least screech." Still no response. "I don't want to sleep. I don't want this night ever to end. I wish I could see Roisin, not in my dreams. As she is now."

The bird tried to shake loose of Rowan's grasp, fighting her. It dug its beak into her thumb, and Rowan let it go, yanking her hand back. The bird landed in the grass and hopped crookedly away, toward the little brook just to its left.

Brook?

Rowan jumped to her feet and spun in a circle. Her bench was gone, her roses were gone, the castle was gone. She was in a forest. A forest she knew. It couldn't be.

Hesitantly, reverently, Rowan walked forward to the clearing she saw up ahead. Walking toward a small singing voice.

It couldn't be.

Within the Guard of Trees

"*I*n the Fairy circle, moonlight paints the ground, and all in one big circle, the toadstools dance around. In the Fairy circle, late into the night, little fairies come to dance, beneath the starry light."

Rowan paused in the shadows of the trees and simply watched. She was perfect. Her hair was nearly to her waist, with barely any more color to it than a moonbeam, and she had three red freckles beneath her right eye. She was a tiny thing, barely more than three feet. She looked so happy and free, dancing and spinning in little jumping loops around the Fairy circle—just as Rowan had foreseen the day Roisin was born.

"In the Fairy circle, you will come to me, and we will pass the midnight hour within this guard of trees." She had a soft, sweet voice, full of faith and joy. "In the Fairy circle, all lost things are found, for Fairy leave their treasure here scattered on the ground."

Rowan thought she should step forward and say something, but what if it was just a dream? She might step forward and find herself in the rose garden again. What did one say to one's long-hidden sister? It had been five years; Roisin had barely been more than a baby. She might not even remember.

"Aren't you going to come and dance?" Roisin asked, still in a singsongy voice, continuing to twirl and leap. "You danced in my dream."

"Did I?" Rowan stepped out of the shadows. Roisin had dreamed of this, too. Maybe she did know. "Do you know me?"

"Of course. You are the fairy who made this place for me to find." Rosin stopped spinning and turned toward Rowan. "I am the only one who ever finds it. So you must have made it for me. Are you going to take me away and replace me with a changeling?" she asked, seeming more intrigued than frightened.

"No. Who told you I would?" Rowan asked, more than a little disappointed that her sister did not simply run into her arms.

"My Auntie B, when I told her I found a Fairy circle. I couldn't bring her, so she told me a story about the dark fairy." Her voice took on a dramatically animated quality; she leaned forward with wide eyes, as though she were imparting a great secret. "About the traps they lay for naughty little girls who go and dance under the midnight moon."

Rowan was completely charmed. Roisin didn't know who they were to each other, but she knew well enough that she was safe.

"She was trying to frighten me." Roisin stood straight again, looking at Rowan with resignation, as if to say, this is something grown-ups do and I tolerate.

"But there is no frightening you?" Rowan asked.

"Not of you." Roisin walked right up to her sister and took her hand. "I have dreamed of you for always. I knew you would come."

Overcome, Rowan bent down and wrapped her sister in a tight hug. "I have dreamed of you for always, too."

When she finally released her little sister, there were tears on Rowan's cheek. Roisin let out a little shudder running a finger along the armor Rowan wore.

"That's cold."

"Oh, sorry." Rowan stepped back and, with a bit of effort, removed the armor piece by piece, laying it on the grass.

"Ooo. You are so beautiful," Roisin said in awe when the last of Rowan's armor was gone. She stood before her in the dress Maureen had made.

Rowan laughed; no one ever called her beautiful.

"I wish I could be tall. But Auntie A says I will not be, and I mustn't give Auntie B the satisfaction."

Rowan chuckled at the thought. She had only met the aunts once, but they had left a lasting impression.

"You are beautiful. In fact, you are perfect, just the way you are," Rowan said, resisting the urge to run her finger along the freckles under her sister's eye.

Roisin smiled and held out her hand again. "Come here; I must show you something." She pulled Rowan over to the ring of mushrooms, yanking her to the ground in front of it.

"See here." She pointed to a little hole in one of the mushrooms. "There is a frog who lives there. He is no bigger than your thumb, but he is very old," she confided in an educational tone. She was such a funny creature, her sister.

"He was having a spot of trouble with a rabbit. The rabbit wouldn't have eaten him, you understand, but he was so much bigger, he nearly killed Ally; that is his name, Aloysius Frog. I call him Ally. The rabbit nearly killed him, twice, by not looking where he hopped. So I suggested the Fairy circle; it seemed to me to be a very safe place to live. I assured him that you and I were good friends, and I was sure I could explain his dire need sufficiently so that he might stay."

Rowan bit the inside of her lips to keep from laughing. Rather than attempting to speak, she nodded sagely when Roisin looked to her for an answer.

"I knew you would be kind." Roisin beamed.

"Well, I shall try. Do I have any other tenants?"

"A few, yes," Roisin said in a very adult voice. "I must admit, they are not all quite so small and unassuming."

"You don't say. You haven't any dragons hiding here, have you?"

"My, no. They are much too large; they would frighten Aloysius. There is only Finn, the three-legged fox, and his two children. They lost their mother, and I have a soft spot for things with no mothers, as I have none, either."

"You have no mother?" Rowan had a sudden flash of memory—Gwyneth rocking Roisin to sleep in the nursery, with such an open, loving expression on her face, as Rowan hid watching from the hall like a thief. She had always been jealous of such moments, but Roisin would not have those, either. Rowan's heart twisted, and her hands tingled with a desire to pull Roisin into a tight hug. What had the aunts told her?

"None to speak of. My aunts say she was lost to me because of a powerful curse. What is your mother like? I have wondered what it would be like to have a mother."

"So have I," Rowan said sadly. It had never occurred to her that Roisin would grow up missing a mother.

"You have no mother, either," Roisin said gently, and she laid her hand on Rowan's shoulder. "I am sorry. Have you never had one?"

Rowan smiled. All her life, everyone had known everything about her. How her mother died, how clumsy she was, how she got her name, that her grandmother wanted nothing to do with her, that it was her fault her sister had been cursed. Now here she was, lying in the grass beside her sister, who had no idea who she was. For the first time, Rowan could simply tell someone her story.

She had never realized how very much she wanted to do just that.

"I have never known her. She died as I was born. I am told she was able to hold me for only a moment before she passed."

"Only once." Roisin looked off into the trees.

"Every year on my birthday, her oldest friend comes and tells me the story. I was born into a raging storm, she says..." Rowan drifted off into silence, thinking about the words. "They all talk about how I was born into sadness and storms and battle. They think I don't understand peace." As the words slipped out, Rowan felt oddly resentful of the story, all the things her family thought her lacking. If she was "born" to it, why did they insist on acting as though it was all her choice?

"Do you?" Roisin asked, rolling onto her side.

Rowan rolled onto her back and stared up at the sky and the passing stars, releasing her frustration on a sigh. "This is peace. I understand it fine. I simply do not have it very often."

Roisin nodded, then rolled to her back, as well.

"Do you know?" A thought stuck Rowan. "You remind me of my mother. Not her exactly, of course; I never knew her. But she was soft and trusting and loving like you—and beautiful. Sitting here, it's as though I can remember how it felt when she held me just once. Safe and happy and...loved."

"Yes!" Roisin nodded excitedly. "That is just how I feel. Like I am home again. I have often wondered what they were like, my mother and father. I can remember that they loved me and I loved them, but I cannot remember anything else."

Her mother and father only? She couldn't remember a sister? It ached. But she loved her; Roisin loved her. Rowan could feel that, even if Roisin had no idea who she was.

"Well, your father is a large man, very tall like me, and strong, but sad for missing you. He has loved you from before you were born, and every day he grows to love you more, even as he searches for a way to bring you home. And your mother…" What good could she say of Gwyneth? "Your mother loves you more than she loves herself or any other thing in the world. She was always a gentle and…good woman, but when she looked on you for the first time, she became truly beautiful. She held you in her arms, and she laid her forehead against yours and kissed you. For a moment, you were one heart." Rowan could still see it clearly, and her own heart longed for such a memory. "Since the curse took you away, she is a bit lost, alive, but only with anticipation of the day you will return to her."

Roisin was sitting up now and watching her sister with a pensive expression, weighing some deep decision. After a moment, she shook her head and laughed.

"That story won't do. Far too sad and lonely."

Rowan chuckled. "Well, you may have a point."

"No, what happened was this. My mother was a beautiful creature, loved by all. One day a powerful wizard saw her and fell immediately in love." Roisin spoke with such verve and awe, it was impossible not to be drawn in. "But she did not love him, so he put her under a deep love spell and tricked her into marrying him. Even though her love for him wasn't real, as long as she was under the spell, he was happy, and he treated her with all of his love, so she was never sad or lonely. When she became pregnant, the wizard was overjoyed. Now he would have a whole family. But he didn't realize that every day, my mother began to love me. And that love was real love. The more real love she felt, the weaker his spell became. Every day she loved him less and me more, and the wizard grew frightened and jealous. When I was born, the curse broke completely. My mother became angry with the wizard for having held her there for so long. They had a terrible fight, and in the middle of it, the wizard cursed my mother to be…always outside of her own time!"

Rowan loved the way Roisin's entire face came to life as she made up her little fantasy, one word at a time. She was so completely alive. There was no one like her. Was it any wonder she would be loved by everyone she ever met?

"So she wandered the earth, but she was never mother to her own daughter. Even if she met me, she wouldn't know me. In that way, the wizard separated her from the thing she loved most in the world, just as she had done to him by breaking the spell." Her eyes grew wide and sad, as though surprised by her own story. Then she opened her mouth, and her expression shifted to hopeful again. She could not stay downtrodden, her sister.

"Nearly as soon as the curse was done, he regretted it, because he truly loved them both, daughter and wife. Knowing he must be punished for his crime, he sent his daughter away to be raised by his three sisters in a forest, while he worked to undo his spell. But he still didn't understand that true love, like my mother had for me, couldn't be conquered by a curse. Every year, for one night, mother and daughter meet in the middle of a Fairy circle. They don't know each other, but their hearts know each other. In this way, they are never alone—even as we search for each other."

Roisin's face was raised toward the sky and the stars. From the ground, it seemed to Rowan, the whole of the night had wrapped itself around her, bathing her in the soft glow of eternity.

"You're right," Rowan croaked. She had to cough to clear her throat of tears. Roisin was a wonder. It was perhaps the sweetest story in all time. So sweet, Rowan did not have the heart to tell her they were not mother and daughter. "Your story was much better."

Roisin looked down at her with an angel's smile before plopping onto her back alongside Rowan.

"Yes, I rather thought so."

Rowan laughed through her tears. They lay there together in silence for a while, watching the stars go by, hand in hand.

"Will you dance with me before you go?" Roisin asked as the sky began to warm with flecks of pink.

"I do not think I have ever danced before," Rowan said, surprising herself.

"It isn't very hard. I will show you. We must dance, to show we are grateful for the night and the stars and the safety of the Fairy circle."

"All right. Show me how." Rowan pushed up to her feet and followed her little sister—jumping and twirling in loops around the ring of mushrooms, laughing all the way.

"In the Fairy circle, moonlight paints the ground, and I will sing the Fairy song till morning light is found," Roisin chanted. Rowan followed along.

When the first rays of sunlight touched the trees, the girls stopped dancing. Suddenly Roisin looked sad; rushing, she threw her arms around her sister.

"Will you promise to come again?" she begged.

"I do not even know how I came to be here. Didn't you bring me?" Rowan asked anxiously. She had felt nothing but calm and contentment for hours; now all her old fears came rushing back. What if she never found Roisin again? What if this was a dream?

"You brought yourself. I only waited for you," Roisin said, confused.

"I couldn't have. I never do magic right. I must have had help."

"It was just you; I felt it."

"But…When I am around, magic either goes terribly wrong or simply doesn't work. I have tried and tried."

"Perhaps it was never important until tonight," Roisin said so simply and hopefully that Rowan could barely breathe for looking at her.

"No, nothing was ever as important as tonight."

"Then you will come again?"

Rowan nodded; lifting her sister into the air, she twirled her around joyfully. That had to be it. With a breathless laugh, Rowan returned her sister to the ground and dipped down for one more hug.

"I will come again," she whispered in Roisin's ear. "I love you eternally…" Rowan drew back to look her sister in the eye, but all she found was empty air. "Little sister," she finished in a whisper, letting the words fall upon the air.

She was back. She spun around; there was no sign of Roisin anywhere. Her breath shuddered out as though she would cry, but she shook it off.

That was no dream. She had seen her sister. Spent the evening laughing and telling stories with her. There was nothing sad about that.

Rowan walked to her mother's roses, running her fingers along the buds as she passed. The rows were not neat and orderly here like they were in the shrub garden on the western side of the place. They curved and wound, as though her mother had been dancing when she planted them and the roses couldn't help following the motion. There was no great sense to be made of the order either; every bush was a different shade, white beside orange, beside a many-hued pink, beside yellow and red. Each rose was...unique.

Halfway down the row, a pale yellow rose reminded Rowan of the moonlight playing in Roisin's hair. Rowan stopped beside it, running one finger along the pattern of the petals, and bent her head to breathe in the sweet scent. With no thought but holding on to the memory of the night, Rowan snapped the bloom off the bush, cradling it gently in her palm.

"Rowan? Rowan?" Her father's voice came from just beyond the wall.

"I am in the garden, Father."

"Have you been out here all night?" he asked, coming forward and taking her face between his hands to examine her.

"I lost track of time," Rowan said, unable to banish the smile on her face. From the corner of her eye, she saw her armor and sword lying in a pile beside the bench and her bird sleeping with its beak tucked into one wing beneath the bench.

"Are you all right? You haven't taken ill, have you?"

"No." Rowan laughed. "Yesterday was the best birthday I ever had. I didn't want it to end. Thank you." Impulsively, Rowan pulled her father into a quick hug. "I must go change; I am late for practice!"

"I know," the king called after her. "Colum nearly sent the knights out to search for you." Shaking his head, the king walked over to the bench to collect Rowan's birthday presents. It was good to see her smile so much. He should take her riding more often.

Unwilling Servant

2,790 days until Roisin returns

By the time Rowan had changed and run to the courtyard, she was so late that Colum was already training the real knights. It would be easy enough as princess to simply walk over and interrupt. But when Colum chose knights for her, they would be uncomfortable enough fighting a woman and especially fighting the princess; she did not want to complicate matters with them disliking her for unfair treatment. So she walked to Maureen's home.

Magic lessons changed dramatically when Maureen became a mother; the children were in her mind at all times, even when they were not underfoot. So she would never risk harming them with dangerous spells. Instead, she attempted to teach Rowan to exert her will over other creatures. To force truth or obedience or deference, as Rowan had failed to do with the Fairy messenger the day before. She was not particularly good at it.

But today, despite not having slept and having worked hard the day before, she was certain she could do it. Today was different. Today she was different.

The children were not underfoot when Rowan arrived, having followed their father to watch him train the knights.

"My, my, perhaps we should let you sleep late more often. Look at that smile on your face."

"Yesterday was wonderful; I didn't sleep a wink. I wanted the day to go on forever, and now it will."

Maureen chuckled. "I hope you don't intend to remain awake forever just to continue enjoying your birthday."

"It wasn't that it was my birthday, or gifts. I was different. Do you think… maybe I am terrible at magic and a clumsy oaf because it was never important not to be?"

"Well…" Maureen cast about for a way to answer. "You are not a clumsy oaf. You haven't been clumsy at all for years."

"That isn't the point." Rowan waved her off. "I have always had something else I could use, something I was more confident with than magic. But when magic was the only way, I used it. Without even thinking."

"What do you mean?" Maureen drew back, startled.

"Last night, I went somewhere," Rowan said excitedly; she wanted to tell Maureen everything. But as she opened her mouth to speak, the words would not emerge.

"Where?" Maureen asked, but her voice was different, far away. Not her own.

"I…to the rose garden," Rowan said cautiously. "Like I do every year on my birthday." There was something odd in the air, sinister, a nearly imperceptible tickle of cold raising the hairs on her arm; it stopped her from saying all she wanted. "But it was different this time. I felt closer to my mother."

"Well, that's lovely, dear," Maureen said, and her voice became her own once more. Perhaps it had all been Rowan's imagination; she examined Maureen for signs that she was different, but her smile was warm and understanding as ever before.

No point risking it, though. Rowan had kept many a secret before. At least this one was good.

"All I really meant is…" Rowan caught herself waiting for the cold again and shook the feeling off—this was Maureen. "Today, I feel eternity. Perhaps we should try something new."

"If you like." Maureen nodded slowly, watching Rowan, but she made no comment about Rowan's hesitation. "Why don't we try a shade spell? It allows you to look into the heart of a thing, to what is kept hidden."

It did not take long for Rowan to become frustrated. She tried looking into the heart of the castle, into the heart of her new bird; she even tried looking into her own heart. But it simply wouldn't work. It was silly to think that just because she had seen her sister, she could do other magic right. Maybe Roisin was wrong. Maybe she had not brought herself to that Fairy circle. Her stomach dropped, and she fisted her hands against a sudden fear—what if she never found her way back?

"Well, nothing that's worth doing is very easy," Maureen sighed.

Rowan watched her walk across the room to take her seat. She was always tired now. The children wore her down. Maureen might not look it, but she was fifty-eight years old. She had been nurse first to Sinead and her twin, then to Rowan. And had given birth very late in life. It was little wonder she was not as sprightly as she had once been. Perhaps Maureen would prefer to simply abandon the cause of teaching Rowan to use magic.

What do you hide? Pull back the shade; show me your truth. Rowan thought the words of the spell. She only thought them. And Maureen closed her eyes, leaned back against the chair, and began to speak, entranced.

"This may be pointless." Rowan's heart froze in her chest as Maureen continued speaking. "No fairy has ever given its powers to a human, as you did with your sister. You may have none of it left. And that girl...it is not as though she did not have everything that should have been yours already. And you gave her your power." Rowan shrank away from the words, from the tone that sounded like resentment of Roisin.

"You are so like your mother, sometimes, in all the worst ways. Giving all of yourself away to someone who will never give back. You knew what it was to feel eternity, both of you, and you threw it away."

Rowan drew back, biting her tongue to keep from speaking, from crying. She felt like a child again, wanting to shrink away from the disappointment she'd caused, but where to? She'd always shrunk into Maureen's arms.

Maureen began to stir; without thinking, Rowan laid a hand on Maureen's shoulder.

"You need your rest," she said gently, and watched as Maureen settled back into sleep.

Two spells in as many minutes. Would her magic always come in fits and starts? Perhaps when she woke, Maureen wouldn't remember what she had said. And nothing would need to change. Nothing but what Rowan knew.

"Hasn't anyone ever told you?" Sorcha's voice poisoned the air, making Rowan jump. The voice hadn't come from Maureen, she spun around seeking the source. On a tree branch, just outside the open window a sparrow sat, staring in.

At Rowan's glance it cocked its head sideways and Sorcha's voice emerged once more, "Be careful what you wish for. Or you are bound to get it." Its message delivered, the bird flapped away with a cackling song.

Rowan stood where she was, waiting for the chill to pass. She had long been aware that Sorcha could use birds as spies, but speaking through them was somehow more sinister than Rowan had imagined. And what happened earlier, with Maureen... Rowan clenched her fists against the swirling fear in her gut. Sorcha knew what had happened here, though she had not been in the room. Did Sorcha know about the Fairy circle? Roisin said no one but she could find it, not even the aunts, but what if Rowan had brought some part of Sorcha with her? Would she even know?

Maureen would know the answer. But Rowan couldn't ask her. Tears stung her eyes as she watched Maureen sleep on; it had not been her imagination earlier. Sorcha had spoken through Maureen when Rowan would have told her about the Fairy circle. There could be no asking for help with this. Maureen was right; Sorcha had spies everywhere, sometimes even unwilling ones.

Rowan ran a thumb across the scars in her palm. *You knew what it was to feel eternity, both of you, and you threw it away.* A weight so heavy it might never be lifted settled on Rowan's chest as she fought the need to cry out. She couldn't let Maureen be right. She had to prove her mother's sacrifice was worthwhile. She would do it alone, and make Maureen proud.

Rowan walked from the house with mixed feelings. On the one hand, she had performed a spell just right—two, actually. On the other hand, she had invaded the private thoughts of her surrogate mother, thoughts she did not want to know. And she knew now that Sorcha was watching her very closely, that she could use fairies as spies against their will. Because there was no way, whatever Maureen's conflicting emotions, no way she would willingly betray Rowan. A bit of the weight rose from Rowan's chest as the certainty settled within her. She hadn't realized until just then that not all of the pressure came from disappointing Maureen; some of it was from doubting her, and that wouldn't happen again.

Three tiny fireballs hurtled past Rowan toward the house.

"Stop," Rowan ordered, and shockingly all three froze. She would need to have care with exerting her will over other people. "Your mother is fast asleep," Rowan whispered, coming down on her knees before the trio. "We have all been wearing her out. What do you say I take my three favorite children for a walk?"

"Walks are boring." Ferdy kicked a foot in the dirt, throwing a look over his shoulder. He would like nothing so much as to run inside and wake his mother.

"What if we go and throw wet hay at the knights to distract them?" Petal suggested with a bright innocent smile, as if she did not know this was a terrible idea.

At once, Ferdy began nodding his head, and Keagan shook his.

"What if we compromise? I shall take two naughty children and one good," Rowan said with a nod at Keagan. Petal and Ferdy only smiled at being called naughty. "And I throw them into the pond."

"Yeah!" All three screamed excitedly; even shy little Keagan looked over the moon with excitement. They loved the water.

They played for a few hours; it was new to Rowan, taking time out of the day to simply do something fun. She saw a different side of the children when they were playing. Ferdy became milder when he was not being reined in. Petal became a bit of a bossy shrew, ordering her brothers around and stomping her foot when they wouldn't listen. Keagan's new demeanor was the most dramatic: gone was the shy, obedient child; he joined forces with his devilish brother to torture his sister, throwing water at her and chasing her around the pond.

Rowan mostly just watched from beneath the shade of a tree, calming them when they would go too far, as little children will. When some time had passed and Rowan could tell they were becoming grouchy, she rounded up her reluctant troops and headed back to the house.

"Don't push, Ferdy!" Keagan screamed at his brother. They returned home at less than half the speed they had gone with.

"Don't push, Ferdy!" Ferdy repeated, quick to know what would most annoy his brother.

"Don't copy."

"Don't copy."

"You're going to get in trouble!"

"You're going to get in trouble." Ferdy stuck out his tongue.

"You're making my head hurt," Petal said, rubbing her temples.

"See! You made Petal sick!" Keagan yelled, stopping altogether to shout at his brother.

"I did not; it was you."

"All right." Rowan turned to put a stop to the little squabble, but before she could reach the boys, they shouted in unison, charging past her.

"Petal!"

Spinning back around, Rowan saw Petal stretched out across the grass, with her hand on her head and her eyes closed.

"Oh no. Petal!" Rowan shouted, coming down beside the siblings and reaching for Petal. "The one time I watch you alone." She pulled Petal up into her arms, feeling her head for a bump or some sign of what was wrong.

"I'm fine." Rowan heard the tiny whisper. She pulled Petal back to see her face. Petal opened one eye and winked at Rowan before letting out a little groan and slumping even more.

Rowan didn't know whether to be offended or impressed. Both, she supposed. The boys, who moments ago were ready to come to blows, were practically wringing their hands in fear.

With a disgusted humph, Rowan stood, keeping Petal in her arms. No reason to spoil the effect before she had all three hooligans home.

"Come on; we must get her home." Rowan was impressed to see the boys moving quickly and quietly along beside her.

"We will discuss this atrocious behavior later," Rowan said firmly. Beside her, the boys nodded ashamedly. But Petal knew whom she was speaking to, and though her eyes remained firmly shut, a little smile grew on her lips.

When they reached home, Maureen was awake, making the children a meal. Her eyes caught Rowan's sadly; she looked away almost immediately. She remembered. Rowan's arms tightened reflexively around Petal; she fought the fear of facing Maureen and her true feelings.

"Mama, Mama, something is wrong with Petal!" Keagan yelled anxiously.

"Oh?" Maureen said skeptically.

Rowan nearly chuckled; so this was not the first time. The devious little girl.

"Go wash up. I'll fix Petal," Maureen added when the boys would have hovered over their third. "Just drop her anywhere," Maureen said once the boys were out of the room. "She might as well have something in need of fixing."

"I was only trying to help, Mama," Petal said, pulling herself up in Rowan's arms.

"Lies are never helpful. You keep up this behavior, and your brothers will never trust you—with good reason. Go get clean."

Rowan put Petal down and watched her run out of the room.

"I'm sorry," Rowan said once Petal was gone. "I should never have…"

"*You* are sorry?" Maureen shook her head, near tears. "Rowan, I am sorry. The things I said to you."

Rowan rushed to reassure her, desperate to brush aside and forget all Maureen had said. "It's all right. I—"

"It is not all right." Shaking her head, she walked to the chair where Rowan had put her to sleep earlier and patted the one next to it. "Come here. Let me explain."

Rowan sat; Maureen still did not look her directly in the eye.

"Your parents' marriage was part of a contract between Sorcha and your grandfather. He promised her fealty from himself and his people, and she promised him Fairy blood to make his dynasty strong. Sinead was raised knowing she would marry your father. When the time came, she married him the same way she did everything else, with all of her heart. She was not a woman who knew how to hold anything back. I did. I hold many things back." Maureen met Rowan's eyes sadly.

What else had she hidden?

"I knew from the first your father was not as comfortable with the arrangement as your mother was. I tried to tell her, but it was too late. She had already decided to love him. I watched her do what I watch you do, devote her entire life to someone who would never do the same."

"It isn't Roisin's fault. She doesn't know us, any of us. That is why she is safe."

"I know. I know it is wrong of me to blame that little child, but don't you see? You have nothing in your life but her. And *she isn't here!*"

"I have other things," Rowan protested. Taking Maureen's hand, she smiled with teary eyes. "I have you."

"Rowan, I love you, and I know you love me and my family." Maureen shook her head slowly, squeezing Rowan's hand. "But you come to me for help to save your sister. You go to Colum for the same reason. What do you do just for the joy of it?"

Rowan smiled, shrugging. "I can't help it. We may not be twins or even whole sisters, but we are two pieces of one whole. If she were gone forever and I had no hope of seeing her again, I would be no better than Sorcha. I might even be worse," Rowan said in a near whisper, thinking of all the resentment and dark desires to hurt those who had hurt her, all kept at bay with the promise of Roisin. Of perfect love one day.

"That is exactly my point! I do not want you to give up fighting for her or to forget her. But I see in you a willingness, a determination, even, to die saving her. You do not even imagine what you will do when there is no longer a threat. I know I can't dissuade you. I could not dissuade your mother from giving all her power over to you. You, neither of you, seemed to see yourselves as worthy of having someone sacrifice for you."

"I would have…"

"Oh no, you don't. I do not mean that you should have died and your mother lived. I should have been able to save her. Had she held even a little of herself back, she might be here *with you*. But she loved with everything that she was. If you won't hold something back, at least promise me this: enjoy yourself now. Your sister is."

Lady Knight

*I*t had never occurred to Rowan that loving with her whole heart was a bad thing. She was not sure she could ever see it as such. But Maureen had a point. Rowan loved the hours she spent doing nothing with the children; would it be so terrible if she had more hours like that? Both Father and Colum had said similar things to her.

Rowan approached the practice field where the young knights were sparring with their mentors, and stood back watching. She used to love following knights around. One knight in particular, Bran, she had trailed for an entire year; he took to calling her his page. He left, a part of the third campaign to kill Sorcha, and never returned. Rowan had cried for a week when her father informed her. There were no more campaigns to kill Sorcha after that. Still, whenever Rowan thought of it, she felt hollow for the loss of her friend with his indomitable spirit and complete faith in her ability.

Before he left, he took her aside and told her he would expect to find her the kingdom's first lady knight when he returned. A real knight, he said, loyal, brave, strong, and honest. He would accept nothing less.

Rowan watched the fighting. Sometimes, she supposed, being brave didn't mean facing death; it meant facing rejection, insult, even hatred if it meant doing what was right.

Rowan walked forward, pausing long enough to pick up a practice blade from the pile beside the field; she continued out until she stood in the center of the field.

"Who will fight me?" she demanded when the clang of swords had died down and she had the attention of every knight.

"You do not want to practice with men, Princess," an older knight, the size of a small mountain, said condescendingly. "You would be better off with your practice poles."

"I am Rowan, high princess of Stonedragon, and your future queen." She swallowed; her chest was pounding, and there was a buzzing beneath her skin that felt exactly like riding Yseult as fast as the horse would carry her. Her chin rose a bit higher. "If you are too cowardly to face me, you may call me Your Majesty. But any who are willing to face me may call me whatever they choose. The only oddity I am is a lady knight."

"All right, Sir Rowan," a young knight, perhaps a year older than Rowan, said from behind her. "I will fight you."

Rowan grinned and motioned him to advance. She saw Colum leaning against the fence on the far side of the field. He would not interfere, but his expression was grim.

It really was different from sparring with Colum. His intent was to teach, to show her weaknesses she needed to protect. This knight was young, he was determined, and as were many of the other young men of the kingdom, he was shorter than Rowan. His intent was to win. To prove to her she did not belong on the field. He attacked with all his considerable power and energy, and Rowan spent the first of the encounter simply blocking his blows.

His sword struck hers like a hammer; she sank back a bit, absorbing the strikes with her core. Every strike was harder than the last and just a bit higher than it needed to be, so that when his sword fell, it forced her lower, as though he would pound her into the ground. Rowan's chest expanded like a shield and her legs firmed, making herself taller.

All the eyes on her should have made it harder, but they didn't. They wanted her to fail. She was not very good at giving people what they expected from her. It only galvanized her to fight harder.

More than that, the adrenaline from knowing someone would hurt her if she did not stop him was electrifying. She felt unstoppable, and that feeling awakened the power within her.

She fended off the young knight's attacks until she could see him growing weary. Then she charged, striking out at him with equal force and determination.

Now he was the one who could only defend. She beat him back until she saw her opening, swinging her sword down to connect with his side in what would be a mortal wound with real blades.

He dropped his sword and his head at the same time, fighting to hide the murderous anger in his eyes.

Rowan nodded her thanks. She looked back at the crowd; so overpowered by the adrenaline and success, she was smiling. "Who is next?"

"Why not fight someone your own size?" The young knight's partner stepped forward. Rowan remembered him from when she was younger— Ardal. He was indeed one of the few men on the field taller than Rowan.

She smiled and nodded at him, still hyped from the previous fight.

This fight was different. Ardal was a better knight. He did not rush out to beat her, but took his time. Also, he did not seem as intent on hurting her; he would, if it meant winning, but he was equally willing to win by outlasting her. He was not as affected by the adrenaline as she was.

They seemed evenly matched. Rowan saw Colum from the corner of her eye. He did not look particularly impressed. She remembered the first time she had sparred with him. She had lost miserably within seconds and complained about the unfairness of how weak she was.

"It isn't about strength, Rowan; tiny forces drive back huge ones over and over. It is about determination and logic. Never go to your opponent; make him come to you."

Rowan began stepping back, leading Ardal to her. *Think, Rowan, what do you have that he doesn't?*

"Never use a large amount of energy when a small amount will work. The blade works for you; don't let it carry you."

When Ardal swung out at her powerfully, Rowan dropped to one knee and stabbed upward, slamming the practice sword into his gut.

Ardal stumbled back, laughing. He turned to the knight he mentored. "That is how you beat a larger opponent, and make your teacher look a fool. Well done, Lady Knight." He bowed low.

Rowan was panting and aching a bit when she got to her feet, but she bowed her head respectfully to Ardal before searching the group at large.

"Next?"

The first knight who had spoken to her stepped forward. "What tricks have you for me, Princess?" he asked snidely.

He was an older man. Perhaps even a bit older than Colum, and very large. Rowan was sure she should know his name—he had been a knight of the kingdom for many years—but she didn't. She was not sure she had ever seen him fight; this would be difficult.

"*Don't let your opponent into your head.*" She heard Colum's voice again. "*Then you do his work for him. You are as powerful as you believe.*"

The knight stepped onto the field in front of Rowan, bowing, as one did in a formal duel, and tossing off a superior smile. Rowan smiled and made a curtsy, well able to interpret his look.

Many of the younger knights laughed. This man would put the girl in her place.

He knew what he was doing. The practice sword, just as heavy as a broadsword, but dull, rested in his hands as though it weighed no more than a stick. And he was a man who knew how to learn an opponent. From the first strike, he was attacking Rowan's weakest points. He circled her, never allowing her to situate her footing, leaving her scrambling to keep up as her skirts, despite the long slits on the sides, bunched between her legs. He'd swing just short of her knees, so in avoiding a strike, she'd be tripping. Balance was ever her worst enemy. She had no time to attack. He moved rapidly from one attack to the next, barely bothering to defend himself. He struck her leg hard, and then swept his sword up to strike her shoulder, the impact jarring her entire skeleton. Never a fatal blow, but you could beat an opponent with small strikes.

"*Sometimes you simply cannot win,*" Colum told her once. "*But that does not mean your opponent has to. You must decide how much you are willing to sacrifice to be certain your opponent does not survive.*"

Rowan braced herself for what would be a very painful hit if she were any judge of the man's intent. He liked hurting people. Rowan lowered her sword just enough to appear weak. As he moved to take advantage, she brought her sword up under his arm. Just as his sword struck her full in the chest, hers connected with his throat. A draw.

There were several gasps from around the field. The young knights, who had been prepared to cheer, saw where Rowan's sword rested. Rowan stood still, panting as she faced her opponent. Neither moved their swords at all.

Colum was already on the field coming toward them. He walked right up to Rowan and removed the sword from her hands. The older knight pulled his own away and stepped back.

"Tomorrow, you will arrive on time," Colum said flatly. "And you will do that again, until you can beat him. Do you understand?"

Rowan nodded, but her eyes never left her glaring opponent. "Yes, sir."

"Good."

The knight stared her down a moment, then executed a short, stiff bow. "Sir Rowan," he growled and walked off the field.

Rowan bit her cheek to keep from grinning. She might not have won their skirmish, but that "Sir Rowan" was a victory of a different kind, an acknowledgment of her skill, her right to be here.

"What is his name?" Rowan asked.

Ardal was walking forward to congratulate her. He threw a look over his shoulder at the retreating man, then back to Rowan. "He is Lord Donovan. Your stepmother's uncle. Have you never met him?"

"No." Rowan watched the man retreat. "Her family is afraid of me."

"With good reason," Ardal said with a chuckle. Ardal was likely a similar age to Colum and Donovan, in their later fifties. But he seemed much younger for his constant smiling and laughing. Standing as they were, side by side, Rowan noticed Ardal was only slightly taller than her, perhaps no more than a few inches. He was not of the bulky build many of the knights had. Certainly nothing like Donovan; that man looked like a large pile of rocks that had sprouted a face. Ardal appeared strong, but his strength seemed to simply be.

"You are one determined princess," Ardal said, breaking into her thoughts.

"I like 'Sir Rowan,'" she said with a smirk. "Grandma said I have a boy's name." She started to laugh but stopped when she felt her ribs pinching.

Ardal hit her on the back in a friendly fashion that still managed to tweak her ribs. "You'll be sore tomorrow."

"Tomorrow?" Rowan stretched her sore muscles.

"Well, you took that last hit like a m——"

"Like a man?" Rowan asked, raising a brow.

"That is what he meant," Colum said from behind them. "Let us be clear." He drew Rowan's attention. "Tomorrow will not be so easy. They have seen you fight and will not underestimate you again."

"The boys will be determined to make a name for themselves beating you," Ardal added.

Rowan glanced at the retreating young men. Wasn't the boy she fought determined? There wasn't a Bran among them, was there? Her heart sank a bit, but then she caught Ardal's friendly smile and returned it. He liked her.

"Donovan as well will want a piece of you. That last hit was designed to hurt in a lingering fashion. He'll hit harder if he thinks it will stop you," Colum growled.

He was angrier than Rowan had ever seen him. Angry that he had ever begun to train her. Maybe even disappointed in her for coming here. The part of Rowan that most wanted his approval longed to just back down, to smile and tease like the child he'd loved. But she met his gaze steadily and nodded; he would understand eventually. This was Colum; he always understood her. The certainty of it overpowered even her soreness.

"I understand."

"Then get rest. They will be well rested and ready to take you on tomorrow; you must be the same."

"I will." She fought to appear confident despite her racing heart. Tomorrow would be harder. It filled her with a mix of dread and anticipation, and made the magic only more anxious to get out.

With Mother's Assistance

2,789 days until Roisin returns

As Colum predicted, the next day was not so easy. Every man on the field wanted a piece of the princess, but Colum would not let them have it. He picked her opponents and the order. Sore as she was, Rowan did not quit the field until the other knights had done so. She practiced no magic that day and spent no time with her father and his advisors preparing the treaty, as she had the day before. She knew to leave would be to admit defeat, so she powered through.

When the knights broke for the day, Rowan walked, slowly with her head high, refusing to look left or right, straight into the castle. It was not until she reached the safety of her room that she let the pose drop and fell onto her bed, sore, tired, and bruised.

She had fought seven men over the course of the day, four of them young knights. Even though today's practice was done without a gallery of spectators, every time a knight had landed a blow of any kind, there was a round of cheering. She had beaten every one of her young challengers, with some difficulty; they were excellent knights.

She had not, however, beaten even one of her senior challengers. Two draws and one loss. The only positive she could find in those matches was that she had not lost to Donovan. She had not fought him. Her loss was to Ardal. It felt similar to losing to Colum; even as she lost, he was instructing her on how to prevent a similar loss in the future.

At the end of the day, when the knights were leaving the field and Rowan's head was nearly spinning with relief, knowing soon she could let go, Ardal and Colum had approached her.

"We think it best to give you a mentor. Like the rest of the young knights," Ardal said conversationally. Rowan watched Colum; this was his idea, but Ardal voiced it. Did Colum really think she would accept kid-glove treatment any better from someone else? She needed to fight men who were willing to hurt her. "Only one knight to spar with regularly. Bouncing among opponents this way may not work."

"Is Donovan interested?" Rowan asked with false innocence.

"I was suggesting myself," Ardal said matter-of-factly, but he had an eyebrow in the air, acknowledging the sarcasm of Rowan's question.

"No. I like you, Ardal, and you like me. You will not purposefully put me into danger."

"You are not meant to be in danger on the practice field. It's a learning place," Ardal pointed out with his usual jaunty smile.

"I will not be leaving the palace on campaigns, like the young knights," Rowan pointed out. "Here is the only place I can learn what real danger is. I will rotate."

"Rowan." Colum spoke now, the voice of reason. "You are better than most of the boys, but eventually they all get lucky. Alternating this way gives each of them a chance to learn your weaknesses before fighting you. If you do not want Ardal for a mentor, I will choose someone else. You cannot take beatings like this every day."

"Yes, I can," Rowan snapped. "When she comes, Sorcha will not kindly assume proper dueling poses. If I wanted the knights to like me, I could have charmed them."

Ardal chuckled, covering his face.

Rowan pointedly ignored Ardal's skepticism. "I challenged them, knowing what I would get for it. I will alternate."

Rowan lay in bed now, aware that there were tears on her cheeks, but not up to the task of wiping them away. They were right; she couldn't do this every day. Certainly not when she was in this much pain.

She wanted to call for someone, a maid, a nurse. But anyone she called would tell someone else. She couldn't let it get back to the knights that she was weak. On her window ledge, Mother, the bird Ferdy had given her, paced back and forth, screeching disapprovingly.

"There, there now," came Maureen's soothing voice from the side of the bed. "I won't tell a soul."

"Maureen." Rowan was horrified to hear her voice emerge as a sob.

"Yes." Maureen came to the top of the bed where Rowan lay and gave her a brief hug. "I've a warm bath here for you. Between us, we'll soon set you to rights."

"You won't tell Colum?" Rowan begged. She could not give him one more reason to try to stop her.

"Dearest, long before you started calling me, Colum said I should come see to you." She eased Rowan onto her side and began untying her dress. "He knows every blow you feel. He also knows if he doesn't let you do it on his field, you will find someplace more dangerous."

Rowan sat up with some help from Maureen.

"I knew it would hurt, but..."

"Cursed swine! What have they done to you?" Maureen screamed, seeing the deep purple bruises on Rowan's arms, legs, and chest. "Why didn't you come to me at once?" she demanded, sounding so angry, it seemed like someone else's voice, especially as she very carefully helped Rowan to her feet and over to the tub. Rowan smiled, allowing herself to sink closer to Maureen, as she would as a child, to be loved and protected. Maureen was ever her fiercest protector.

"I'll kill every last one of those cowardly curs!"

"No. Ohhhh, this feels so much better," Rowan sighed as she sank into the tub. "I will be all right. Anything they can take, I can take."

"Nonsense. To begin with, they do not hit each other this way," she snapped. "They are trying to beat you, to scare you. This isn't normal training. And you are not a man. You are tall, you are strong, and you have trained in manly arts for years. But you are still a woman. And the simple fact is men and women are just different."

Mother screeched her agreement.

"I'm different," Rowan sighed, beginning to drift to sleep. The water was so comforting to her sore muscles. And the more Maureen stirred little circles in the water, the further away her pain felt, until it was almost as though it had never been. "In all time, there has never been another like me. My mother told me that."

"When?" Maureen wanted to shake Rowan awake and demand an answer. She remembered every word Sinead had whispered to her baby girl, and those were not among them.

But she wouldn't wake her. It would be easier to work on her injuries with her asleep. Kneeling beside the tub, Maureen rolled her shoulders, letting all her anger and fear slip away. She had told Rowan she was good at holding things back. She had held back love, even from this sweet little girl, worried what it would cost her. But no more. If those men could beat her down with their fears, the least Maureen could do was shield Rowan with her love.

The next day, Rowan woke to find her bruises and soreness gone. She felt physically wonderful. She should have felt embarrassed for needing Maureen's help—knights took care of themselves—or sorry to have asked it from someone who had given her so much already. But her mind drew her to the aunts' parting words for Gwyneth. That she would never survive until Roisin's sixteenth birthday if she did not learn to trust. Perhaps Gwyneth was not the only one who needed to trust someone.

Before Rowan went to practice, she ran out of the castle through the courtyard to Maureen and Colum's little cottage. The family was sitting at breakfast together. As soon as Rowan entered the house, the children jumped up and ran to greet her. When they were settled down and Colum had them clearing a place for Rowan, Rowan went to Maureen and simply hugged her.

"Thank you."

"Dearest." Maureen took Rowan's face in her hands, looking up at her so that their eyes met. "I helped deliver your mother into this world; mine were the first eyes she saw. I decided then that I would love her forever, as a daughter. You are the daughter of my daughter; whatever is mine is yours." Tears slid out the corners of her eyes.

Rowan took a deep breath. "Sometimes I am so scared, it feels like I am the only person I can trust. But I can trust you. I won't let her take that from me," Rowan said fiercely.

"She could never take it from you," Maureen said.

So Rowan told her what had happened two days before. Told her about Sorcha's presence, and how it had seemed her voice came out of Maureen. She took a seat at the table as she spoke, with the children and Colum gathered around, listening.

When Rowan reached the end of her story, Maureen smiled gently.

"You were a frighteningly powerful child."

"What do you mean?" Rowan gave a half laugh, shaking her head. "I cannot do any spells right."

"Two days ago, you performed the shade spell on another fairy, which is very hard, and you did it before I even taught it to you."

"No, I didn't; it was when you were tired."

"No. That was the second time. Sorcha has dominion over the Fairy; it allows her, if she focuses enough, to see and hear through any fairy of her kingdom. It is called the window; she can look through, she can hear, but she cannot fully control them. And as far as I have ever heard, it is undetectable. You looked back through the window. You should not be able to do that." Maureen was smiling, so broadly Rowan thought she might burst of pride.

"How did I? It seems as though I only do magic well when I am not thinking about it."

"You perform magic best when you simply let it flow through you." Colum nodded as he spoke. "When you open up enough to embrace what it is you need, there it is before you."

Rowan leaned back on her chair and thought. Embrace what she needed, and it was before her. Her father had said something similar, about just letting the magic come. Could it be that even people without magic understood it better than she?

"You said something last night." Maureen interrupted her thoughts. "Something you said your mother told you?"

"That there had never been another like me." Rowan spoke absently; then, as if catching what she had said as it slipped by in the air, she looked up and met Maureen's eyes. "That isn't a part of the story."

"No," Petal said, drawing everyone's eyes. "That was from before."

"When?" Three adults asked at once.

"When you went to get her father, Mama," Keagan answered casually, as though it was the most natural thing in the world that he should know this.

"But how do you know?" Rowan demanded in wide-eyed shock.

"Because we helped you remember." Petal spoke again.

"You asked for help," Ferdy said, much more seriously than Rowan had ever heard him. "Mother heard, told me you needed to remember."

"I told you no such thing," Maureen said with a humph. Not for a moment did she doubt her children's powers. But that did not mean she wasn't annoyed to be left out of what they'd done.

"Not you, Mama," Petal interjected.

"Mother. The bird Ferdy gave Rowan," Keagan finished.

Rowan looked from one member of the little family to the next, her eyes finally coming to rest on Colum. She had asked for help, without even wanting to; she had asked, and she had found herself here.

"What if"—Rowan thought as she spoke—"I rotate among all the knights until the summer, when they go off to the trials? But I only practice for half my usual hours?"

"What will you do the rest of the time?" Ferdy asked, sounding very formal.

"I imagine I shall spend some of it with you, imp. And some helping my father battle the curse. And a bit learning magic with your mother."

"And the rest?" Maureen urged, dissatisfied with the still battle-oriented list.

"I don't know. Whatever I need." Rowan caught her eyes, smiling.

Maureen nodded.

Colum looked at her steadily. "Many of the knights will view this as conceding defeat." It was a challenge.

"A real knight does not let taunts and challenges lead him." Rowan quoted her teacher. "He is his own man, who does what he must for the good of the world, not for the glory of *herself*."

Colum smiled.

The Knights of the Rose

2,694 days until Roisin returns

*I*t was much harder handling unscheduled time than Rowan had imagined. The first few days after making her plan, Rowan wandered about with her free hours, wishing she was training. And it was not nearly as easy to ignore the taunts as she had anticipated.

They came from everywhere. On the field as she fought one knight after another:

"Had enough, little princess?"

"Ready to hide behind Daddy, Princess?"

"Have a pressing dance to attend, Princess?"

Princess became one of the leading taunts. No one but Ardal called her Sir Rowan any longer. It seemed almost as though, practicing less, she was injured more often, and more painfully.

Matters only got worse one day three months later, when Balder saw his daughter limping in from the practice field with blood on her face and hands. He did not approach his daughter, just charged out to the field where the knights practiced and confronted them. He finally saw the harm of letting his little girl trail excitedly after men who lived by the sword.

"Colum!" The king did not pause, storming across the field, oblivious to the men dropping to their knees as he passed. "I did not give you permission to nearly kill my daughter with your training. She is bleeding! Limping! What have you done to her? Who was she fighting?"

"She fought Lord Donovan, Your Majesty." Colum bowed quickly and lowered his voice, attempting to back off the field so the men would not hear. "Rowan will recover."

"She should not be in a position to recover. You know better than anyone; I only ever meant for you to humor her." The king was seething. Girls were not supposed to limp to their rooms with blood running down their faces. He had allowed this to happen; now he would put a stop to it. He should never have trusted Colum; he would not make that mistake again.

"You are through influencing her," he shouted at Colum. Then to the group at large, "If another of you harms my daughter, he will find himself facing the full penalties of treason."

He marched off the field, as completely unaware of the sniggers and chuckles as he had been of the bows. Most of the men on the field were ecstatic; they had won. Rowan had run to her father to hide after the beating Donovan had given her. But there were some among them who exchanged discomforted looks.

Rowan was so busy learning from Maureen how to heal her own wounds—a dislocated ankle and several small cuts—that she knew nothing of what had gone on until the next day.

She arrived on the practice field ready to fight, but no man was willing, and Colum was gone.

"Your father ordered us not to harm you," Ardal said hesitantly. "He might be right. You are the future queen; we should not be putting you at risk."

"Yes, Princess," Donovan jeered, coming up beside Rowan and giving a deep, mocking bow. "This is no place for such a delicate lady. So many places to trip and fall."

Rowan bit down hard on her tongue to ignore the jeer and focused on Ardal. "Where is Colum?"

"Your father removed him as leader of the knights. He will settle down, Rowan," Ardal whispered, taking hold of Rowan's arm when she would stomp off to confront her father. "Do not make things worse."

"You know what a poison you are. Wouldn't do to get your only friend killed," Donovan taunted.

Rowan faced him slowly, jerking free of Ardal's hand. There was not a sound anywhere. The knights on the field did not even breathe. For most, she could tell it was fear that held them silent. But several looked on Donovan with disgust. He had taken his taunts too far.

"What is it about me that so frightens you, Lord Donovan?" Rowan advanced on him slowly, pleased when he took an involuntary step back. "Do you fear what I am, half Fairy, half human, never fully either? Does it keep you awake at night? Wondering exactly what I can do?" As she spoke, Rowan stretched out a hand, and the sword of a nearby knight flew from his grasp into hers. A startled gasp went up from around the field.

"You are nothing. You should never have existed," Donovan snarled.

"You aren't the first to say so," Rowan said offhandedly, but she heard Sorcha's voice in her head and shied away from it, calling forth her anger instead. She nodded her head at Donovan's sword. "Raise your sword. That's when you are at your strongest. When you have your pointy little shield to rely on."

"You have no right to the throne."

"Take it up with your king." Rowan nudged him with her sword as he continued to retreat.

"I won't fight a changeling."

Rowan laughed. "You fought me yesterday. Seemed certain you had the advantage. Won, even. Why so frightened today? Draw your sword, Donovan."

"Rowan, stop." The king's voice rang across the field.

"Not until he fights me." Rowan did not even look at her father. All around, men were taking to their knees, but Rowan had eyes only for Donovan.

"Rowan, this wasn't his doing; it was mine. Come here."

She turned to face him. "I will be his queen." She was eerily calm. "But he will not follow me. I am his sovereign already, but he affords me no respect. He will fight me, now, or he will leave this kingdom forever."

Balder looked into his daughter's eyes across the field. Were she his son, he would not argue. But she wasn't his son. And that man was bigger than she, more experienced. He had murder in his eyes.

But the other men watched the exchange as well; if he denied Rowan her right as sovereign now, who would follow her in the future?

Balder nodded his head once. "It is your right to demand this."

"Her right to demand it?" Donovan shouted. "She usurps your position even now, and you allow it. She is a poison. Her own blood sees this——"

"You will not speak so of the princess again." Ardal stepped between them. And behind him, a few knights took to their feet threateningly, as well.

"She has no place here!"

"Then lift up your sword and prove it," Rowan said steadily.

"And have you strike me down with a curse?" Donovan shook his head and threw his sword at her feet. "I fight men."

"Not in this kingdom," Balder said firmly. He did not allow the quiver of relief he felt to coat his words. He nodded at Ardal and the other standing knights. "He may have his horse, two days' food, and any belongings he can carry. But he is to be gone from my lands by daybreak tomorrow. Rowan, I would speak to you."

Rowan walked off the field with her father, feeling defeated. What had responding to Donovan's taunts done for her? The knights had one more reason to despise her. And by acting the queen and banishing the one man who stood against her, she gave them exactly what they expected. Colum would be ashamed. She was ashamed. Hurt and temper had gotten the better of her. How would she recover from this?

"You should not be fighting with the knights," Balder said as soon as the door closed behind them in his private study. "You are not as strong as they. Eventually you will be hurt beyond your magic to repair."

"You are right, Father," Rowan said sarcastically. "Better I not prepare at all and be easy prey for Sorcha."

Balder's eyes cut across Rowan angrily, and he fisted his hands on the desk, leaning forward to drive his point home. "Sorcha will not come after you with a sword. If she comes after you at all."

"She will come. There can be no doubt. She will not let us defeat her curse, and cower away into the shadows. She will want revenge, and I want her to come for it here."

"A sword will not kill the queen of the Fairy. But it may kill you."

"I will not stop training. I must be ready with every weapon I can find. The aunts said I must find a weapon she does not know."

"They were speaking of magic," he bit out between clenched teeth.

"How do you know? You have never understood magic."

"Fine. I do not understand magic; I do not know how to use it or what it means. I do not even know where it comes from. But if swords and armor could defeat Sorcha, she would have been killed by the horde of *real* knights I sent after her to their deaths."

Real knights? Rowan drew back. She knew no one else in the kingdom saw her title as anything other than a courtesy to a child, but she had not thought her father felt so.

"Balder!" Gwyneth barged into the room. Rowan and her father remained staring at each other. "Tell me it isn't true. You could not have banished my uncle, Donovan."

"No," Rowan said snidely. "He did not. I did. And you may tell the rest of your relations that I will do the same to them if they move against me." Not waiting for a response, Rowan stormed from the room.

2,689 days until Roisin returns

By the next day, Colum had returned to leading the knights, but he was following her father's edicts, refusing to let his knights fight her. He barely spoke two words to Rowan before sending her away.

She walked away with her head held high, so the men would not have one more reason to snigger and smirk. But her stomach churned with the shame of letting him down, and the fear that she had, with one stupid mistake, lost her best friend.

The jeering did not stop; it grew more insidious. Whispered between men when she passed, rather than shouted in her face.

Gwyneth would not even look Rowan's way. She curtsied and kept her eyes on the floor.

In the end, it was the return of Ardal and the knights who had escorted Donovan out of the kingdom that settled things. Rowan was practicing, blindfolded, in her old practice ring, with the triplets throwing obstacles at her. The four knights rode straight up to the ring and dismounted.

"Your Majesty?" Ardal called out. "May I have a moment of your time?"

Rowan tore off her blindfold and walked to the edge of the practice ring, catching the dirt clod Ferdy had thrown and crumpling it in her hand.

All four men knelt as Rowan approached, startling her. People rarely bowed to her outside of formal functions, much less knelt.

"We had time to think as we rode. And we have decided to respectfully request to be Your Majesty's personal knights."

"My knights?"

"We would gladly defend and *spar* with our future queen," Ardal said with a wink.

Rowan looked around the group. None of these knights had ever been particularly keen on putting her in any danger. They would challenge her, but all very safely. But if she refused, she was fighting dirt clods and padded sticks.

Rowan nodded. Then, catching their very gallant poses, Rowan curtsied.

"Keagan, get my sword." Rowan tossed aside her practice sword and took her special rose-hilted sword out of its sheath.

"Ardal, Liam, Sean, and Cassidy, insomuch as you have honored your future queen with your offer of service, shown your valor in defense of your kingdom, and without regard to the risks to your person, freely offered your fealty, I anoint you all Knights of the Rose. And bid you rise, my friends."

Distraction

Rowan resumed practicing with her knights without informing her father. For a few days, the whole of the palace held its breath to see what would happen, but in the end, nothing did.

Whether Balder felt guilty for what he had said in the midst of their fight or he trusted these men to keep her safe, it didn't matter. She was left to train, and that was all that mattered to her.

Every day she spent several hours riding Yseult or reading accounts of kings past, to prepare for her future, or simply sitting in her rose garden, thinking. All because people kept telling her she needed something in her life besides waiting to face the Fairy queen. But whatever she did, her mind always drifted back to her sister in that field or the Fairy queen and what she must be like. No matter what she imagined, it never seemed quite right.

Every day seemed a bit longer than the last. She understood her magic better. She felt it coursing through her in her sparring matches; when she was closest to losing, it rose up to push her forward. Even when she lost, she never went down easy. And in the evenings as Maureen helped her heal her wounds, magic rolled out of her in soothing waves. But Rowan had not returned to the Fairy circle. The more she tried and failed, the more she began to think that she was right originally; something other than her magic had carried her there. Whatever it was, it wasn't taking her back.

Several months had passed when Rowan received her second letter from the high prince of Turrlough. She was in the great hall with her father and Gwyneth when it arrived. They were hearing peasant disputes; everything from farmers convinced their neighbors were stealing to traders frustrated with higher costs of setting up stalls was brought before the king to be settled. It was incredibly dull and frequently petty. The same messenger as before brought the letter. He held her eyes as he approached and seemed to sniff the air around her.

"Your Majesty." He bowed low, as he had before, holding out the letter. "A bit bigger," he commented. "But not big enough by far."

Rowan wanted to ask in which way she had grown—power, age, or understanding—but Gwyneth's voice preempted her.

"What on earth do you mean?" Gwyneth demanded.

"The letter," Rowan replied before the messenger could. She did not want anyone else to know this man was Fairy. "He thinks the prince a bit short of words."

"I cannot see that it is his business."

Rowan took the letter, coming to her feet. "I would like a moment to read this, Father. Perhaps our guest should be given some food," she suggested to get him away from Gwyneth.

Rowan went to a small room off the great hall where she frequently read, and settled into an alcove to read her letter.

Dear Princess Rowan,

I must begin by apologizing for my somewhat vague proposal. My mother informs me that men frequently take for granted the things they most need to explain. As such, it is not entirely my fault; I am, after all, a man.

Rowan smiled, curled her legs beneath her, and pulled her long braid over her shoulder.

Allow me to clarify. I propose you visit Turrlough at any time in your convenience and get to know both its people and its ruling family. It is my hope that, having met us, you will feel compelled to accept my proposal of marriage.

A marriage between us may offer you little, but it can definitely offer you a trip down that lovely stretch of the Liadan you mentioned.

My brothers and I used to sail it on a flat wooden raft we built. We pre-tended we were fishermen. Until our nanny discovered us, and our great aspirations were chopped into firewood before our very eyes. I promise to offer you a much sturdier vessel.

Rowan released a small laugh and glanced around the empty room to be sure she wasn't caught. He was just so alive this Prince Gavin. He seemed genuinely happy.

I did not realize circumstances existed to prevent you leaving Stonedragon. It had been my understanding that, aside from a hidden princess, all was well in your kingdom. Perhaps that was thoughtless. While I have frequently wished to drown my brothers, I cannot imagine the turmoil that would grip both family and kingdom if even one of them were to be lost to us for several years. You have my deepest sym-pathies and great hopes for a peaceful and happy resolution of your current troubles.

I read your letter several times, particularly the beginning, and I believe you were jesting when you inquired if I was in fact a real knight. However, I believe it is the right of a queen to know what sort of man asks for her hand. I trained with the knights of the palace from a young age. I competed in the first three trials of the sword, before withdrawing from the final stage.

It was not my desire to withdraw. I wished to prove myself to the men who would follow me. But my father, and various other counselors, convinced me it was not in the best interest of the monarchy to risk its future king in a game of honor. I was knighted without completing the final challenge. You are free to make of my title what you will.
I remain your servant,
Gavin, High Prince of Turrlough

Rowan began responding without even thinking.

Dear Sir Gavin, High Prince of Turrlough,

Please take no offense at my sometimes odd humor. It is rarely understood in person, so why I should think it would carry better on the page, I do not know. I only meant to tease, as I thought you were about my title. I have heard of your many knightly qualities. Sir Colum spoke highly of your performance in the trials.

I knew you to be a knight in truth before I teased. It is the reason I felt comfortable doing so, although I should remember we have never met.

I have met both your younger brothers, however. Your youngest when he attended my sister's birth celebration with your parents. And Prince Owen as he traveled with your knights before his trials last year. So I must inquire, which is it you would have drowned? The dynamics of siblings always fascinate me. I never had the time with my sister to grow sufficiently annoyed with her to wish her harm. But I observe that it is somewhat common with close siblings.

I would have liked to know Roisin long enough for us to have aspirations of peasanthood together. I have never even thought to imagine myself a fisherman. But the image your story conjures is very peaceful. It is a shame I shall never see what I can only imagine was a terrible death trap built by three small boys.

Rowan stopped there for a moment, truly caught by the image. The triplets would do something like that. Build a raft and float down a river, as if time meant nothing. What would that be like, to simply float away, worrying for nothing?

It seems sometimes as though the people of Stonedragon, in an attempt to keep my sister's memory alive, will trap her forever in their minds as a three-year-old girl. They plan for a return that is seven years, three months, and ten days away as though it is tomorrow. I will sometimes enter a room where it is clear that all the inhabitants are asleep, even as they walk about and speak to one another. On good days, they re-member the spell and the time that has passed. They remember that we must continue to live our lives as we wait for Roisin's return. But there are other days.

Rowan paused again, brushing the feather end of her quill back and forth across the page. If she were entirely honest, she didn't care much if the curse took her subjects. But only a few months ago, while she and her father had been at odds over her training, avoiding each other to avoid the fight, she'd come across him in the hall. He was right before her, so she knew she could not ignore him.

"Father." She greeted him with a curtsy, a formality she only observed when they were fighting or attending a formal function.

He'd looked at her, right into her eyes, and was clearly lost. It had prob-ably only been a few moments, but with her breath achingly still, the time stretched on until at last she saw recognition dawn. He shook free of the confusion and nodded his hello as if nothing had happened, but Rowan could not forget it so easily.

What would happen if she left the kingdom? Would he remember her at all?

Those days are the reason I cannot leave at this time. Though your of-fer is a tempting one. I shall keep it in my thoughts, should I sense any change in my people.
Your intrigued correspondent,
Rowan, high princess of Stonedragon

Once the letter was sealed, Rowan focused her mind on the servant who had brought it and found herself in front of him without moving. It was a trick Maureen had been teaching her. One she had used without understanding when her father used to burn the rose garden. She had not found much use of it before now.

"Displaying your powers for my benefit?" he asked over the hunk of bread he was devouring.

Rowan did not respond; focusing on the little man, she thought the words of the shade spell: *What do you hide? Pull back the shade; show me your truth.*

The messenger chuckled. "Don't concentrate so hard. I can hear your intent a mile away. I'll take that." He yanked the letter from her grasp, vanishing before Rowan could react.

Rowan ignored the stares of the kitchen staff, all impressed by the fairy who mocked the future queen. She marched back to the great hall. It occurred to her as she walked that while reading the letter and responding to it, she had been thinking of nothing else, only the letter. Not the curse, breaking it, the battle, or the Fairy circle. Just the letter, that moment. And maybe, what it would be like to lie on her back on a poorly constructed raft and let the current take her where it would.

Her correspondence with the high prince of Turrlough quickly became the thing Rowan most looked forward to, aside from her sister's return. The letters came more frequently—it was rare for more than a month to pass without a message—and the more frequently they came, the more informal they became.

Every time Rowan saw the fairy messenger, a jolt of power rushed through her; here was a chance to try her hand at spelling him again. And she would get a chance to visit with Gavin. That was how his letters felt, so lively and present it seemed he was there with her.

The messenger appeared one afternoon just as Rowan was set to enter the rose garden.

"Your Majesty, I've a—" He broke off as Rowan lurched forward, wrapping her hand around his own, outstretched with the letter.

What do you hide? Pull back the shade; show me your truth.

He smiled cockily. "Apparently surprise is not the key for you."

"Humph." Rowan snatched the letter, annoyed, and marched into her garden to read. She forgot everything, even the annoyance of failing to spell the messenger, for the complete absorption in…fun that Gavin's letter offered.

> *Dear Princess Rowan,*
>
> *I wanted to drown them both at different times. I pity you greatly that you've never had the chance to wish the same on your sister. If you*

are truly saddened that you cannot see the doomed raft, I am sure I
could construct an even more dangerous one on my own...
Prince Gavin

Dear Prince Gavin,
  I have changed my mind; you are clearly a terrible brother. And it
leads me to believe you would be a most unfeeling monarch.
  I trust this fisherman fantasy was your only one. Or were you al-
ways shirking your responsibilities in your dreams
Rowan

Another time the fairy interrupted her training with the Knights of the Rose. She was fighting Sean, with Liam, Ardal, and Cassidy shouting directions as they watched. Sean was something of Ardal's and Colum's age and nearly Rowan's height, but he was the most solidly muscular of all her knights. He could beat her in power every time—so Cassidy urged her to be faster; Liam urged patience, insisting power burned more energy; and Ardal thought she should best him with cunning.

For her part, Rowan thought she would fight better without their assistance. She was stepping, swinging her blade down, to block a gut strike, but couldn't hear herself think for the knights arguing behind her.

"Sweep his leg, Rowan; bring him down," Cassidy called out.

"She'll never bring him down that way," Liam argued. "Stomp on his toe. Those boots are ancient." The two men chuckled.

"Why not use your magic?" The fairy's voice so startled Sean that he dropped his sword arm, glancing past Rowan. She'd been swinging toward his left shoulder, but at his sudden distraction caught him full in the neck with her blunted sword.

"Ugh chhh!" He gave a strangled cry, his hand flying to his neck.

"Sean!" Rowan dropped her sword, rushing forward to check on her friend. But he was already smiling wryly.

He coughed to clear his throat. "Guess you found your opening. No harm done." He shoved her playfully in the shoulder, nudging her in the messenger's direction. "See what your beau has to say. He can't seem to get enough of your letters."

Rowan felt a blush suffuse her face and hid a grin, looking at the ground.

"The only way she'll catch a man's attention is with a sword to the gut," a passing knight scoffed.

Rowan jerked up straight from the stab of self-consciousness at the comment. Before she could respond, her knights turned on the man. Cassidy was closest; kicking him to his knees, he unsheathed his sword and swung it fluidly to rest just at the man's throat.

"You will show the princess her proper respect," he snarled.

The man nodded, his eyes full of resentment as they skated away.

Rowan glanced away, trying to banish the sudden shaky feeling, and caught the fairy glaring in the man's direction as well.

He seemed to sense her eyes and glanced up. Smiling kindly, he bowed. "From the High Prince of Turrlough, Your Majesty, with all his compliments."

Rowan smiled, oddly touched by the fairy's attempt to comfort her. It was unsettling; she had not been so affected by such insults before there was someone in particular she wanted to impress. She reached out a hand for the letter, wondering what was wrong with her that she was so easily manipulated. As soon as her fingers brushed the page, a jolt of anticipation rushed over her.

Her magic reached out to the fairy before she had even thought of it. But he only shook his head, as if pleasantly unsurprised by her attempt to spell him.

"Closer, little queen. But still I anticipated your intent."

Rowan only laughed. Not so bothered by failing this time, she took the letter.

> *Dear Rowan,*
>
> *I shirk my responsibilities almost daily. But I imagine, as princess, you never have to sit through peasant disputes and find yourself envying the farmer whose vegetables have been devoured by his neighbor's goats. And I thought, if I could only spend a day beneath the sun, hoeing land, I should be a happy man...*
> *Gavin*

Dear Gavin

   I cannot say I often consider what would make me a happy man._
I have, however, listened to a number of peasant disputes. I find myself
more taken by the complaints of the sheepherder who says one lost sheep
is not such a problem when she left that morning with fifty. After all,
if you had all those hills to wander, wouldn't you find it hard to be
constantly counting, when there are a million more fascinating things
to watch than sheep...
R—

Some letters were short and seemed more like an excuse to get a response than
an actual letter, but others were pages long. Rowan had stopped reading the
letters as manipulation into marriage and begun to simply read them as correspondence with a friend.

   But it was quickly assumed that if there was not yet an understanding
between Stonedragon and Turrlough, there very soon would be. And it was not
just the members of their respective kingdoms who had taken notice.

Grand Plans

2,427 days until Roisin returns

The day before Rowan's sixteenth birthday, she was informed that there was a prince waiting to meet her in the great hall. Rowan was shocked and thrilled. She could not believe he had come. She had invited Gavin to visit Stonedragon, but he had insisted it was impossible.

> *I would happily make the journey today. If only to spar with you, so I can decide for myself if you are simply modest, as your knights claim, or a poor example of a knight, as you insist. However, my father has been poorly for some time now. We every day worry it will be his last. At the moment, I am prince in name but king in duty. Should my father recover, I will make the journey at once. But I simply cannot leave my kingdom in such uncertainty even to visit a fine friend.*

Rowan assured him that she understood and wished his father great health and a long life. Perhaps the king had recovered; that was the only way he would come.

Hearing a prince was there, Rowan rushed in from the south fields, where she had been practicing the joust in full battle armor, and went straight to the great hall.

She made quite the noisy entrance, armor clanking against itself. As she walked into the nearly empty room, with its vaulted ceilings, it sounded as though a whole battalion was walking in. From across the hall, she saw the prince look up in surprise. He was not what Rowan had expected.

He was about her height, with light hair the color of wheat stalks and a somewhat sweet look about him, with a heart-shaped face, fluttery hair, and wide, innocent eyes. It was not that he did not look strong, but Rowan could not imagine this was the same knight Ardal had described as a giant in the ring.

Rowan wondered, catching his expression at her approach, if she should have spent a few moments changing. As quickly as she could, she removed her helmet, stuffing her gloves into it as well, and smoothed the stray hairs off her face. It would startle most men to see a lady dressed in full armor, she supposed.

"Princess Rowan?" he asked rather hesitantly.

"Yes. I am sorry; I was practicing the joust. Give me a moment; I will return."

"Oh, no, no, that is not necessary." The prince rushed forward, worried he had offended her.

Rowan had ceased to be offended by people's expectations. It was perhaps a little galling that her very close friend, Prince Gavin, would be quite so superficial, but she was uninjured by it.

"I heard you were a knight," the prince said, stepping up and lifting Rowan's hand. Rowan wanted to draw her hand back, but refrained, watching the prince cautiously. He had a nice face, rather like she imagined Ferdy might look all grown up, but not like she had imagined Gavin. Perhaps she had spent too much time with men far older than herself.

"I assumed it was merely a courtesy title, like it is for my brother. But I suppose it is wise for a woman ruler to understand how men make war."

At this point, Rowan drew her hand away and took a step backward for good measure. Where was the Gavin she corresponded with?

"Is your father much recovered?" she asked as politely as she could.

"He was well when I left him."

"I am so glad. I was concerned for you and your family."

"Thank you." He looked at her cautiously.

"Are…" Rowan opened her mouth to ask a question and was suddenly struck by the prince's lack of armor or crest, or servants. A high prince was not left alone in the great room of an allied king. And he looked younger than Gavin should, at nine years older than Rowan.

"Your brother was given his title as a courtesy, you say. Which brother was this?"

"The only one I have. High Prince Rory of Anwyn."

"Ah." Rowan nodded, feeling the fool for her mistake, and her disappointment. "Prince Braden, allow me to express on behalf of the king and queen what a pleasure it is to have you as a guest. It has been many years. How long will you be with us?"

"That all depends on you." He gave Rowan what could only be called an uncomfortable smile.

"Well…It is rude of me to keep you here so long without offering refreshment," Rowan said, casting about for an excuse to leave. "I shall have someone show you to a room and bring you something to…refresh you." Rowan fled the room like a coward and didn't care a bit.

Ardal was in the hall, with a broad smile, eavesdropping. "Thought he was someone else, did you?" He snickered. Teasing Rowan about her correspondence with Gavin had become a favorite activity for all her knights.

"Shut up," Rowan hissed, blushing. "He is strange, don't you think?"

Ardal laughed. "Have you never met a man who was not a knight? That's what they look like, scholars. Soft and friendly."

"I don't know that I would call him soft. Not terribly comfortable, though."

"You are carrying a sword and a helmet."

Rowan chuckled. "So, the scholar was frightened of the big bad lady knight?"

"Yes."

"Um," Rowan mumbled skeptically and walked off.

That evening after Rowan and her family had eaten with her guest, he asked her to take a walk with him. Rowan left her armor aside for a dress, but refused to shed her sword. It slapped against her leg gently as they walked along the east side of the castle.

"Princess Rowan, it can be no secret why I am here."

"Then neither can it be a secret what my response will be," Rowan replied, unnerved again when Prince Braden took her hand. She felt like slapping him.

"I hoped you might reconsider. There needn't be any inconvenience to you. If you agree to a favorable marriage contract, I will merely remain here for the period of our engagement so that we might become acquainted. We could be married within a year. Once your sister is returned, we could take a bridal trip to my kingdom."

Rowan felt suddenly sick. "My, how neatly you've arranged everything."

After your sister is returned, we could take a bridal trip...

"What if I do not want to leave when she returns?" Rowan asked. "I have not known much of my sister. Am I never to know her?"

The prince paused, taking a deep breath. It was a practiced speech, she realized. He had never had anyone poke holes in it. Why did Anwyn suddenly want her tied to them so badly?

Rowan knew what her answer would be. What her answer always was. But standing here, looking at this prince, hearing his expectations, she realized what it was everyone meant when they asked if she had even thought about the future. She had not. The future was some vague happy place where Roisin was returned and there was a wonderful party that lasted into eternity.

But what would it really look like?

Blank.

Rowan could think of nothing that would fill up the vast empty space of peaceful eternity. Except maybe an afternoon lying on a hill watching the clouds. But that was one afternoon. This man, boy really—he couldn't be more than two years older than Rowan, making him just eighteen—he had planned a life for her.

"What would we do after this bridal trip?" Rowan asked, truly curious. What did other people see in the future? People whose lives were not defined by curses.

"Well, we would spend some time studying the roles of king and queen of Stonedragon that we would one day assume. And set up our own home, have children."

"How many?"

"I don't know—two."

"Genders?"

"I would rather think that isn't up to me," Prince Braden snapped, beginning to sound annoyed.

"Oh. I wasn't sure there were things that were not up to you," Rowan said with false innocence. "One point of clarification: you would not be king here. It will be written into any marriage contract I sign that my husband will merely be a means to getting an heir."

"Would you prefer I call you the king?" Braden bit off.

"If it would make things clearer for you." Rowan was being unkind. It was no more his fault than it was hers that the whole of their lives were planned out this way. But she could not keep her mouth shut, and all that came out were her frustrations.

"I think I would like seven children," Rowan said, imagining the giant brood with a tickle of delight. Siblings must be the best way to grow up certain you were loved; she only had to look at the triplets to know it, even Gavin with his brothers.

"Seven! Are you insane? When would you have time to rule?"

"Well, if we are talking about what *I want*"—she emphasized the words—"never. I think I might enjoy being a sheep farmer." She finished with a broad smile. She had never fantasized about being a peasant before Gavin's letters, but the idea had a certain appeal.

Prince Braden stared at Rowan for a full fifteen seconds, then burst into laughter. "The sword would frighten them."

"Yes, well, I imagine in this far-off mystical day, I shall hang up my sword and armor, and Rowan the Eternal shall cease to exist."

"Hmm. It is certainly an intriguing plan." Braden's smile lingered after his laughter. It was a nice smile, a sign that if nothing else, he had a good sense of humor. "So you will be a sheep farmer, with seven children. How will you feed them?"

"Do you know, that is an excellent question. I don't think my plan is as well-formed as yours. Still, I like mine better."

The prince made his formal proposal before the night was over and received his formal rejection. But they parted that evening as somewhat reluctant friends.

2,426 days until Roisin returns

On her birthday, a letter and a present arrived from Prince Gavin. After thinking for a few moments that he had come to see her, it was a bit disappointing. It was a painting of the stretch of river she had mentioned wanting to see in the first letter she sent him. It was likely to be the only way she ever saw it.

> *Dear Rowan,*
>
> *I wish you a beautiful and abundant birthday. I looked for this painting so that you might be able to see the lovely stretch of river you mentioned. Though it may take you some time yet to sail down her.*
>
> *Did you know the river was named for a young woman? A lovely one, who wanted to wander the world. You see, the ocean and the wind had called to her, promising to show her all their wonders. But when she told her father this, he locked her away, determined to marry her off. Her husband apparently locked her away, as well, afraid she would flee from him.*

Rowan's heart slowed as she read, and tears not of sadness but…well, she couldn't say what, just tears wet her eyes.

> *She was a wild thing, unsatisfied with only one view. So she sat at her tower window, staring into the world, and wept. Her tears fell every day and every hour, growing so numerous, they became the river.*
>
> *The river cut across the land, straight for the sea, and flowed out into it and around the world. In that way, her soul was carried off across the world, though her body remained locked in the tower.*

Rowan wiped aside a few tears and cleared her throat. He had such a way with his stories. As if he reached across the world and spoke only to her. Sometimes, reading his words, it felt like he was beside her, speaking. And other times, like today, he felt so real but so faraway, she wished she could have him here, see his face as he told the story, know the sound of his voice. She wished she could escape her tower.

When Liadan eventually died, they set her body adrift on a raft and set it afire. Bits of her are scattered up and down the river.

It is a sad story, but I thought you might appreciate it.

It is a year now since I first wrote you. It has had very different results from what I first intended. I am pleased that it did. I wanted to gain my kingdom some of your good fortune and myself a bride. I think it is much better that I have found my kingdom a valuable ally and myself a true friend.

Your Friend,

G—

It was startling; Rowan had not realized before now, his first letter had indeed arrived on her birthday. It felt almost…fated. Rowan was not overly fond of fate. It made her suspicious. What could it all mean? She tried to banish the thoughts as she wrote a response.

Dear Gavin,

I am pleased as well to have found a friend in these correspondences, which I first considered merely a new, somewhat clever, maneuver to win a princess. It seems sometimes that the days that pass between our correspondences are somehow less real, less important.

As your friend, I feel confident I can call you out as a liar. I have never heard any such story associated with that river. Admit it; you invented the tale out of your very fertile imagination to entertain me. And I was entertained, moved even.

Rowan paused, torn between a desire to ask him how it was he understood what even her family did not, and a desire to play his story off as if it were nothing.

It was a hauntingly lovely story. I will treasure it, treasure your sharing it with me. Inventing it for me.

I always find myself around people of great imagination. Able to make a story out of a leaf on the wind. I am ever enthralled—and jealous. I have not a single imaginative bone in my body. It is a great talent you have.

Thank you so much for your thoughtful gift.

And please give my wishes for his speedy recovery and long life to your father. I know how it must worry you, and I can only hope he re-covers and you are able to share many more days together.

Your Friend,

R—

As Rowan went to find the messenger, her mind drifted again to fate. It was such a monumental year for her, and Gavin had been a part of it from the first. What did it mean?

"Sometimes, little queen, things just are." The fairy messenger read Rowan's thoughts, as usual.

Rowan simply handed the fairy her letter. She did not attempt to spell him or threaten him. Her thoughts were too consumed.

"What is your name?" Rowan asked suddenly as the fairy was about to depart.

He looked up at Rowan, a twinkle in his eye. "Now how is it a year today since first we met, and only now you think to inquire?"

He did not really seem to need an answer, so Rowan gave none, contemplating instead what it said of her that she never asked for introductions.

"My name is Eachann." He bowed. "Your servant."

Rowan curtsied properly back, as though he were a lord and not a servant, pleased to see his broad smile at the honor. She stopped him once more when she thought he would leave.

"Eachann, the king, what is it that ails him?"

"Oh, the weight of his sins," the fairy said with a shrug.

"Are they so very bad, his sins?" Rowan was unsure how to take this answer.

"Not so much worse than other men. But it is not always the degree of the sin, but who one sins against that weighs."

"The Fairy queen?" Rowan asked, though she already knew.

Eachann nodded. "For one."

"What did he do?"

"He took up with the losing side in a battle for the Fairy throne. That alone was bad enough to see him dead, but when she won, the Fairy queen gave him a choice, a deal for the lives of his people. He took it. Others did not. That weighs on him, as well, but most, the deal was not for him alone to keep. The Fairy queen comes now to collect."

It was vague, but Rowan could tell he would not be much clearer. Even now, it was hard to say on which side the fairy stood. If she asked the right questions, Eachann would answer her, but which were right?

"That is why the crops die, the flooding, because of the deal?"

"Aye, little queen. And much more." His voice was flat, and his eyes held, for a moment, the hollow look of one who has known much grief.

It was a wide reach her grandmother had. Wide and deadly.

"Are there many others like that?"

"Oh, yes." Eachann nodded, seeming to look off into eternity as he spoke. "A great many."

Rowan and Eachann stared at each other for a moment. Taking each other's measure.

"You grow every day in wisdom and understanding," Eachann said after a moment. "In power, too, I think. It is good."

A tingle of pride rushed over Rowan's skin, followed quickly by embarrassment. "But not in age?" Rowan teased, to distract him.

"No, you are but seconds old in my lifetime. And not even so very old in your own," he said with a nod and a smile.

"Promise?" Rowan asked it with a smile, but it did not reach her heart. He understood so much, this fairy, and she was slowly coming to trust him; surely he would know other things. Know if she would succeed, know if she would ever escape her tower in life, or if she would have to die like Liadan of Gavin's story. How very long would she live?

Eachann shook his head with a laugh, refusing to answer. He winked and vanished. Rowan's breath shuddered for all the unanswered questions. She might have no way to answer the questions about her own fate, but Rowan's questions about Sorcha and her reach, those she might just have the tools to answer.

For Me

Rowan departed Eachann with a plan, only to be caught halfway to the courtyard by her stepmother. Gwyneth had been avoiding Rowan in the months since Donovan's banishment. They spoke the absolute minimum, tolerating each other's presence, but never attempting to clear the air between them. So it startled Rowan when her stepmother cornered her in a hall, looking excited.

"Rowan, there you are." Gwyneth stepped into her path, blocking her, and reached for Rowan's left arm. "I have been searching for you everywhere. Come with me quickly; I have a wonderful surprise."

Rowan took a step back, her right hand settling over the hilt of her sword instinctually. She did not like the smile on Gwyneth's face. Gwyneth was a slender woman with perfectly straight, soft-looking, blond hair and dreamy brown eyes. Her appearance was in no way threatening, but neither was the Fairy queen's. Oddly, the taller Rowan had grown, the more uncomfortable she became with Gwyneth's soft looks.

"Why?"

"For your birthday. I had a wonderful idea. Please, come see." Gwyneth looked fanatical in her excitement.

Rowan tried to banish the visions of a hundred men waiting with lances to run her through, or her grandmother waiting with a poisoned goblet, or wild animals to pull her apart.

Gwyneth wasn't stupid. Surely she would know better than to kill Rowan in any way that could be traced back to her.

"What are you waiting for? Come along."

"Where to? What is this surprise?"

"I cannot tell you; that defeats the purpose of a surprise." Gwyneth smiled with sharply impatient eyes, as though Rowan was not an especially bright child.

"You overestimate my desire for surprises," Rowan replied flatly, her stance unyielding. "I hate them. I won't go anywhere with you until you tell me what it is you have planned."

Gwyneth rolled her eyes at Rowan's stubbornness. "I thought you might enjoy having your first ball," Gwyneth said between her teeth. "We never had a prince here at your birthday. I convinced Braden to stay longer; the great hall is being readied for the festivities as we speak. I want you to come with me to be fitted for a special dress."

"A ball?" Rowan said, at a loss. There had not been a single proper celebration of any day since Roisin left. Why now?

Gwyneth captured Rowan's free hand between both of hers and spoke excitedly, trying to imbue Rowan with her enthusiasm. "I so want to give you your first ball. Please let me. I remember my first ball. It was at this castle, in the great hall. I was about your age, and...I remember the glow of the candles and the swell of the music. You have no idea what it is like to spend an entire night dancing and have every man in the room vying for your attention."

Rowan chewed on the inside of her cheek, resisting the twin urges within her to yank her hand back and to get excited by the idea right along with Gwyneth. It made no sense. Why would she suddenly try to win Rowan over? Did she think Rowan could be persuaded to let Donovan return? Was she afraid of the threat the aunts made? What did it matter, anyway? No matter what Gwyneth did, Rowan would not be fought over by men as Gwyneth had been.

"Please, Rowan. You will enjoy it, I promise."

Shrugging, Rowan allowed Gwyneth to pull her away to be fitted. She didn't want to get excited; there was bound to be a trick in all of this. But as she was being fitted, the servants around her chatted excitedly. They seemed as awed by the idea as Gwyneth; at last there was something to do besides wait. The more they spoke and smiled, the more Rowan was drawn into the excitement.

When she was at last standing before her mirror in her beautiful new gown, with all of her hair let loose for perhaps the first time in years, Rowan allowed herself a moment of pure undisturbed excitement. There had never been a celebration just for her in the castle. Never. And tonight there would be.

Perhaps she had let Gwyneth's words from so long ago remain too much in her mind. Perhaps they had just been the foolish words of a frightened mother. That didn't mean she really meant them. Until today, as they stood facing each other alone, Rowan had not realized she still waited for the day Gwyneth would try to kill her, to save Roisin. Maybe it was time to let it go.

Still, Rowan strapped her sword on her waist as she was leaving her room. She did not feel quite herself without it.

When she arrived at the great hall, two servants pulled the doors wide for her and announced her.

"Rowan the Eternal, Princess of Stonedragon."

She stepped through the doors, and a cheer went up around the room. It felt unreal. Rowan wanted to yell at them all to stop pretending. *I know what you really think of me.* But she smiled and stepped forward, searching for a face in the crowd that she could trust, ignoring every eye but those she sought. Maureen, Colum, and the triplets were nowhere to be seen.

Ardal and the other Knights of the Rose were along the wall to her right. As she stepped into the room, they came forward and fell into form behind her, escorting her through the crowd to the dais that held the thrones.

Before Ardal stepped back, he threw her a playful look and whispered, "Trust you to be the only princess in history to wear a sword to her first ball."

Rowan grinned. Even if everyone else in the room was putting on a show, she had her knights.

The music and dancing resumed as soon as Rowan had taken her seat. Gwyneth sat on Rowan's left, with the king just beyond her. Rowan saw her father's eager smile and questioning look. And returned both with a smile; he wanted her to be excited, so she would try.

Braden claimed Rowan's first dance, inciting several playful looks from her knights, who remained at the side of the dais. Rowan threw them a brief glare as she stepped out onto the floor with the prince.

Only when she was on the floor did it occur to her, she had no idea what she was doing.

"I take it," Braden whispered sarcastically when Rowan stepped on his toe for the third time, "dancing is not something future queens are required to know. Perhaps it would work better without the sword."

"Knights dance with swords all the time," Rowan said. She concentrated hard on the couples around them, trying to distinguish the pattern while dancing herself.

"Hmm." Braden tried to catch her eye but couldn't manage it. "Are you looking for an attack?"

"I wore the sword because I don't like to be without it."

Braden laughed at that remark, finally managing to catch her eye. "I meant the way you're looking around the room. Not the sword."

"Oh." Rowan blushed. She hated, more than anything, to be caught at a disadvantage. It was why she had completely abandoned the spear and would soon abandon the joust as well. Her aim with both was particularly bad.

"People tend to look at each other when they dance. Or at least pretend to."

"I don't know the dance," Rowan returned tightly. Everyone was staring at them.

"I could tell. Don't worry; no one will say anything. You are the future queen."

"You're saying something," she said between her teeth and stumbled over his feet again.

"Yes, well, you made it clear yesterday I have no chance to win you. It was because I was startled by the armor, wasn't it?"

"I said to you what I say to every proposal." Why did he insist on talking? She couldn't concentrate. She tripped again and caught Gwyneth's unnervingly eager look.

"No." He shook his head knowingly. "You seemed particularly disappointed when I did not pass your little test."

"There was no test," Rowan bit out, angry to be stumbling once again. "Must we dance?"

"Of course not." Braden bowed his head; leading Rowan off the floor, he lowered his voice. "It was a test coming to see me in the armor. I was startled. Is that so bad?"

"Why do you care? Do you want to marry me?"

"Not particularly. But I will. You seem nice enough. And my parents are determined it is for the best."

Rowan rolled her eyes. "It was not a test." She sighed; why not tell him the truth? "I was not expecting you. I was told a prince had come to call on me, but I was not told which one."

"Who did you expect?"

"Gavin, of Turrlough," she mumbled.

Braden laughed, leaning a shoulder against the wall as they reached it. "He would not have been surprised to see you in armor?"

"No. He is a knight, as well. He has asked if we may spar when we meet."

"I am a knight." Braden straightened away from the wall, offended. "I passed the trials. All of them, unlike Gavin the Cowardly."

"Cowardly?" Rowan demanded, offended on Gavin's behalf.

"I didn't give him the name. But some of us are willing to complete the whole trial."

"If you are a knight, why are you frightened when I carry a sword?"

"I am not frightened of the sword!" His voice took on a higher octave. "I have no use for weapons. I participated in the trials because my father wished it. Once I had proved myself capable of defending my people, he allowed me to pursue my own interests."

Rowan looked at Braden as though he were some bizarre creature that had wandered into the room. "You trained as a knight because your father required it. You will marry me, against your wishes, because your father requires it. You dance with me because my stepmother expects it. What do you do without instruction?"

"What do you?" he challenged.

"Everything. My father and I argue at least once a week about my knight-hood."

"Your Majesty." Ardal's voice interrupted the argument. "Might I have the honor of a dance?"

"I am terrible." Rowan shook her head at Ardal. "Ask Braden the Obedient."

Ardal barked out a laugh, and just as quickly covered his mouth.

"I am sure Your Majesty is simply out of practice. We rarely have the opportunity to dance in Stonedragon." Ardal barely managed to get the words out past his hilarity.

Rowan shook her head at all the overly polite conversation. Turning her back to Braden, she stepped into Ardal's arms.

"Not enjoying your first dance?" he asked, suddenly sounding exactly like a father. Not her own. More like Colum. Most times, Rowan could forget that Ardal was older than her father, and think of him as her fun-loving friend. Then out of nowhere, he would become protective or serious, reminding her that he was just one more in a long line of men who didn't think she was up to the task ahead.

"No one will ever truly see me as a knight, will they?" Rowan asked, unaware she was actually managing to dance moderately well.

"You have never seemed to care much what people think."

"Prince Gavin completed all but the last trial. Because it was unsafe for the crown prince. They call him Gavin the Cowardly. I will never even participate in the trials. What do they call me?"

Ardal grinned broadly. "Are you worried about what they will call you? Or offended by what they call your beau?"

"He isn't my beau," Rowan bit out, glaring at her friend for her heating cheeks. "And both."

"What was the first lesson Colum taught you?"

"That I am who I choose to be. Being a knight is a matter of character, not a matter of title," she recited, looking around the room for Colum and the family again. "Is he still angry with me? He has not been the same since I banished Donovan. I know I should not have lost my temper that way, but I thought he would forgive me. He barely speaks to me. He does not even return home in the evenings if I am there."

"He isn't angry with you." Ardal cast a dark look toward the thrones and shrugged. "He is angry with himself. He hated seeing you hurt, at least as much as your father. He feels now that he should have stopped you from the first."

"He couldn't have," Rowan said flatly, not really believing Ardal. If it were something so little, Colum wouldn't be so distant, he'd be supporting her or trying to dissuade her from fighting.

"This I know, Sir Rowan. Now, see." He smiled arrogantly as he led her from the floor. "You danced that wonderfully. Just as I said, you needed practice."

Rowan danced the next several with her knights; some dances Rowan knew she managed admirably, but others felt abysmal. But the worse she danced, the more fun she had. Her knights would laugh or try to show her the steps until they both ended in giggles, dancing their own steps.

Between dances, Gwyneth approached Rowan cautiously.

"You seem to be enjoying yourself. I am so glad. Prince Braden seems taken with you."

Rowan restrained her skeptical remarks on that topic and simply smiled. "It is a lovely celebration, thank you."

"Good. I am so glad." Gwyneth looked off toward the king, then back at Rowan. "Do you think there is enough light? I originally thought I would use twice as many torches, so the light was brighter, but your father thought this would be better."

"There is plenty of light," Rowan said noncommittally.

"Good. You seem to like the less formal dances better. Do you think it is the lively music or the steps?"

"I…the music, I suppose," Rowan replied slowly; this was an odd conversation.

"Yes. I always liked the formal dances when I was young. They seemed so lovely and magical. I should probably be sure to have a bit of both. I suppose she will be more like you."

"She?" It took Rowan a moment—but when the pieces fell into place, everything that seemed strange hours ago made sense. And Rowan felt the force of it knock her backward, like the lances she had imagined earlier, driving her from her horse so she lay on the ground gasping for air. How had she let herself be drawn into this?

Gwyneth just wanted to test it all out. Practice the party she would throw for her daughter. Of course she had. Why Rowan had thought it could possibly be for her was the only mystery.

"Roisin." Rowan nodded, fighting back the tears that threatened to overwhelm her. "I imagine she will love anything you prepare. When one is being welcomed home with genuine love and warmth, the love is all that matters."

Dance Lessons

"Rowan. Rowan!"

Startled out of her thoughts, Rowan shifted slightly on her throne to face her father.

"Are you enjoying the party? It is not quite as intimate as last year's. I hope you don't mind. Gwyneth was so taken with the idea of giving you your first ball."

"It is lovely." Rowan forced a smile.

"You don't have to like her, Rowan," the king said, surprising his daughter. "I don't have to like her. But we must allow her the chance to make up for past mistakes."

With a ball? She can make up for suggesting you kill me, *with a ball? That isn't even for me?*

The words screamed in Rowan's head as she turned away from her father. She had enjoyed much of the ball. Perhaps she should just focus on that.

Braden was dancing with Gwyneth; they made for a much better couple than he and Rowan had. Gwyneth was tall enough to just reach past his shoulders, and as he spun her around the room, they looked comfortable. With Rowan, he had been just a bit shorter, and both of them had danced stiffly, uncomfortable with each other.

But perhaps her height had nothing to do with it. Across the room, Liam, one of her shorter knights, was dancing with a woman several inches taller than he, and they looked at ease with each other. When he had danced with Rowan earlier, who was nearly half a foot taller, he had seemed perfectly at ease.

"Would you do me the honor of a dance, Rowan?" her father asked, stepping in front of her.

"Of course," Rowan said automatically, standing to take his hand.

A cheer went up as they stepped onto the floor together. Rowan stiffened, rattled by the attention, but allowed herself to be pulled into the steps.

It was…uncomfortable. Rowan spent half the time trying to force herself not to notice the stares and the other half thinking how odd it was to be this close to her father. They were never an overly demonstrative family, but since Roisin was taken, they rarely even hugged. It was as if they had agreed, without speaking, that it would be best not to become too close.

When the dance was over, the king kissed his daughter on the cheek. He bowed low before retuning with her to the dais.

Braden returned Gwyneth to the dais shortly after and asked Rowan for another dance. She agreed reluctantly.

"Your stepmother would have us married tomorrow, she is so sure we will suit."

"Ha," Rowan scoffed. "She would have us married before you can be thoroughly frightened away. She doesn't realize you are so obedient." She couldn't say why she was taking her frustrations out on this near stranger.

He just seemed to fall in line with everyone so easily, as she never could. He represented everything that had her on edge, and was very purposefully annoying her.

"Does it disturb you so much? The idea of someone being bound by their duty to their king?"

"No," Rowan said, and then thinking the better of her answer, "Yes. Because it is only duty. Not loyalty or devotion or…anything. You are not a knight or a man. You are a soldier."

Braden shrugged. "You were the firstborn. I was the third. Firstborn children are reared with the knowledge that all they see belongs to them, as they belong to it. By the time one gets around to a third, the child is a servant to king and kingdom and everyone in between."

"I am sorry you were made to feel that way," Rowan said kindly, trying to force a bit more patience with him. Obedience was not the worst flaw.

"Do you know, I would never have considered Gavin a clever man. He takes such pride in being a knight. It is hard to imagine him thinking. But he figured out well enough how to court a lady knight."

"Oh?"

"Since it is knights you want, I will agree to spar with you, if you will agree to dance just once without your sword."

"If it is unnerving you, all you needed to do was say so." Rowan abandoned Braden on the floor, marching over to Ardal. "The prince is afraid I will skewer him," Rowan commented, removing her sword and handing it to Ardal.

He laughed, looking over her shoulder to where Braden stood openmouthed. "Did you tell him that was not the only weapon you had on your person?"

"How did you know?" Rowan asked.

"I know you."

Rowan smiled evilly and returned to the floor.

By the end of the evening, Rowan had quite enjoyed herself. She had danced with people she had never met. She had thoroughly disturbed Braden by slipping a knife out of the long sleeves of her dress in the middle of their dance, so much so that he stomped off. And she had managed to learn the complete steps of one dance.

She put away any thoughts of why Gwyneth had decided to give her this party or what people would call a lady knight who had never completed the trials and simply had fun.

She danced herself down to her rose garden to sit and talk with her mother, as was her tradition. No sooner had she twirled into the garden than she found herself back where she had tried to get all year, in the Fairy circle.

It looked different. There were holes in the ground and in several of the trees. Rowan spun in a circle looking for her sister; she was nowhere to be seen. What or who had made the holes? Had Sorcha found her sister?

No, it couldn't be that. Rowan felt sure she would feel it if Sorcha had Roisin; no matter how far away they were, she would feel it.

"I'm coming!" Rowan heard the voice from in the trees. "Don't leave. I'm coming."

Roisin burst through the trees into the Fairy circle with a small fleet of animals trailing in her wake. Giggling, she ran straight up to Rowan and threw herself into her arms, talking a mile a minute.

"I was so afraid I would be late. Auntie B said I could not go out tonight, and there was a rather long argument. Even once Auntie C had taken my side and said if I had seen it, there would be no stopping me, no one would stop arguing. And then, as I was coming, I found this poor badger trapped in a hole in the ground. I had to stop and help him, even though I knew you were coming tonight. I have been waiting so very long."

Rowan did not really hear half of what her sister said; she was too busy basking in the glow of this simple, genuine hug. This was love.

"You've gotten taller." Rowan ran her hand down the hair resting on the sides of her sister's face. "You will be a lady soon."

Roisin laughed and spun away. "A lady like you."

"Better; a lady like you."

"My Auntie A wants to know if you think this is wise."

"She said that?" Rowan stared after her sister. *The aunts knew?*

"Yes. Do you know her? I did not think you knew her."

"I met her once," Rowan said, considering Alma's question. "You can tell her I don't know."

"That's what I said. How can you know if something is wise or not until you have done it?"

Rowan laughed; it sounded exactly like something Ferdy would say after jumping off a roof.

"There are ways," Rowan said, looking around at all the holes in the trees again. "Did the animals make all these holes?"

"Oh yes. You have several more tenants now."

"Umm." *Was that wise?* Rowan was not precisely certain how a Fairy circle worked, but she had a feeling it depended on the circle being intact. Would this affect it, all the missing pieces in trees and in the ground? All the animals?

"When did you meet her?"

"Who?"

"Auntie A."

"Oh." Rowan thought for a moment about how to answer. Roisin had not been told the truth of who she was. And Rowan was certain that was for her protection. She did not even use the aunts' full names. But Rowan didn't want to lie to her. "I met her a long time ago. She came to help me with a curse."

"I see." Roisin looked at her feet when she said this. She wanted to ask more but was resisting.

"What do they call you?" Rowan asked, thinking of Eachann; it had taken her a year to even wonder about his name.

"They call me darling girl. Auntie C says it is not my name, but a name is a powerful thing, and we do not want the wrong person to hear it. What is your name?"

A name is a powerful thing.

There were little ears all around them—squirrels, birds, frogs, rabbits. Could Sorcha use them to hear things?

"Why don't you call me friend? And I will call you darling girl, like your aunts."

Roisin stared at her sister, suddenly serious. Rowan wondered if she would pout, as the triplets did at times when they could not have their way.

"You are not my mother, then?"

"No. I am sorry, darling girl." Rowan took the three steps to her sister and wrapped her arms around her. "I did like your story better. But I am not your mother. I do love you very dearly, though."

Roisin returned the hug, squeezing her tightly, and shed little tears on Rowan's gown. "I love you dearly, too. The most dearly."

She held on for less than a minute; stepping back, she dried her face with the back of her hand and smiled up at Rowan with shining eyes.

"Come along, friend. I will introduce you around the neighborhood."

Rowan allowed her sister to pull her from one little animal family to the next. She used the shade spell, silently, on each animal. She found no trace of her grandmother, but it did not entirely banish her concern.

Later they danced around, singing the song of the Fairy circle that Roisin had invented. Rowan taught her sister the steps of the dance she had learned. They even lay for a while under the stars. Later Roisin told another of her imaginative little stories—about an ogre prince.

The ogre prince didn't want to scare the villagers; he wanted to be beautiful and loved by all. When he met a traveling witch, he bought a potion to make him more beautiful than anything in the world. He swallowed the potion and fluttered apart into bits of light, the first rainbow. Rather than being upset by this turn of events, the ogre was overjoyed and followed the rains, bringing joy to all he met.

At dawn, Rowan found herself once more in her mother's rose garden. She sat on the bench where she was born to watch the sun rise.

Beyond Our Borders

2,334 days until Roisin returns

*R*owan launched a campaign to discover more about the Fairy queen's reach, dispatching her knights to different kingdoms on the island and its surrounding islands to gather information. It was to be done quietly, in the guise of missions of aid to neighboring kingdoms. Each of her four knights was allowed to choose others to accompany him and took a small force of soldiers, but only the Knights of the Rose knew the true mission.

With all four of her knights gone, Rowan approached Colum to see if he would once more allow her to train with his men. Both Colum and her father fought her on the idea, but in the end relented. She could practice in full armor and only with blunted swords. It wasn't what she wanted, but it was something, so she took it.

In the months before Rowan began to receive word from her knights, she applied herself to searching through Stonedragon's history to see what she could learn. She often barricaded herself in the library, poring over her grandfather's records and old reports from his generals.

The hardest part was not having anyone to ask about it. Her father put her off whenever she spoke of the Fairy queen. Whether it was an effect of the curse or simple fear didn't matter, as he would not answer. Colum could analyze old treaties and troop movement the same way she did, but didn't offer up any deeper knowledge; if he had any. And Maureen was reluctant to discuss the Fairy queen for fear that it would draw her ear.

When Eachann arrived with a letter from Gavin, Rowan was as eager to speak with the fairy as read the letter.

"You are brimming with questions," Eachann said before Rowan could get a word out. "Choose well; I cannot answer all without drawing her ear."

Rowan spoke carefully, avoiding actual questions and watching Eachann's expression. "It seems from reading my grandfather's letters, that Fairy and human soldiers fought on both sides of the Fairy War. And my grandfather took the Fairy queen's side from the first."

"Not precisely. He took no side until it was clear who the victor would be and he had made a deal with the Fairy queen."

"Cowardly." Rowan drew her shoulders back stiffly, discomforted more by having a cowardly grandfather than one on the wrong side of the war.

"Or wise."

"They are at times the same thing," Rowan said derisively.

"Ah, so you feel better a brave fool than a wise coward?" Eachann laughed.

"I feel it is better to be a foolish man of good character than a wise man of none."

"An old debate. Much older than you. Please, your other questions."

"I understand my grandfather's deal was for the fealty of his people. But it seems more like dominion over them. They are not aware of it, but they obey the Fairy queen."

"A limited dominion." He shrugged. "They cannot actively stand against her, but she does not control their every action, and they can stand against her allies."

"But I am exempt."

"You—are special." Eachann smiled. Rowan grinned back, tickled by the compliment. "Take the letters, little queen. I will wait with the children," Eachann said, indicating the triplets, playing a few feet from where they stood. Apparently he had reached the end of his answerable questions.

Ardal must have been in Turrlough when the prince was sending a reply, because one of the letters Eachann handed her was from him. She tore through it first—the mission always came first—and...it would allow her to savor Gavin's letter.

Your Majesty,

Aside from the troubles we have already heard of in Turrlough, I have discovered some other troubling news. The king has not spoken in over two years. Your young prince rules in his father's place. Because of old deals his father made, he cannot assume the throne. If the old king were to abdicate without fulfilling a rather mysterious deal with the Fairy queen, all his offspring would be killed and the kingdom given to one of the children of Arrnou of Ulm.

Rowan's breath caught, and she reread the sentence, sure she must have misunderstood. Sorcha would *kill* Gavin, *kill* his siblings—the bright, kind, happy family she was coming to know through Gavin's letters. Her stomach roiled, and she stiffened her spine to keep from sinking into her chair in fear and disgust. How did someone become such a monster?

More disturbing still, I discovered from a woman here that every year a group of Fairy come and steal the ten-year-old girls. None have been returned. This has happened for three years now.

All the ten-year-old girls. Her own home had been so completely altered, hushed, when Roisin was taken. Even strangers lived on hope of Roisin's return. And she was only one girl. How quiet must that kingdom be? How lonely?

Your young prince first attempted to fight the Fairy off, but this year has tried a different tactic. He has hidden all the girl children near that age. I have not attempted to discover where; the queen might find them through my search.

There may be other, more deeply hidden troubles here, and I will return to them. As you have left it to my discretion how I complete my mission, I have decided to take a short leave from Turrlough. I believe I may have found the lost Creelan people; I mean to leave and investigate.

I prevailed upon your prince to deliver this message for me so that it might reach you sooner.
Sir Ardal

If Rowan could ignore Ardal's rather annoying habit of calling Gavin *her* prince, it was a very useful, though unsettling, letter. What would Sorcha want with female children? And if she would give the kingdom to the children of Arrnou, then Ulm must have been her allies in the war, but Rowan had found nothing to indicate they had participated at all. It was troubling. The Fairy queen would kill Gavin and his siblings if the king were to abdicate. What if he died? Would it have the same result? Gavin—dead.

Rowan's chest felt overgrown with thorny points of fear, slowly draining her oxygen like a sieve. He'd seemed somehow *beyond* the battle with Sorcha; she knew his people suffered from droughts and poor fortune, even knew Sorcha was the cause, but still he seemed untouched by her evil, protected. But even he was not safe.

Gavin's letter was not nearly so troubling, but it left Rowan wondering about their *great friendship;* perhaps it really was just a clever trick to win her with happy fantasies.

Rowan,
I cannot for a moment believe that you are lacking in imagination. After all, I would never have imagined that there would one day be a lady knight. I do not think any man would. I have concluded, after talking to one of your Knights of the Rose, that you simply do not have sufficient time to utilize that imagination.

I am told, in the course of one day, you look to the daily business of running a kingdom with your father, train for several hours with your knights, care for three small children, and research your family history. That, I understand, is on one of your idler days.

So I have decided to do your imagining for you.

You should imagine yourself a sea captain. You would visit many and varied locations, have a constant group of people to order about, and have nature and her changing moods to contend with, so you would not grow bored.

Thank you for your thoughts for my father. They were gratefully received by him and all my family.

G—

Rowan took more time with her response than she had since perhaps the first letter they exchanged. She needed to know if they were truly friends. Nothing Gavin wrote indicated the severity of his father's illness. Nor did he mention the trouble with Sorcha. Yet Rowan held almost nothing back in her letters.

Dear Prince Gavin,

I have greatly enjoyed our correspondence. Every scenario you write of is more diverting than the last. But I do not deal well in imagination.

It was not I who first imagined me a knight, but my father. It was his attempt to calm my fears after I met my grandmother for the first time. She said I would poison everything I touched, just as I had poisoned my mother. That it would be me, and not her curse, that would destroy my baby sister, Roisin. When she left, I was afraid to touch Roisin. It did not help when my stepmother suggested I be sent to the Fairy queen to do with as she would, so that she would remove the spell from my sister.

My father, to soothe me, placed my sister in my arms and named me her protector. Told me I was the only person who could stop the Fairy queen from hurting her. At seven, I held my sister and looked into a future when the woman who was my grandmother would return and I must be the one to stand against her. I vowed to never be as powerless against her as I had been that day. So began my mission to be a knight. It was reality I faced. It is reality I have understood every day since.

I will happily continue to write you and enjoy your fertile imagination, if that is all you want. But if we are truly the type of friends you say, we can afford to face reality together.

I did not realize until very recently how selfish I had been in my plans for the Fairy queen. I knew one day I would face her—but only for myself, only for my sister. I am learning that I am perhaps the least of her victims. I have lost a sister who I know to be safe, while others have lost homes and safety, and perhaps if the stories are true, their very humanity.

I have decided, therefore, when I face the Fairy queen, I will not be facing her just for my sister. I will be facing her for us all. All the victims of her curses. Perhaps you will be a good enough friend to help me do this.

Your Hopeful Friend,

Rowan

Eachann smiled when he took the letter from Rowan. "Aye, now you grow in age as well."

The Proposal

2,149 days until Roisin returns

Months passed, and Rowan began receiving reports from her knights but heard nothing from Gavin. She wanted to write again, to tell him to forget what she had asked, so if nothing else she could have her friend back, but she forced herself to wait. Her knights continually assured her he was at least alive, but the rest of their reports grew steadily worse. From them, Rowan was able to piece together the basic players from the Fairy War. It was not hard to see that the kingdoms that prospered now had been on the Fairy queen's side. Others, who were beset by disasters of nature, loss of life, and everyday sinking fortunes, must have been her enemies.

The hardest places to gather information were the kingdoms where all was well. People there were not inclined to upset their good fortune by speaking to the Knights of the Rose.

Rowan found a way to begin gathering information from one of those kingdoms when Braden returned for a third time to Stonedragon. Every time he came, he made the same offer. Every time, he was declined. But for some reason, his visits grew longer and longer.

They were becoming friends, after a fashion. Braden had not kept his promise to spar with her, but he occasionally watched, even offered advice. And though he teased her constantly about being a knight, he did not stand for it coming from others.

For her part, Rowan enjoyed his presence once he had delivered his mandatory proposal. On his second visit, when she found him and Keagan sketching together, she decided to approve of him. Few people could coax that little boy out of his shell, or even bothered, but Braden shared a common interest with him in the form of art.

On his third visit to the palace, after his proposal was out of the way, Rowan attempted to interrogate him. She was certain it would be easy enough if she was subtle. But while he did not seem to be catching on to her intent, Braden was either criminally unobservant or purposefully obtuse. He did not seem to know much of anything that had gone on in his kingdom in the past few years. He had no idea what part it had taken in "The Great Fairy War," as Rowan was calling it.

It seemed as if he did not even realize it had taken place. Rowan had all but given up on Braden, deciding he was too selfish or too stupid to know anything, when Keagan came to her the morning before Braden was meant to leave.

"Rowan." Keagan stood very properly, outside the door of the map room Rowan was using for her research. "May I speak to you?"

"Of course. Come here. What is it you need?"

"I am worried about Braden. You don't seem to like him. And if you don't like him, you won't help him."

"I like Braden because he is your friend." Rowan smiled encouragingly. She was sure whatever problem he thought Braden had would be easily fixed. "What does he need help with?"

"He's very scared. He needs you to marry him."

"Did he ask you to say that?" Rowan got to her feet, incensed. How dare he use a child this way?

"No. No, he didn't tell me. I just know how worried he is." Keagan rushed to explain. "His father is a mean man. He is very angry that Braden isn't keeping his part of the bargain. And if he doesn't keep it, bad things will happen."

"His part of the bargain," Rowan repeated. "You heard his thoughts, Keagan?"

"Yes. I'm sorry, but when we were sketching the birds, he got to worrying so much, I couldn't help it."

"It's all right. It's very good. Thank you, Keagan. I will find a way to help him."

"Rowan?" Keagan took her hand to stop her, looking up into her eyes sadly. "He isn't bad. Sometimes people do bad things, like Ferdy does bad things, but you like him. Because he isn't bad. Braden isn't bad, either. But...no one likes him, no one at all."

Rowan nodded; her heart twisting sympathetically, she squeezed Keagan's hand. She would have to handle this delicately.

Braden was in her rose garden. Just seeing him there after what Keagan said, Rowan wanted to fight him and be done with it. This was her sanctuary; people were not supposed to come into her sanctuary. But she had let him in, because she thought him harmless.

Rowan watched him for a minute. He was sitting on the grass, sketching Rowan's bench and the tree behind. He seemed harmless. *He hadn't held up his part of the deal.* That could mean anything. It was ridiculous to assume that all deals had to do with Sorcha. But Keagan also said he had done bad things. Bad things and deals, and the fact that he was from the kingdom that was most blessed—it could not all be coincidence.

"Have you ever noticed the shape of this tree? It's very unusual," Braden said, continuing to sketch.

Everything inside Rowan was ready to rush forward and attack, but this was Keagan's friend, and he had asked her to help him.

No one likes him, no one at all.

Rowan knew that feeling. What would she have done if some part of her hadn't felt eternity reaching out to assure her things would be different?

Walking over, Rowan sat beside him and looked at the tree.

"Did you know I was born there?" Rowan stared at the bench. "My mother died there." She said it absently, not noticing when Braden looked her way. "I used to sit there like I expected her to materialize out of the bench. She never does. I hated her for the longest time. She left me here, alone, to deal with her mother. My grandmother thinks I poisoned my mother to death while she carried me. It doesn't matter how many times I say it; I still don't know how to prove her wrong."

"You think you poisoned your mother?" Braden asked, appalled.

Rowan shrugged. "Doesn't really matter, does it? She's dead. But I won't let Sorcha be right about the rest. I won't kill my sister. I won't let her do it, either."

Braden shook his head and went back to sketching. "You sound exactly like a knight. All of you, so stupidly confident that you're invincible. You've spent the last week asking me all kinds of questions about the Fairy War. But you don't seem to get it. They lose. People who oppose her lose. Soldiers, knights, kings, Fairy—everyone who dares to threaten her throne loses."

Rowan raised an eyebrow; apparently he was purposefully obtuse. "So what, you will just sit here in the garden and sketch, and ignore what she does? Kidnapping children, starving people, turning people into animals?"

"Did you know she locked her son inside a crystal she carries around with her?" Braden dropped his sketch to the ground as he spoke, growing more animated. "When people even look like they will question her, she takes out the crystal and passes it around the room. She forces people to try their hand at freeing him. Smiles the whole time."

"Wait! You've met her? You've seen her, spoken to her?" Rowan demanded.

"Yes," Braden said, shuddering, as though trying to banish a specter. "We brought her here to your sister's celebration. We brought her, and we took her back."

"I thought she came by magic," Rowan muttered.

"The whole way here, she spoke so sweetly, and she looked so beautiful. I remember thinking how lucky I was to sit beside her. I was gloating about it to my brother as we walked through the line to see your sister. And we were the last ones to see her, my family and I. I doubt I would have remembered her, otherwise." As he said it, Braden handed Rowan the sketch.

She had thought it was just a picture of the garden, but she looked closer; Roisin's face was in the center of every rose, in the curve of the tree trunk. Her sister's face as it had looked as a baby, chubby little cheeks and overlarge wide eyes that sparkled even in Braden's charcoal sketch. Rowan couldn't pull her eyes away; more than any portraitist, Braden had caught her sister's spirit, from one meeting. Rowan's skin tingled with cold.

"I can't banish her face now. We saw her, she laughed, and then the queen came. And I couldn't see the beautiful woman I rode next to. She was hideous, twisted, angry, and dark. She cursed that laughing little baby, who never hurt anyone." He paused then, looking away. When he spoke again, his voice was distant. "Then we rode back together, and I sat next to her. Squeezing myself into a corner to hide. You can't stop her. Not because you are a woman or not a good enough knight. But because even on that carriage ride home, when I was wishing her dead, I would have jumped to her defense if she'd asked. Rather than risk her surviving, and having to meet her wrath. And I'm not the only one."

Rowan shrugged; that came as no surprise. She'd seen it when Sorcha cursed Roisin; it wasn't only magic that held those guests still. Rowan stared down at the sketch. The tree was an odd shape. It looked almost like...a dragon. A dragon that had guarded her in her birth.

"What if you don't oppose her? What if you don't even lie?" Rowan whispered, thinking as she spoke. "What if all you do is court me, wisely? By answering my questions. Keagan says you need to marry me. I take it that means Sorcha wants it?"

"Yes. She said I was to court you, convince you to give up being a knight, and marry you."

"Did she say why?"

He shrugged. "Only that you were hard to distract. She thought being courted might distract you."

"For someone who is so afraid to fail her," Rowan said slowly, "you don't try particularly hard to do what she asks."

Braden shoved to his feet, towering over Rowan. She simply lay back further, so the sun was not in her eyes, and watched him. "I won't challenge her. I still feel her fingers gripping my wrist as she forced me to hold that crystal. She told me if I could free him, I could do anything I wanted. I don't have the benefit of being half Fairy, like you," he spat out, shaking his head. "But that does not mean I want her to win. As long as I return from every trip and say I honestly tried to distract you, I haven't betrayed her."

Rowan smiled. She shoved to her feet, shaking off the bits of grass that clung to her dress. She had never felt so certain she could defeat Sorcha.

"So court me. Put effort into it." Rowan walked over, slipping her arm through Braden's. "Do you know what would really make me want to marry you? Information. I want to get to know my grandmother…" Rowan led Braden out of her rose garden, laying out her plan. Leaving the sketch forgotten on the ground.

She would have a spy.

Rowan had begun to wonder if a response was coming at all when Eachann finally arrived with Gavin's letter.

> Rowan the Eternal,
>
> When I wrote you the first time, I had heard your name, and hoped. I needed help for my people. I was convinced if I could win you as a bride, I could gain my people just enough power to hold against the Fairy queen while I found a way to destroy her.
>
> It has not worked out that way. But I hesitated to tell you, because the woman I intend to destroy is your family. I knew of the curse, but never exactly what she said to you. I am sorry. It explains a great deal. My mother returned from your sister's celebration and came straight to my sick bed, bringing both my brothers. She held us all for hours, crying. I had never before, nor have I since, seen anything so thoroughly terrify my mother. I cannot imagine what it must have felt like to you. But you do not bow down.
>
> We could use a bit of eternity here. It seems every day the Fairy queen sends some new trouble for us to combat. But it is good that you remind us we are not the only ones who suffer.

I will help you however I can. But I will also continue imagining for you. Too much reality, I am afraid, leaves one confined to a bed, unable to speak from the weight of it all.
Eternally Your Friend,
Gavin

Rowan was near tears when she finished the letter, but she did not cry. *She held us all for hours, crying.* And it had not even happened to her children. Rowan could not remember a hug from that night. Plenty of assurances and sympathy, but no arms locked around her as she cried. Because she did not bow down.

Rowan's response included some of what she had discovered, without mentioning Braden by name. It seemed best to keep their assistance secret from each other. With the combined knowledge of all her allies, Rowan said she hoped they might hit upon Sorcha's weakness. Braden had agreed to join forces; he might not think it much, but his role was perhaps the most important. And the most dangerous. He would be returning to Sorcha, telling her lies. He might not know it, but Braden had just made the bravest choice of his life. And it was up to Rowan to be sure he remained safe doing so.

When I Close My Eyes

1,697 days until Roisin returns

On the night before her eighteenth birthday, Rowan awoke from an old dream—the same one that had haunted her sleep since Sorcha's first visit.

Rowan was walking down a hall in the palace; it was dark ahead of her and all around her. But behind her, she heard music and saw the faintest hint of candlelight. She walked away from the music and the light, following a voice that called to her.

"Rowan, Rowan? Where are you?" the voice whispered, teasing Rowan, always one step ahead of her or just around a corner.

"Don't you want to be loved like that? Wouldn't you like to be beautiful?"

Rowan didn't know why she followed the voice. There was something wrong with it. A chill ran through her veins, but she could not seem to stop walking, stop following the voice.

Suddenly she wasn't in the castle at all, but in her rose garden. The roses glowed, surrounded by an unnatural blue light. Her fingers stretched toward the glow; she wanted to touch one.

"They'll forget about you. They've already forgotten you. But you can change all that. You can be the most loved of all."

Rowan plucked one of the flowers, feeling the thorns press sharply against her skin but never puncture it. No matter how hard she squeezed, the thorns couldn't pierce her skin.

"That's not for you. You're too special for such a little rose. Give it to your sister, the thief. She's taken everything that should be yours. Their love, their admiration; she'll take your throne too, if you let her. Why should she have everything? Give her the rose. It's the sweetest poison she'll ever smell."

Rowan felt herself walking; she did not even fight. She just walked, back to the lights, back to the music. Back to her sister, surrounded by admirers, by her father and mother, and every person Rowan had ever known. They smiled at Roisin, fawned over her, offering her gifts and dances, and love.

Rowan walked through the crowd, feeling it part as she came, jumping back as though she was on fire. Until she stood before her sister and there was no one but the two of them.

She didn't say a word, just stretched the glowing flower toward her little sister, who smiled up at her with her three-year-old face, and trust.

"Thank you," Roisin said in a child's voice, reaching up.

But she didn't look like a child any longer. She was a young woman, just as Rowan had envisioned her on the day of her birth, stretching out her hand with a serene smile on her face. One finger extended farther than the others, aimed for a thorn.

Rowan watched the finger's approach until it rested, barely touching the tip of the thorn. Three little drops of blood fell from her sister's finger and landed on the rim of her dress. The flower was gone, and in its place a tiny spindle sat in Rowan's hand.

Roisin looked up at her with forgiving eyes, then crumpled to the floor at Rowan's feet.

"You poison everything you touch," Sorcha's voice mocked.

Rowan jerked awake, biting her tongue to keep from screaming. Her hands were balled into fists around her sheets, and tears ran down her face. Rowan counted to ten before releasing her tongue. With sobbing breaths, she buried her face in her pulled-up knees.

You poison everything you touch.

No. Not Roisin. Never.

Rowan could not say how long she sat there, crying into the sheets over her knees. She heard Mother screeching again and again, her call growing farther away, but ignored the bird. When it became apparent that she would not sleep again that night, she leaned back against the headboard and stared off after Mother, a tiny shape on the horizon.

When Rowan first trained with the real knights, almost three years ago now, she had slept every night without the dream. It felt like she was on the right path. But the dream was back; it never changed, but it felt worse every night.

She never told anyone about the dream. Well, she told Colum once, but she knew he mistook her. He thought she meant she dreamed of her grandmother dying at her feet every night. Rowan hadn't corrected him, couldn't. He would wonder, wouldn't be able to stop wondering, if maybe some part of Rowan wanted it to be true. He'd sat right there and asked if she loved her sister more each day. If she explained about the dream, he would start to watch her as the servants did, as Gwyneth did. Waiting for some sign of evil, so they could kill her to protect Roisin.

Rowan paced away from her thoughts and toward the stars out her window. The closer she got, the farther away the stars were, and suddenly it wasn't cold stone she felt beneath her feet but damp grass.

Rowan sighed and nearly began sobbing again. She shouldn't be here. Not now.

What if that was what Alma meant, asking if it was a good idea? Maybe Roisin wasn't safe with her.

"Don't cry." Roisin stepped up from behind her sister and wrapped her in a gentle hug.

Rowan stood still, unable to open her eyes. She didn't want to bring the darkness of the dream here. She didn't want any part of it to ever touch her sister.

"I knew you would come early," Roisin said, not stepping back, content to simply hold Rowan as she spoke. "You needed a friend."

"I am sorry," Rowan whispered, not sure if she meant she was sorry for coming troubled. Or for having killed Roisin in her dreams.

"I am not." Roisin smiled against her sister's shoulder. "I am proud that you would trust me to comfort you. No one ever trusts me with their troubles."

"We want your life to be untroubled," Rowan said. Returning to herself, she pulled her sister back to see her. "You are ever a beautiful child." Eleven now, Roisin was barely over four feet tall, and her once moonbeam-thin hair had thickened into rich waves of gold. But by far Rowan's favorite feature was still the three freckles forming a half circle beneath Roisin's right eye.

"Beautiful, sweet, darling," Roisin said flippantly. "But not strong. No one thinks I am strong, or they would tell me things, tell me the truth."

Rowan shrugged, smiling with her sister's struggle against her idyllic life.

"We are opposites, then. I have been called strong, bossy, unattractive, and poisonous. But no one has ever thought me any of the things they think you."

"Will you tell me why you are sad?" Roisin challenged her sister, rather than sympathizing with her.

"I had a dream," Rowan said, unsure how much to share. "A dream of someone dying because of me."

Roisin dropped her defiant demeanor all at once, reaching for Rowan's hand with both of her own and pulling it to rest at her chest. "It was only a dream. You are too good to kill anyone."

"Am I?" Rowan laughed without meaning to. "Thank you."

"I am sorry," Roisin whispered. "Auntie A says she should not have left me alone with Auntie B for so long. She has been a bad influence on me."

Rowan chuckled at the thought. "Wait—alone? Where did the others go?"

"They will not tell me where. Only that it is no longer safe to assume people will not notice them. Every so often one or two will leave, for a month, to see that we are safe."

"I see." Though she did not see at all. Wasn't this supposed to be a safe place?

Roisin let go of her sister's hand, walking a ways away, chewing on her lip as their father sometimes did.

"They are wrong. The people who said those unkind things about you," Roisin said fiercely. "You are the most beautiful woman I have ever seen, and you are very kind to me. You could never be poisonous."

"Thank you. But it is easy to be kind to you. You do not harbor an unkind bone in your body."

Roisin scuffed her foot on the ground in front of her, annoyed by the comment.

"Can you teach me to be a knight like you?" she blurted out suddenly. "I want to be strong. I want people to trust me. I can help." She spoke fiercely, planting her hands on her hips.

"I...I can try. But we only see each other once a year. There would be a lot to teach in such a short time."

Roisin nodded resignedly.

"Have you told your aunts you feel this way?"

"No." She shrugged. "Auntie C says I am proving to be as impatient as the rest of my family. She wishes I would simply remain a little girl awhile longer. So I suppose she knows, but I don't ask. They wouldn't tell me anyway."

Rowan's gut twisted, seeing her sister so disheartened. More than anything, she wanted to pull her close, tell Roisin who they were to each other, tell her how much she was loved, but she had to believe this was for the best. She had to keep to the plan.

"There are things you cannot be told. Not because you aren't strong, but because it isn't safe to speak of them."

Roisin walked away, looking almost angry. The Fairy circle looked about the same as it had the last time Rowan was here. But the animals were either asleep or in hiding, not scampering at Roisin's feet.

Rowan watched her sister walking around, pouting. For someone who said she wanted to comfort other people, she did not stay focused for long. It wasn't her fault, though; it was not something she had been given much practice with.

"Will you tell me about your life here?" Rowan asked. She knew it was not perfect. Roisin seemed to miss her mother and father, and aside from the aunts and the animals, Rowan doubted she had any friends.

"Will you tell me about yours?" Roisin challenged.

"Yes."

"Oh." Roisin was momentarily startled. Shaking her head with a laugh, she plopped herself onto the grass and patted the spot beside her for Rowan.

Roisin painted a lovely picture. She and the aunts lived in a little cottage in the middle of a forest. They grew their own food in a garden behind their house and had several fruit trees. Every day, they sang songs and read stories. Bride's entire room was filled with books; books for shelves, books held up her bed, and books lined her walls, and sometimes a new one would simply appear. Cianna was teaching Roisin to weave with spider silk and make lace patterns. Alma kept the gardens and didn't sleep in the house at all, preferring to be under the stars. She kept a little hammock covered over in peat moss and clovers, and was teaching Roisin the names of every plant and animal they came across. They took turns cooking and teaching Roisin about the world outside the forest. Four times a year, they would all go out and celebrate the changing seasons with a dance beneath the rising moon.

"I taught them the dance you showed me. We had so much fun spinning in circles and kicking up our feet. I don't think we did it right."

"Sometimes it's more fun to do it wrong," Rowan said through a smile. She was lying back on the grass, not looking at her sister. It sounded like a wonderful life, but Roisin was fighting it. It was difficult to understand.

"Do you know who I am?" Roisin asked flatly. Rowan heard the desperation and hurt behind the question.

"Yes."

"Why can everyone know but me?"

Rowan pushed up onto her elbows and looked into her sister's eyes. She had such a soft face, smooth and a little chubby; she hadn't yet grown into it. Leaning on one elbow, Rowan lifted a hand and ran a finger over the three freckles under Roisin's eye.

"You know in your heart. But until it is safe, even your heart must keep the secret. You are too precious to risk," Rowan whispered.

"What if I don't want to be precious? What if I just want to know?"

"You can't. I'm sorry it hurts you. But that is how it must be. You don't have much longer to wait. I promise, one day soon you will know. You will know who you are. You will know your family. You just have to wait."

"But I don't want to," Roisin pouted.

"Well, that's too bad," Rowan said, growing frustrated with this new whiny Roisin. "I don't particularly want to wait, either. But if I tell you too soon and the evil person searching for you hears, finds you, and you die, I will die as well. Die for the loss of you. So you will wait! And wait patiently, never forgetting to be thankful that there are so many people that love you who must wait as well."

Roisin drew back. It was possible no one had ever chastised her before. The shocked, slightly hurt look on her sister's face brought the dream back in full force.

You poison everything you touch.

Rowan shuddered, fighting back tears. She was barely able to look at Roisin. "There, you see, I am unkind."

"No." Roisin shook her head, looking at the ground. "I am sorry. I…I just miss you so much when you are away."

"I miss you, too. Sometimes it seems the days pass so slowly when I am without you that I may go insane." Rowan pushed to her feet and looked down at her sister fiercely. "I made you a promise once, and I will make you another. I will bring you home, darling girl, no matter what it takes. I will bring you back to your family."

Roisin jumped to her feet and hugged her sister tightly. After a few moments, Rowan pulled away smiling and asked to see the wrong steps to the dance. Dragging Rowan along behind her, Roisin ran to the center of the Fairy circle and began to dance in wild uncontrolled spins and kicks around the ring of mushrooms. Soon she lost herself in the dance and the euphoria. As she jumped and spun, her feet left the ground and stayed in the air. She spun and sang and clapped and danced in the air.

It was the most beautiful thing Rowan had ever seen. Her sister with her long hair flying out behind her and a smile of pure jubilation on her face dancing in the air, completely weightless.

Special

1,696 days until Roisin returns

Rowan's birthday was uneventful. Gwyneth had planned another ball, but for a week later, when Braden would return for another visit. The king, while he seemed to remember the day's significance, was unusually quiet. He gave Rowan a gift in the morning, then retreated to his office, where he remained for the rest of the day. In the evening, Rowan was expected at Maureen's house for a special birthday dinner, but that seemed a long way off.

Eachann arrived with a letter, but as if controlled by the mood of those around him, he did not laugh or joke as he usually would. And Rowan wasn't up to the effort to draw him out.

She began to wonder if perhaps there was something hanging on to her, some darkness she carried around, infecting the people she spoke with.

You poison everything you touch.

Why couldn't she banish the dream today?

Dear Rowan,

I have some news for you, but it will have to wait for another letter, as today is special; today you were born.

My mother used to come into my room on my birthday and wake me. Any other day it would be a nanny or a servant. But on my birthday, she would come into my room and wake me, and she would say it was the most special day of the year, because it was the day I was born.

It can only be doubly true of today, because you are such a special creature.

Rowan's eyes slipped off the page as a blush spread across her cheeks. Smiling, she pulled her legs up into the window alcove with her and read on.

I have decided that I tell you far too many sad stories. So I shall tell you a funny one today. But you must keep it a secret. No one outside my closest family knows this story.

Rowan's heart beat faster. She leaned into the page, as though it were Gavin, waiting for his whisper.

With good reason, my mother would kill anyone she heard repeating it, and she is a very gentle woman.

The story goes like this: When my father was a boy, he had two older brothers and so was certain he would never be king. So he could be incautious, and he was. He went out dressed as a peasant and ran away from the kingdom. He had a crime spree, stealing horses, clothes, and food as he wandered about the country, looking for something to excite him.

He came across a group of travelers, a whole tribe, it seemed, no less than ten families. And they were keen-eyed travelers, watching him warily as if they knew it was his intent to steal. My father, being the incautious boy that he was, saw this as a challenge. An opportunity for a great adventure. So he pretended to be very hungry and sickly, and one of the group took pity on him and invited him to share dinner with them.

He ate with them, all the while making his plans, looking about to decide what was worth his while to steal. He had decided on a beautiful red shawl with a lacy knotted pattern that hung on the side of one wagon, and was only waiting for his opportunity to grab it, when a few of the travelers took up instruments and began playing.

Now this is a story I have heard many times from my father, and many things in the story change, but never the words he used for what happens next, so I must quote him: "As soon as the big man who looked the size of a mountain took to playing the flute, one tiny bare foot appeared at the entrance of the wagon I had been watching so intently. A woman's, and on her ankle, she wore a strand of shining bronze bells. They tinkled as she stepped daintily out to the front of the wagon. I could feel her eyes on me, so I looked up. She was the most beautiful thing I had ever seen. Dark and mysterious, and haughty, she returned my stare boldly. As if she had read my mind, she slipped one hand past the door and lifted the shawl, draping it around her shoulders, and hopped from the wagon. She seemed to land silently but for the jingling of the bells. What was I to do? I decided then I would wipe that haughty look from her face, and steal both the shawl and the bells, without her being any the wiser."

Rowan giggled. Fighting the braid she'd unconsciously wound around her left hand, she nearly dropped the letter trying to turn to its second page.

He has never said as much, but I do not think my father's original intent was marriage. My mother has said it, though. Frequently. When she warned my brothers and me against playing with intelligent women. She says she saw every tiny thought in his brain as clearly as she could see his face. What's more, she says, she could tell he was a terrible thief. She claims, always with a provoking smile and her fingers entwined with my father's, that she took pity on him and had her father, the mountain-size man with the flute, force him to marry her.

Rowan felt an oddly pleasant sort of longing fill her chest. Usually when she wanted what others had, it felt like jealousy; this felt more like—hope. Perhaps it could be hers one day.

> *They have argued over it my whole life, who tricked whom into marriage. But for my part, I have to believe my mother. They lived rather happily, traveling with her family, until one of my uncles died and the other forced my father home. When it was discovered that he was married, my uncle decided to hide my mother's heritage, calling her a lost princess from the island of Weere.*
>
> *That is how I came to be. Since I know you think I invent all my tales, I offer you this proof as a birthday gift. My mother's bells.*
>
> *Have a truly special day.*
>
> *G—*

Rowan couldn't help but smile. It was such a sweet tale. How wonderful it must have been to grow up with parents who loved each other and loved their children. To have a mother who would wake you up simply to tell you that you were special. But how much harder it would be for them now that the king was ill.

Rowan held the anklet up in her hands, shaking it so that the bells tinkled softly. *One day.* Even the thought left her a bit breathless. She wondered if his mother knew Gavin had given away something so special. It was like being invited into the family. And what a lovely family to be invited into.

Rowan felt a bit cheated to have never heard such a story from her father. His marriage to her mother was arranged, but had there not even been one moment?

Rowan stared at the bells, shook them, and let the jangle pull her away from reality for a moment. It was bizarrely, beautifully implausible, but when she read Gavin's letters, and only then, she felt certain there would be a *one day*. And when it came, Rowan must have stories of who tricked whom into marriage, all told with joy to her horde of happy children.

Dear Gavin,

You were very lucky to have such a family. Have you ever met your grandfather the size of a mountain who plays the flute? It would be a rather fascinating thing to watch—a giant man playing a tiny instrument. I think I would enjoy learning to play.

It is a beautiful story! Thank you for sharing it.

The trouble is, now you have given me an idea that I cannot help but think is the best yet. When this is all over, I shall be a wandering thief like your father. I shall never get bored with so many places to see and so many chances to get caught. What do you think? Would I make a good thief?

I probably should not keep your mother's jewelry. You did ask her permission, didn't you? I shouldn't keep it, but I think I will. Every time the bells ring, I shall think of your story and smile.

Thank you for the smiles.

R—

That evening, Rowan approached Maureen's house with the bells tinkling softly at her ankle. Colum was putting away the practice swords and padding. Things had not been the same between Colum and Rowan since the day her father had marched onto the practice field. He did not joke and laugh with her; he did not just sit with her and listen. Every time she saw him taking some young knight under his wing, she grew jealous. But when she tried to speak to him about it, he said nothing was wrong.

Rowan approached him instead of the house. He looked around at the sound of her bells, eyeing her strangely.

"Where did you get those?"

"A present," Rowan said awkwardly. She didn't want to talk about the bells or Gavin or anything other than Colum and herself, and why he did not seem to care for her any longer.

"Much more womanly than knightly," Colum said with a smirk.

"Are you angry that I formed the Knights of the Rose?" Rowan asked baldly.

"No." Colum shook his head. "They are good men, ones I would have recommended."

"It isn't as though I chose them," Rowan said, sensing a hidden depth in his comment. "They volunteered, after they escorted Donovan away. I know I shouldn't have lost my temper that way," Rowan rushed to explain when she saw Colum growing distant. "You trained me better than that. And I am sorry I banished him, but...will you ever forgive me for it? It was a mistake."

"It was not a mistake." Colum spoke as harshly as Rowan had ever heard him off the training field. "I was never angry that you banished him. You are his queen for all intents and purposes, but he never treated you with the respect you deserve. When it came to that, you did the right thing. But it should never have come to that, Rowan." Colum stepped forward, pulling Rowan's eyes from the ground she was nodding at.

"You allowed it to get there. And so did I. That first day, when you challenged twenty men to fight you, I should have stopped it then. But I didn't. And you gave them permission to insult you and treat you as less than you are. For what? To get a sparring partner?" Colum shook his head angrily, walking away. "I thought you did it as a kind of strategy—let them tease you until they felt like you were one of them. But you didn't. Even with Donovan, you wouldn't have banished him if you were not angry that no one would fight you. It wasn't the insults or the lack of respect that fired you off at him, was it? Was it?"

"No," Rowan muttered, shaking her head. "They don't mean anything. Really, Colum. It doesn't hurt me. I was mostly just angry that you were gone and it was my fault."

"That's exactly what I am angry about. You sat in my home and made me a promise—to take time for yourself, to enjoy yourself. But you don't even try. You will fight for anyone but you."

Rowan drew back; he was angry that she would defend him.

"Even your knights. They should not be Knights of the *Rose*. They should be Knights of the Queen. You, Rowan, you are deserving of defense, of respect. But you don't see it."

Rowan bit the inside of her cheek, clenching her fists. She didn't know what to say. Of course she was deserving of respect; everyone was. But if she fought every person who disrespected her, she would be fighting all the time. It wasn't worth the energy.

"I…"

"It isn't your fault. We did this to you," Colum said, shaking his head. "Every single adult here who had a responsibility to see you loved and cared for. We were the ones who let this happen. I should have stopped you following me around from the first. Worked to make other people treat you properly. So you would never have been on that field."

"You want me not to be a knight?" Rowan asked, aghast. This wasn't the Colum she had always known.

"It has made you treat yourself carelessly. So, no, I do not want you to be a knight."

Rowan nodded her head and turned away. "Then you don't want me to be me."

Dinner was a quiet gathering. The triplets picked up on their father's and Rowan's moods and were unusually subdued. And Maureen was near tears the entire night. When it was over and Rowan was walking home, she wondered why she had even gone.

She wandered into her garden. She didn't sit; she just walked among the roses and looked at her tree. Would there ever be a day when she wouldn't hate her birthday at least as much as she looked forward to it?

You poison everything you touch.

Her mother had died tonight, eighteen years ago. Eighteen years. Rowan stopped and stared at the bench. Eighteen years; her mother had been eighteen when she died. Rowan was eighteen tonight.

She nearly sat but couldn't, not there. Not tonight.

No.

There would never be a day she wouldn't hate her birthday.

Today is special. Today you were born.

Her mother had said something like that.

In all time there has never been another like you.

Rowan left the garden. The bells at her ankle tinkled as she walked. But she wasn't smiling. She was wishing that she had been born into a different family.

She was special. All special really meant was different. And people don't understand different. Sometimes even the people you love the most.

Days Pass Slowly without You

The days dragged on endlessly. Since Rowan launched her mission to find out all she could about her grandmother, her knights were rarely at the palace, and never all together.

She stopped practicing with the young knights. They were all frightened to hurt her, so it was barely any exercise. And after her talk with Colum, she didn't want to train with him any longer.

So she found other ways to practice. She took to leaving the palace in disguise and starting fights on the roads if none of her knights were present. But she couldn't do it every day; it would quickly become obvious. So she frequently just practiced with poles or ran through poses.

Even working with Maureen, though no longer as frustrating, was much less rewarding. She was loved there; Rowan knew it. But it hurt to see the way Maureen would smile at her children or scold them. It seemed no one looked at her that way. Every day there was a greater distance that Rowan knew she alone was responsible for.

She spent more and more of her time poring over the letters and journals of the previous kings, and less and less time with people. Waiting.

All she ever did was wait, it seemed. She waited for news from her knights. She waited for Braden to return. She waited for Gavin's letters. She waited for her birthdays to visit the Fairy circle. She waited for the curse to strike. For the day that she would either fail at the only thing she had ever worked for, or kill the woman who had given her mother life.

Rowan never thought she cared one way or another about her grandmother. But as the days passed and she grew more alone, Rowan began to wonder if her grandmother might not be the person she was closest to in all the world. Who else could understand this terrible stretching feeling, as though one moved as slowly as the sun through the sky, dragging its way into night—only to repeat the process all over again with the dawn. Would it ever end?

She lived her life from letter to letter or visit to visit. Hating everything in between, but unwilling to say it.

Dear Rowan,

The May Day draws near again, and I am at a loss for ideas. If we fight, perhaps we kill a few Fairy and a few men, and still the girls are taken. If we hide the girls, they are found. We have had no luck in our searches. They must be in the Fairy court. There is no other explanation. But how to retrieve them? I begin to wonder if I only believe them to be alive because I need to feel less of a failure.

My father, despite his failings and sins, was a good king. Our people could not have been happy with a king who would simply bend to the Fairy queen's rule. Although I begin to see that those who chose safety were not entirely wrong.

I have fought for so long to keep my brothers from my plan; they are young, and I preferred to see them sheltered. I cannot keep it from them any longer. They must help; there is no other way for it. It will take us all.

We must find a way between us to bring others into our plan. The more we discover, the more I am convinced that the first attempt to remove the Fairy queen was a failure because the factions were too divided. Worried more for their own concerns than what would happen once they gave the Fairy queen so much power.

It will be hard to win support. I know you bear some of the burden of a queen, but it is difficult to understand until you alone are responsible for the lives of all who serve you. Every girl that is taken is my responsibility; every soldier lost, I have killed. I understand what it is to be tempted to simply submit to the Fairy queen and assure, if nothing else, the safety of my people.

But I cannot do it. If I submit to her now, what is to stop her from taking even more? Who is to stand beside you and face her?

I am convinced we need more people on our side. I do not like this plan of ours. Too much of it still falls to you.

Your Friend,

G—

Dear Gavin,

You are not alone in believing that the young girls must be alive. She has some plan for them that we do not know. There would be no reason to kidnap them if her intent were to kill. It would be far simpler to kill them where they slept. She is keeping them alive, and we will get them back.

It is not the same, I know, but it weighs on me too that she takes them. It weighs on me that my men go out in my name to find answers, risking themselves where I alone should be at risk. I am every day more frightened for my spy. Between his reports, my dreams are plagued worse than usual. I even worry for you. For what will happen if your father dies before this is settled.

You say too much of the plan rests on me, but who else is it to rest on? My father might not have meant it when he said I alone could defeat my grandmother, but it is every day clearer that it is true.

We could challenge her now. Send out troops to the edge of her kingdom and declare war. But we would likely lose. And cost many men their lives in the process. Who among your men would be able to fight her were she to drag the girls she has taken onto the field and threaten their lives?

It is me. It has always been me. Even, I think, before I was born.

You are right; I do not feel the responsibility of a king. I feel very little loyalty to my own people. In all the world, there are perhaps a dozen to whom I feel I owe anything. But—my grandmother fears me. And that makes me responsible for everything she has done, everything she does until I stop her.

It eats at me, this waiting. But if there is one thing I have learned in all my training, it is not to go rushing into a fight. If you rush forward, you give your opponent power. They get to decide the location, they see you coming, they reserve their energy.

It has to be here. It has to be the day Roisin returns. Sorcha will come here if we defeat her curse. When she does, we will have laid a trap. It is the best way. She thinks herself safe here, because my people cannot fight her. She will come. And I will kill her.

We do need more allies. Not to fight her, but simply to refuse her. The more people she wins over with her promises and threats, the more powerful she becomes.

I am no great diplomat, but I thought to begin with the next ball Gwyneth offers. She has become so fond of them. Every occasion she can get, she throws another to practice for Roisin's return and to reminisce about her first such experience. I thought I might send the invitations more widely than we usually do. It will give me a chance to try to win over more supporters.

If you truly mean to include your brothers, perhaps they could do something similar. They must be invited to events frequently enough. Recruiting supporters is a safer way to be involved.

Despite the fact that this practicing a ball is Gwyneth's idea, it might be wise to experiment with the best way to position the men you will send for our trap when it is time. So nothing is left to chance. Think about it.

R—

1,510 days until Roisin returns

When Braden visited again, Rowan had not practiced with a real knight in months. She informed him that she would never consider his proposal unless he sparred with her.

Braden agreed with evident reluctance, which Rowan ignored; she only cared that he fought her, not how he felt about it. She took Braden out to a field behind the castle, where they wouldn't be disturbed while fighting. She was hiding, but she didn't care. She might kill Braden accidentally if she fought him with everyone watching. Every knight who thought they had won because she no longer trained with them.

She had barely fought with him a minute when Rowan grew frustrated. All he would do was stand there blocking her blows.

"Damn it, Braden—attack! I can get a better workout from a training post."

"You're a girl." Braden's sword rested between his toes, held loosely in his left hand. He shrugged his shoulders, looking distinctly uncomfortable.

"Really?" Rowan demanded sarcastically. "I had no idea."

"Why can't you just fight with the others, like you used to?"

"They're afraid to hurt me. My father and their master are threatening them."

"So you think it's better that I be the one they go after when you wind up injured?"

"Watch." Rowan pulled back the long sleeve of the dress she wore and sliced deeply into her arm with her sword. She dropped the sword and placed one hand calmly over the spot as Braden rushed forward. Lifting her hand away, she revealed a completely unharmed arm. "If you injure me, I will fix it. Now attack."

Braden didn't move. "So you can heal a scratch. It's impressive, but it doesn't mean anything. What if it's a more serious blow? How much can you heal?"

"Short of killing me, I can heal," Rowan spat out. It wasn't precisely true—she'd never been that badly harmed—but Braden didn't need to know that. "Fight me. You're defying the Fairy queen, whom you're terrified of, but you're going to balk at swinging a blunted sword at me? Quit being a coward."

That did it. Braden refused to be called a coward. Lifting his sword, he charged forward, attacking Rowan. She laughed, meeting his strike.

Braden nearly beat her twice, which just went to show how out of practice she was. But it was still the most fun Rowan had in months. She charged, he charged; they fended each other off. He was good, better than Rowan expected, as he apparently abhorred weapons. In the end, when they both gave in, calling it a draw, they were laughing.

"You really enjoy fighting, don't you?" Braden asked as though the idea were ludicrous.

"I love being in motion, working toward a goal. Every day I'm feeling more and more—stagnant. When the time comes, I might be a statue for all the action I've been taking."

Braden nodded. "I understand that. Half the time when I am home, I want to march up to my father, or the Fairy queen when she is there, and tell them I am no longer theirs. At least that way I can see it coming, whatever they will do to me."

"I am not going to let them harm you," Rowan said fiercely, her stomach twisting at the thought of him openly challenging Sorcha. She should not have put him in this position.

Braden laughed. "How will you stop them? Powerful as you apparently are, you cannot be everywhere at once. You are not able to stop her kidnapping those children; how will you stop her hurting me?"

Rowan's stomach was a twisting, burning knot. She couldn't protect Braden or the girls. She had shown Braden Ardal's first letter and asked him to find out anything he could about the kidnapped girls. So far, he knew nothing. Sorcha was no fool; she told Braden very little. So Rowan was impotent to do anything but wait. It all came down to the one plan. One option.

"I would put a spell on you if I thought it would work," Rowan whispered. "But I worry she would know, and attack you."

"I know." Braden chuckled. "In a way I am glad you can't protect me. If you could, I would let you. Even knowing that it would distract you from the bigger plan. I want to be safe. But taking the risk without protection, it makes me feel more a man than any sword fight or trial I ever had to endure."

"You are a man. The bravest I know. I just wish I could trade places with you or my knights or those little girls. Anyone." Rowan's hands were fisted on the grass, and her gaze burned the distant hills with its intensity.

"I know." Braden nodded. "If it makes you feel any better, I don't think any of us would be willing to trade with you."

"It does not," Rowan said, leaning over to shove Braden onto the grass.

He came up laughing, yanking at Rowan's braid. "What? I thought you liked being the bravest knight in the land."

1,443 days until Roisin returns

Braden sparred with her every day during his visit, but it didn't last long. One week, and Rowan was on her own again.

She was never without something to do. But when Eachann came again, she could not remember a thing she had done since waving Braden off.

"My lady grows older by the second," the fairy said, handing Rowan the letter.

"But it is no longer good?" Rowan asked, interpreting his tone.

"All the Fairy are old, but they have a child's heart. It is your heart that is aging."

"Well," Rowan said coldly, offended, "I am not Fairy. I am something else."

"That you are." Eachann nodded. "So is your grandmother, I think."

Rowan yanked the letter from Eachann, her stomach throbbing as though she'd been kicked, and stomped off.

Dear Rowan,

I would not for the world offend you, but I think I have. When I wrote of the burdens of kingly responsibility, I did it unthinkingly. Of course you understand. You take on responsibility in much the same way my father has.

Before he fell into this ceaseless sleep, he would speak of his blame in the matter. He felt responsible for the curse placed on your sister, the curse on our lands, the loss of Creelan. Everything the Fairy queen did since the war. Sometimes he would sit for hours in the same spot, staring at a painting on his wall. As if waiting for the dragon in it to come to life and rescue us. Every year that went by, he grew worse, weighted. Until all he could see were the dark things, his failings; and he could no longer speak.

Please do not let this struggle consume you.

Eachann's words rushed beneath her skin again, making her cringe; she nearly crumpled the letter. *It is your heart that is aging.* Was everyone right? Was there nothing to her but this struggle? She did feel lonely and frightened and so tired, but she didn't know any longer how to be anything else, because no matter what, she could not just give up and trust her sister to fate.

Rowan smoothed the letter, drawing herself up; she was not waiting for rescue. The struggle would not consume her, at least not until she'd saved her sister.

Maybe it wasn't selfish, wanting only to defeat the curse on your sister. Perhaps all that is needed of you is to break the one curse. And the rest of us must take responsibility for our own.

You wrote that every small way she fails weakens her more. Because her powers come as much from what people believe them to be, as from magic. Perhaps all that is needed is for you to weaken her, and for the rest of us to simply stop believing.

Stop believing, and poof, Sorcha is gone. Rowan shook her head, incredulous. Stop believing and steal Sorcha's power, stop her evil. Was their belief so strong? Rowan felt a little bad for scoffing at Gavin and his limitless hopeful belief. But it would not be so; the sunken mass in her stomach assured her: stopping Sorcha would not be easy.

I have done what you suggested and sent my brothers out as ambassadors for our cause. Subtlety is not something either is known for, but I have impressed upon them how very secretive this mission must be. I think they understand. I hope they understand.

I will keep to the plan, but I think we must consider others; it is good strategy.

G—

Dear Gavin,

I was not very offended. A little, but not much. You do not just have the responsibilities of a king; you have the responsibilities of a son to an ailing father. I understand there are things in your life I simply cannot comprehend. Do not worry about my feelings; they are sturdier than that.

I thank you for your concern for my safety—and sanity. I will take your feelings into consideration. I will even consider other plans. But—are there not things you simply know inside of yourself to be true?

There are for me.

Once I knew, before even my stepmother, that I would have a sister and that she would be beautiful. I knew my mother's nurse would have three children. I knew, before I saw her face, that my grandmother had evil on her mind. And I know, though I cannot explain it, that my grandmother's fate will be decided by me.

What I don't know is how. I doubt a sword will be of much use to me, but it is the only human weapon afforded me that I have any skill with. And I cannot imagine that it will be my great and powerful magic, either.

Every day I am capable of more magic, but she has lived and breathed magic her entire life. I do not even fully understand how it is I perform magic. My sister, for all that she was not born a Fairy, is more Fairy than I will ever be. She can dance on the air and call all the creatures of nature around her. And when she sings...I would swear that all of nature stops to listen.

Rowan paused, ready to crumple the page and begin anew. She shouldn't mention her visits with Roisin to anyone. But she hadn't exactly claimed to visit. And she had told Gavin many dangerous things; if he wanted to betray her, he could have long ago. He was on her side. He understood her, she needed someone to understand her—completely.

She, who has no Fairy blood, is Fairy. And I—I am something else. Both human and Fairy, but still I am neither.
  I don't know how I will stop Sorcha. I just know that it must be me.
  If I could have your father's dragon by my side, I would take it. But I have not heard of there being dragons since before the Fairy War.
  Don't worry.
  R—

Gavin sent a reply unusually fast; only a week elapsed before she had it in her hands.

Rowan,
  If a dragon is the only thing you will take with you, then I will find you a dragon. You will not be alone.
  Gavin

Rowan held the note in her hand and felt tears running down her face, but could not move. Her eyes were caught on the words *You will not be alone.*

How had he known that was the only thing she needed to hear? Every day she felt more alone, but she wasn't. It didn't matter that she had never seen his face or spoken to him; she had Gavin.

Rowan's response was only two words.

Thank you.

After the note, Rowan's mood was much better. She still did not practice with the knights. She still did not spend as much time with Maureen. But she knew she was not alone, and that was enough.

She took to wearing the bells that Gavin gave her everywhere. Every ring was a reminder that she was not alone.

On her nineteenth birthday when she visited her sister in the Fairy circle, they danced and laughed and spoke of nothing in particular, just enjoyed each other's company, and that was enough.

Whenever one of her knights returned to the palace, they sparred with her, planned with her, and most importantly laughed with her. Eventually she even got a few more volunteers to join the Knights of the Rose. As she neared her twentieth birthday, the Knights of the Rose had eight members, excluding Rowan.

The time was drawing near. Rowan could feel the unrest growing in the air as the world itself prepared for the coming battle. Where before she had simply trained and waited, planned and waited, and waited even more, now things were getting serious.

Whenever she grew anxious, scared, or desperate to start the battle, Rowan jingled the bells at her ankle and banished her grandmother's voice with Gavin's words.

You will not be alone.

Because I Will Ask Her To

1008 days until Roisin returns

R owan was slowly gathering supporters with the help of her knights and the three princes of Turrlough. Almost none of the supporters were willing to openly defy the Fairy queen, but they all agreed not to assist her. Rowan was growing impatient with them; she wanted to hold Braden up in front of them as a shining example of bravery, but she couldn't. None could know of his involvement. Even Gavin only knew him as Rowan's spy.

Braden visited four times a year, but every time he left, Rowan worried for him more. He would be visiting in her birthday week, but in the month before it, Rowan began to worry it would not be soon enough.

Things had suddenly become very serious. Two of her knights, Sean and Declan, had returned home barely alive after being attacked by a flock of birds. Sean had been trampled and lost an arm, and Declan lost an eye and a great deal of blood from his numerous small injuries. Rowan felt sick and guilty visiting them, but could not do otherwise; these were her friends, her men. She had failed to protect them but would not fail to cheer them.

Ardal had not sent word in months and had not been seen by anyone. The knight Rowan dispatched to search for Ardal had not been heard from either. The longer she went without word, the less Rowan was able to eat; she wanted to cry herself to sleep, more every day. But even that felt wrong; she didn't want to abandon hope of her friend returning, what little hope she had.

Gavin's monthly reports also grew much worse. Since the year began, there had been four attempts on the king's life. Two by servants who had worked for the royal family all their lives. Gavin reported a decided lack of children at all in his kingdom. Families had simply stopped having children for fear that they would be girls. Other families, with small children, had left the kingdom. They knew it was unlikely to do much good, but fled all the same, a last desperate hope.

> *I cannot blame them. I have not proven myself capable of protecting my people. It is better they leave. There is just shy of three years left until your sister returns and we hope to defeat the Fairy queen with our trap, and suddenly things are worse everywhere.*
>
> *I offered escorts and food to any who chose to leave. And they will be welcomed back if ever they return.*
>
> *My youngest brother is to be married in a month. To Kayla of Heige. She is on our side, braver than most, even; she has convinced her father to take in many of the people who are fleeing my kingdom. An island away, perhaps Sorcha will not bother with them.*
>
> *We have maybe five families with small children living in Turrlough. There are other girls, though—two orphans, both nearing the age of ten. Kayla has promised to adopt them. They will be citizens of Heige on the day of the wedding.*
>
> *I can only hope that does the trick and that they are safe.*
>
> *Things must change.*
>
> *G—*

Gavin,

> *They will change, I promise.*
>
> *Ardal, before he left, brought me all the information he could find on Creelan. There is little to suggest that the stories are true. The only proof is a pack of wolves that seemed to take over the ruins of the great city. But I do not think those wolves were once human. My grandmother is not that powerful. Everything he discovered suggests they left as a people. Picked up and abandoned their home in search of a better one.*

Rowan froze with her quill poised above the page; her stomach was churning in revolt against what she must write next. Her letters with Gavin were no longer the lighthearted teasing that had drawn her in; reality had invaded her safe space. Still, the idea of losing the letters completely, of losing Gavin, left her sick—unreasonably frightened.

> *Though I would hate to lose our correspondence, leaving as they did is something to consider. I would aid you any way I could. I will no matter what. If you want armies, I will raise them; if you need food, gold, a friend, anything.*
>
> *Tell me how I can help.*
>
> *R—*

980 days until Roisin returns

The plan was crumpling around her. It was like a siege, all this waiting for the right time to strike. And Rowan had forgotten the first rule: only begin a siege if you can outlast your opponent. Eternity was a very long time, and Sorcha, despite her reputed impatience, had an eternity to wait. No one else did.

Rowan could not believe how stupid she had been. She had decided to fight for others and had not adjusted her plan to suit that. She would fail everyone at this rate.

The feeling was only heightened when she received Gavin's response.

> *Rowan, my friend,*
>
> *I have considered leaving. But I cannot ask my people to abandon their homes to the Fairy queen any more than I can ask them to surrender their will to her. That is what she wants, us defeated, bowing to her. Every challenge she forces on us raises our determination to triumph.*
>
> *Several fairies fled Sorcha's court and took refuge here after the war. One of them gave me an idea last year. Rescuers. We would plant*

fairies among the families, disguised as young girls. The opposite of the changelings, fairies are reputed to leave in cradles.

Rowan smiled, impressed both with the clever plan, and the inherent insult. Sorcha would have been enraged. Maureen had told Rowan about the old legends of fairies trading their own, sickly children for healthy human babies. Told her how humans looked on Fairy as evil beasts, and blamed them for every misfortune that befell them, raised their children on cautionary tales of being eaten by dark Fairy. Every time Maureen spoke of it Rowan heard the pain in her voice. If this plan had worked Sorcha would have had to recognize the insult for what it was, Fairy calling her evil, seeing her as every despicable prejudiced image the world had ever concocted of Fairy. But if Gavin wrote of it with so little hope, it must not have worked.

I did not tell you, because I feared even writing it. But it failed. The fairies were left behind. I do not know how to ask it of human children. How would they even help? They have no magic. I do not know how to ask it of any child, but I will.

Eachann spoke of three children, half Fairy, half human, like yourself. Nearing the age of ten. And one of them a girl.

Rowan froze, nearly dropping the letter. Her eyes tore across the words a second time. He couldn't mean it. Petal.

I know what these children mean to you. And you must hate me for asking, but we are quickly running out of options. Eachann says they are powerful, and just human enough to fool the Fairy. He thinks she will be safe.

On May 1ˢᵗ for the past several years, Fairy have come and spirited away our ten-year-old girls. May 1ˢᵗ is but seven months away. Seven months of no hope, only heartbreak, as we prepare to part with those we love.

You asked what you could do. Ask her to help. Please.
She may be our last hope.
Your Friend,
G—

Rowan couldn't believe it. How dare he ask that of a child? Of Petal. She had barely begun to live. She swooned to stop people fighting. Had an irrepressible crush on Braden, would follow wherever he went. And she was a little thief, stealing everything from food to weapons to hearts. How could he ask that?

The boys will stay, and she will go away.

No. Not this way.

Rowan left her writing room to find Eachann.

"This was your idea?" she demanded, walking toward Eachann, waving the letter. He was leaning with his legs crossed on the inside of Rowan's garden wall, facing the bench. He did not bother to look up, just waited for Rowan to come and stand in front of him.

"It was," Eachann said simply. He had the look of a man who knew he was in for a fight. Rowan was happy to give him one.

"How dare you? Do you know what a risk she would be taking?"

"No more than the girls the queen already takes."

"Much more! She wouldn't belong. Every girl Sorcha has taken would know it. What happens when Sorcha realizes who she is?"

"You said if she wanted them dead, she would kill them where they slept."

"If she wanted little girls from Stonedragon, she would take *them*."

"What would you have him do? This is the only choice."

"There is always another choice. I sent him one already. Take his people and leave."

"Now you are in favor of cowards?" he challenged. "I thought it was better a fool who fights than a wise man who lets someone else fight his battle."

"It isn't his battle!" Rowan screamed, her entire being shaking with rage and futility and utter confusion. "It never was."

"No? Whose, then? Yours? It cannot all be about you, little queen. Ask the girl. Perhaps she thinks it is her fight, also."

Rowan paced away, ready to throw a punch to stop Eachann talking. She knew what Petal would say. All three of the triplets saw this battle as theirs. But she wanted to keep them from it.

"She is only a child."

"How old were you when you were given an adult's task? Life is no more careful with children than adults."

"Life isn't careful with anything," Rowan snarled. "But we are supposed to be." Here she was nearly panting in frustration, trying to make Eachann understand her, and he would not even look her way. She looked over her shoulder to see what held his attention so completely. Her bench?

"Did you know my mother?" Rowan demanded; he was more interested in the bench than in what she was saying.

"I did not have that pleasure." Eachann straightened away from the wall, bowing to the bench. "It should have been my great honor to know her, and her brother, if not for the war."

"Oh." She didn't know what she had expected to hear. Not that; for a moment it startled her right out of her anger.

"We are each of us born with a purpose," Eachann said, walking to stand between Rowan and the bench. "This may be Petal's."

"The boys will stay, and she will go away. She will go to the Fairy court."

"How do you know?"

"Because I will ask her to."

No. She couldn't. How many people could she continue putting at risk to save one person? There had to be a limit. She loved Roisin, more than anything. But to risk Petal? Was it worth it?

You poison everything you touch.

"There will be no response." Rowan walked out of the rose garden, not waiting to see what Eachann would do.

She wouldn't risk Petal.

Because I will ask her to.

You poison everything you touch.

Seeking Comfort

*R*owan could not say what had taken her there—surely nothing she'd done—but she found herself outside her father's study with her hand rapping gently on the door.

Any other time, Rowan would go to Maureen with a problem like this, but the triplets would be there. They could hear thoughts, Keagan the best of the three, and he would tell Petal. And Petal, sweet, fearless Petal, would go.

She couldn't write to Gavin about it. She knew where he stood, and as much as she loved their friendship, she hated him for bringing her to this. She absolutely could not speak to Colum about this. And all of her knights were away. No, there was only her father.

"Come in."

Rowan stepped into the dark room. The curtains were drawn, and her father sat by the fire, cradling a small portrait of Roisin. This happened more and more frequently of late. Rowan had stopped bothering to try to slow the progress of the curse with him.

It was odd. Where at first his growing love for her sister had simply meant a distracted king, now his love for her smothered him beneath a dark depression. He rarely smiled, rarely left this room. Sometimes he would not even sleep. It had grown steadily worse since her last birthday.

Another person Rowan had failed.

You poison everything you touch.

"Rowan?" Her father looked up, confused. "Is it your birthday already?"

"No, Father." Rowan walked over to the fire and sat across from him. Did he think they could only speak on her birthday? "I just wanted to see you."

"Oh. That's good. I promised I wouldn't forget." But he looked away, distracted by Roisin's portrait.

"What makes one life more worthy of saving than another?" Rowan couldn't say why she spoke; even if he heard her, her father was too far gone in the curse to care.

"She's not worth more than you," the king said absently, running a hand along Roisin's portrait. "But you aren't worth more, either." He said it as though the idea troubled him, a giant puzzle he simply couldn't solve. Rowan knew it wasn't fair, but she wanted to shake him, wanted to yell at him. What had Roisin ever done but remain safe, and Rowan had made her that way. Why wasn't that worth more?

"I love you both."

"I know." Rowan swallowed her unworthy bitterness. "That wasn't what I meant. I just…"

"I have time yet. Your birthday. She said I had until your birthday. What gift shall I give you?" he asked, suddenly frantically animated.

"I don't need a gift, Father."

"Oh, you must have a gift. I love you; I must show you. Then you will understand." He let go of the portrait, heedless as it clattered against the floor, and grabbed Rowan's hands in his. "You will understand, won't you? I love you both. But I have not seen your sister since she was a baby. I have to see her at least once more."

"Of course." Rowan worried about her father's health. He was not making sense. Sitting in this dark room, next to the sweltering heat of the fire. "Come with me." Rowan pulled her father to his feet. "You need sleep."

"She said I must choose." Balder talked to himself as Rowan led him out of the study. "I did not think I could. How do you choose one child over the other? At first I thought it must be you. I know you. I love you. I see you every day. It must be you. Your sister is a stranger to me. Then I saw the portrait. She doesn't look like that anymore. It would be as if she died all those years ago. And I promised we would all be together again. She will allow that, only for a moment, but she will allow that."

Rowan stopped halfway up the staircase and faced her father; he was looking right through her.

"Who do you mean, Father?" Rowan asked slowly.

"Your grandmother." He looked up at Rowan as though she were the one speaking nonsense.

"What did she say to you? When?"

"On your birthday. She came the night of your nineteenth birthday. She was tired of waiting and said I had to decide. She will let me have one daughter preserved forever, just as she is at the moment I agree."

"And the other?"

"The other would have to die."

Rowan did not understand why she was just standing here, calmly breathing in and out, holding her father's hand as though he were a sickly child. He would make a deal to trade her life for her sister's. Not even her sister's life really—*preserved forever*, that wasn't life.

"How will she preserve her?" Rowan heard her voice as if from far away. Why was she not upset? Why was she holding his hand?

"In a crystal; she will float there, in no pain, forever."

Just like her son.

"And you took this deal?"

"Not yet. She comes again on your next birthday. She will bring Roisin back to us."

"Did you tell her where she is, Father?"

"No. Not until your birthday. When she returns. You do understand, don't you?" He spoke so fervently, his eyes misted over.

"Of course, Father," Rowan said flatly. "Come along. We've two weeks yet before Sorcha comes."

"Yes. I should sleep."

Rowan led her father into his room and tucked him in. She sat at the side of his bed staring down at him. She must be asleep. It was the only explanation for the fact that she could not seem to feel anything.

Laying her hand on her father's forehead, Rowan closed her eyes and began to whisper, "While everyone slept, some dark form came for her. You do not know who; you do not know where. Every day you worry, and every day you search for some sign of her. But you have no idea where Roisin was taken. You cannot give Sorcha what she wants, because you do not know."

Rowan sat at her father's side for a long while. She had not been in here since she was a child. Every wall had another image of Roisin, laughing, smiling, sleeping. A three-year-old girl.

He was willing to trade Rowan's life simply to see his other daughter grown.

Rowan left the room. Left the palace. Walked back to the rose garden. She didn't know what pulled her, but she marched forward, right up to a rosebush and grabbed hold as tight as she could to the thorny stems; she shook the bush with all her might.

It did not even prick her; she barely felt the pressure.

You poison everything you touch.

"No. You do!" Rowan shouted to no one at all. "You want me cowering in a corner crying like a child, and it won't happen. I'm going to destroy the only thing you have left. Then I'm going to kill you."

Hiding Out

979 days until Roisin returns

*H*er father was much better the next day. Stealing knowledge from him had soothed his mind. He did not lock himself away or mope. He simply went about the business of being king. But Rowan was not convinced it would be enough; there were others who knew, or could at least describe, where the aunts had taken Roisin.

Over the course of the day, Rowan found a way to steal the memories of that night from Maureen and Gwyneth. The only people left with the knowledge were the aunts and herself.

The hardest person to steal the memory from was Maureen. Rowan stood at her threshold for nearly a minute without knocking. Maureen was expecting her for a magic lesson, but Rowan didn't want to move. There was something sacred about this home, and Rowan was about to violate that.

Maureen opened the door with a teasing smile on her face, but it faded almost at once. Reaching out, she took one of Rowan's hands between both of her own and brought it to her chest.

"Dearest, what is it? You look so strange; you can tell me anything." Her eyes filled with tears, and Rowan's began to cloud over as well, her heart longing to confess all and hide from the world in Maureen's arms. "Truly, I will understand."

Rowan's breath hitched; brooking no refusal, Maureen dragged her indoors, shutting the door behind them, and led the way to a pair of seats. Rowan should speak, tell her about Gavin's request and her father's deal with Sorcha, tell Maureen what she planned to do, but she couldn't open her mouth. There was no way Maureen could understand it all, not when Rowan could not understand it herself. It was betrayal.

But Rowan had to do it. If she did not take Maureen's memories, Sorcha could come for them, threaten her children to get at the memories. Rowan couldn't let Maureen be put in such a position. But stealing memories was so much worse than hiding feelings or keeping her distance. Why had it not felt half this wrong with her father?

"Maureen, do you think she still watches me?" Rowan whispered. Maureen stopped halfway to shoving Rowan into a seat.

"Sorcha?" she asked, tightening her hold on Rowan, as if the name alone was a threat.

Rowan nodded.

Maureen nudged Rowan into a chair and sat across from her. "Yes. I am certain she looks in on you from time to time." Maureen's voice sounded choked, and she watched Rowan's hands instead of her face. "Is that what keeps you from me for all but magic lessons—fear of her seeing you?"

Rowan didn't respond, couldn't, biting her lip as a few tears escaped. She had herself convinced Maureen didn't even notice the absence.

Maureen sighed, wearing a tearful smile. "My dearest, I do try to give you your space. But I will never fail to miss your presence in my home."

"I'm sorry." Rowan squeezed Maureen's hands, infusing the one apology with the wealth of her regrets.

"You know…" Maureen released Rowan's hand, settling back in her chair with a far-off look. "I used to hope Sorcha would look in on you, look in and, with time, come to love you."

"You did?" Rowan heard the tiniest thread of hope in her own voice and was appalled by it. Was that really something she wanted? As evil as her grandmother was, did some part of Rowan want her love? Was she such a fool?

"That was my hope."

"But it will not happen." Rowan drew up straighter. Maureen met her gaze and smiled comfortingly, knowingly.

"No. And it will be perhaps the greatest loss she ever suffers." It was the sort of thing Maureen could always be trusted to say, and the words drifted through Rowan like a tender balm. "Why did you want to know if she peeks in?" Maureen asked; in her eyes Rowan saw wheels turning.

"I want Sorcha to know something. I want to be *certain* she knows."

Maureen nodded quietly, not even attempting to discover what that something was. She knew Rowan would not tell, and she allowed her space.

"You were wanting, perhaps, to use me for this certainty?" Maureen spoke casually, as though both unsurprised and undisturbed by the question.

"Would you mind? If it can even—"

"I can touch her mind," Maureen interrupted sharply, but she wouldn't meet Rowan's eyes and her hands were fisted. "But you must..." She shook her head, clearly having great difficulty with something. Rowan held her breath.

All at once Maureen's eyes pinned Rowan in place, and she reached out, latching onto both her hands. "I would never betray you."

"I know that!" The words exploded from Rowan on a sob.

"Do you?" Maureen's reddened eyes searched Rowan's. "You hide so much, dearest. I understand the need to protect your sister and yourself. But you forget, you are not alone in this."

Tears rushed out of Rowan's eyes now, and she sobbed so hard she could not breathe. Maureen leaned forward and ran a hand along Rowan's cheek. The gentle comfort of Maureen's love, her magic, rushed out to settle Rowan and calm her sobs. Maureen kissed Rowan's cheek and settled back onto her chair with a smile and a nod.

"Come, dearest, use me for your cause. It would be my honor."

She did not even ask what Rowan wanted, just gave herself over to the cause, and as comforted as she was, Rowan felt so much worse for it. Look at all she took from the people she loved most.

All the same, Rowan sent her magic out, searching Maureen's mind for the memory of the night, nearly ten years ago, when the aunts came for Roisin. Rowan plucked the memory out, so Maureen could only remember resting that evening. When it was done, Rowan settled back to wait for Sorcha, wondering if it would be different this time. Would she even feel Sorcha peeking in now that she was invited?

She needn't have worried. Freezing cold raced, sharp-edged, through Rowan's veins and across her skin. She stiffened. It was different than before; it was worse. It brought tears to Rowan's eyes with worry for how it must hurt Maureen.

"Well?" Maureen's lips moved, but it was not Maureen speaking; it was Sorcha.

This was Rowan's plan, exactly what she'd asked for, but she couldn't force the words out. The cold of Sorcha's hatred was all around her, smothering Rowan. It terrified her, this hatred of her, for no sin but living.

"I asked once before if you were dumb, child. Need I ask again?"

Rowan wanted to vomit, hearing the words from Maureen. Rowan had asked for this, and this recoiling feeling was exactly what Maureen had feared. Rowan stiffened her spine; it was Sorcha. *Sorcha*. Maureen wasn't here right now.

"I defeated one of your spells," Rowan growled between clenched teeth. "My father can tell you nothing. And it is only a matter of time before I defeat all your magic."

"Oooo. I'm quaking." Maureen rolled her eyes dismissively. "There are others who can be made to speak." Sorcha lifted Maureen's hands, looking at them with a broad grin; she tilted her head to the side smugly. It looked nothing like Maureen, not a bit. Rowan found it oddly comforting.

"No. There are not. I saw to that." Rowan nodded sharply.

"One little triumph won't stop me," she snarled, lunging forward as if to bite Rowan. "My plan is already in motion. And we both know, despite what you play at, when the time comes, it will be your hand delivering the poison unto your sister."

The cold was gone, but Rowan couldn't stop shivering. Slowly Maureen became herself again. Breathing slowly, she sat forward.

"It worked," Maureen said, observing Rowan's wide eyes and clenched fists. Carefully, being sure not to frighten her, Maureen reached out and touched Rowan's arm. Rowan turned her arm beneath Maureen's touch and gripped her back. Slowly warmth suffused Rowan's body, chasing away the remnants of Sorcha's hatred. But not her words.

"Sorcha has a very disheartening effect on one," Maureen said into the silence. "But I have faith in you. When the time comes, you will be stronger than she."

Rowan shivered at Maureen's words, so unintentionally similar to Sorcha's.

When the time comes, it will be your hand delivering the poison unto your sister.

Rowan wished she had Maureen's faith. Anyone's faith. But it didn't seem to be in her, not with all she still hid from Maureen. Not with both Sorcha's words and her father's entreaty still fresh in her mind. So she retreated to her garden to hide.

In past years, when she would have given anything for her father's company, he had remained shut away from her. And now that she wanted nothing so much as to never see him again, he seemed intent on spending time with her.

Rowan should not blame him. The blame for anything he would have done belonged to her grandmother. She put a fever on him and made him mad with worry. But no matter how she tried to rationalize it, Rowan felt betrayed. He had taken Gwyneth's side in the end.

Rowan found any excuse to avoid her father and the triplets. But no one seemed inclined to cooperate.

Rowan was hiding out in her garden, reading. She felt too chaotic inside to focus on anything real; all her rage and confusion rose up, but with nowhere to go, she only became more frustrated. So she had taken to rereading "The Song of Branduff." It was Gavin's favorite poem; he'd sent it to her years ago. For the longest time she'd read it over and over, sung the words, trying to love it as he did.

The words were lovely, but the story didn't much suit Gavin. It was the story of a farmer who finds a starving beast, rescues it, befriends it, loves it even; but when the people of his kingdom see and try to kill the beast, it kills several of his people defending itself. At first Branduff hides it, but eventually, to stop more people dying, Branduff betrays and kills the monster he loves.

It seemed more like something Rowan would pick herself than Gavin's taste; perhaps it reminded him of her. It was too depressing a story for times such as these, but Rowan kept coming back to two lines: "Come now, be at peace in this place; there will be many great hours for grieving tomorrow." She read them again and again, waiting for the peace to find her.

It never did.

The garden gate was locked, but the triplets found her.

"Petal doesn't fight well," Ferdy said by way of greeting, startling Rowan so she fell off the bench.

"How did you get in here?"

"The same way you used to," Keagan said as if it were obvious. "With magic. Ferdy's right; you must teach Petal to fight."

Rowan looked at Petal, the only silent member of the party. Very unlike Petal.

"Why?" Rowan asked, pushing to her feet.

"Because the girls in Turrlough always fight when the Fairy come for them, and I must be convincing."

Rowan caught her breath. They knew, but she had been so carefully avoiding them. How did they find out?

"You should know how to protect yourself," Ferdy snapped, oblivious to Rowan.

"I will be safe."

"Petal…" Rowan began, only to stop herself. She didn't want Petal to go. But she knew, sooner or later, circumstances might conspire so she would ask her. Wasn't that what made her angriest?

You poison everything you touch.

Better Petal be prepared. "I will teach you to fight. It will have to be with a dagger or other small weapons. Hiding a sword might be a bit hard."

Rowan trained all three of the triplets for hours every day, hidden in her garden. Ferdy was by far the fastest, and Keagan the strongest. But it quickly became apparent that sweet little Petal was the most cunning. Years of fainting to calm her brothers had left her quite good at throwing her little weight around, and she could steal her brothers' blades right out of their hands.

It was fun being the master instead of the trainee. She loved showing Keagan how to hold his balance or tempering Ferdy's impatience. She loved best of all that Petal had none of Rowan's old insecurities. If Petal was not the best at something, she just shrugged it off and worked harder or found ways to complement her brothers, but it never made her feel less worthy. Rowan was surprised but pleased to find her own teaching style a combination of Colum's steady instruction and the playful sparring she'd shared with her knights. She only wished she could banish her growing sense of dread; every time she saw Petal holding her fake blade, trying to slice her brothers with intense focus, her heart shook a little.

973 days until Roisin returns

One week after she had sent Eachann away empty-handed, he was back.

> *Rowan,*
>
> *You can say no. Can decide I am a monster, as low as your grand-mother. But answer me this, what makes your Petal more important than Colleen or Erin or Finnola, or any of the fifty-eight girls your grandmother has taken in the last five years?*
>
> *I did not want to ask this. I tried many other things before I did.*
>
> *We need someone inside her court. I need this, and so do you.*
>
> *G—*

It was so like what her father said. That Roisin was not worth more than Rowan, but that Rowan was not worth more, either. Perhaps it was something about men; they didn't seem to understand that nothing could justify sacrificing one life for another.

> *Gavin,*
>
> *Do not pretend this is an option you have been putting off to the last. Sorcha takes ten-year-old girls. It was not an option until this year.*
>
> *You have given me your request; at least have the decency to own that you know what you are asking. There are other options.*
>
> *Even you think she will not come again after this year. There are no girls left.*

Rowan did not even sign the letter, just folded the paper in half and handed it to Eachann. She would have walked away, but the fairy stopped her.

"Your qualms are good. But do not punish him because his are not the same. You have not been in his place."

"Yes. I sit here safely hidden from the horrors. I cannot possibly feel as useless and frightened as he for those girls because they are not my own. Right? He knows what it is like to be powerless and frightened. But what he is asking of me is not the same. How many has he ordered into what could be their deaths?" Rowan asked, incensed. "One of my knights lost an arm because I sent him to study the Fairy queen. Another will never see the same again. Every day I risk one of my closest friends, sending him back to Sorcha as a spy. The best of my knights has been missing for months, and the young knight I sent after him is missing as well.

"His fifty-eight girls may be gone from their families, but not from this world. I know them to be safe, and so does he. So I will not pretend, and neither will I allow you to do so. More is asked of me. I alone am responsible for their lives. And he asks me to risk a child now. I will take my time with my qualms, thank you. To do less would be to surrender even my soul to this cause. And I won't do that."

Before Rowan could make good her escape to the garden, her father found her.

"I can never seem to find you anymore," her father said as he caught her. "I begin to think you are avoiding me."

"What can I do for you, Father?"

"Nothing. I merely wanted to speak to you. Are you all right, Rowan?"

"Fine."

"You can tell me anything. I am your father; I love you. Did you have an argument with your prince?"

"Which one?" Rowan asked sarcastically.

"Gavin. I know Braden is here often, but you seem more like brother and sister than anything else."

"Yes, we are arguing. But it is not important."

"Rowan," the king called as his daughter started to walk around him, "anything that is important to you is important to me."

Rowan drew in a breath to keep from crying. "It will pass, I'm sure," Rowan said, meeting her father's eyes. "But I find it hard to look at you."

The king's eyes widened, but otherwise he did not move, frozen in place, staring at his daughter.

"Do you not remember telling me?" Rowan asked, her voice cracking. The sound only made Rowan angrier. She stiffened her spine, glaring at her father. "Explaining to me why it was I would have to be the daughter who died."

Balder sucked in a horrified breath and stepped away from his daughter.

"I understand. I did, after all, volunteer when I was seven. Do you know how very stupid and trusting children are?" Rowan ranted. "They look their executioners in the eye, seeking approval of how well they've laid their head on the chopping block. The trouble is, it seems, with age comes a desire not to always be sacrificed for one's sister."

"Rowan, I..." Her father's eyes were wide, horrified, and he shook his head helplessly, never quite looking Rowan's way.

"I don't care. I know who is the more worthy of us. And I will forgive you. Just not today." Rowan walked around her father, furious for having allowed herself the outburst.

It was more about Petal and what Rowan thought of herself than it was about her father.

Was it too much to ask for one piece of good news?

Petal

969 days until Roisin returns

*B*raden arrived a few days later. After every piece of bad news she had had lately, Rowan was so relieved, she rushed forward and threw her arms around him, holding on tightly as he stood stiffly in her arms.

"Rowan?" Braden choked out, his voice squeaking. "Rowan, are you all right?"

"I am so glad you are back." Rowan released Braden and stepped back. "You are all right, aren't you?"

"All in one piece," he said with a chuckle, looking around awkwardly. "Are you all right?"

Rowan simply stared at Braden, nodding her head, though she wasn't certain what he said. She was oblivious to the stares of his escorts or the servants around them. All she could see was that he was back and unharmed. One person she hadn't failed—yet.

"Come on." Braden took Rowan's arm, urging her away anxiously. He led her toward her rose garden. "What is wrong?"

"What isn't?" she said once they rounded a corner. "Ardal has been gone longer than you have and has not been heard from. I sent Tom after him, and he has not been heard from. I had Sean and Declan trailing Sorcha once she left your father's palace to find the entrance to her court, and they were attacked by a flock of hawks. Sean was thrown from his horse and trampled. He lost an arm. Declan lost an eye and a great deal of blood. He has been back two months, but only yesterday was he even able to sit up.

"I put people in danger." She shoved off Braden's hand, walking ahead of him. "It's bad enough what I asked of you, and so...cavalierly. As though it was nothing. But to ask it of..." Rowan drifted into silence. She couldn't say it.

"Can't ask it of whom? Never mind. It doesn't matter," he said when her face began to crumple. "You've never treated what I am doing cavalierly," Braden rushed to assure her. "Do you think I cannot tell how much it worries you? Your knights all volunteered. We know the risks and are proud to do it. Do not diminish our choices by acting as though you left us none."

"You are a man; my knights are men." Rowan and Braden stopped walking just outside the rose garden. She shook her head, trying to find the words to explain what she was thinking. "I don't mean to diminish your sacrifices. I know you want to stop my grandmother. But, how might you have done it differently if I had not been the one commanding? I do not think I ever want to be queen, not if this is what it asks of me."

"I wouldn't want to be queen here, either."

Rowan laughed, dropping her head. Trust Braden to make her laugh at a time like this.

"Read this." Rowan pulled Gavin's letter out of her pocket. She had taken to carrying it around with her. Looking at it at odd moments, trying to think of a better way.

She had never revealed the true nature of Gavin's letters to Braden. It was too dangerous for both of them. But if she did not tell someone, she would go insane.

"Petal," Braden said in shock. "He wants Petal? But she is just a girl. Barely more than a baby."

"I am not a baby," Petal snapped, appearing in the gateway to the garden.

Rowan groaned, her muscles knotting. Could she not protect the triplets from even the conversation?

Petal put her hands on her hips and glared at Rowan, more than a little hurt. "You are late."

"I am sorry. I forgot when Braden arrived."

"Humph."

"Petal," Braden began in a pleading voice, "I did not mean it that way. You know I think of you as a young lady. But…I would not let my sister do this, and she is married and has a child."

Petal, with a glare that would have suited a woman three times her age and all the dignity to go along with it, walked to where Braden stood and simply held out her hand for the letter.

"See here." She waved the letter about triumphantly. "It says I am powerful."

"It says we are powerful," Ferdy said from up on the ledge of the wall, startling Rowan. How was it she never sensed Ferdy? She could usually sense the others.

"You can read it from there?" Braden asked, impressed.

"He could hear me reading it in my mind. We can hear one another."

"Only if you let us." Keagan emerged from the garden.

"So she will be all right, because we will know when something is wrong," Ferdy said.

"And we can always find her," Keagan added.

"You have never been that far apart," Rowan pointed out, crouching so she was on the children's level. "I know you are powerful." Rowan looked Petal steadily in the eye. "You are by far the three most amazing creatures in the world. But you don't know what waits for you there. No one does. And you are only nine. There are so many things you cannot understand yet."

"You were made a knight when you were seven," Petal said in such a pleading voice that it was impossible not to see how very small and fragile she was. "I can be like you. I promise."

Rowan laughed sadly, wiping a tear away from her eye. "That is just it. I do not want you to be anything like me. Your father and mother would hate me if I let you become like me."

"They won't hate you." Petal reached forward to touch Rowan's hand. "Mama already knows I will go."

"She does?" Rowan drew back, appalled. Why hadn't Maureen come and told Rowan she hated her, tried to kill her? She should be furious.

"She said you told her before I was born. So when the fairy came to us and told us the prince's plan…"

"He went to your home? Without my permission?" Rowan jumped back to her feet, ready to kill.

"Rowan." Petal grabbed for her hand. "I want to rescue the little girls. No one else can help them."

"You will be the little girl there. All the others will be older than you. What makes you think you will even be able to persuade them to listen?"

Petal said nothing; she just smiled, with her head cocked to one side with an eyebrow raised.

Rowan laughed. "Swooning will not work as well with girls."

Petal shrugged, smirking. "I will think of something."

Rowan nodded. Petal looked at her expectantly, and her brothers did the same. All of them waited for her to turn to Petal and ask her to do this. But she wouldn't. Not yet.

"Come along." Rowan walked around Petal, past Keagan, and into the rose garden. "You need more practice."

Braden practiced with them that day and was thoroughly bruised by the end of it. None of the triplets appreciated Petal being called a baby. But once they had thoroughly injured him, they returned to liking him again. They were creatures of easy forgiveness.

There was to be a ball in three days' time, and Rowan had not yet said one word to her father. Whenever she had moments to herself, Rowan thought about that and the triplets' easy forgiveness.

It was not as though she could blame her father. She would pick Roisin, too, most days.

Then there were the days when she hated herself, more even then she hated her grandmother, because she was jealous of her sister. She would give anything to be loved so completely without reservation. With no one watching her in fear or wanting her to just be a little bit more ladylike or a little bit less pushy. Or just—better.

When she visited the Fairy circle last, she wished to trade places with her sister, live somewhere like that. In near solitude, with little to worry her besides the concerns of the local groundhog family.

Still, on her good days or bad, Rowan could not bring herself to forgive her father. He was the one person who should never turn on her. He was the thing within the walls of her home that stood between her and the growing number of Gwyneth's friends. All of whom were more than willing to sacrifice her to save the Rose Princess. Now, it seemed, she was alone.

966 days until Roisin returns

On the morning of her birthday ball, Rowan convinced Braden to train the triplets alone, so she could sneak away to see Maureen. There had been no chance to see her privately since Braden arrived. It was not a meeting she looked forward to.

When she entered the house, Maureen was waiting for her in her favorite chair with two cups of tea and a pot between.

Rowan walked in and sat. For a while it seemed they would remain so forever, silently regarding each other.

"I did not think seeing the future was a part of your gift," Rowan said for something to say.

"All Fairy sense little things. My gift is mostly for healing—you are right. I don't see the future. But I was holding my arms out to you when you entered the world. I can feel when you will come to me. And today I could feel you were troubled."

"I am sorry," Rowan said. And she did what she could with no one else— broke down sobbing. "I am so, so sorry. I won't ask her! I wouldn't do that. I won't."

"Oh, my dearest." Maureen came over to rest on the arm of Rowan's chair and wrap her in a soothing hug, softly brushing Rowan's long hair away from her face. She kissed her forehead. "I love you. That simply is; it will not stop."

"Why? Why do you love me?"

"Humph. Nonsense. Why do I love you? Why do you love your sister? Why do I love my children? Love does not need a reason; it doesn't even need to be returned. It's just there, like rain or sunshine, sometimes feeding us, sometimes beating us down."

Maureen shook her head, moving back to her seat as Rowan began drying her eyes. "I haven't always done well by you. It hurt so much to see you after your mother died, and your father never liked me. So I let that be a reason to leave you to him. I didn't know you very well until you were already such a lonely little thing. Do you remember the day you told me about your sister? Fourteen years ago. You told me about my children then, too."

"I know. But…"

"Let me finish. I didn't believe you. I had never seen you as powerful before, but also because of the way you said everything. As though you had peeked through some door into the future, and everything was beautiful. I'm not used to bright futures, but when you spoke, I heard peace in your voice. You weren't lonely any longer, because of what you had seen." Maureen nodded, squeezing her hands together until her fingers turned red. "Petal will be safe. You and I will be terrified and sad as we wait, but Petal will be safe."

Rowan didn't say anything. What could she say? Neither of them could know that. Rowan remembered her words from that day, but not what future she'd seen. And she had never been able to choose what parts of the future she saw. Just watching Maureen, her clenched hands, how very still she held herself, when she was never completely at rest even sleeping—Rowan could tell she knew it. She was trying to reassure Rowan.

Reaching out silently, Rowan lifted the cup to her lips and sipped her tea.

Eachann appeared before Rowan as she was heading down to the ball. She said nothing, not trusting herself to speak; she just took the letter out of his hands and began reading it there in the hall.

> *Rowan,*
>
> *I am asking you, despite all I know you already carry, to ask a small girl, you love, to take a risk with her life to save many others and help us to defeat a great evil. I ask, knowing full well that I could indeed flee with my people. And allow them to live as beggars*

210

and refugees among yours or any other people who would take them. Knowing as well that you may never forgive me.

I want those fifty-eight girls home. I want my people to have their homes, and some of their pride. But I could perhaps risk these things, depending on the success of your plan, because I trust you. What I cannot risk is you, forced to face the Fairy queen alone.

I have found no dragons.

I am searching. I have knights and soldiers searching, though they begin to think me insane. But I have found none.

It was a good plan when Eachann suggested it. But the part of it that appealed to me most was that here, at last, was a way to be assured, wherever you meet your grandmother, you are not friendless.

I am eternally your friend, and hopeful that you remain mine as well.

G—

Rowan folded the letter, slowly repeating the words in her head. How many times would she need to read them before she let his explanation be enough? Once was not enough.

"There will be no reply." Rowan turned away.

"Let it never be said that you do not know how to pout, little queen."

"Well, there you are then, Eachann." Rowan let her voice trail behind her as she walked away. "I am childish once more."

The ball was oddly festive, considering that the king did not speak, the princess felt like crying, and Petal, who was far too young to be there, was dancing as though she would never return.

Sadness and fear were good motivators for festivity. It lasted far longer than any of Gwyneth's other balls. Rowan, the triplets, and Braden simply refused to let the musicians leave. Petal never stopped dancing; Braden, playing the gallant knight, would not allow it.

When at last Petal began to fall asleep on her feet, Rowan carried her home, with Braden behind her, holding up the boys, who refused to be carried.

"Aren't balls the most wonderful thing in the world?" Petal yawned.

"Only when one is a girl like you, whom everyone wants to dance with," Rowan whispered to Petal, nearly asleep on her shoulder.

"Rowan," Petal sighed, settling her head on Rowan's shoulder and shutting her eyes, "if I work very hard, do you think I can become a knight before I go away?"

"I think," Rowan said slowly, "you can do anything you choose."

Enough Love

965 days until Roisin returns

*R*owan turned the corner into her rose garden, and she was once again in the Fairy circle. She did not want to be here tonight. It was not one of her better nights.

"You're late. It's nearly dawn," Roisin's lilting voice accused from behind Rowan.

She swung around; her sister was sitting on a low-hanging branch of a tree. Roisin looked different. Her hair hung long past her waist in a smooth wave, and even leaning as she was, she looked graceful.

"And you've changed," Rowan said flatly.

"Auntie A says this year has been good to me, but she does not think I will grow much taller," she said, looking down at herself. She had one leg folded up under herself and the other on the ground for balance, so it was hard to say exactly how tall she was—at least a foot shorter than Rowan.

"You are tall enough," Rowan said almost disinterestedly. There were many more complicated things on her mind than her sister's lack of height. "Women are expected to be delicate. You fit the description well."

"You are angry with me." Roisin shrank back a bit against the tree as she said this, her eyes swelling with tears.

"No." Rowan took a deep breath. What was wrong with her? She was turning into her grandmother, blaming Roisin for the curse. "I am sorry. It has been a long day."

"I did not think you would come," Roisin said flatly, straightening away from the tree to stand a few feet to Rowan's left.

"I thought you always knew?" Rowan asked, confused. Didn't she see the future?

"I used to dream of you all the time." She wouldn't face Rowan; as she spoke, she walked from tree to tree, running her hand along the trunks. "I don't as much anymore. Every time I dream of you here, you seem farther and farther away. I can barely see your face."

"But you do see me?"

"Yes. It's just..." Roisin's voice was choked, "in my dream, you didn't want to come. You wouldn't look at me."

"Well..." Rowan didn't know what to say. She should not have brought these feelings here. Almost better that she not come at all. "I am here now. And it's you who won't look at me."

Roisin looked over at her sister. She was fighting back tears, the way Rowan always had. Rowan had never seen her sister do so before. Roisin always accepted her feelings as natural. Without a word or a thought, Rowan walked forward and wrapped her sister in a tight hug, laying her lips against the top of Roisin's head.

"I am sorry. I have been very sad lately." Rowan spoke into her sister's hair. "I do not think I am always a good person when I am away from you. I miss you terribly. Sometimes I fear I will never see you again, or that I will, but you will see how ugly I am and won't want to see me ever again."

"It couldn't happen," Roisin said, pushing back far enough that she could see Rowan's face, but not leaving her arms. "You are the most beautiful, wonderful person in the world. I love you best of all."

Rowan's breath shuddered out as she bit back her tears of happiness. "I love you best of all too."

"Will you tell me why you are sad?"

"I..." Rowan was tired of hiding things, but here, now, was not the time to risk it. "I am sad because...I want someone to love me the way I love you, but he can't."

"The boy who gave you the bells?" Roisin asked excitedly.

In their last visit, Roisin had begun showing a decided interest in all things male or romantic. Since Rowan knew she had never met a boy, she had to assume the ideas came from one of Bride's books or Cianna's stories. Rowan shook her head at her sister—such a normal girl. It was odd. Rowan was twenty and rarely allowed herself to contemplate men, marriage, anything but the battle. When she did, it was always Gavin, but that was before. Now there was nothing but the battle on Rowan's mind. Roisin, however, at only thirteen, thought of little but love.

"No. Not him." Rowan laughed, almost resentfully. *Not him.*

"Who?"

"My father. He loves me; he just doesn't love me best of all."

"I'm sorry." Roisin wrapped her arms around Rowan.

"I'm not." Rowan kissed her sister on her head. "Not anymore. I just forgot for a while."

"Forgot?"

"That there is more than enough love to go around."

Dawn came only a few minutes later. It was their shortest visit by far, but Rowan thought perhaps it had been one of their best. Roisin was growing up; she would be a lovely young lady soon.

Rowan was no closer to making a sacrifice of Petal for her sister, no matter how innocent she was. But she came out of the Fairy circle willing to forgive her father. It had been so painful hearing his words that Rowan had forgotten how much more she had than he. She knew Roisin was safe, knew where she was, and most importantly, she knew who she was. Her father couldn't say the same; of course he would need to see Roisin grown just once.

When Rowan reached her room, there was a small box waiting on her bed with a note.

> *My Darling Rowan,*
>
> *I do not know how to ask your forgiveness. There is nothing I can say to explain or excuse what I did, what I said. I never knew fear until the day you were born. I stood beside your mother, holding her hand, every second terrified that you would not survive. Then I held you in my arms, so helpless, and I could only imagine the millions of ways the world might hurt you, the ways I might hurt you.*

This is one way I could not have imagined.

I should have taught you to celebrate your life, but I don't seem to know how. I've been too busy wallowing in all the ways I have already failed you. Letting your mother die, letting your grandmother near you.

I thought it was all a dream. A horrible, disgusting dream, the conversation we had. Everything I said to you. I am so sorry.

I allowed myself to believe it was a dream, because surely if I had said such things to you, you could not have been so calm. So loving still that you would just lead me off to bed as if I had not wounded you irreparably.

I have no words to fix this. I still cannot say you are worth more than your sister. My love for both of you will not allow that. But you are worth a million of me. Or any other person I know.

This crystal pendant belonged to your grandmother, my mother. She wore it all the time. It was given to her by the last of the dragons before they left this land. A gift for freeing their children from captivity. I was never allowed to wear it. I had not proven myself a defender of those weaker than I.

I should have given it to you when you were seven. No one, even my mother, is more worthy than you.

I love you.
Your father

Rowan opened the box and lifted the necklace up by its silver chain. At the end was what looked like a hollowed-out prism. In the violent orange light of the morning, filtering through Rowan's window, it glowed like fire.

She reached out a finger and ran it along the smooth surface, not at all surprised to find it warm to the touch.

Rowan had seen her grandmother depicted in a portrait wearing this necklace, with her baby son in her arms. That grandmother had been a warrior, too; it was clear in her stance, though she had appeared very womanly. Standing before the rowan tree that was in the rose garden, with her son in her arms.

There were no bench or roses in the portrait, but Rowan knew that tree well; she could never mistake it.

Rowan slipped the necklace around her neck; the crystal rested against her chest, warming her. She felt more a part of her own family in that moment than ever before. It was enough.

Rowan found the triplets practicing with Braden in the field beyond her garden and stole Keagan for a special project. He was oddly hesitant for a boy who read minds. She led him off into a private room in the palace and sat him down.

"I have a favor to ask of you. I don't know if it can be done, but if anyone can do it, it would be you."

"I will do whatever you say," Keagan said bravely, looking as though he would be asked to die.

"Can you see people's thoughts?" Rowan asked. "Or only hear them?"

"I don't know. Sometimes I see things, memories they have."

"If I thought about a memory, very hard, do you think you could draw it?"

Keagan sat very still, focusing on something. "Show me," he said.

Rowan thought about Roisin as she had first seen her last night perched on the tree branch.

Keagan nodded. "Let me get my things. I can draw that."

Several hours later, Rowan went to her father's private study. He watched sadly, afraid to speak, as Rowan approached. Rowan laid Keagan's sketch on the table.

"This is what Roisin looks like now," Rowan said. Before he could question her, she rushed ahead with the story she had made up. "I see her in my dreams, talk to her, even."

"Rowan…" He did not even reach for the picture; his hands curled up on the desk, as if forcing himself still. Rowan clenched up, unnerved.

"I said it would pass," Rowan said with a shrug; she did not want to talk about what had happened. "Thank you for the necklace. You never talk about your mother. I almost forgot I had another grandmother."

"I know." The king sighed. "I will do better."

He looked like he would speak again, and Rowan felt it would be another attempt to explain. She had forgiven him, but she couldn't stand to hear it one more time.

"She loves animals," Rowan interrupted him, pointing at the picture. Slowly he looked away from Rowan, lifting the sketch and absorbing it, letting it feed him. "She misses you and her life here, even though she doesn't really remember it. She is beautiful, but she doesn't seem to think so. It's strange; you would think someone so beautiful would be unable to doubt it. She wants to be taller; she only just reaches my shoulder."

"That isn't so short," the king said, looking up from the sketch and attempting a smile. Willing as well to change the subject. "You are a tall woman."

"I know." Rowan looked away for a moment. How much more could she tell him? "I know you worry for her, but you cannot repeat any of this to anyone. If my grandmother comes to you again—"

"I will not tell her. I do not know how she tricked me before. She kept talking about how you would suffer, how you both would suffer, if I did not help her. After a while, it was as though I thought death would be better than whatever she had planned for you."

Rowan nodded but did not respond. Of course death would be better. That did not mean they should give in.

"I promise, I won't tell her anything. I won't tell anyone."

"Even Gwyneth," Rowan said firmly. "She is even more susceptible than you. It is too big a risk. She could get Roisin hurt trying to help her."

"Not even Gwyneth." The king nodded.

As she spoke with her father, Rowan caught herself rubbing the old thorn scars on her right palm. She remembered that day so clearly. The fight, the absolute sorrow as the roses burned, as if he was killing her mother right there in front of her. And then, even through the sadness and pain, how safe she felt when her father lifted her into his arms and carried her away. When had that changed? Not when he told her about his deal with her grandmother—before that. They had been growing apart for a long time now.

It would probably never be like that again.

"Do you know," her father said, breaking into Rowan's thoughts, "you remind me of my mother? She had hair like yours; that cool brown, with bits of fire running through it. And she had this way about her of either completely putting people off or making them love her."

Rowan let out a half laugh. "Well, I'm certainly good at the first part."

"You're loved, Rowan. Well loved." They were exactly the words she should want to hear, the kind that should comfort her, fill her with joy, but there was something missing. Rowan could not say what, but it stopped the words from truly warming her.

"I think...as worried as I was to see you fighting with the knights," her father continued, "what bothered me most was how much they all love you. Colum, Ardal, Cassidy. They look at you like you are their little girl. I suppose I worried you would grow to love them more than me."

Rowan shook her head, not sure what to say. There were times when she wished one of them was her father. Not because she loved them more, but because they understood her as her father never would.

"Well, we should both stop worrying," Rowan said with a shrug. "There seems to be enough love to go around."

From My Treasures

*R*owan trained with the triplets every day for three hours. But she insisted that every day, for as many hours, they all play together. They went horseback riding, climbed trees, hid in halls or behind trees, and launched sneak attacks, throwing globs of mud or stewed carrots or buckets of water on unsuspecting passersby. It was more fun than Rowan could ever remember having. Not for the first time, she found herself jealous of everyone who grew up with a sibling.

All four knew they were simply delaying what would come. But it did not seem to stop them from embracing the momentary joys wholeheartedly.

955 days until Roisin returns

Braden remained an extra week; still, Rowan did not want him to go.

"I have a bad feeling. I don't think you should go back."

"I'll be safe. If anything, I'll be safer than before. For all my guards to see you ran up and threw yourself into my arms. They're not going to keep that to themselves. It will appear I'm winning you over."

"Just promise you will be careful. Do not openly disobey anything the Fairy queen asks of you. She has to think she has you cowed."

"I know, Rowan. I have been doing this for some time now." He nodded, holding her gaze soothingly and squeezing her hand between his own.

"So had Ardal," Rowan said flatly, and her stomach dropped in fear for Braden.

"He may yet return."

Rowan nodded. But refused to speak. She had no hope of that. But those were not the words one left a soldier with when one sent him into battle.

"Just take care of yourself. You are no good to me dead."

"Words to live by." Chuckling, Braden rushed over to where his guards waited and stopped her speaking more. He seemed to want nothing more than to be away from her.

With Braden gone, it was harder for Rowan to distract herself from the passage of time, every day closer to April. To the day she would have to decide, once and for all, if she would ask Petal to go or not. It didn't help that Gavin continued to write her, even though she would not respond.

> *Dear Rowan,*
>
> *I noticed something in your old letters. A few things; I have taken to rereading them, since you've stopped writing me.*
>
> *You always refer to the Fairy queen as your grandmother. It seems odd. You only met her once, and I cannot imagine it left a positive impression on you. Why claim her as family?*

Rowan's mind stalled, and her grip on the page loosened; even now, when she hated him, Gavin had a way of reaching inside her and making Rowan face herself. She had to call Sorcha her grandmother for no reason more than that Sorcha refused to claim her.

> *Another thing I realized—you do not want to be queen. Many people fear the responsibility, but I cannot imagine that is the case with you. What is it? You are not one who runs from a challenge. Honestly, after everything you have done and plan to do, I cannot imagine being sovereign will be any challenge.*
>
> *I wonder if you don't feel at home in Stonedragon. You write about being less Fairy than your sister, and never fully human, as though these are bad things. They are part of what makes you who you are. You have*

always stood apart. Always will. Can't you see that standing apart, being something new, gives you so many more possibilities? You can be anything.

No. Rowan forced back tears, shoving them beneath her anger, her resentment. She could be only *one* thing. Do only *one* thing. How was it he failed to see that? Even as he was asking her to risk Petal toward that *one* goal.

There are no limits set on who or what you can become. It is up to you to set your limits.

Rowan, I am sorry for what I asked. I would not have done so if I did not think she would be safe. I cannot make you any promises. So I cannot expect you to simply agree. I expect nothing from you. If your answer is no, I more than understand.
I remain, as always, your friend,
G—

Dear Rowan,

I have not been doing any imagining for you lately. I have trouble myself coming up with any stories that end well. The world is troubled, and it makes for troubled stories. But I do have a true story, which I find quite amusing.

I told you my brother was to be married. What I didn't tell you is that my mother was vehemently opposed to the union. I believe it is because my father still remains silent. It is arduous trying to pry her from his side.

In any event, to put off the marriage, my mother insisted that my brother's bride be put through the princess trials. "It is an old family tradition to be certain a woman is ready to rule," she insisted to our guests, but every member of the family knew at once that she was lying. The princess trials are something my uncle invented, to make the people of our kingdom accept my mother as a princess.

They are secret tests, in three parts, said to determine if a woman possesses the three traits of womanhood most desirous in a queen:

gentility, grace, and delicacy. My mother, it is assumed, would never have passed these had not my uncle told her exactly what to do.

Kayla, on the other hand, is everything that is gentle and ladylike. She had no difficulty passing the tests. Rather absurdly, my mother jumped to her feet and declared Kayla a fraud. My mother, the original fraud.

There was a great uproar, as she did this in front of Kayla's family. It took days, and me explaining that my mother was naturally distraught over my father. But eventually all was straightened out, and they are indeed married.

But my mother is still unsatisfied. She is demanding I come up with other tests to prove her worthy. Or, I imagine, to prove her unworthy.

I hope you enjoyed the story.

As ever, your friend,

G—

It was the sort of letter that would have left Rowan curled up in an alcove, rereading it time and again, laughing and wishing she were there. Would have, but she read it all numbly now. Angrily. Relating better to his mother than anyone else. Of course she wanted to be rid of the girl. The man she loved was trapped, there but not, never a part of their lives. How did they just keep going on? It horrified her, the idea that if she did as Gavin asked, one day Ferdy, or Keagan, might fall in love and marry without their sister there to see it. She shoved the letter into a box with the rest of them, more from habit than anything else. Once they were her escape, but not so anymore.

878 days until Roisin returns

It was January; every day Rowan felt worse and was disgusted with herself for feeling she had the right to feel bad at all.

If anyone had a right to feel bad, it was Petal. But she refused to show any fear. She tried to appear stoic, modeling herself on Rowan. The more she tried to be like Rowan, the worse Rowan felt. This was the little girl who always had a smile on her face. The girl who never met a problem she could not charm her way out of.

In the second week of January, Rowan watched Petal, in an attempt to be brave and adult, refuse to cry. She had slipped while practicing with Ferdy and slammed her head against the ground. Rowan watched her struggle to her feet, biting her lip to keep from making a noise, and decided she had seen enough.

"Boys, go home," Rowan ordered and walked over, scooping Petal into her arms. For once, the boys did not even make a peep; turning away, they marched home.

"Pretty soon you will be too big to carry this way." Rowan held her with one arm around her back, Petal's head resting on her shoulder, and the other arm under Petal's knees to keep her steady.

"Where are we going?" she asked in a tiny voice, fighting back tears.

"To the place where I keep my most sacred and secret possessions."

"Like what?"

"You'll see." Rowan leaned her head against Petal's as she walked, not speaking. Petal sniffled, burrowing her head into the crook of Rowan's neck.

She carried Petal into the palace and up two flights of steps—not quite panting, but well aware that she soon would be—and all the way into the old family wing of the palace. It had not been used since Rowan magically crumpled away her wall when she was six. It could not be fixed properly. The king worried that something must be wrong with the whole structure and ordered it closed. Rowan carried Petal right into her old room, stopping to set Petal on the bed.

"This used to be my room." Rowan walked to the long wooden, folding doors that stood in place of her old wall. She pulled the doors aside, so they rested against either wall. "I did this," she said with a bit of awe and a great deal of amusement, indicating the empty space where a wall should be.

"You did?" Petal slipped off the bed, walking over to Rowan, a foot from the sheer edge, and slipped her hand into Rowan's. "Why?"

"I was angry." Rowan sat, dangling her legs over the edge. Petal sat beside her, hesitantly, trying to force herself to stretch her legs over the edge. "No." Rowan gently pushed Petal back a bit, turning to her right so they were facing.

"You are not me, Petal. No matter how strong or stoic you become, you never will be."

Petal's face began to crumple. Rowan resisted the urge to hug her, smiling down at her instead.

"When I did this, I was angry because my father wouldn't let me go to your parents' wedding. I destroyed the wall and sat here pouting, waiting for my father to come and find me so I could show him he could not control me. I could have hurt someone. I could have been hurt. But I didn't care, because I was sad and angry. I still do stupid things like this." Rowan shook her head, looking down the hill from the palace clear into the valley. There were several rolling hills, and the tiny shapes of the village a few miles away. Rowan glanced back at the crumbled edge of her wall, thinking of all the stupid things she did on a regular basis because she was angry or hurt.

"One of my favorite things about you, Petal, is how very different you are from me. You can charm anyone. You have a smile that is brighter than the sun, and more devious than Ferdy's."

Petal laughed in spite of herself.

"I love *you*. Not a tiny version of me. That's who I need you to be, Petal. Spectacular, powerful, devious, happy Petal."

"You mean I can't be a knight?" Petal said sadly.

"I mean you have to be your own knight. But I think…maybe no more fighting."

"Why? I like it."

"You do not," Rowan said with a laugh. "Ferdy likes it. Keagan tolerates it, and you hate it. The Petal I fell in love with, before I even knew her, fainted to avoid conflict and charmed people with her smile when she was caught robbing them blind. Be that Petal."

"But how will I save the girls if I am not strong like you?"

Rowan paused. Whenever Petal pushed the topic to any specific mention of what was to come, Rowan deflected. Putting her off made it feel less real.

"You will do it by being strong like you." Rowan forced herself to say the words, to consider what she didn't want to. "You bring out the best of goodness and talent in everyone around you. That is what you will do with the girls. You will help them to rescue themselves."

Petal made no response, laying her head on Rowan's shoulder.

"Is this your most sacred and secret possession?" Petal asked after a minute.

Rowan laughed. Pushing Petal even farther from the edge until she was against one of the walls, Rowan stood and walked back to her bed. She bent down. "Come here to me, my heart," she whispered, and a box slid out from beneath the bed into her hands.

"Now, some of these you will recognize," Rowan said once she sat and pulled open the box.

Petal dug through the box, lifting out each thing and holding it up for Rowan to explain. "The shamrock I gave you! And Keagan's picture. A rose?"

"I picked this rose because it reminded me of my sister's hair. And this is a ribbon your mother braided into my hair one year as she told me the story of my birth. This dagger, your father gave me when I was eight. I was following him around, doing everything he did; he sat down and began eating an apple with this, cutting it up into little pieces and handing them to me. He handed me the knife when the apple was gone and asked me to hold on to it for next time. But I hid it away instead."

Petal smiled. "You are a thief, too."

"Yes. But not nearly as subtle." Rowan chuckled.

"Who are the letters from?"

"My friend Gavin." Rowan shoved the letters aside. She did not want to think about him just now. "And here is a little portrait of my mother that my father gave to me when I was a baby. And this rose..." Rowan picked up a slightly burnt, dried rose. She lined its thorns up along the scars on her right hand. "This rose made these scars. It was the very last rose left the first time my father burned my mother's garden."

"How sad." Petal ran one finger along the burnt edge of the rose petals. And a tear escaped her eye. "Why would he burn something so beautiful?"

"He thought they would swallow the castle whole."

"They were only trying to protect it."

"I know. But he didn't understand that," Rowan said, amazed as always by how this little girl understood things that baffled adults. "Sometimes when people don't understand something, they get scared and try to destroy it."

"Is that why the bad queen wants to destroy your sister? Because you gave her your magic, and she doesn't understand?"

"Do you know, I have never thought of that. But you just might be right."

Rowan stared out the open wall into the distance. Could it all be so simple? And her own fault? Would it never have happened if she had not given Roisin a little bit of eternity?

"Rowan." Petal drew Rowan's attention back, and looked earnestly into Rowan's eyes. "Mama said that it hurts you inside to think of asking me, because you do not want me to go. But you don't have to ask. I will go."

"Oh, Petal. You are the sweetest creature in all the world. But it can't be that way."

"Why?"

"Because you and I are friends. We should have the truth between us. And because there is something distinctly powerful in doing something for someone you love simply because they have asked you to. And for one other reason." Because she wanted something from her grandmother. Something bad that she had tried not to want. But something she was going to ask for nonetheless. "I will tell you after dinner."

"Why after dinner?"

"Because right now, you are here for a reason. I brought you to choose a talisman. Something that will remind you why you are doing what you are doing and will keep you safe."

"From your treasures?" Petal's eyes widened, and her voice took on a reverent tone.

"From my treasures," Rowan agreed, pushing the box a bit closer to Petal.

Petal sorted through each thing very carefully, taking her time to lift up and examine each piece in its turn. Once she had touched each and every piece, she pulled her hands out of the box and sat back, observing Rowan hesitantly.

"Could I have," she began, pausing just a moment to look in the box as if reaffirming her choice, "just one petal from the burnt rose?"

"Petal, you may have the entire rose."

"No. Just one petal will be fine. Like me. I am only one petal."

Rowan let out a small puff of charmed laughter.

"All right. A petal for Petal it is. But we must come up with a way for you to carry it. Will you show me how you made the ball that carries my shamrock?"

"Ooo, it isn't a ball. It's a dewdrop. We shall have to find another."

"Let's go, then."

With Petal leading the way back down the stairs and out of the palace, they searched for a dewdrop to hold the one pink rose petal with a burnt tip that Petal had chosen as her talisman. Petal showed Rowan the art of calling a dewdrop to float in the air and blowing bits of air into it until it stretched out to the size they needed.

When it was finished, Rowan kept the talisman, saying she would have it hung on a chain, and she sent Petal running home with a message. There was to be a small dinner in Petal's honor at the castle that night, and the whole family must come by the king's finest coach, as they were the honored guests.

It Is Done

*C*olum found Rowan in the great hall, organizing, shortly before it was time for the dinner.

"What is this about a dinner?" Colum asked. "The children said we're to come to the palace by coach. It's barely a great enough distance to fit a horse and coach into."

Rowan laughed. "Your home is not quite that close. I wanted the children to feel as special as they are."

"I see." Colum looked a bit awkward. He and Rowan had not been on the best of terms lately. He regretted what he had said to her. But there was no going back. "What happened to the sickly and frail boys you promised me?" He tried to lighten the mood. "Both my sons came to me today, demanding to be made squires. They told me if they did not start soon, they would not be made Knights of the Rose in time to help."

Rowan shook her head, looking away. He was trying to have their old friendship back. And she was going to betray it. Tonight.

"Colum, I am sorry that I am not more careful with myself. But there was nothing you could have done. Even before I met you, I was this way. I felt invincible, so what need was there for caution?" He looked taken aback; she could not blame him. Rowan rarely admitted that someone could be right where she was wrong.

"I am not careful with myself. Or much of anything. I am sorry you cannot approve of it, but it does seem to be who I am. I want you to know, before things change, I understand why it is you cannot accept my...recklessness. And I love you all the same. You, your whole family, you have been my family, and my friends, when I felt I had none. I will always be grateful for it. I am sorry I couldn't do what you wanted. It never mattered to me what the knights called me. Nothing could be worse than my grandmother calling me poison. Or people who should have loved me most telling me I must sacrifice myself for my sister."

"Rowan, I was harsh. All I ever meant to say was that I worried your allowance of the taunting and disrespect was a sign that you had begun to believe some of it." Colum leaned closer as he spoke, lowering his voice as his eyes pled for Rowan to contradict him.

Rowan shook her head. "Well, I do tend to ruin perfectly happy lives."

Colum stepped toward her, reaching out. "Rowan, Ardal may yet return." Rowan stiffened, fighting the urge to cry. This was so much worse than Ardal. "Even if he does not, you are not a poison," he said firmly.

"Yes, I am." Rowan shrugged. "But I begin to suspect I will need to be in order to stop my grandmother."

"Rowan. Stop this. I will not allow you to say these things about yourself."

"Wait until after dinner." Rowan fled the hall. She couldn't tell him, not face-to-face, what she would do to his little girl.

Rowan would have liked to exclude Gwyneth from the dinner, but it was rather difficult to exclude a queen from eating at her own table. The rest of the guests Rowan had selected herself. Only her closest allies were invited: every Knight of the Rose in the kingdom: Cassidy, Liam, Declan, Sean, and their families, Maureen and hers, and of course her father.

The long table was strewn with rose petals of various colors, and the hall was lit by hundreds of flickering candles. Rowan made certain every other guest had arrived before she sent word for Petal and her family to be picked up. Colum was right. The distance was tiny. No sooner had Rowan ordered the carriage than her guests were announced. Everyone in the great room took to their feet to cheer.

Rowan thought she might have made it all just a bit too extravagant, but the look on Petal's face reassured her. It didn't matter what anyone else thought.

When the dinner was nearly over, Rowan nodded to her knights; one by one they slipped from the room, Rowan last of all. They went to a small antechamber where servants waited with everyone's armor and Rowan's crown. It would be the first time she wore the crown with her armor, as a king would when knighting one of his men. It was a strange feeling. Heavy, but this was the right time.

The knights returned first, taking up positions behind Petal and her family. Before Rowan stepped out, she sealed the room with a spell so that none but the guests could hear the words.

Rowan stepped onto the dais that held the thrones. Everyone quieted.

"Thank you all for being present on this important occasion." Rowan looked around the room. She had a speech prepared, but she wasn't sure she could get through it. "For much of my life, I had trouble understanding what it means to be part of a family. I stand apart. For many reasons: I will be queen, I am a woman, I am half Fairy." Rowan looked from group to group as she said this. "But whatever the reason, that separation taught me to take on my challenges alone. Over and over I failed to understand that I needed help or how to ask for help. But time and again, in my hour of need, whether I had asked or not, some member of this special family found me and came to my aid. Because that is what a family does."

Rowan looked from one member of the family to the next through gathering tears. *It has to be done. It has to be done, and I must do it.*

"Today, at last, I have learned my lesson, and I will ask for the help I need. We all feel the battle coming. It is building in the ground and in the air, so we walk through the fog of our anticipation. I would face it all alone." Rowan was not sure if she was trying to assure them of the truth of her words or begging them to understand. "But I fear I would fail you."

Rowan looked around the room at all her greatest supporters, noting with sadness the people who were not there. And the things that had already been lost by those who were.

"This battle will require something of all of us if we are to succeed. I called you here today to witness an act of enormous courage and to join me in honoring the greatest among us. Petal, please step forward."

As soon as she said it, her knights fell into two rows behind Petal, the front two, Sean and Cassidy, helping Petal stand. Once she stood centered in front of the knights, they escorted Petal to the dais.

Ferdy and Keagan watched it all with great excitement, brimming over with pride. On their right, Maureen struggled to contain her tears; Colum sat on the other side of the boys and looked confused, agitated. Rowan would not put it past him to march to the stage and grab his daughter back. She half hoped he would.

"Come; stand beside me, so everyone can see." Rowan held out a hand for Petal.

"Petal, child of my friend and sister of my heart, I stand beside you humbled by your bravery, to offer you the gravest of thanks for the risk you are about to take. That you, the smallest of us, should take upon yourself so much, not for glory but for the good of others, exalts you above us all. I offer you this small token as a show of my gratitude."

Rowan stopped speaking and lifted a small pouch that hung from her side. She reached two fingers inside and lifted the silver chain that held Petal's talisman.

"For you, by your choice, I offer this talisman. A petal, off the last rose from the first burning of the garden. A resilient petal—for our Petal. May it keep you safe when we cannot." Rowan bent down and placed the necklace around Petal's neck.

"Kneel, Petal." Rowan turned to her throne; a red rose, with a stem two feet long, lay across it. Rowan lifted the rose like she would a sword, with the flower for the tip. "You are no ordinary child, and no ordinary honor would suit you. Petal, for the great honor you have done us with your offer of service and for the wholesome goodness that resides within your heart, we lay upon you our greatest honor and bid you rise. Petal the Powerful, Knight of the Rose, and Duchess of Stonedragon. We are in your debt."

There was a moment of startled silence. No one knew exactly what was happening. Cassidy's eyes darted between Petal and her father, his friend, anxiously. Others looked dumbfounded. But once the king stood and began cheering, the rest followed suit. Rowan had not told him what was happening, but of late, he made a habit of simply supporting whatever Rowan did. Once the applause had died down, Rowan took a knee next to Petal and turned the beaming girl to face her.

"Petal, I must ask you to take on a dangerous task," Rowan said more quietly, her voice breaking. Around the room, there was absolute silence. "For several years, the Fairy queen has taken girls of your age from the kingdom of Turrlough and spirited them away. We...I ask you to go to Turrlough and allow yourself to be taken to the Fairy queen. To attempt to free the girls she has taken. And also, if you may do it without danger, to steal from the Fairy queen something that will help us to free others from her evil."

No one but Petal would know exactly what it was Rowan wanted stolen. She barely allowed herself to think of it. It was too dangerous. But if anyone could steal it, it was Petal.

Rowan had prepared this speech for hours, but there was no way to prepare for how acid and vile the words tasted on her tongue.

Petal nodded, having lost her voice.

"You are deserving of greatness, Petal, and this is only the beginning of what I shall give you when you return safely to us. I am now and forever in your debt."

"You cannot do this!" Colum charged out of his seat toward the stage. "She is only a child. You cannot ask that of her."

Rowan did not even attempt to defend herself. She motioned Cassidy off when he moved to restrain his friend. Colum climbed the steps of the dais, grabbing hold of Rowan's arm, pulling her to her feet before him. Around the room, people were on their feet to restrain Colum or to support Petal; Rowan could not tell which. She did not care, either; all there was in the world was her and her oldest friend at odds.

"This is what you meant?" he shouted. "This is why you go to such extravagance for her? A last meal?"

Rowan shook her head, horrified and oblivious to the tears rushing down her face. "No..."

"Colum. Enough." Maureen stepped through the knights, laying a hand on her husband.

"Enough? Enough? It can never be enough." He knocked aside his wife's hand and continued to shake Rowan. "You are asking of my little girl what you would never do yourself."

"That isn't true, Papa." Petal tried to step between her father and Rowan. "She can't do this."

"Can't?" He scoffed. Releasing Rowan's arms, he took a step back, gazing on her with eyes full of disgust. "So this at last is the one thing Rowan the Eternal cannot do. How convenient. Well, you cannot have my daughter."

Rowan nodded once, silently. Her eyes never left Colum's face, but he would not look at her any longer.

You poison everything you touch.

"I already promised, Papa," Petal said in a pleading voice.

"You are a child; you do not make your own decisions!" Colum yelled.

"My love," Maureen whispered. "I should have told you before now. Come; I will explain."

"Explain?" Colum threw off his wife's hand, staring at her with dawning horror. "You are a part of this? You? Her mother? You would send her to the place you swore never to return?"

Rowan stood frozen and watched Colum turn on his wife with disgust in his eyes. Her doing.

You poison everything you touch.

"Thank you!"

Rowan jerked around at the words. Gwyneth was down on her knees in front of Petal, grasping her hand as though it would save her from death. "I am in your debt forever. Thank you."

Rowan looked on, oddly detached. Gwyneth did not stop at thanking Petal; she threw herself at Maureen's feet, as well, thanking her and blessing her for raising her children. At the feet of a servant—Gwyneth had never done something so humble.

The king, too, stepped up to Petal, bowing before her.

"You honor us all."

Rowan saw the knights come one by one to the stage and bow in front of Petal, praising her bravery. But through it all, she felt Colum, her oldest friend, looking at her with hatred.

Two days later, a letter arrived again from Gavin. Without opening it, Rowan walked to a desk and penned a short response, handing it to Eachann without a word.

> *Gavin, High Prince of Turrlough,*
>> *It is done.*
>> *One spy or one sacrifice will be yours by the end of April.*
>> *I hope it is worth the cost.*

My Oldest Friend

*I*t took over a month to even convince Colum to hear his wife out. In that time, he slept in the stables, going home only to see his children and collect his clothes. He tried every day to convince Petal she could not go, that she did not have to. Rowan hoped he would succeed. People never saw solutions unless they were forced to. Perhaps if she were forced, she would find a way around sending Petal.

When Colum finally sat down to listen, it was clear he did this only because he knew of no way to stop his children doing anything they had set their minds to. Ferdy and Keagan, despite their father's sudden insistence they would never be knights, had continued to train. No one saw very much of them except the knights they were squired to, and Petal, who refused to be very far from them until it was time for her to leave.

There was a first conversation. That ended much the same way as the dinner. And a second, in which he threatened to kidnap his daughter, if it required putting her to sleep with potions and keeping her that way for the next two years. And a third, in which he broke down and sobbed. But nothing changed. He refused to come home, Petal refused to stay, and Maureen and the boys refused to stop supporting Petal's decision.

You poison everything you touch.

Rowan could no longer banish the words. Even for a moment. When she breathed, the words came into her with the air; when she slept, they settled over her like a blanket. She could look nowhere without seeing something to remind her just how poisonous she was.

The happiest family in the kingdom was in tatters—her doing. Two knights missing, probably dead—her doing. Two knights irreparably injured—her doing. A friend in danger as a spy—her doing. A child about to be the same—her doing.

The only positive things to be seen were so bizarre, Rowan didn't know what to make of them. All she knew was they were definitely not her doing. Gwyneth had taken a personal interest in Petal and her family, in all the Knights of the Rose. She made certain they had everything they needed, acting as everything from nurse to servant to friend. She could not speak of them more kindly—of Rowan, also. Everywhere she went, she spoke of what a good sister she was, what a fine queen she would make, what an excellent leader.

The more kindly Gwyneth spoke of her, the more Rowan wanted nothing to do with her. After all these years, for it to only now occur to her stepmother that everything she did was to see Roisin safe, was offensive, and more than a little suspicious.

808 days until Roisin returns

Rowan approached Maureen's home one morning almost a week before Petal would leave, and saw Colum storming out of the house in the direction of the stables. She planned to hide from Gwyneth at Maureen's for a few hours, but changed her mind. Colum was her friend, and he was right. She could not let him remain so alone.

She followed him into the stables, as she had as a child. And just like before, no matter how quiet she was, he knew she was there.

"I want nothing to do with you, Your Majesty," he snapped with his back to her.

"I know. I am sorry."

"Do you think your regret changes anything at all?" he demanded, spinning around to yell in her face.

Rowan stood her ground. "No."

"How could you? How could *you*? After everything you were put through, everything that was asked of you? How could you put this on her?" He was only a little taller than Rowan, but in his anger, he towered over her. "Answer. I want to know. How could you do this?"

"Because she would have gone anyway."

"No. Don't you dare feed me excuses like that. You asked her. Knowing she would do anything for you." Rowan shut her eyes, seeing Petal's earnest little face promising that she could be just like Rowan, and her heart sank. "Why? Are you that selfish?"

Rowan couldn't speak. Her stomach was roiling in revolt; she didn't want to hear any more. Colum was the first person who ever seemed to have any faith in her, ever seemed to understand her. And he hated her now.

You poison everything you touch.

"Yes," Rowan choked out, "I am. My grandmother took everything away from me. And I want to take the last thing she loves." Rowan barely held back the rage that had been eating at her since her father told her of Sorcha's deal. Barely held in the secret of what Petal would steal, snarling, "Petal is the only one who can get it for me. So I asked her."

"Do you even hear yourself?" Colum shook as he spoke. "Sorcha didn't take anything from you. She didn't have to. You are already throwing it away!" He turned around and marched out of the stables.

Rowan stood for a long while, just staring after him.

Was that what she was doing, throwing everything she had away?

Rowan received a letter from Gavin that day. She almost didn't open it. But what if he wrote that the girls had miraculously returned home?

> *Dear Rowan,*
>
> *I take it no one has ever said this to you.*
>
> *It will be worth it. If it helps you, spares your life, it will be worth it. You alone are worth any cost. Even if that cost is your friendship.*

Eachann tells me you did not read my letter before responding. And your silence since tells me you have not read it at all. Read it. Answer my questions. What am I to do with your knights?
G—

Rowan tore through her desk until she found the still unopened letter from Gavin. Scanning it quickly, Rowan found what she looked for. Two knights had been found near death and brought to the palace.

They were alive! Tom was alive, and so was Ardal.

Rowan nearly began crying as bits of hope bubbled up inside her. All was not lost. Ardal was alive! She hugged the knowledge to her heart, one lone assurance that she might still win: they might all be together again—happy.

Unbanished Words

*T*he news that Tom and Ardal lived changed everything. Plans were made quickly. Maureen would go for the wounded, nearly dead men, and heal them as best she could. But that meant she would not be here when Petal left.

Unless Petal went early.

"I will take Petal with me now," Maureen informed Rowan amid a flurry of activity. Maureen was racing about her cottage, gathering things she might need and setting everything to rights. She didn't look Rowan's way, even as she spoke, so Rowan knew the idea left her on edge. She was coming to better read the little things Maureen hid.

"She was meant to be here another week." Rowan wasn't so much protesting as she was trying to calm the churning chaos within. How was it she had continued to hope something still might prevent Petal going? If she was such a frantic mess, how badly must Maureen feel? How would Colum feel? "We were to have a ball in her honor when Braden arrived."

"Save the ball for her return," Maureen snapped and froze just as she was, with a cup in one hand and a scarf in the other. Her whole body was shaking.

Carefully Rowan walked forward and wrapped her arms around Maureen, hugging her from behind. Maureen raised a hand to her lips to stifle a sob.

"She will come home," Maureen whispered, her body shaking even harder. "I don't know why; I was so calm before, but now..."

"She will come home." Rowan forced her voice to be strong and confident, even though she felt weak and shaky within.

"Colum!" Maureen screamed and shook off Rowan's arms. "I must tell him."

"I'm sorry," Rowan whispered, her eyes skating away from Maureen. Things had not improved much between Colum and Maureen; she shouldn't have to tell him. "He is only going to be angrier with you."

"Rowan," Maureen sighed, "would you love him quite as well if he were not furious with us? This is not an easy situation; he should be angry. But…I think my going with her, at least in this beginning, will be a comfort to him. She will not leave home for the first time completely alone." Maureen reached out for Rowan's hand and squeezed. "I must hurry if we mean to leave this evening. I will always love you, and so does he."

Rowan nodded and watched Maureen vanish from the room. Rowan wasn't so sure Maureen was right about Colum's feelings toward her; he'd made his anger quite clear. He would never forgive her, at least…Rowan's stomach churned violently as she turned toward the family rooms. The only hope of Colum forgiving her was if Petal came home safely.

Rowan found Petal in her room, packing a small bag.

"Petal." Rowan stood in the doorway, her whole being at war with what she was doing. "I know what I've asked of you. But you do not have to do it. I will love you as much, even more than I love you right this second, if you decide to stay."

Petal shook her head. "I see the little girls sometimes when I sleep. They are scared; they need me."

Rowan nodded.

"What am I to steal?"

Rowan held Petal's eyes, sending the words to her silently. *On the queen's scepter, she carries a crystal with her son shrunken and trapped inside. If you can get it safely, I would like that crystal. But only if you can get it safely.* "You know what I say to Braden," she said aloud.

Petal laughed. "I am no good to you dead."

"Exactly." Rowan pulled Petal to her and held tight. What was wrong with her? How could she risk Petal? "I love you so much," Rowan whispered desperately.

You poison everything you touch. You will poison the one you love most.

Rowan drew away from Petal quickly, hiding her hands behind her back. Petal regarded her sadly.

Everything was packed and ready to go in less than two hours. Ferdy and Keagan, without being told, had abandoned their knights and come to be with their sister. The king and queen also made their way out to the bailey, along with several knights, to bid Petal farewell.

Rowan watched from a distance as everyone said their good-byes. Ferdy looked ready to cry; most people would expect that of Keagan—he was so quiet and serious—but Ferdy was a deep feeler, too. Colum joined them; for almost two months now, he had stomped around, fighting against Petal going; now that the moment was upon them, he simply walked over to his little girl and picked her up in his arms, holding fast. Ferdy and Keagan walked over and wrapped their arms around their father's waist, where Petal's legs hung, hugging them both. After a moment, Maureen joined them, as well, laying a hand against her husband's cheek and whispering something Rowan was too far away to hear.

It was the sort of beautiful display their family was known for. Like the greetings Rowan had been so jealous of. She should not watch, but could not look away. Would they ever look so again?

They remained that way for some time, oblivious to the crowd, so absorbed were they in one another. When they finally released from the hug, they did not stray far. Colum put Petal on the ground, but stood directly behind her, as if he could not bear having any space between them. Without looking to see that she was there, Colum reached out and wrapped his hand around Maureen's, squeezing it.

Gwyneth came walking over a few moments after, and crouched in front of Petal.

"I brought you this." She shook out a traveling cloak with a hood and fur lining. "I know it isn't much, but it was mine when I was a girl. I thought I would give it to my daughter. But I would be honored if you wore it." Petal bent forward and let Gwyneth put the red cloak around her shoulders.

There were tears in Gwyneth's eyes when she stood. "You are a wonderful girl."

Only moments later, Colum was helping his wife and daughter into the coach, and the crowed stepped back. He turned to scan the crowd, and his eyes came to rest on Rowan. He simply looked at her for a moment; then his head jerked ever so slightly, motioning her over.

Rowan walked to the carriage, forcing a smile. She stopped at the doors and leaned in.

"Rowan." Maureen leaned forward, placed her hands on either side of Rowan's face, and kissed her on the head. "All will be well. Remember." She brushed a stray hair off Rowan's face, smiling into her eyes. "You are loved."

"I love you too. So much." She lifted a hand to Maureen's wrist and squeezed. "Be safe."

Maureen sat back. Rowan turned to face Petal.

"Will you tell Braden how brave I am being?" Petal asked fervently. "And how grown-up?"

"I will," Rowan promised. "I will even tell him that you are to be a duchess, with a very large fortune. How's that?" Rowan returned, teasing.

"Oh yes. That is an excellent idea." Petal wore an adorably conniving look. "Don't worry, Rowan." Petal sat back, playing with her necklace, to all the world looking perfectly content. "Your mother's rose will protect me."

Rowan's chest locked up with hope and fear. She longed to reach out and touch the talisman, to feel some measure of Petal's certainty; but she had a sinking suspicion the certainty came more from the wearer than the talisman itself. "I will think of you every day until you return. Be very careful with yourself. I love you dearly."

Petal smiled warmer than the sunshine. "I love you too."

Rowan did not realize, until the carriage was gone, that she stood with Colum and the boys. None of them able to move. When the carriage was out of sight, Rowan looked over her right shoulder to where Colum stood; he did not look her way. Turning in the opposite direction, Rowan walked away.

Rowan walked to the castle, smashed under the weight of what she had done, wanting to cry, but unwilling. She was nearly there when a little hand slipped into hers. Rowan stopped, startled, and looked down into Ferdy's tear-streaked face. Without a word, she knelt down in the dirt and gathered the boy into her arms so they could cry together.

807 days until Roisin returns

Braden arrived the next day. Rowan had never seen him as angry as he became when he realized Petal was gone. He released the full force of his feelings on her, screaming in her face and eventually mounting up and leaving the same day.

Rowan considered it no less than she deserved, and retreated to her room to feel sorry for herself. She had wallowed in her sadness for only half an hour when a visitor arrived.

"Rowan." Gwyneth hesitantly peered around the door she was opening, unannounced.

"What do you want?"

Gwyneth walked in, perching herself very delicately on the edge of Rowan's bed. Rowan had the urge to simply stretch out her leg and kick Gwyneth from the bed, but she resisted, clenching her fists to have something to focus her anger.

"I knew you must be hurting. I wanted to come and…comfort you."

"What for?" Rowan asked with a brittle laugh.

"Rowan, I know you have not always liked me."

"Not liked you?" Rowan scoffed, aghast. She could not be that stupid, could she?

"Yes. It is entirely my fault."

Rowan raised an eyebrow, but refrained from speaking. She was bound to hit Gwyneth if she kept trying to put her dainty little shine on the hatred between them.

"But I want to change all that. I don't know how to thank you for what you did with Petal."

"Don't. You. Even. Dare." Rowan pushed herself up, swinging her legs over the side of the bed as she spoke with great precision.

"But, I have to say this. I...did not realize before how very much you really do love your sister." Gwyneth's head rose, as if carried by the joy of her discovery, and she smiled so lovingly that Rowan could almost forget she was a monster to this woman. Almost.

"Get out." Rowan stood, pointing to her door.

"I know you..."

"Get out now!" Rowan felt as though something was trying to claw its way out of her gut—something dark and angry and resentful. "Nothing I have ever done was for you."

Gwyneth's gaze slid away, softly accepting. "I know that. Do you think I don't know you can never forgive me?" Gwyneth shook her head sadly. "You have no reason to. What I said was unforgivable. I am just so grateful that you will not punish Roisin for my mistakes."

Rowan spoke in a voice low and tight with anger. "You are as undeserving of my kindness and forgiveness as my grandmother. Everything you do is selfishly motivated. You are small and greedy and cowardly. My sister is *nothing* like you. And there are times when I think it would be better for her if I killed you before she returns so you can never influence her."

Gwyneth drew away, sucking in a breath.

"If you think being grateful that I would risk Petal's life will win me to your side, you are not only wrong; you are repulsive. I will save Roisin. But not because you want it. She is my sister, and I have always loved her. Now leave my room, and do not ever speak to me of Petal or your enormous gratitude again." Rowan's every muscle was coiled tight, her hands fisted at her sides, as her entire body shook, enraged.

Gwyneth ran out. Rowan couldn't stay in the room; the stinging sweet scent of Gwyneth lingered, making her stomach roil. She fled the castle, walking to her garden to shut herself away from everyone.

You poison everything you touch.
You poisoned your mother, like you poison everything you touch.
You will break her heart. Then you will poison the one you love most.
It will be your hand delivering the poison unto your sister.
You poison everything you touch.

The words were everywhere, following her into the garden. Seeming to be written in her mother's blood on the stone bench where Rowan was born. Where her mother died. All the voices followed her.

Her grandmother's:

You poisoned your mother.

Colum's:

She is only a child. You cannot ask that of her.
So this at last is the one thing Rowan the Eternal cannot do.

Braden's:

They all lose...Everyone who dares to threaten her throne loses.

Even her father's voice followed her here:

You will understand, won't you? It is only that I haven't seen your sister since she was a baby.

And back, always back to where it all began. Her grandmother's voice, under every other word that existed within her. Would it never go away?

You poison everything you touch.

Rowan couldn't stand it. The voices beat at her. They were everywhere. She ran, ignoring everything and everyone she passed, until she came to the only place the voices had never followed her.

She sat in her old room, her legs dangling over the edge of her wall, and read through Gavin's old letters, one after another. They had always been an escape. Maybe they would be again.

The light was growing dim when Rowan came to the end of her letters. It had worked while she was reading. But the moment she laid down the last letter, the voices came rushing back, bombarding her with all her failures.

Rowan walked to her old desk, searching for paper, something to write with. She wrote without thinking.

Why is it so very hard to hold on to the good voices? I must have been told a million times that I am loved. Yet when I am alone, it seems impossible to call up those words. But other words—painful, repulsive, angry words—those return without effort. They are always there, haunting me.

You poison everything you touch. You poisoned your mother. You will break her heart.

I hear them every moment of every day.

Every time I look at my father, even though I have forgiven him for saying it, I remember how he explained that he loved me, but I must die, so he could see my sister once more. Just see her.

Why can't I banish that?

I sent a ten-year-old girl, barely alive yet, to face my grandmother. Something I have not done. To fight my battles.

I've dispatched men who either do not return or do not return whole. I risk someone I have come to care for as family every day. I have lost my oldest friendship. For what?

I may yet fail. But I don't allow for that possibility to stop me when sending men and children to die. Why?

Because I still believe what I did as a child?

My father told me what he thought I needed to hear. He didn't believe I would stop my grandmother. No one did. Only me. Because I needed to. Because I needed to be something special. As if that could make up for all the things I wasn't. Beautiful, delicate, good. Wanted. There is a difference between being loved and being wanted. I have always been loved, but not desired above all, so it was never enough for me.

Why do I continue believing what I know was only meant as reassurance?

What if I fail? Fail at the only thing I have ever thought about, the only thing I have ever worked for. I would be nothing. Worse than nothing, I would be like my grandmother, using other people for my own ends and remaining safely shut away.

My stepmother came to me today to thank me. To thank me for sacrificing Petal to save Roisin.

All I could think, all I could feel, was disgust. But not at her—at myself. I did it. I did what she wanted to do to me. I just did it to Petal. I am worse than this woman I have hated most of my life.

I walk the halls, and all I see on every wall is Roisin's face. Everywhere I turn, her face. And I grow to hate it. To hate what I have become for her. So I ran to my sanctuary, to sit on the bench where I was born. But all I see there is the place where I killed my mother.

There is nothing of me here. I want so badly to simply get on my horse and ride away. But where? There is nothing of me anywhere.

I wonder sometimes if the reason I have no imagination for the future is because some part of me knows the only way to make all of this right—everything I've done, everyone I've sacrificed. The only way all of this ends well is if I die with my grandmother.

If we simply take the poison with us and vanish from the world.

I am sorry. This is a terrible letter. I should not send it.

But—I want someone to know.

Selfish to the end,

R—

It was the first time Rowan dispatched a letter to Gavin with her own servants. It would not get there quickly. But she needed to send the words. And if it made him feel bad, so much the better. He had put her through hell asking for Petal. He deserved to have a bit of it back.

Side by Side

805 days until Roisin returns

*B*raden hadn't gone far. He returned to the palace two days after leaving. Rowan was on the south lawn, where they sometimes sparred. She had a pile of journals and letters spread out in front of her and writing equipment on her lap.

"When did you become studious?" he asked, sitting down on the grass in front of Rowan as though nothing had ever happened. Rowan didn't allow herself to be drawn in, waiting instead for the hammer to fall. He couldn't possibly have forgiven her; she could not forgive herself. But she was glad to have him back; it released a bit of the pressure in her chest.

"A long while ago." She didn't look up as she spoke. "I've been so busy gathering information, I have not bothered to organize it all."

"And this can't be done in the palace, at a desk?" He watched as she spilled drops of ink on her dress, carrying the quill from the inkwell to the open journal in her lap. She wouldn't look at him.

"No. I am thinking of having a small home built here." Rowan glanced across the flat empty field with her back to the castle and all its inhabitants. "It needn't be anything more than a single room."

"Rowan?"

She looked up finally.

Braden had an eyebrow raised, looking vaguely exasperated until their eyes met. He drew back a bit, looking at her sympathetically. "I'm sorry I yelled at you."

"You were right. Everyone is right." Rowan shook her head. "If that is possible. I was right to send her, but I was also wrong to do so. It makes no sense, but it's true. And it doesn't matter."

"What do you mean?"

"Right or wrong, it's done. All that is left now is for us to make her risk worthwhile."

"So that's what you're doing? Making her risk worthwhile?"

Rowan nodded, looking at all the information she had spread out before her.

"I have acted as if all I can do is wait. But I can also make sure nothing like this happens again." Rowan was not really looking at Braden. "I am writing it all down. The history of the great Fairy War. All the mistakes, all the information I can gather, in one place."

For the longest time Braden was silent. When Rowan looked up, he wore a playful grin. "You know, you look exactly as you did when you first demanded I spar with you. Unshakable." One corner of his lip lifted a bit higher, so his smile was lopsided and fond. "No one but a *crown princess* can go through life so certain nothing can sway her.

"Do you need help?" he asked, shaking his head.

Rowan nodded. "I am having trouble organizing things. Those journals are my grandfather's, and these my grandmother's. They had very different perspectives on the war. I am quite certain they did not like each other much at all. At first I planned to combine their thoughts and represent a clearer picture. But at times they say such different things about the same moment that I don't know what to do. Over here"—Rowan stretched out her hand and pointed to a pile of letters—"I have reports from my knights, but none of it is anything other than impressions."

"I see." Braden did not seem particularly thrilled that Rowan wanted his help with organization. "Well, what have you done so far?"

"I made a timeline out of the information. And a list of what we know about the stances different kingdoms took and who was ruling at the time. Just now, I was making up family biographies for each kingdom. Who was born, who died, how they appear either blessed or cursed since the war, and a list of all the marriages."

Braden blinked several times, looking around as if for an escape. "You know, I'm better with the big picture."

"You volunteered," Rowan snapped. "Anyway, aren't you supposed to be the scholarly one?"

"I don't know where you got that idea." Braden laughed.

"You abhor weapons!" Rowan threw up her hands, exasperated and unwillingly amused.

"There are more choices in life than scholar or soldier," Braden argued, puffing up his chest. "I am an artist." Rowan rolled her eyes; of all the utter nonsense, what sort of life choice was that at a time like this?

"I don't know anyone who isn't better with the big picture, Braden. But," Rowan sighed, shoving her open journal into his hands, "look at this. Did you realize your father only began ruling the year the Fairy War began? His father died of an assassination, in which the culprit was never discovered. Even stranger, your father's first wife, who was much older than he, was the only unmarried daughter of the king of Ulm, who it appears was the first supporter of the Fairy queen, though never a participant in the war."

"You are saying what? That it was planned?"

"I am saying, it appears as though the Fairy queen might have been manipulating people with deals and favors long before the war began."

Braden clenched his teeth as though he would argue more, but shook it off with a jerky shrug. "How does this help you?"

Rowan shook her head; her eyes skimmed everything before her, searching. "I don't know yet."

Rowan and Braden sat on the south lawn for several hours a day, every day, compiling the information as best they could. Rowan at first found Braden more frustrating than helpful. They approached things very differently. She made lists and diagrams, wanting everything in its place before interpreting, while Braden was unable to focus on one thing for that long and would flip back and forth between her grandparents' journals, comparing their opinions and jumping to conclusions as a result.

They found their rhythm the second day of his visit. While organizing a timeline of the war's pertinent events, Rowan had come across several missing pieces of information. She knew the kingdoms of Turrlough and Creelan, along with some Fairy, had attacked the Fairy court, but didn't know their specific leader. Or what grievance exactly led them to war. There were no contested lands nor accusations of unfair trading; it was as though all the kingdoms had been coexisting peacefully until one day in the middle of August in the year 358, when two kingdoms declared war on a third.

Rowan made Braden a list of the things she most wanted to know: who commanded the attacking forces of Creelan and Turrlough, what made those two kingdoms so committed to the cause, and which side was right. Braden, using his uncanny ability to find an important comment amid a wealth of arbitrary information, sought what Rowan needed.

It was slow going and a bit frustrating, but Rowan had made up her mind after writing that last letter to Gavin. Until Petal and Roisin were returned to their families safely, Rowan was not going to complain about a single thing. She had no right. If the only plan she could come up with was the one they already had, she would focus her considerable time and energy on perfecting it. Making sure nothing could happen she did not anticipate.

The only useful thing Braden had discovered was that the king of Creelan had been puffing up his kingdom in every way he could but land expansion. He built up his cities and armies and expanded his trading as far as Ether, the large land to the north of the island. He wanted to make his kingdom the most respected the world over, and his strongest competition was the Fairy.

A letter from Gavin arrived the second day of Braden's visit, making it just four days since she had sent hers off. It would have taken her messenger at least three days to travel that distance. Meaning either it had been sent before her messenger arrived or Eachann had exerted considerable power to get here quickly. It was easy enough for a fairy to move short distances by magic, but the nearly three hundred miles between kingdoms was no short distance.

Eachann found Rowan and Braden on the south field working.

He looked from one to the other, seeming somewhat annoyed. "I was told there was some haste required," he complained. "As usual, humans are wont to exaggeration."

Rowan blushed, annoyed with herself. She had wanted to call the letter back nearly as soon as it was gone. Just writing it had helped, but it was too late.

"I am sorry I was not lying in a pool of my own blood so your effort could be worthwhile," Rowan remarked, avoiding Braden's gaze.

Trying to do so subtly, Rowan closed the journal she had been making notes in with the quill stuffed inside to keep the ink from running. She stood to face him. Rowan had yet to find any understanding for this particular fairy and what he had done behind her back, so he was hard to trust.

"I don't tell tales," Eachann snapped with a tired sigh. "I am on your side."

"Are you?" Rowan demanded, and her voice took on an eerie, faraway quality, stretching out with her magic. Over the years Rowan had come to trust, even like this fairy. But in light of recent events she was unsure, and blind trust was too big a risk, especially with Petal. She needed to know, once and for all, where he stood, while there was still time to call Petal back.

Eachann's entire attitude altered. His condescending smile and cocked head vanished, replaced by a sad, cowed look.

"I am Your Majesty's servant. Whatever you need, I shall provide."

Rowan recognized excitedly that she had this fairy, at last, under her spell. But she did not succumb to her excitement, focusing all her energy on holding him in her power.

"What side did you take in the war?"

"The side that lost."

"Who led you?"

"The king of the Fairy, my brother."

"King? Are the Fairy not always led by women?"

"Yes. But he was Nessa's husband. He thought Sorcha had killed his wife. When she came to claim the throne, as was her right, he ordered her imprisoned. But she had seen him coming. She always knows when Fairy speak against her." He looked frightened as he spoke the last words, even as he remained within her spell.

Rowan took the letter from his hand. "Go into the palace and rest. I will have food brought to you. Thank you."

Rather than vanishing, Eachann walked away, something he had not done since their first acquaintance.

"You are very frightening sometimes," Braden said breathlessly. "You made him speak, didn't you?"

Rowan nodded. She was not so much impressed by her magical powers as she was interested in what Eachann had said. *The king of the Fairy.* It had been the biggest missing piece, the incident that took people from contention to war. The leader.

"Why did you let him stop?" Braden asked when Rowan remained silent. "We had a firsthand witness. He could have answered all our questions."

"She always knows when Fairy speak against her," Rowan repeated, looking down at Braden on the grass. "I don't want her eye on me. Particularly not when you are with me." She thought of how close she had come to putting Braden in serious danger. She needed to come up with firmer walls between her various allies.

"Her eye?" Braden scoffed.

"She has a window through the eyes of any fairy." Rowan sat again and opened the letter slowly.

"Even you?" Braden asked, straightening.

"I'm not Fairy," she assured Braden, the letter lying open in her hands.

"No? She does that, you know? Pulls the truth from people."

Rowan raised an eyebrow but didn't respond. She could tell Braden a number of other ways she was like her grandmother. It changed nothing; they had all of them chosen their sides. All that remained was to live with them.

"Is that why you'll rule here? Because Fairy are always led by women?" Braden asked.

Rowan shrugged. "I suppose. My mother forced my father to make me his successor before I was born. But it isn't as though he ever had any sons."

As she said it, Rowan saw a flash of her father and Gwyneth huddled together; both looked older. They were staring into the eyes of a baby boy who lay in her father's arms.

As quickly as it came, the vision faded. When she came back to reality, Braden was staring at her in a distinctly disapproving manner.

"What?"

"You're going to read that?" His tone was bitter as he indicated the letter. "You still write to him?"

Rowan shrugged, dropping the letter on the grass. She picked her journal back up. If she was going to read it, she would do so later. Away from judging eyes.

"What will he ask for now? Ferdy and Keagan sent to him as shields?"

Rowan smirked at the ground; it was nice to have a friend who held a grudge as well as she. Better, maybe.

"How can you forgive him?" Braden growled. Rowan glanced his way but quickly let her eyes fall away; he was rarely intense, as he was now, his breath heavy and his eyes intent on her. Whenever he looked this way, Rowan felt distinctly uncomfortable.

"Who says I have?" Rowan asked on a sigh. She didn't know if she'd forgiven him. She only knew she couldn't continue to ignore him.

"You're still wearing the bells he gave you. You're writing to him. As soon as I read that letter, I knew you would send Petal." His voice rose as he spoke; he was suddenly unable to hold in what he had pretended no longer mattered. "He asks for something, and you do it. No matter how horrible. Don't you see he is bad for you?"

Rowan didn't speak for a long time. She stared at the letter on the ground, the words she had sent to Gavin swirling around in her brain, leaving her embarrassed and oddly eager to read his response. He always seemed to understand her, sometimes better than she understood herself. Was it possible anyone could understand that much?

"I'm the one who needs to be forgiven. I asked her. I sent her. I didn't do it because he asked. I did it because..." Rowan drifted off. She couldn't tell him Petal's secret mission. Some things were just too dangerous to share. Instead, she looked into Braden's eyes steadily. "How can you forgive me?"

"I don't know," Braden snapped. He looked like he wanted to storm away again. Then he shook his head, blowing out an exasperated breath. "But I have."

Rowan nodded. Tears of relief filled her eyes, she looked away before he noticed. "Thank you. Oh, I forgot," Rowan continued excitedly. "I was supposed to impress upon you how very grown-up Petal was behaving. And how brave."

Braden smiled.

"I think she's pleased to have a mission so like yours."

"She probably is the more grown-up of the two of us," he commented, laughing.

"When she gets back, I'm going to have some competition for your hand in marriage."

"That will be a relief for you," Braden muttered.

Rowan glanced his way, shocked by his, perhaps bitter, tone. He must be teasing. Surely. He was her friend, maybe her very last one; she needed him to remain so. Needed that one relationship to be unchanged. Rowan laughed, then Braden, both a bit awkwardly. They went back to their respective studies without further comment. The letter lay on the ground undisturbed.

What All Fairy Fear

Dear Rowan,

You are not poison, and you know it. But this letter is the final time I will say that or anything like it to you.

R owan nearly refolded the letter and shoved it into her desk right then. Clearly she did not know any such thing. If she did, she would not have sent the letter. And if he thought chastising her for the feeling would scare it away, he did not know her as well as she'd thought.

The sad thing was that her heart pounded faster, with fear, as she read the phrase *the final time*. Surely she would need to hear it at least once more. Perhaps a hundred more times. Even knowing he did not think her poison, while vaguely comforting to the far-off Rowan she kept within, did not convince her it was so.

If you don't know within yourself how wonderful you are, then the Fairy queen has already beaten you.

You have brought people together, Rowan. Given us hope and purpose, when all we were able to think of was survival. Every one of those people you wrote of, who are at risk, would have chosen that risk for themselves, because you inspire it. Do you think there is even one of us that does not know you would gladly die to save us?

It is time you start expecting the same treatment.

Do not let her words become so much a part of you.

Rowan's breath caught, and she bit her tongue to keep a sob from escaping, as her tears had. There was the comfort she'd hoped for, but where such words usually made her feel closer to Gavin, right now they left her even more resentful of what he'd asked than she was an hour ago. He knew her. Understood her as no one else did. How could *he* have asked such a thing of her?

> *You are in the center of a very deadly battle, but being at the center does not make you its cause.*
>
> *Come up with something—it doesn't have to be imaginative—just one thing that you want for yourself alone, when the battle is over. Find it and hold on to it, because when this ends, you will have a great deal of time on your hands, and I don't think you will be prepared for it.*
>
> *You will not die.*
>
> *Your Friend, G—*
>
> *P.S. I have met your Petal. Her mother has decided to stay until April with her daughter. She thinks it would be best that your knights not travel just yet.*
>
> *Petal is truly remarkable, at once a child and an old woman. She informed me I must apologize at least once more, in every letter, until you write and say that I am forgiven. And then two more times, not in a row.*
>
> *I must do this, she said, because I am your friend, and friends do not ask each other to break their own hearts.*
>
> *She has a point. In doing what I think must be done, I forgot to do what should be done.*
>
> *I am truly sorry. More than I can ever say.*

They were the right words, she supposed. But they did not quite reach her. Rowan sat in her old room, at the desk. She had taken to sleeping here. To spending all her time inside the palace right here, with the wall open to the elements and her door shut to the world. A world she had managed to keep Gavin separate from for so long.

In one letter, he'd gone from chastising her for feeling bad, to demanding she make plans for her future, to apologizing for making her miserable. She wasn't sure how to respond to it.

It wouldn't be forgiveness.

She had no plans for the future.

While she was no longer dwelling on her feelings, they weren't gone.

She thought of the flash she had seen that afternoon. The future? Or her imagination? If it was the future, it was different from any way she had ever seen it before. This vision had flashed in front of her, then vanished. In the past, she had seen details, felt the air, so she knew the time of year, heard water or wind. This was only an image. If it was the future, didn't that mean it was one she wouldn't live to experience?

> *Prince Gavin,*
>
> *Thank you for informing me of Maureen's and Petal's safe arrival. They are both uncommon women, worthy of great praise.*
>
> *My letter was probably somewhat startling. We have very different lives. Be assured, whatever my feelings, I have no intention of giving in to them. There are simply some days when I feel it all.*
>
> *I have been compiling information for a history I am writing. A history of the Great Fairy War. It occurs to me that while we have often discussed your father and the general consequences of his bargain with the queen, I do not know the specifics. Nor do I know precisely how your father came to be king. Information from wartime is hard to come by.*
>
> *It would be very useful to have all the information you can give me. Specifics of the deal, a brief family history, of at least your father and his brothers. Did any have spouses, are they living or dead…*
>
> *Anything you can think of.*
>
> *R—*

Rowan dispatched the letter with Eachann the following day. He seemed much recovered.

"You managed to spell me at last, little queen." Eachann smiled in a friendly, almost proud way. "You must be pleased."

Rowan shrugged. "I am all-powerful when in the presence of exhausted Fairy," she commented.

Eachann chuckled. "At last you grow in humility."

"Oh, was that required?" Rowan laughed. "Then by all means." Rowan curtsied so low, she was touching the ground. "I am your servant, sir."

The fairy was shaking his head when he froze suddenly. He bent down, reaching for the chain on Rowan's neck, and pulled the pendant free from inside the bodice of her dress.

"Where did you get that?"

Startled, Rowan straightened, clasping a hand around the pendant. She always wore it so it hung beneath her dress. It would be in the way when she practiced otherwise. And she found she liked the feel of it, always warming her, right next to her heart.

But seeing Eachann's reaction to it, she suddenly felt she should have kept it better hidden.

"Why?"

"That is dragon magic," he said, eyeing her hand as though waiting for something evil to spring from it. "Dragons are dark beasts."

"And Fairy are thieves and tricksters," Rowan returned, unnerved by his stare. "There are no dragons; they either left or were killed years ago."

The fairy shook his head. "All Fairy fear dragons," he said cautiously. "But I forget, don't I?" He took a step back. "You are something else."

He vanished before Rowan could question his cryptic comment again. She gripped the pendant tight in her right hand, feeling the crystal warm her. Then she tucked it into her bodice again, to be sure it was safe.

When she looked down at her warm palm, her scars were gone. Startled, she rubbed her hand, as if the rubbing would reveal the scars. But it was as if they had never been there. Or as if they had simply—melted away.

All Fairy fear dragons.

Well! That was worth looking into.

Rowan gave Braden his new assignment when she met him on the south fields. Find dragons. Any reference he could, particularly if it was mentioned in conjunction with the Fairy, or what had happened to the last of that once great race.

"Your grandmother was a funny woman." Braden flipped though one of her journals.

"Oh." Rowan didn't look up. Braden made a habit of talking about useless things. Rowan had found it was best to simply nod along and pretend to listen. Trying to refocus him only distracted him more.

"This is from just before she was married. She hated your grandfather." He chuckled. "Apparently he was an 'angry, little, selfish, ancient man.' She was particularly disturbed by the old part. Here she was, twenty, considered almost beyond marriage because of her inability to 'bend her tongue to her father's will,' and your grandfather was nearing sixty, with her his third wife without children. She didn't like the idea of having to marry a man who was older than her father."

"Umm." Rowan refused to be distracted, focusing all her attention on making a map of the reported dragon kills from the kingdom's old logs. Searching for a pattern.

"So she goes out of her way to make him opposed to the wedding. Flirting openly with his male servants. Calling your grandfather a murderer, because of his stance on dragon hunting. She even goes so far as to sabotage one of his parties, releasing the baby dragon they were going to use in a slaying skit."

"They were going to kill the dragon in front of guests? For entertainment?" Rowan demanded, suddenly interested in what Braden was saying.

"Yes. It was a common practice here. They would kill the parents, wherever they found them, because they were too threatening to bring back. But they kept the children or the eggs. They were trying to see if dragons could be broken like horses. The runts or the overly aggressive ones were killed for entertainment and served to the guests."

"That's disgusting. Babies." Rowan shuddered, shaking her head. "So you've found where the dragons present her with the pendant?"

"You mean the whistle. Yes, that's much later, just a few years after your father is born. This is before the marriage."

"If you found it, why didn't you show me?" Rowan grumbled impatiently.

"Well," he shrugged, "it's a story that needed context. I was looking for the things she referenced."

"Like what?"

"Like the baby dragon she released at their engagement party. She said…" Braden tore through a pile of journals he had stacked upon one another open to specific pages, grabbing the one on the bottom. "'I did not always care for their plight as I should. I thought them monsters, capable of ripping me apart. They were merely a means to escaping my husband. But the first time I looked into the eyes of a dragon, I became changed. That baby was frightened, and as I gazed into its eyes, I saw a soul. Any vessel that houses a soul cannot be evil. I had to help it, help them, or abandon my own soul.'"

The words knocked the air from Rowan, as though she'd been thrown from her horse, so she sat, separate from herself and numb but certain she'd feel the sting in a moment. Her grandmother was a *good* woman, another person she would never live up to.

Father said Rowan reminded him of his mother. It didn't seem likely. She was good enough to help a creature no one cared for simply because it had a soul. Rowan wasn't like that. She planned to kill someone, her other grandmother. And no matter how bad she thought Sorcha, she knew she had a soul.

"There's more," Braden said hesitantly, putting the book on the ground. "But I am not sure you want to hear it."

"Why?"

"It's about your father."

"Tell me." Rowan nodded.

"All right." He sighed. "She says this just before the dragons give her the whistle: 'I should feel shame at my betrayal, but I cannot. In the midst of this horror, we made something beautiful and changed each other for the better. Balder's father, who I once thought to be the lowest of men, is now the best. I have given my son a good man for a father; there can be no shame in that.'" Braden looked up expectantly.

"Okay?"

"Well, her opinion of her husband hadn't improved. It had grown worse." Braden spoke slowly, waiting for Rowan to catch on. "She talks about wishing to run away, but worries that many dragons would die as a result."

Rowan said nothing. She sat back on the grass thinking of the implications. Her grandmother had had an affair.

Rowan began laughing; it started small and grew wild. "We aren't actually heirs to the throne. Any of us." She fell forward, laughing. "And my grandmother wasn't even a noble, was she?"

Braden shook his head, watching her carefully. "She was the daughter of a knight."

If anything, Rowan laughed even harder. "I'm not a princess. I've never been a princess. Isn't it wonderful!"

"Um."

"This we have to celebrate." She started to rise, but noticed the journals. "Later. We need to finish our work. But later, we must celebrate."

"Are you sure? I mean I really don't think you should tell anyone."

"Oh, I won't tell," Rowan said on a laughing sigh. "There is enough turmoil here. But...I've never felt like a princess. I was never graceful, or soft, or sweetly spoken, or pretty. And now, it doesn't matter, because I know the truth. I'm the granddaughter of a fairy. The great granddaughter of a knight. Who was my real grandfather?"

"Well, he started out as a dragon hunter, but she won him over and he began helping the dragon's escape instead."

"Wonderful! I am the almost eternal, granddaughter of a, dragon defending, knight. Isn't that so much better then being a princess?"

"Well, you are still a princess. Your father is the child of the queen of Stonedragon; whether he's the king's offspring or not, he is still heir to the throne."

"Nope." Rowan smiled, shaking her head. It didn't matter what his argument was; she had the affirmation she always wanted. So it had no hold over her.

"And even if you ignored that," Braden pressed on, "you are the granddaughter of the queen of the Fairy. So you are a Fairy princess."

"I don't know about that. I'm half human. I doubt if I'm heir to any throne." Rowan had her head high in the air, and a gleeful smile stretched her lips. "Give it up. I'm not a princess; do you have any idea how wonderful this feels?" She threw her head back, shaking her long braid out behind her.

Braden laughed along with her. "Yeah, I suppose it would be fun to discover I was not my father's son."

"Exactly! Now if only you could prove, by reading someone's journal, that my mother was not actually the child of the Fairy queen, then everything in the world would be nearly perfect."

"I'll work on it." Braden smiled, his gaze lingering intently on Rowan's face.

The Ground between Us

*R*owan did not think she could explain to anyone but Braden how that one little piece of history changed her entire perspective. Even Braden, while he could sympathize with the desire not to be connected to one's family, did not quite understand. He seemed to be waiting for some bad side to hit her.

But the knowledge was completely freeing. All of Rowan's failings that made her fear ruling were unimportant. She found that thing in the future she could look forward to. Never, as long as she lived, becoming queen of Stonedragon. It was not hers, not her responsibility. Now that she knew they were not in fact her people, she could abandon the responsibility she never wanted.

More than that, nowhere in any of the journals did it mention this mysterious dragon hunter–turned–dragon rescuer dying. He could be out there somewhere. And if he was, when this was over, she could go and find him, a grandparent she could like.

Braden stayed only five days. Rowan was as ever concerned when he left, but her newfound inner contentment helped her manage the fear. Before he left, she stole his memories of Petal's mission, to be safe. She could return them later. But for now she needed firmer walls.

Rowan continued compiling her research. Reading everything she could get her hands on that might help. Even stealing her father's old journals from his desk.

She trained with her knights again; Sean and Declan were not up to their old standards yet, but it helped them, as well as her, to have the practice, and a few others were home now.

She barely saw Ferdy and Keagan but from a distance. They were so busy as squires. Colum would not speak to her, though she saw him often. Once he looked at her for longer than a second. Not much longer, but a little. Long enough for Rowan to hope for the future, and as always followed hope, ache for the present.

797 days until Roisin returns

The days were passing quickly enough when she received her next report from Gavin. He had done as she asked, sharing the exact nature of his father's ascension to the throne and giving her the details of the bargain with the queen. She wished there was one person with whom she could discuss everything, from Braden to Petal to all of her research, even Roisin, but she had yet to find that person.

Gavin's letter ended with another apology. Rowan wondered if he would continue to do so forever as Petal instructed. It reminded her of when she had first met Braden and called him Braden the Obedient. Did all men need instruction?

With Gavin's letter, Eachann delivered several others, from Maureen and Petal. One for each family member. All he gave to Rowan.

"Why don't you deliver these while I consider my response?"

"No, madam." He did not even meet her gaze, looking at a spot on Rowan's shoulder. "My instructions were very specific. The bossy fairy servant said you and you alone could give the letters to her husband and children. She said to tell you she would know if you did not."

"Maureen is much more than a servant. And you will treat her respectfully," Rowan snapped, taking the letters. Trust Maureen to force everyone to speak again. Still, Rowan doubted it would do much good.

She found Colum sitting on an old stump outside the little practicing ring where he trained her so long ago. He had stopped training the knights, working with the squires, instead. Rowan originally assumed it was a ruse to spend more time with Keagan and Ferdy, but as she walked over, she began to see other benefits of the job. Colum was somewhere around his early sixties. She didn't know Colum's exact age, but he was getting on in years. Soon he wouldn't be able to train anyone. This was a less taxing job.

He looked up as she walked over; for the first time in a long while, he did not look so much furious as tired.

"I have letters for you from Petal and Mau—"

Before she had finished her sentence, he was up and grabbing the letters from her hand. He turned away as soon as he had them and walked to his stump, his back to her.

She nearly left so he could be free of her, as he clearly wanted to be. But the Maureen who lived in her head stopped her. Colum was her oldest friend, and Maureen asked her to deliver the messages so they might mend fences. Rowan stayed.

Colum consumed the words, oblivious to the young boy in the ring. Oblivious even to Rowan's presence.

Since she could tell he would take a while with his own letters, Rowan walked a few feet away to stand under the shade of a tree and read. She opened Petal's first.

> *Dear Rowan,*
>
> *I have never been so far from home. It is wonderful; on the first night of our journey, I did not sleep a wink. There were too many things to see. I saw a wolf! I think I should like one as a pet.*

Rowan giggled quietly, bending into herself so as not to disturb Colum.

> *They have lovely eyes. Do you suppose it used to be a person?*
>
> *Has Braden returned yet? You did remember to tell him, didn't you? Mama says he is not for me. But I do not see why I can't have him if I want him. You said I could do anything I liked.*
>
> *I met Prince Gavin this morning. He was very gracious and appreciative. He is not nearly as handsome as Braden, but he is well enough looking.*

Well enough looking. That could mean anything. Rowan shook her head, amused and frustratingly curious despite herself. Declan, with his eye patch and claw scars, was well enough looking for a man surviving a bird attack. And eighty-year-old Adam, with one hand, seven teeth, and a hunched back, was well enough looking for a man half in the grave. Where were the details?

Oddly, Petal's vague comment sparked Rowan's interest, when it should no longer matter. There could be nothing between them after what he'd asked, after what Rowan had done.

So he was well enough looking for a prince who had convinced Rowan to use a ten-year-old as a spy.

> *I met his mother, too; she is very sad. I think her husband may die soon.*
> *He is very sad, as well; he cannot speak, but I can tell he wants to. If*
> *Keagan were here, he would know what he is thinking.*
>> *Rowan, I know it is a great favor to ask. I am only ten and he is*
> *so much older, and you like each other very much. But will you please*
> *not agree to marry Braden until I have returned and can have a chance?*
> *I Love You*
> *Petal the Powerful, Duchess of Stonedragon*
>> *I love my title very much!*

Rowan folded the letter with a smile on her face. Petal had a vibrant sense of joy about her. She only hoped it would survive what was asked of her.

She looked over to where Colum sat; he looked very serious, reading what appeared to be a five-page letter. It must be Maureen's. Rowan opened her own.

> *My Dearest Rowan,*
>> *We have arrived safely in Turrlough. I had an opportunity to look*
> *in on both of your knights; it is indeed quite bad. They were both starv-*
> *ing in a cave when discovered. The frost was cruel. I have great hopes*
> *for Tom's full recovery; he is young, and he was never as badly injured*
> *as Ardal.*

> *But, my dear, you must prepare yourself. If I am able to bring Ardal*
> *back alive, he will never be the same man you knew.*

Rowan closed her eyes, blocking out the words a moment, and her hand tightened on the page. She'd held barely any hope of Ardal returning, and now he would. It was a miracle, but her heart ached for her friend, for the man Maureen said was gone.

> *He cannot walk. He cannot even sit on his own. His legs were ampu-*
> *tated to save his life before we arrived. And though I have healed many*
> *of his other injuries, I cannot heal the injury to his spirit. He refuses*
> *food and will not speak of what happened.*
>
> *He knows he will not die in battle. And for a man like him, who*
> *has done nothing but soldiering since he was a boy, it is a fate worse*
> *than death. I will do my best to return him to you; I know how much*
> *you love him.*
>
> *I have decided to stay here until the end of April. It would not do*
> *for me to be in Turrlough in May, when the Fairy come, but I cannot*
> *leave Petal before then. And it is better for Tom, who is still recovering*
> *from the damage of the frost and a poorly healed stab in his left side. I*
> *hope you will understand my decision.*
>
> *I also looked in on the king while I was here. Like Ardal, his ill-*
> *ness is not something within my power to heal. It comes from the weight*
> *on his heart and perhaps a bit of magic I cannot penetrate. The queen*
> *rarely leaves his side, and this is what helps him most.*
>
> *Now, dearest, I want you to consider something. I have told the*
> *interfering fairy that you are to deliver all of the letters. You said, when*
> *you honored Petal, that you do not know how to be part of a family.*
> *This is how: you forgive.*

Rowan felt her eyes burning and pulled the letter away before her tears could mar the words. Even hundreds of miles away, Maureen had the power to reach straight for Rowan's heart and release her sorrows, her fears.

It is not an easy thing for either of us. We wait for someone to decide they do not love us any longer and go away. But you must do it. Forgive Colum for the way you feel he abandoned you.

Rowan caught her breath, shocked. It hadn't occurred to her that Maureen understood how she'd been feeling toward Colum lately.

The trouble was, she thought she had forgiven him. But that didn't take away the feeling that here again, she would never be loved for just exactly who she was. She didn't want to spar around him, because he did not want her to be a knight. It hurt worse than any taunt she'd received over the years.

I know you, dear, and I know what you feel. Forgive him.

Once you have done this, you will simply do what you worry no one will for you. You will refuse to give up on making him forgive you. Family isn't perfect. There is anger in it, and sadness and betrayal. But in the end, the most powerful tool family has to stand against the challenges of life is its ability to forgive. To accept.

Put the things that have hurt you, that would hang upon you and make you desire to always stand alone, into your past, and forgive them. Love with all your heart as I watched you do as a child. Love will save you as much as it will save your sister.

Your Loving Friend,

Maureen

Rowan faced into the tree so no one could see her cry. There was simply too much in the letter. Ardal—funny, carefree, wonderful Ardal—was broken and did not want to heal. Her friend didn't want to heal. And all Rowan's pain and disappointment with Colum, Maureen was saying to forgive him, that Rowan had to simply let those feelings go. She wasn't sure she could do that. Colum would surely never forgive what Rowan did to Petal, to his whole family.

Rowan dried her face with her hands and refolded the letter, stuffing it into her sword belt. She turned around to watch Colum as he continued to read.

The Breach

At length, when Colum finished, he glanced toward Rowan, leaning against the tree. He stood and walked to her; she started forward, as well, so they met halfway.

She did not know what to say. "I'm sorry" again? He already had said her feelings changed nothing. She couldn't think of a word that wasn't useless. So she said nothing.

"What will you do about Ardal?" he asked after a few moments.

Rowan shook her head. "I am not sure." She opened her mouth to say something about how she had done this to him, but stopped. Colum was looking for something constructive. "I must get him home. I will write to him, see if I can impress upon him how very important he still is to me. Then...I will know better what to do once he is here, I think."

"That is probably true." He nodded. "It would not hurt to mention that you love him. Ardal has loved you for some time. Even before you made him your knight or began training with us, he would watch you work, impressed by your determination—said you reminded him of his first love."

Rowan nodded. Ardal had always been a good friend; he teased her about boys, and she was much more comfortable dancing with him than even dancing with her father. "I love him very much. I will make sure he knows it."

She looked at the ground, unsure what to say next.

"I love you very much, too!" she blurted out. "You have always been my very best friend. I can never take back what I did or ask you to forgive me, but I am so sorry, and none of it was because I do not love you."

Colum watched her silently for a moment; Rowan worried she had said the wrong thing. What if he just walked away?

271

When he continued to remain silent, Rowan found herself speaking again. "Even if you can't forgive me, you must forgive Maureen. She loves you so much, more than she has ever loved anyone. And she only kept it a secret from you because—"

"Please do not try to explain my own wife to me." Colum raised his hand for silence. "My anger with her has nothing to do with you and everything to do with fears I thought she had banished years ago." He clenched his teeth, breathing between them. "But that is between us."

Rowan nodded, her eyes filling. She looked away.

"Rowan, we were not at our best even before this. In many ways, that was my fault. I looked at you like a child, but expected you to act and understand as an adult. I decided I would love you like my own before I met you. The first time Maureen spoke of you and I saw her love, I decided it would be the same for me."

Rowan looked up at Colum then. He was smiling at her in a sad way, looking through her into the past.

"Then I met you. And you were trying so very hard not to cry. You had knocked something over. A servant was muttering about how there had never been such a clumsy princess. The more she muttered, the sadder you grew, until finally you got so frustrated, you stuck your hand out and knocked over everything she had picked up. Do you remember what you said?"

Rowan blushed, embarrassed of the memory, her behavior. "Now there is."

"Yes, 'Now there is.' I couldn't help it; I burst out laughing, and you looked up at me with such a surprised smile, so big and warm. And I loved you just for that." He smiled at her then, as he used to do, and for a moment, Rowan thought perhaps it would be this simple. They could simply go back.

"And then things changed, and every day there was a new problem. I watched that smile disappear bit by bit. By the time you were ten, you were a little grown-up. Everything I did, I did to make you smile, and because I wanted you to be able to protect yourself. The world tells women to wait for someone to come and protect them. But that someone doesn't always arrive in time." He drifted off into silence, gazing through her. Was he thinking of Petal? "I wanted you as safe as I could make you. But I never, not for a moment, imagined you would actually find yourself one day facing the Fairy queen. Not until you sat me down and told me you would not have it any other way."

Colum paced away, all of his frustrations having returned. "I sat there watching you, and I could see it. That look you get that makes it clear nothing short of death is going to stop you. And all I could think of was you, dead, in a million horrible ways. Lying on the ground dead, before you ever allowed yourself to live. You may be twice Petal's age, but you are just as much a child," he snapped, coming over to stand in front of her again.

"It made me so angry. I couldn't do anything to change your mind. And you went and got stupider. Challenging a field full of men, and I had to stand there, watching them hurt you. You made me watch as they hurt you." He put both his hands on her shoulders, shaking her, and Rowan longed to reach up and just hold on, but her arms felt too weak. "Do you know how much that hurt me? Watching you take their beatings and insults, knowing if I stopped you, you would only find another way. I have been frustrated and angry and lost as to how to help you, for nearly five years now. And just when I think to myself I can put that aside and help you the way I did when you were a girl, so that if nothing else, I can have as much time with you as I am able, then you do this." He jerked away, waving his arms, and Rowan nearly stumbled after him.

"And Petal...Petal, the happiest little girl in the world, looks into my eyes with that same expression. Ready to risk herself, ready even to die. What the hell did I do wrong? What sort of father raises his girls to go out in the world to *die?*"

"You didn't—"

"Didn't I? You cannot possibly imagine what it feels like to have both your girls look into your eyes and say they don't need you, because they think it is their job to die for someone else. I won't have it! But I can't stop it."

Rowan bit her cheek to keep the tears from falling. She had never seen him like this, even when he yelled over Petal. He had never seemed so...fragile.

"You think this is me failing to love who you are. Or not being able to forgive you, but it's so much worse," he said in a low voice. "This is me, being torn apart piece by aching piece as you make me grieve for you both, even as you're standing in front of me."

One giant sob escaped Rowan as she breathed, and before she could break down completely, she ran. Tearing past him. She had to get away. She did not make it very far; ducking into the stables, she stumbled into an empty stall and allowed herself to weep.

Colum found her there, with her face shoved into the hay to hide her sobs. He lowered himself to the ground next to her and gathered Rowan into his arms.

"It's okay," he whispered, running his hand down her hair. "You're allowed to cry. I've done it quite a lot myself of late." Rowan seemed only to cry harder. "You know, a long time ago, this kingdom was known for its knights, men who went out and conquered beasts. Now it's known for its curse. But I begin to think it should be known for its women. Too brave for their own good, they go out and risk themselves for others. And for what's right." He said it flatly, coming to some realization as he spoke.

"I will never stop hating that. I would much prefer to see you married with a bundle of children and no more worries in life than the next mother. But I love you still. I will always love you."

Rowan wrapped her arms around Colum's waist and hugged him as tightly as she could. Her crying began to lessen. After a few moments, she drew back, using her sleeve to dry off her face.

"I'm sorry."

"Let's have no more apologies between us. All right?" His arms remained gentle around Rowan's shoulders, and Colum's red eyes revealed his own tears, but there was a sternness about him, a distance.

Rowan nodded once. "I will do better."

"I will do better also."

Colum and Rowan went together to find the boys, and all four walked to the family cottage to answer their letters. Each found a corner of relative privacy to write in, but it helped that they were all together.

Rowan wrote to everyone who had written to her. And to Ardal; she did not know if she could convince him to heal himself, but she had to try.

Dearest Petal,

I give you my word that I shall not accept anyone's offer of marriage until both my sisters are home to advise me. And to have their chance with my suitors.

You said Prince Gavin was 'handsome enough.' Was this meant to imply that as I am not as beautiful as you, I do not need a very handsome man? If so, I am quite hurt. I would never say such a thing to you.

Rowan smiled at her little bit of teasing; Petal would enjoy it. She would laugh at it or grin slyly. How long would it be before any of them saw that smile again?

You are very much missed, Petal the Powerful. I love you eternally.
Rowan

Dear Maureen,

You are always fixing us, even the hurts beyond your magic to repair. Thank you. It is much better now that I can speak to Colum. I have a secret to tell you when you return; I cannot send it in a letter, but it makes me very happy, this secret. I miss you. I have not been without you this long since I was six. Be well...

Dearest Ardal,

I am overjoyed to find you alive. I had begun to despair of ever seeing you again. I have asked a great deal of you, because you have always been the greatest of my knights and one of my closest friends.

Please come home to me. I love you dearly.

But also, I have a mission I can trust to no one but you. I know you cannot walk, and if I cannot find a magical solution, I will find a human one. You are invaluable to me, as a friend, as a knight, and as a member of the only family I have who knows me as a person, not a princess.

You are the strongest man I know. If any could recover, it is you. Recover; I need you.
Rowan

Dear Gavin,

I am all out of clever things to write. I have never had so many to correspond with. Thank you for the information you included in your letter; it will be very helpful.

Please take care of the family I have entrusted to you.

R—

It was not the shortest letter she had ever written to Gavin, but it felt the most incomplete. Rowan could not explain why. Perhaps, having forgiven Colum and being forgiven by him, she wanted to do the same with Gavin. But something held her back. She could not say what it was she wanted from him, but she had not received it yet. So the words of forgiveness wouldn't come.

World-Altering Ideas

791 days until Roisin returns

*O*ver the next few days, Colum and Rowan slowly grew more comfortable together. Things did not simply go back, but they worked toward a new friendship.

After a week of speaking to each other in friendly, if slightly awkward, ways, Rowan brought Colum the bulk of her research on the Fairy War to have the benefit of his perspective. It was a great relief to share it with someone who thought as she did.

"I've not had a chance to examine the journals I stole from Father," Rowan remarked as Colum read over one of Rowan's timelines. "But I think what came before may be more important."

"And your father is alive. You could ask him your questions, instead of stealing."

Rowan shrugged off Colum's judgment.

"What is the matter, Rowan?"

"I doubt I would trust his answers. Most times, he avoids any question I ask about the time before I was born or before Roisin was taken."

"Perhaps he tries to protect you," Colum offered encouragingly.

Rowan thought of her father's words that night in the stairwell. "He is trying to protect himself."

"You've brought quite a lot to examine," Colum said after a moment of non-invasive silence. "Where shall we start?"

"I don't know," Rowan admitted. "I have so much information, but not all the information I want. So it is hard to know what is important."

"You picked a place to start your war timeline."

"Yes." Rowan took the page Colum held out; it was lined with every link Rowan had found to Sorcha wining the Fairy War—all beginning with a contract between Stonedragon and the Fairy nation for the eradication of dragons. "The dragon pact of three hundred and fifty was the first mention I found of Sorcha making deals that affected the outcome of the war."

"How so? It occurred eight years before the war, and Sorcha was not even the Fairy queen at the time."

Rowan's hand went to the chain at her neck; she felt the warmth of the pendant even with so little contact. "Eachann said all Fairy fear dragons. I do not think the war could have happened if the dragons had remained."

"But we cannot attribute that to Sorcha alone; she spoke as her sister Nessa's emissary," Colum pointed out. "Sorcha did arrange the match between King Flint and Queen Danu. Assuring Flint an heir constituted the Fairy half of the bargain."

Rowan scoffed, and received a quizzical look from Colum.

She opened her mouth to tell Colum everything. With all Sorcha knew, she must have realized Flint's heir would not be his child. Colum would find it as funny as she; he'd always shared her humor. He might even know who her grandfather was; he'd lived those years. But...Her heart sank; Colum's expression was stern and unamused. He was helping her and he cared, but they were not friends as they once were. This was work.

"I'm sorry." Rowan cleared her throat. "You were saying..."

"I was saying, it was Nessa who wanted the dragons eradicated." Colum finished with an eyebrow in the air, his tone firm and full of deeper meaning Rowan didn't want to delve into.

"It is not only the dragons leaving that came from that pact," Rowan defended. "Father was born in three hundred and fifty-three. If Flint had no heir to bargain into marriage, Sorcha might not have pulled him into the war six years later."

"Ahhh." Colum smiled, tilting his head sideways approvingly. "It is an interesting point. King Flint had not been much inclined to enter the war—too comfortable trading with both sides and busy searching for his missing queen."

"Missing? Queen Danu?" Rowan demanded, thrown. Was so much of her history still missing? "When? It is in neither of their journals."

"The queen vanished only months before the war began," Colum commented, steady as ever despite Rowan's rising agitation. "In the early summer of three hundred and fifty-eight, taking the last of the dragons with her."

"But..." Rowan tore through the journals. Her timeline was all wrong. "I thought the dragons left in three hundred and fifty-six, when they gave Danu the pendant."

Colum shook his head. "There were two others—three, actually. They were kept secret; one imagines the dragons who left believed them dead. There were two infants and an unhatched egg." His voice took on a faraway, almost empty quality, and he crossed his arms over his chest. "For a long time, we hunted dragons for sport; the kingdom was founded by such sport, driving their kind farther inland, away from what we claimed as ours. But after Sorcha's visit, hunting dragons was a knights-only duty. Kill dragons; bring back their eggs."

"You hunted them?" Rowan asked in a near whisper. It didn't fit with the Colum she knew.

"All knights did. Ardal, Liam, Donovan, and myself worked together."

"Oh." Rowan felt uncomfortable, an intruder on a secret she didn't want to know.

She could tell Colum sensed her disapproval, but he said nothing of it. "Most of the dragons had been driven into hiding, after years of being hunted. The adults we found were killed immediately, and the infants brought back so trainers could break them."

"He wanted a weapon against the Fairy," Rowan said, aghast.

Colum nodded.

"But my grandmother, Queen Danu, she spoiled it," Rowan said through a half smile, oddly proud of this stranger who was her grandmother.

"As I've said, we should be known for our women. It was a...contentious marriage," Colum said diplomatically. "She tried to free the dragons, believed herself successful. Once she discovered the other three she vanished with them. When she returned, she was imprisoned for the duration of the war and put to death shortly after. Your father could not have been more than seven."

"And he was left to King Flint to raise."

"You do not claim him as a relation." Colum chuckled. "I take it you have a great dislike for him?"

"Everything I read leads me to believe he was a bad man. Why should I claim him?"

Colum shook his head, smiling. "If you are right and the dragon pact started it all, do you believe Sorcha foresaw the war so far in advance and did nothing to save her sister?"

The way he asked it, Rowan knew he looked for some deeper answer than yes or no. But she didn't have it. She nodded her head yes. Sorcha knew too much; of that Rowan was certain.

"Hmm." His eyes remained on hers, waiting. After a moment his gaze slid back to the timeline. "You listed King Alistair of Anwyn's first marriage; why is this important?"

"Sorcha arranged it," Rowan said sharply, chafing a bit from Colum's dissatisfaction. "Two years before the war, but I am not sure what it gained her—support in the war perhaps."

"So she not only foresaw, but informed an ally?" Colum said skeptically.

Rowan shrugged. Colum appeared unimpressed, but did not push.

"We can safely say that Nessa's death and Tyrone's accusation of murder are important."

"Yes," Rowan agreed. "But Nessa died in May of three hundred and fifty-eight, and Tyrone did not declare war until late in August."

"It is time-consuming gathering supporters," Colum said dryly. "You say Sorcha banished her sisters in November, more than a year later, just about the time Sorcha was bargaining for Stonedragon's support with your parents' arranged marriage. Had they supported her so long into the war?" It wasn't a question. With Colum, nearly all expressions were subtle variations of his steady regard, but with his left brow tilted upward and his eyes challenging her, Rowan knew he meant the words as a prompt. A clue to the deeper understanding he was urging her toward.

"I cannot say for certain they were on her side, only that they were not opposed to her. They didn't think she killed their sister. Even once she banished them." Rowan thought back to meeting the aunts; they still did not seem to truly oppose Sorcha. "Things that actually went on inside the Fairy court are hard to discover."

As if the Fairy court were rejecting her. Robbing Rowan of that portion of her history because she'd spent her life rejecting magic. Or worse, because it considered her unworthy. Rowan ground her teeth, grinding down the sting. It was far more likely that she did not know her history because she had not sought it forcefully enough, had shied away from it even. But other people didn't have to seek their history. Other people *knew*.

"Have you asked Maureen?" Colum inquired with such quiet depth Rowan wasn't sure what he wanted her answer to be. "She was there."

"I worry it will pull Sorcha's eye to her. It may be too large a risk."

"Hmm." Colum's eyebrow rose skeptically. Rowan held her breath, waiting for his anger to return. After a moment he nodded and steered them back to the point. "Why do you think King Mathis's abdicating is important?"

Rowan released her breath, pulling Gavin's previous letter to the top of the pile. "From all accounts, he was a fair king up to that point. It was Thaddeus who convinced him to take sides with the Fairy king, Tyrone. Then suddenly Mathis abdicates and flees the kingdom. I think he betrayed them. Listen to this." Rowan searched for the pertinent passage in the seven-page letter. "'*It was early December of three hundred and fifty-nine that my uncle, King Mathis, without explanation, abdicated the throne and fled the kingdom, perhaps the island, if indeed he survived his flight. My father believed Mathis could not countenance all the deaths on his hands. So many more men were lost in the war than Fairy. We lost nearly a quarter of our troops attempting to take Ulm alone. No Fairy from Tyrone's force were sent with us to retrieve his secret tool to undoing Sorcha, a tool I would share with you if I knew a way. Fairy lives were apparently of more value than the weapon. In any event, had my uncle but remained* three days more*, he might still be king. Tyrone's hideout in the caves of our small sea village of Mobe was discovered by knights of Stonedragon, who had entered the fray only one short month before the war's end. Tyrone was found and killed on the spot. His body returned to the shores of Liadan, where she meets with the trail of Everspill, and Sorcha declared the war at an end.*'" Rowan lowered the letter. "He goes on a bit about his father assuming the throne at seventeen and the deal with Sorcha."

Rowan let her words drift to a stop. It was strange; during all her research, it never felt so real that the men she had loved all her life had been a part of this war. Might have died. Why did they never speak of it?

"Colum, you fought in the war."

He smiled. "Yes. But I was not among those who killed Tyrone. Only the best of Flint's knights were trusted with such a task."

"Not if they did not take you," Rowan snorted, when in truth she was glad he hadn't been among them. That felt too dangerous, even now, thirty-eight years later.

"I was a much younger man. Fighting in Creelan with the three I mentioned earlier. The men sent for Tyrone are long dead."

"Long dead? So we may never know how they did it."

At this, Colum chuckled. "Rowan, have you ever known a knight who does not boast of his conquests?"

"You."

"I am an old man."

"No, you aren't," Rowan said fiercely, fighting the impulse to reach up and hold on to Colum for dear life. Old men died. Even if they were never friends, as they had been, she couldn't lose Colum completely.

He shook his head, smiling gently. "There were five in all. Four knights of Stonedragon, and one Fairy sent to conceal them. When they found Tyrone, three fought off his guards, and Adomnan took Tyrone's head. It is the only certain way to kill a fairy."

Rowan swallowed. She couldn't find words or air enough to speak.

Sorcha was such a small woman, slight, at least a foot shorter than Rowan. A quick two-handed swing should do the job cleanly, but—Rowan couldn't see it. Her blade kept stopping short of the woman's throat in her mind. Rowan hated Sorcha, had spent her whole life training for just such a moment, but she couldn't even see it.

"It is a bloody, ugly thing, war." Colum spoke as if knowing her thoughts. "No side is wholly right. Only think how Prince Gavin writes of his father's ally."

Rowan barely heard him. *The only certain way.*

"Rowan?" She shook herself free of her reverie and looked up at Colum. "You believe Mathis betrayed them?"

"Yes." Rowan forced Sorcha, and what must be done, into the back of her mind. "There is even something in Sorcha's deal. Her insistence that Thaddeus never abdicate. And compared to what Creelan reportedly suffered, it is a nearly lenient deal. All they had to agree to was to disband half their army, pay recompense with one third of their autumn crop for fifty years, and never take up arms against her." Colum nodded. "And...the deal gives her the right to claim their lands and divide them between Arrnou of Ulm's children, but she hasn't."

"No, but perhaps something they did triggered the girls being taken," Colum said as though it were a question.

Yes. Rowan had begun corresponding with Gavin around the time the first girls were taken. But if Colum didn't say it, when it must have occurred to him, Rowan wouldn't bring it up either.

"But why not take the land, as well?" Rowan wondered aloud. "If the girls are indeed punishment, she must know they are resisting her."

"It is strange King Thaddeus agreed to this if he was so opposed to Sorcha." Colum seemed genuinely lost, searching the empty air for explanation.

"Sometimes people agree to things in a moment"—Rowan's shoulders folded inward as she forced the words up out of her rough throat—"hoping to come up with something better before time runs out."

Colum looked at Rowan deeply. Was he recalling things she had agreed to? The things that still lay between them? "What is it you hope to gain from this?"

Rowan watched Colum a moment longer, her mind not having quite caught up to him. Reluctantly she turned her gaze back to her pile of information.

"A few things. Perspective. You always said I must know as much as I could about Sorcha—how she fights—so I can anticipate her. My second goal is not so much for me as for people who come later. This is a poorly documented war, perhaps because it was so recent. But I think it would be helpful for future generations to consider the mistakes of their forbearers. And here, in all my research, are the things Sorcha understands: manipulation, contracts, betrayals, murder. I feel the weapon she does not understand *must* be here, as well. Perhaps in Ulm." She glanced back at the letter.

Colum shrugged. "Perhaps, but what? Even Prince Gavin does not know." Colum nodded at the table. "Your second goal is much more long-term, and if your journals are any indication, you are well on your way to achieving it. What should concern us are your first and last goals. Take a step back, Rowan. Consider what you have assumed without proof."

"I have little proof of anything," Rowan said absently, annoyed.

"Before you began, you made one assumption that guides all the rest. You must throw that assumption away if you mean to understand the Fairy queen."

Rowan's stomach knotted in slow protest. They were back to that deeper knowledge he wanted.

Colum took Rowan by the shoulders, holding her in place before the table. She looked at all the information she had compiled: there were three timelines about Sorcha, one for the war, one for the deals that came after, and one of all the curses and deals Sorcha had made that Rowan had tracked down.

Rowan held herself stiff and forced out the words she thought Colum wanted—"You mean putting the Fairy queen in the center of it?" His every "hmm" and questioning gaze had been leading her, resisting, to acknowledge that she was too focused on Sorcha to see any deeper truth.

"Look again." When Rowan remained silent, Colum leaned around her, picking up the war timeline. "What are the things that either do not fit or cannot be explained?"

"The match she arranged for King Alistair. That Sorcha was not the one to declare war. That her sisters never turned against her. That her deal with Turrlough seems lenient and oddly enforced."

"What about those things is similar?"

What was it Colum wanted to hear? Why didn't those fit? What was she missing? Rowan's stomach roiled, and she fought the urge to pace away. She needed to face the knowledge she'd been hiding from. Rowan clenched up as her mind found Colum's answer.

"They imply"—Rowan said slowly, more confused than ever—"Sorcha is not completely evil."

"Exactly. That is the assumption you must set aside."

"No," Rowan shouted, unreasonably enraged. She yanked up the timeline of Sorcha's deals and curses. "Look at all this. If she is not evil, what is she?"

"An excellent question. The one you should be answering," he said firmly.

Rowan was boiling, seething acid inside. "She locked her son in a crystal she takes out and passes from person to person, offering them immunity against her if they can free him."

"She offers them 'anything they desire,'" Colum corrected. "You are viewing it as a show of her power. What if she truly wants him free and cannot do it herself?"

Rowan wanted to stomp her feet and throw the papers in Colum's face, shake him even. *Sorcha is evil!* The words shuddered beneath her skin. They were the truth Rowan was most certain of, the knowledge around which she'd shaped most of her world. If that was wrong...

It was so frustrating. Rowan felt like her child self again, with magic she didn't understand and family that terrified her and the walls of her home so large and confining she couldn't breathe inside them. Colum had been her safe place, her understanding. If he would take Sorcha's side, defend her, say Rowan was wrong about her evil, then Rowan didn't know anything anymore.

"Consider all the matches you have her making." Colum nudged her back toward the table. "Several led to no help whatsoever in the war. How do you explain them?"

Rowan fisted her hands. She went to run her thumb over the scars on her palm as she always did when she was confused or nervous, but her skin was smooth. The scars were gone. Rowan opened her hand and stared into her smooth palm; even gone, she felt the scars. Felt the moment the thorns tore through her skin.

That day had changed her in more ways than just the scars; it forced her to face a side of the world she hadn't wanted to see. Forced her to face a fear she had not even been able to voice. But it had also given her a different kind of strength.

"All right." Rowan rubbed her smooth palm. "Let us assume she isn't evil." Those might have been the six hardest words Rowan had ever spoken.

It changed everything.

The Road Back

Colum placed a hand on Rowan's shoulder and squeezed, drawing her just a bit nearer to him. Her whole life, Rowan had known three things without a doubt. That she loved her sister more than herself. That she was the only one who could protect her. And that her grandmother, the Fairy queen, was an evil woman who must be destroyed. What would it mean to her plans if that wasn't true? What would it make her if she continued plotting murder?

"What does it mean?" Rowan asked tightly. She wasn't comfortable with the assumption, but she had to consider every possibility. It was the only way.

"I don't know yet," Colum admitted. "But now that we are considering it, we will find out. By your estimation, what is the worst curse she ever made?"

It was hard for Rowan to consider any curse but the one put on Roisin the worst. But she must consider them all.

"It depends..."

"From her perspective. If you were she, which would be the worst?"

"The one on her son," Rowan said without hesitation. The strongest feelings of guilt and self-disgust Rowan ever experienced were from sending Petal, because of her love for her. "Nothing is worse than cursing your own child."

"Then we will start there. Maureen told me of it. It happened just before your mother and father married; it nearly killed your mother."

"How?" Rowan demanded, startled.

"They were twins. Your uncle was angry with his mother and the deal she had made that would see his sister married to a human man she had never met. It is not the custom among Fairy. He accused his mother of being blinded by fear of power, claiming that was why she had banished the 'very best of the Fairy,' her three sisters."

"Oh." Rowan did not want to feel sympathy for her grandmother. She much preferred Sorcha remain evil. But having constantly been compared to Roisin and found the lesser, she knew how much it would hurt to hear that from one's own child. "That is when she did it?"

Colum nodded. "She said he might not consider her the best of the Fairy, but he would learn not to speak against her. She imprisoned him—apparently meant to banish him—inside the crystal, but your mother intervened, insisting he would learn the lesson better if she kept him always at her side. But when Sinead tried and failed to free her brother, she became very distraught and would not leave her bed until the wedding."

Rowan paced away from Colum; it was the most information she had ever received about her mother in one sitting. And it did not paint her as the sweet, self-sacrificing woman Maureen always said she was.

Too much was changing today. Rowan thought she might be sick. Maybe she should take to her bed and let someone else take over. She nearly laughed, or maybe cried, at the thought. She couldn't tell what she was feeling—how could she? Everything she had used to build her self-image was wrong, ripped apart in one conversation.

"That was all she did?" Rowan demanded. "Made sure he was not *thrown* away, and took to her bed?"

"Your mother's powers were very much tied to her brother. Being without him made her weak, and she was always more cowed by her mother."

"But...he was her brother. She just gave up."

"No. She didn't give up. She continued to live while she looked for another solution."

"And failed!" Rowan shouted, frustrated. She hadn't realized how immense and perfect her mother was in her imagination, not until the image faltered. Sinead was the ultimate example of what one did for love, unsurpassable in goodness. It had seemed like a connection between mother and daughter, the sacrifice she had made, the one Rowan planned to make for her sister. But if in a similar situation her mother had just given up...Was there no one in her family who felt as she did? No one who would stop at nothing to see their family safe?

"Rowan," Colum said in that same steady voice he used when she was a child wanting desperately to fight something, if only so she wouldn't cry. Rowan closed her eyes and let the comfort sink into her; it had been so long. "You know better than that. Your mother didn't fail. She had you and gave you everything—her determination to free him, her magic, her love of family. Everything she had, she gave to you."

You mean put on me. Rowan released a pent-up breath. *And I put it on Petal.*

Rowan felt hollow, adrift in the sorrows she'd sworn not to feel until this battle was over. Until her sisters were home.

"Finish the story," Rowan sighed.

"There is not very much more to tell. The Fairy queen took to carrying her son with her everywhere. Maureen said there were days when all Sorcha did was stare at her scepter. She did not begin passing him around until after your mother had died."

"When he was the only family she had left." It seemed wrong to hurt for someone she'd hated her whole life, but Rowan couldn't help feeling lonely for her grandmother.

Colum shrugged. "The only family she acknowledged."

Rowan nodded, a bit numb now from all she'd accepted. What did it tell them, really? Sorcha had a temper that she would come to regret. She seemed to love her children, however poorly. She wanted family.

Who didn't?

"Who was her husband?" Rowan asked, too empty inside to feel hopeful, but curious all the same. "I have read nothing of him."

"Sorcha had no husband. Several lovers, though. There were accusations that one lover was Nessa's husband. Which would explain some of the contention between the two sisters."

Rowan shook her head, walking away. Of course there was no answer; she was still unworthy of Fairy secrets. Rowan shoved her disappointment aside with work.

"It might explain that, but it wouldn't explain why he tried to seize the throne from Sorcha."

"Maybe not. Maureen always seemed..." Colum shrugged. "Maureen may have believed Tyrone and Sorcha were lovers, or she may not have; her anger at the past makes it hard to say."

"It just seems strange. Sorcha gave birth only a few months into the war. The turnaround from lovers to warring with each other seems very fast."

Colum bobbed his head from side to side, smiling. "You've never had a lover. It is not always a harmonious relationship."

Rowan made a face, completely uninterested in that part of Colum's life. "I'll take your word for it." She smiled, feeling lighter, relieved that she could still feel playful.

Colum chuckled. "Maureen has never told me which lover fathered Sorcha's children, so shall we say, your grandfather's identity is a mystery?"

"Why not?" Rowan said with a little laugh. "It seems to be a habit."

"What does?"

Rowan opened her mouth to tell him, but changed her mind. What if he did know? What if Donovan was her grandfather? Colum said they once hunted dragons together. Could she tolerate the idea of being related to that man? Of being related to Gwyneth?

No.

Not when she had agreed to think of Sorcha as something other than evil. She would keep it to herself for now. With the mystery came hope. She longed to know what he looked like, who he was, why she'd never met him. But tucked inside her, he could be anything, anyone; he could be the thing that warmed her with a promise for the future.

"Mysteries," Rowan said. "Mysteries are becoming a habit."

Colum laughed. "In life, you will discover, if you do not find three questions for every answer, you have not found the right answer."

Rowan rolled her eyes. "Isn't that just my luck?"

They laughed together. It was a good feeling. Maybe things would never be exactly as they had been, but they would be friends again.

In the Empty Night

By the time Maureen returned in the last week of April, Colum and Rowan had found their new stride. It was quiet in the palace after Maureen's return. For those who knew what Petal was doing, there was nothing in life worth laughter until they knew she was safe. And for those who didn't, the pall on the air was palpable, infesting their moods.

Tom and Ardal both returned. Tom was all but recovered. But Ardal was as Maureen had warned, a changed man. A servant lifted him from the coach, and it was all Rowan could do to keep from crying at the sight of him. She'd known what was coming, but it did nothing to help. He looked so…small, not just in size, though he had lost a good deal of weight, and Rowan couldn't even bring herself to look at the stumps of his legs. But he looked small in person, as though he was ready to die. Rowan wanted to run away; the sick, churning feeling in her stomach was almost too much to bear. This man who was once a giant of personality was barely present.

Rowan had no idea what she said, only that she held on to her overbright smile with muscles so tight it seemed her jaw might snap. He managed a brief smile for Rowan, but it faded quickly and held none of his old humor. She walked with him as he was carried to his new home in the palace, smiling and talking ceaselessly until Maureen shooed her from the room. But the whole time, Rowan felt herself sinking inside, growing small and frightened. Guilty.

You poison everything you touch.

The world beyond them was so big and so deadly. How was she to save anyone at all, when the strongest of her knights wasn't safe?

Rowan spent hours with him each day, trying to cheer him or endeavoring to get his help with her research. For the most part, he simply lay in the bed, barely responsive, but every once in a while, he would smile or make a small joke.

"Did you realize that of the five human kingdoms on the island, only Ulm was settled by people who were not dragon hunters?" Rowan spoke to a spot just over Ardal's shoulder. Her chair stood at an angle against the bed, just past Ardal's thighs, so her back was to the stumps of his legs, cut off just above the knees. She didn't know if this was at his instruction or if someone did it to protect their own sensibilities, but she was glad of it. She couldn't afford to feel like sobbing every time she looked at him; it wouldn't help his mood.

"As princess, should you not know this already?" He spoke toward the open window. Only the blue sky and an occasional bird could be seen through it.

"Well..." Rowan cast about for something to amuse him. "I never paid much attention to history lessons as a girl. I might have known it."

Ardal looked over with half his lip curved upward and shook his head with what must be the tired ghost of his old humor. "Why pay attention now?"

Rowan smiled broadly now, pleased to have amused him and desperate to keep him engaged. "Now that I'm looking for dragons, it seems useful."

"Ah." Ardal's entire body shrank deeper into the mattress, and he returned his gaze to the sky.

Rowan cursed her stupid mouth, her hands balling reflexively into fists in her lap. She wanted to shout at him not to be such a fool, that he was still useful to her. But the last time she'd said the like, he grew sullen, told her he wasn't "quite recovered from the last time she needed his assistance," and wasn't "up to helping further." When he'd asked to be alone, she'd fled to her room to cry; she hadn't the right to want his comfort. This was all her doing.

She didn't know what to do anymore. Every word, every gesture seemed the wrong one with Ardal. He clearly felt no need to fight off death. He was home, but made no effort to remain, to recover. Rowan wanted to shake him, demand he fight, or at least tease her as he used to. She wanted to be the one to cheer him, as he once had her, but she buried her hands beneath her legs instead.

You poison everything you touch.

His spirit had been so large and buoyant in the past. Just being near him had made her feel lighter; now, it seemed, the opposite was true.

When the first of May arrived, Rowan, Maureen, and the family waited with bated breath for something to happen. None of them knew what; they were not in Turrlough, so they could not say what was happening there. They could do nothing but wait.

It passed without word or incident. Rowan knew she would spend the next day, and the next, in exactly the same way if she did not do something about it. So she did what she had been talking about for months. With the help of her knights and Maureen's family, she began constructing a little house on the south side of the castle. But it wasn't for her any longer. It was for Ardal.

Ardal hated living in the palace. He had lived most of his life in the village a few miles outside its walls. Rowan could send him back there, but his wife had died several years ago, and none of his four children lived there any longer. And Rowan wanted him near. She thought his own space might make him happier.

768 days until Roisin returns

They were nearly finished with the house two days after they began it, when Eachann arrived with the first news from Turrlough.

Rowan read the letter aloud to Maureen and her family.

> *Dear Rowan,*
>
> *The Fairy came yesterday. Petal was taken with them. There did not appear to be anything different about the way she was taken. As far as we can tell, all has gone according to plan.*
>
> *We all pray for her here and anxiously await her return.*

She asked that I tell you all she loves you and will be well. She sent no specific messages because she liked the letters she sent home with her mother best.

The two girls my youngest brother and his wife adopted were taken as well. I promise as soon as I have any word of a change, I will inform you with all haste.

We were all sorry to see her go. We have grown to love her—my mother, perhaps, the most of anyone. She was a great comfort to her. She is a treasure.

I am sorry that it came to this, that I asked you for this. And most of all, that I could not take her place.

But I have faith that if anyone could trick or charm her way into the good graces of the Fairy queen, it is Petal the Powerful.
Your Friend,
G—

There was not much said when Rowan finished reading. The family sat quietly together. After a while, the boys went back to the knights they were squired to. Never had two squires been allowed so much time away from their masters. But had a word been said against them, those knights knew they would have the whole of the royal family to answer to. Because she was asked to stay, Rowan remained with Colum and Maureen for dinner. They spoke very little, mostly about what should be done to help Ardal. He was a bit better in the cottage, but not much. Colum suggested sending for one of Ardal's grandchildren to care for him; it was a good idea, but it made Rowan oddly jealous to think of someone else caring for Ardal. Someone he would not resent, someone he might laugh with and tease. No one seemed to eat much, poking uselessly at their stew. And the conversation did very little to cheer them. When she finally left, it was quite late; no one wanted to relinquish one another's company, and no one wanted to sleep.

As she walked away, Rowan heard a noise behind her and glanced around to see Gwyneth slip out of the shadows beside the little house and go knock on the door. Rowan paused to watch, slipping into the shadows herself.

She and Gwyneth had not so much as said hello to each other since the incident in her room. Her stepmother now feared for her life should she get on Rowan's bad side. Rowan had no interest in disabusing her of the idea. She liked having Gwyneth avoid her.

Rowan could not hear what was said between the two women, but after a few moments, Maureen looked over her shoulder at her husband, then turned back and gave Gwyneth a brief hug. Gwyneth clung to Maureen just a moment longer. When she stepped back, both women were in tears.

For once, that old sense of betrayal Rowan always felt when someone liked Gwyneth did not come. She saw Maureen's face in the light; she had tears on her cheeks, but wore a grateful smile. Maureen had not worn a smile for longer than a moment since returning. That alone was enough to make Rowan tolerate whatever Gwyneth had done.

Gwyneth waited outside the house, with the door closed at her face. After only a few moments, Maureen and Colum walked out of the house, Colum carrying a small bundle. Gwyneth motioned them ahead of her, and they all passed Rowan, oblivious.

Rowan followed at a distance. When they entered the palace, she waited outside until she could assume they had settled in. Then she went looking for Gwyneth. She found her walking down the stairs from the guest wing.

"Gwyneth." Rowan blocked her stepmother's path.

Gwyneth executed a brief curtsy, with her eyes fixed on the ground and hands clenched at her sides, but otherwise did not respond.

"Thank you," Rowan said and began to leave.

"For what?" Gwyneth blurted out.

"You invited them to sleep here. It was kind. I would not have thought of it."

She shrugged, a very odd motion for Gwyneth. "It isn't something you would understand. There is nothing quite so heartbreaking as sleeping in the place where your child used to be when she is gone, perhaps forever."

Rowan said nothing, watching her stepmother. There was a hollow look in her eyes Rowan had never noticed before. It reminded her of Maureen; as they spoke at dinner, her soul looked so hungry as to be nearly dying. Rowan felt her heart tightening and her head beginning to pound; before Gwyneth could say more, Rowan curtsied and walked away.

No, she did not know that feeling.

Rowan followed her feet, without much thought, into the old nursery where she had played with Roisin. There were toys lying on the floor. This must be someone's doing, as there was no dust of any kind. She walked over to the exact spot where she stood when the aunts took Roisin away. She remembered the feeling, how hope had fused with heartbreak to the point Rowan thought she might die from it.

The room was exactly the same. Where nearly every other wall or surface in the palace had been covered with images of Roisin, this room had none. Well, not none; it had the childish drawings Rowan had made of herself and her sister, and the little scribbles that could mean anything at all, Roisin made.

Rowan walked around the room, pausing to look at a toy or a picture, remembering her world as a child. She had never come back here. Not once.

There was a chair in the far corner where Gwyneth used to sit and sing to Roisin. Rowan had never been with them; she had watched from the hall. A blanket lay over the chair now; it hadn't been there that day.

What must it be like for the rest of them? Rowan never dwelled on Roisin's absence; there were too many things to do. But everyone else...what did they have but the waiting?

She felt more than heard Gwyneth's presence behind her. Felt it in the stiffening of her spine and the clenching of her teeth. She fought the reaction. For no one else was Rowan such a victim of her emotions, not even Sorcha. But for some reason, when this woman stood in the same room with her, Rowan could not gather even a fragment of serenity.

"Do you spend a great deal of time here?" she asked.

"Yes." Gwyneth walked into the room; still, Rowan did not turn around. "It is comforting to be here."

"Is it?" Rowan looked around. "For a few minutes, I suppose, but then...I would become caught up in the fact that she will not be a little girl when she returns. It would ache."

Gwyneth said nothing. Rowan turned to find her dabbing her eyes delicately with a handkerchief.

"It will not be long now." Rowan moved to walk past her stepmother. There had been no explosion between them, but there would be if she lingered.

"I am sure this will offend you," Gwyneth began. Rowan stopped with her back to Gwyneth. "But you do not like me already, have threatened my life at least once…"

Rowan couldn't help her breathy chuckle at the irony.

"Do you want her back? I know you love her, mean to save her, and woe unto those who stand between you and your intentions. But do you *want* her back?"

Rowan swung around to face Gwyneth. She did not realize the tears searing her eyes were visible, or she would have left. She had sworn, long ago, to never let this woman see her cry. Still, it tore at her. Every time someone hinted she was lacking in love for her sister, every time someone's eyes followed her with disgust as she refused to look on some new likeness of Roisin, it wrenched her soul bare.

"Roisin is in every dream I ever have—wonderful or terrible. When I wake up, I count the days, just as everyone else, seven hundred and sixty-eight days until Roisin returns. I don't understand that feeling you were talking about; I don't. Because my body is all that sleeps in these walls. My mind and my soul sleep with Roisin. I love her, everything about her. I love her laugh and her smile and her optimism, even her childish temper tantrums. She is the only person in the world that understands me without words. And I understand her." Rowan walked away, then, speaking over her shoulder as she went, said, "I will not justify or explain myself to you or anyone else again."

"Rowan, wait."

"What? What else do you want from me?" Rowan spun on her stepmother wildly, her right arm slashing the air between them. "Would you like to know if I think Roisin will like the color pink? Do you want my opinion on what room she would like best? Or perhaps you want me to tell you what food I think she will enjoy?" Rowan spat out bitterly.

"I...no." Gwyneth fumbled, dumbfounded. "I just wanted to offer you comfort."

"Offer your comfort to someone who believes you are sincere."

"I am sincere," Gwyneth insisted with a small wounded voice.

"Perhaps. But only because it is Roisin we speak of. What if I wasn't trying to save her? What if I was simply sad because my friend had come home a different man? What if I acted like the princess you used to despair of ever seeing, who curtsied properly and accepted the suitor her father liked best and spoke only when spoken to, frightened of blades and spiders? Would you care to comfort me then?"

Gwyneth looked at her as though she was mad.

"No. I thought not."

"You don't understand...she still might die. I could get her back only to lose her."

"Yes, you could." Rowan nodded. "I have thought about that quite a bit. We shouldn't have sent her away."

"What?"

"We should have kept her with us, had the years we were promised."

"You would give up?" Gwyneth was horrified.

"No. I would have her beside me every day if I could. Every day as I worked to save her—with her. Sixteen years. That's what Sorcha offered. Sixteen years with her. It seemed such a tiny amount of time, but...Some people do not even get that." Maureen and Colum were asleep somewhere in the palace because they could not stand to be in their home. Because their daughter was gone.

"We could have had a lifetime with her, and we threw it away."

"If throwing it away is what motivates you to save her, I am glad we did."

Rowan laughed. "Why is it always me, Gwyneth? Do *you* want her home? What is it *you* do to save your daughter?"

"*Nothing!*" Gwyneth shouted so loudly, Rowan took a step back. "I'm not allowed to do anything. Don't you understand that?" She advanced on Rowan. "I am useless. I have to trust her fate to someone who hates me. As I do nothing. It's driving me insane. I am sorry you don't want to hear my questions. I have no one else to ask. No one but you visits her in sleep. You don't want my gratitude for taking steps to bring her home. But gratitude, parties, plans, questions, hopes, they're all I have!"

Rowan observed her for a moment stilly. Gwyneth was panting; she didn't realize yet that she was having a loud outburst in a wing of the palace that was never without servants. It had always intimidated Rowan, Gwyneth's apparently innate ability to appear always graceful, calm, and unmoved by the world. Well, not always. She'd been nearly feral after Sorcha's curse. Rowan's nerves shivered at the memory, but she did not allow her muscles to move. The odd thing was, though it had hurt and terrified her when Gwyneth offered Rowan up as a sacrifice, she understood Gwyneth more in that moment than ever again. Until now. This, madness of waiting, Rowan understood. She only wished she did not; she had no desire to understand Gwyneth.

After a moment, Rowan nodded once, shrugging her shoulders. "I will think of something for you to do. Come to my reading room in the morning." With that, Rowan made her escape, rushing around Gwyneth.

Why was she helping this woman? There was nothing about her that she remembered ever liking. And it was a kinder thing Rowan did for her stepmother than she could ever remember Gwyneth doing for her. But if the Fairy queen was not evil and she could forgive her father, why not show compassion to her wicked stepmother?

Reaching for the Flash

*R*owan could not sleep. She sat with her legs dangling over the ledge of her missing wall, staring into the night. Her box of treasures lay open beside her. She had thought to read Gavin's letters, but her fingers found the burnt rose instead. She held it in her open hand, lining the thorns up with the places her scars used to be, and pressed the stem against her palm. She wanted the scars back, the connection with Petal. But the thorns would not pierce her skin.

She would give anything to close her eyes and find herself in the Fairy circle. To at least remind herself what she was fighting for. Some years stretched on so much longer.

It was an odd thing to wonder about, but of all the things she said to Gwyneth, one stuck out. Would anyone love her if she was just an ordinary princess? A woman who did as Colum said the world expected and waited for someone else to do the rescuing, rather than rescuing her own sister? Would they love her if she was not trying to save Roisin?

Probably not.

Roisin would, though. And didn't that just say it all?

In any event, she was not saving her sister to get their love. Roisin's was the only love she required.

"Rowan." Her father huffed and puffed as he came walking into the room. "I have been looking for you all over. Do you not sleep in your room anymore?"

"I like this one better." Rowan returned the rose to the box and shut the lid.

"Which explains why you are sleeping," he remarked dryly, coming to stand just behind her left shoulder. "Are you all right? Gwyneth found me, said you offered to give her something to do to help break Roisin's curse."

"Would you like an assignment, as well?" Rowan offered bitterly.

The king chuckled. "You really do usurp my position even as I stand here, don't you? I thought Donovan was simply a fool."

"He was a fool. Why were you looking for me?" Rowan asked a bit more politely.

"To make sure you are well. I would say that I should never have married your stepmother, and I have said it, but it would mean..."

"That Roisin was never born." Rowan nodded. "No one wants that."

"It was very kind of you to go out of your way for Gwyneth."

"You're welcome." Rowan watched the horizon. Sometimes as she watched the sun rising, Rowan thought she could make out the bump of Mount Kieran, the highest point in the known world, so faraway it was almost a fantasy, beyond the reach of all this sorrow; she longed to reach it. "What makes you continue loving her?"

"What?"

Rowan didn't respond. He heard her, understood perfectly well what she was asking.

"I'm not sure I do."

Rowan looked over her shoulder, raising an eyebrow at her father.

He sighed, moving very cautiously to sit next to her. "She always seemed to like me, as a person, not as a king. Even now, she laughs at my jokes, and she will sit next to me after a particularly difficult day and simply listen, or bring me tea and rub my shoulders. She is a comfort."

Rowan looked away, her head pounding so hard she thought she could see it. *She was a comfort, brought him tea.* For something a particularly good servant might do, he forgave her asking that he sacrifice one child for another. Rowan's throat stung with the scream vibrating inside her. She wanted to curl up in a ball and sob, or stretch out wide and release all her anger and sorrow and magic in a scream so powerful it crumbled the entire palace. She wanted to do anything but just sit here aching and waiting. But what must Maureen want, and Colum, and Petal?

"I do not expect you to like her." Her father interrupted her thoughts. "We do not always bring out the best in each other, never have. But I hope you will consider that not everything is her fault."

"Of course not. Most of it is Sorcha's."

He laughed. "No. I mean not everything in our past." Rowan looked at him, confused. He smiled condescendingly. "I know you stole my journals. I do not think it is a coincidence that I have seen little of you since, and she skirts you like a frightened rabbit."

"She was skirting me because I told her I wondered if Roisin would be better served by me killing her mother before she returns. I do have your journals, Father, but I have not had a chance to read them. What is it you think I have discovered?"

His mouth opened and closed several times, as though he did not know how it worked. Rowan glared at him, all but ready to put the shade spell on him. Then his shoulders shrank.

"You threatened to kill her?" He sighed. "I knew that you...resented her, but I had not thought it this bad."

"Resented?" Rowan spoke calmly, though she felt like shoving her father out the hole and seeing if he could fly. "I will never understand how it is you continue loving someone who asked you, not once, but at least twice that I heard, to sacrifice me. Though you did say the same thing yourself not long ago." Rowan swung her legs back into the castle away from her father and jumped to her feet.

"It must be one of those aspects of parenthood I do not comprehend." Rowan felt shaky, chaotic with pent-up magic, and paced away from the feeling. "I don't *resent* her. That implies jealousy, of her presence or your love for her. I'm not. I'm baffled by it. I used to hide from her; did you know that? When I was seven and eight. I was afraid if she found me alone, she would send me to Sorcha. I hid—feeling like a terrible sister; because I should be willing to die for Roisin, shouldn't I?"

Rowan stared at the wall, not really seeing anything, as the chaos slipped away and left only the giant, hungry hole within. She laughed brokenly. "I am always at cross-purposes. More than anything, I want Roisin home and safe. But"—her voice shattered slowly, until it was a tiny, desolate thing—"in the same moment, despicably, I want someone to say that perhaps she should die to save me." She felt disgusting saying the words aloud, expressing her worst fear. Acknowledging that the Rowan of her nightmares, extending the poisoned rose to her sister, could one day be real. "It is not because I want her to," Rowan rushed the words out, begging understanding, "but...don't you see you don't really love us equally?"

"Rowan." The king pushed to his feet and walked to Rowan, putting his hands on either shoulder. "I don't know what to say."

"No." Rowan smiled through her tears. Her shoulders bowed inward, and her arms itched to close over each other and hold tight. "You never do."

"Listen to me. I love you. I love you, and if the situations were reversed...of course I would feel the same to her as I do you."

But you wouldn't give her up, as she is now, for me, as I am.

Rowan pasted on a bright smile to hide her disappointment, shoving the unworthy emotion into the bleakness within, where no one would ever see it. "I love you, Father. What was it you thought angered me?"

Balder looked on his daughter with fear in his eyes. Whatever his secret, he thought it would turn her against him. What could it possibly be?

He would not speak the words aloud. Rowan did not push. Today had been a long day. She did not care to hear more bad news. She only wanted tomorrow.

"Never mind, Father. I am not angry. I will not kill Gwyneth." She shrugged out of his hands and walked back to the hole. "It will be dawn soon."

"I do love you, Rowan, more than you know."

Rowan watched the sky, her whole being stretching toward the first flash of sunlight she felt in the distance. A new day. She heard her father retreating from the room. When he was gone, she moved to her desk; the bleakness pulled her there.

Gavin,

Have your parents always been what you wanted? Are they always the wonderful people from your stories? Who love you and each other so well? Or do you only tell me the good?

I feel sometimes like my father has never been who I wanted. I can call up only a few moments in my life when I felt that he loved me, as a daughter should be loved by her father. And, as always, I am left feeling that I must compete for worthiness of that love with my sister. I do not *want her to come home to me resenting his love for her. When I dream I am with her, those feelings cannot follow for long. Then I am here again, and I wonder.*

I told my father exactly what it was I wanted to hear, and still he could not say it.

Everyone asks me what I want just for me. Well, here it is. I want children, hordes of them. And I want every single one to feel so safe and loved and happy that if I were to tell them stories of these times and how I felt, they wouldn't believe me. That the idea of such utter confusion and sadness would be so foreign to them as to be completely unimaginable.

Somewhat unlikely, I suppose. But no one said my dreams must be plausible.

I told him what I wanted to hear, and he still could not say it. Could not even lie to me.

This, then, is what we will have between us. He loves me and I him. But incompletely, not as the father and daughter I would have us be. I think I may be fairly contented. I need never again fight for that shred of love he cannot give me. Perhaps we will be better for it.
Rowan

The whispers of morning sun were just threading their way between the distant clouds as Rowan finished her letter. For some inexplicable reason, she felt drawn to her missing wall. She stood there with the rosy morning breeze tugging at her letter. Feeling completely in touch with eternity for the first time in years, she shimmered with a certainty she did not fully understand, but trusted. Rowan lifted the unfolded letter and surrendered it to the wind. It floated before her a moment, one more leaf following the current of the breeze.

As the first curve of the sun appeared in the distance, Rowan's heart caught in her chest; the letter vanished.

Across the island, in a small, quiet castle that was just coming awake, a prince sat up in his bed. He rubbed the lingering sleep from his eyes and gazed out his window, toward the still dim distance and the sea. He could not see the dawn from this side of the castle, but he felt it.

As the first flash of light fluttered across the water, a rose-scented breeze filled his room. A letter fluttered out of the air and drifted to the bed before him.

Gavin reached out, his heart silent in his chest. His fingers brushed the page, and his heart leapt. The first beat of the new day. And for that one moment, from across the island, he felt Rowan's heart, beating with his own.

Rowan's feet were poised, edging over the drop of her wall, into the wind when she felt it. Her heart leapt. No, it was not only Rowan's heart; the pounding in her chest was too large, too hopeful for only one heart. She felt Gavin's heart as well. Her magic had stretched out, connecting them. A smile grew slowly on Rowan's lips as the sun curled its way over the horizon, a smile of inexpressible wonder, and in this instance of fusion, a smile of absolute—*belief.*

The End